THE LIGHTYEARS BETWEEN US

ISBN:
E-book 978-1-915585-35-6
Paperback 978-1-915585-36-3
Hardback 978-1-915585-37-0

Cover Art by: Annabelle Friedrich-Moe

THE LIGHTYEARS BETWEEN US

Shannon K. English

Tiny Ghost Press

Who can fear
Too many stars, though each in heaven shall roll,
Too many flowers, though each shall crown the year?
Say thou dost love me, love me...only minding, Dear,
To love me also in silence with thy soul.
— Elizabeth Barrett Browning, "Sonnet 21"

PROLOGUE

Laika 15 – Day 515 – 13:41

"You...you were never meant to come home, Laika."

Will stared at the dash, the red light blinking, on and off, on and off. Exactly two seconds between each change. Inhuman precision.

She opened her mouth to speak. Closed it again.

What was there to say?

"Can you repeat that, Eden?" Paige's voice cut through the heavy silence; clean and sharp, straight to the truth.

There was a beat. No word from Command. The Eden was silent as a tomb.

"Eden, come in," pressed Paige. "Are you still with us? Request that you repeat your previous statement. There was interference and I'm not sure we heard you right."

There was a crackle as whatever poor unfortunate tasked with manning the Command Module pulled in a breath.

"No Laika has ever returned," Command said finally.

Will wondered perhaps if she had known the person now speaking. The distance and the radio waves rendered the disembodied voice so tinny and distorted that it could almost have been anyone. Will might have seen them at one of her father's parties, might have shaken their hand. Might, in that other life, have counted them as an ally, if not a friend.

"What do you mean?" Paige demanded, glaring at the console as though it personally was responsible for this hideous new facet of reality. Paige knew, she *must* know, as well as Will did herself, exactly what the comms officer meant—but she wanted to make them say it. To hear the self-condemnation in their own words. "They come back. How can we be the first?"

The Eden was silent.

Eyes wide, Paige turned to Will. *I told you so,* her expression said. Her finger stayed pressed down on the Transmit button, relaying the words she spoke aloud back to the station. "We're the first one *ever*? Two or three come back every launch. We've been gone nearly two years—we shouldn't even be the first back from *this* cohort!"

Will dropped her eyes, unable to hold Paige's gaze. Those big brown eyes, blazing with righteous indignation, flecked with tiny spots of amber. Will knew those eyes, every tiny speckle of colour—every fleeting emotion.

Those eyes had been the focal point of her life for the past eighteen months. Paige's face, Paige's expressions, the ceaseless movement of her hair in the low-grav air—these things had been the only changes in the unchanging world of the Laika's crew quarters. The only human features Will had seen in all that time, aside from fleeting glimpses of her own pale, sunken face in the mirror above the waste disposal unit.

Other than Paige, all had been empty. Bleak as the featureless space scrolling past the Laika on the vidscreens displaying the vast blackness outside. Paige had become the weathervane by which Will could measure her days. The very first thing she did upon rising was to look across at the other girl, to try and gauge what sort of morning awaited them. If Paige's eyes were clear and bright, then Will would hum as she prepared their porridge, and the two of them might even laugh as they ate their morning meal. If Paige's hair was rumpled and unplaited, if she kept her face turned to the wall—then Will understood that hope for the day was lost, and the porridge would be eaten in silence.

Those eyes were filling with tears now, pleading, as Paige spread her hands. "Eden, please come in. Please clarify. *Why* were we not expected to return?"

It was a performance worthy of a standing ovation.

There was another agonised crackle from the dash. Will's pity for the poor soul on the other end of the line deepened. They must have thought today's assignment an easy one. Manning a comms station that monitored empty space. It ought never to have made a noise.

"Repeat identification requested," the Eden said finally.

Paige's breath rushed out in one long exhalation: relief at a return to some semblance of normalcy. "Laika Fifteen, Pilots Tarrant and Arrex hailing from Spoke Six, launched year four hundred and fifty-two."

She obviously took comfort in the familiar words, the same callsign she had been repeating once an hour for the past three days, hoping that the Eden would soon be within range. But Will could not feel the same sense of reassurance. Laika Fifteen of Spoke Six, the fifteenth of the little ships from Eden Station. It was a registration that had ceased to have any relevancy the second they had launched. An epitaph more than a name. She had heard the comms officer with her own ears.

You were never meant to come home.

Part I
ENTROPY

CHAPTER 1

Spoke 6, Eden Station – Year 452 – Day 312 – 11:32

"So, once the first sprout shows, who knows what to do next?"

The professor smiled benignly down at the class.

Will knew the answer; obviously she did. Every topic covered in the general classroom she had completed with her private tutors at least two months prior. But no one else needed to know about the hours she had spent writing the material out over and over, until she was certain she knew it by heart. No, let them think it came to her effortlessly. Just as all things should come to a Noble.

Excelsior: ever onward, ever upward. The Arrex family motto was a single word, but it cast a shadow long enough that Will was forever struggling to remain in the light.

So she knew full well that once the potato showed the first hint of greenery the duty of the agro-workers was to turn the seedling once every four hours to ensure even UV coverage. And once sufficiently established, to transfer the shoot to the SoilGro beds and transition to the regular schedule of NutriGen plant feed and light-alteration periods. Will knew this, word for word, exactly as the textbooks laid it out—but she did not raise her hand. An Arrex was superior, but they did not force it on their subjects' notice. Everyone already knew exactly where things stood, and there was no need to flaunt it. Will knew *that* as surely as she knew the optimal growth programme for potato seedlings.

But her deskmate did not.

Beside Will there was a sharp intake of breath. A moment's pause, to let the anticipation build, and then with a rush of air the hand shot upwards and stayed, rigid, vibrating ever so slightly with suppressed excitement.

Will swallowed the sudden urge to sigh—an Arrex was not demonstrative—and contented herself with shooting a sideways glance from beneath her lashes.

Tarrant looked just as she always did: big brown eyes bulging with eagerness, freckled skin flushed with the excitement of *knowing the right answer*, the ultimate goal of Paige Tarrant's existence.

Will blinked, long and slow enough to conceal the roll of her eyes. Since she was four years old, she had attended classes alongside the six other children born in her spoke that year. Since she was four years old, she had been told by her father that as an Arrex, it was her duty to be better. And since she was four years old, Paige Tarrant had made the competition much too close for comfort.

The professor sighed as he saw Tarrant's hand quivering. After a cursory scan of the other students, who kept their gazes fixed firmly on their desks, he surrendered. "Yes, Tarrant?"

Tarrant beamed. "Thank you, Professor! Once the shoots appear the plant will need to be turned ninety degrees three times per twelve hours of light, followed by twelve hours of darkness. Some scholars argue that there should be eight hours of muted light and only four hours of true darkness, but—"

"Yes, *thank* you, Tarrant."

The professor's look was withering, but Tarrant seemed hardly to notice. Too buoyed up on the wings of her own genius, Will assumed.

The professor glanced back down at his notebook. "And once the leaves are out and the young plants are in the regular nursery, who can tell me what NutriGen supplements the potato needs to be given?"

Tarrant's hand shot back up so fast Will was surprised the girl didn't give herself whiplash.

The professor looked past her, to the students skulking in the back of the room. "Erntz? Abbeia? Any ideas?"

Tarrant's hand strained infinitesimally higher.

Lysse Abbeia glowered at her desk, and Erntz just shrugged his burly shoulders, utterly indifferent.

The professor heaved a sigh. "Your mother is an agritech *supervisor*, Erntz. You really have nothing to share on the needs of potatoes?"

Erntz shrugged again, more aggressively this time.

Tarrant made a soft keening noise, deep in her throat.

Eyes skimming over her and skating away, the professor's gaze finally came to land on Will.

"Lady Arrex?"

Beside her, Tarrant deflated, but Will couldn't take any pleasure in it. She was trapped. Once called on to answer, there was no other option within the leeway her father's rules allowed. It was all such a supreme waste of her time.

Sitting up a little straighter in her seat, she met the professor's eyes. *Eye contact is very important, Wilhelmina. It's how we connect with our audience. Our people.*

"Blend AB+ in the first eight weeks, Professor, followed by AAC until maturity."

He smiled, pleasure washing over his plump face like a wave. "Very good, Lady Arrex. Very *concise*."

Will responded with the smallest possible smile. She didn't need to look left to feel Tarrant squirming with fury. It was shocking, honestly, just how much Tarrant let herself *care* about these petty little things. Even on her worst days, Will could not imagine reacting the way Tarrant did, emotions spilling out of every orifice for everyone to see.

"And what are the best crops to share a growing trough with potatoes?" The professor was clearly as tired of the subject matter as most of his students.

"Marrows are the best deep-growers, and any number of topsoil plants mesh well," blurted Tarrant, fizzing with answers and not even waiting to be asked. "Strawberries, gooseberries, blueberries, raspberries—"

"*Thank you*, Miss Tarrant," spat the professor. "Perhaps you could wait to be asked next time, like Lady Arrex and the other students."

Finally quelled, Tarrant fell back in her chair and scowled.

It was her second minor triumph over Tarrant in as many minutes, but Will was more focused on the professor's obvious sycophancy. Was it too much? Should she mention it to her father? It was *unlikely* to lead to resentment strong enough that her classmates would discuss it with their parents, and even less likely that the parents would care enough to alter their opinions—but the Biannual Approval Surveys were coming up, and it never hurt to be careful.

"Of course," Tarrant hissed between her teeth, "us plebeians can't hope to compare to *Lady* Arrex."

After a quick check to ascertain that the professor was facing his vidscreen, Will permitted herself a moment of weakness and stuck her tongue out at Tarrant. It was childish, yes, it was unnecessary, *yes*, but she was only human. And Tarrant was *inhumanly* irritating.

Tarrant gasped, inarticulate with fury, and her mouth opened—to shout for the professor's attention? Surely a waste; he would never believe her—before snapping closed again.

As she bent over her work once more, Will watched her rival visibly stewing with rage, and smiled to herself, small and secret. The same old struggle, just as it had always been. Fire and ice, Arrex and Tarrant, pitted against one another in an eternal battle of wits and wills. Perfect symmetry.

And the Eden was a place of order, of symmetry. Six spokes making up the wheel of the station, rotating in its own stately orbit. In each spoke, six hundred people, united beneath a single Noble family. Seven babies born each year, to parents carefully vetted and prepared.

What a pity that Tarrant had been born in the same year as her.

The professor launched into a lecture on the technicalities of maintaining grow-lights, and with the risk of being called on over, Will let it wash over her without paying too much attention. It wasn't anything she didn't know already. She kept her gaze down, eyeing the debris on Tarrant's half of the desk with distaste. Her own side was pristine: three books only, neat and orderly in their stack, the bottom left corners perfectly aligned. But Tarrant's was chaos—piles of notes scattered haphazardly about, at least five books sprawling open amongst the papers, and another teetering pile of volumes in the corner.

Will tilted her head slightly to the left, trying to get a better sense of what Tarrant was studying. The next lesson was applied engineering—she'd revised her notes on the architectural substructure of the Wheel the night before, as scheduled—to be followed by geology and chemistry. While those subjects made an appearance in Tarrant's vast pile of tomes, the books actually open in front of her all seemed to focus on Terran history. Will squinted again at Tarrant's notes, but could make out nothing beyond the fact that the writing looked as though a worm had escaped from the hydroponics farms, dipped itself in ink, and thrashed wildly across a page.

Tarrant leaned forward, her grey jumpsuit falling open a little. Today's undershirt was crimson with white spots, bright enough to force itself on Will's notice and lend Tarrant's honey-brown skin a warmer tone. The flash of colour at the throat was distracting, catching the eye as it appeared and disappeared between Tarrant's thick curls and the iron-grey school uniform.

Will wondered what it would be like, not to care what clothes you wore. To just grab something at random out of a rainbow of colours and pull it on over your head. The Arrex steel-grey was simple and classical, and it provided exactly the right impression to the people—calm and collected, sensible and sombre. A level-headed, responsible leader, the daughter of another level-headed, responsible leader. *You can trust us,* that shade of grey whispered, just as Will's own face did, almost identical to her father's, and to generations of Arrexes before her. *You can put your faith in us. The Arrex family never changes, never falters.*

It would be something, to bend that unerring line, even if only for a day.

The klaxon signalling the beginning of the lunch hour sounded, cutting Will's reverie short. The door to the classroom slid open and the rumble of noise from the corridor grew to a roar.

Tarrant leapt to her feet so abruptly that her chair screeched over the floor, and shoved her way past. Will hissed under her breath, but instead of looking back for one last exchange of vitriol, Tarrant caught up with Sutsu and suddenly blossomed into a ball of smiles and energy.

"Cara! Hey!"

Will watched her go as surreptitiously as she could, wondering why Tarrant never smiled at *her* that way. She was perfectly nice, wasn't she? Alright, fine—maybe not nice to Tarrant, not *all* the time. But honestly, you would have to possess the patience of a saint to be nice to Tarrant *all the time.*

The room was suddenly bursting at the seams: everyone sweeping books into bags and racing for the door. Joss and Garth darted out hand in hand, already muttering sweet nothings to each other. Lysse Abbeia swept away from Erntz, who panted after her for a few strained sentences before fading sulkily into the background. Tarrant had hopped up onto Cara Sutsu's desk, swinging her legs as they chatted. Will did her best to look calm and unruffled when no one spoke to her.

Best to keep a careful distance, anyway. Slip-ups in youth could be fatal later on: Will's great-grandfather lost the Approval Surveys once when it came out he had cheated on his boyfriend with another classmate thirty years before.

Will had friends. Obviously she had friends. She wasn't an outcast. But Carroway and Xanthe were far away on the other side of Eden, one in Spoke Three, the other in Spoke Two. And sometimes it was hard not to feel a little...envious. Tarrant and Sutsu, heads close together: one silky black, the other a mess of riotous brown curls. What would it feel like, to have a friend that you could trust like that?

"Good morning, Lady Arrex," a bright voice broke into her thoughts, and Will looked up to see Lysse Abbeia, free of Erntz at last and leaning against the desk. Her fingers were splayed carelessly over Tarrant's notes, crumpling them, and Will suddenly wondered if she should try to save them. Otherwise Tarrant's first instinct would doubtless be to accuse *her*.

"Good morning, Abbeia." She kept her voice polite. Disinterested. Neutral. Her vague daydreams about friendship always evaporated quickly when Lysse was the one offering it.

Lysse leaned forward, looking slightly *hungry*, just as she always did when she spoke to Will. If one could become a Noble just by wishing, Lysse would have become Lord Captain of the Eden by the time she was nine years old.

"Did you have a nice evening?"

"I did, thank you." No detail meant nothing to latch on to. Even Lysse would have no reason to elongate the exchange.

The silence stretched, and Will ground her teeth as she realised the only thing worse than allowing familiarity was delivering a snub. Lysse's parents were electors too. She paused, before reluctantly adding, "I trust yours was pleasant too."

If Will had her way, Lysse would have politely nodded, perhaps said *Yes, thank you*, and then headed back to join the devoted Erntz. It would have been over as quickly as it began.

But the other girl smiled delightedly. "Thank you for asking, Lady Arrex! I actually attended a party over in Spoke Four—"

Will could only sit there and think sourly to herself *I didn't ask, actually,* while the blow-by-blow account of the party thrown by the parents of a friend of Lysse's boyfriend's brother, who was studying spacecraft design at the Academy with a focus on gliders, and...oh, it just went on and on and *on*, and it was all Will could do to keep an expression of mild interest fixed in place. She rose to her feet and dropped her three books one by one into her bag, hoping Lysse would get the hint.

No such luck. Lysse's tale of a minor-league glider-racing star turning up *out of nowhere* at this party was only silenced when Tarrant appeared at her elbow and chirped a greeting.

Lysse levered herself off Tarrant's notes with a final smirk for Will. "I can finish telling you about the party at lunch, Lady Arrex. See you there?"

Will only narrowly kept the distaste off her face.

With a sigh, Tarrant dropped back into her seat and began to shuffle her reams of paper. "Got a hot date for lunch, huh, Arrex? Think Johann ought to be worried?"

Will hastily combed through her mental files. Johann, Johann—oh, right. Johann Veel, a sallow-looking boy two years above them. Lysse's latest suitor, presumably.

"No," she said drily, wishing she had been a little faster with her response. "I don't think he's in much danger from me."

Tarrant shot her a look edged with mirth, and one corner of her mouth quirked. "I think *you're* more likely to be the one in danger, huh? Lysse would drop him like a hot potato if you asked."

It was moments like this that took Will aback. Despite Tarrant's dopey friends and her all-consuming desire to be universally acknowledged as top of the class, sometimes Will caught a glimpse of a wicked sense of humour, as sharply pointed as her own. These instances were so out of alignment with Tarrant's general aura of *irritating little freak* they always left Will wrong-footed.

Will attempted a suave, worldly smile, but she wasn't sure it landed.

Tarrant was looking at her notes again, and suddenly huffed in irritation. "Ugh, she's left a great big *handprint* here." She flipped her head round to glare at the departing Lysse, and in doing so hit Will full in the face with her great mass of hair.

Will reared back, her nostrils full of the cloying, over-sweet scent of artificial strawberries. She leant away, raising her hand to fend off the thick curls, just as Tarrant whipped her head back towards the front of the room. The coils of hair slapped Will in the face a second time and she had to shove her hand hastily back to her lap in case Tarrant saw and somehow got the idea Will was trying to *touch* her stupid hair.

Tarrant was muttering darkly about *carelessness* and *disrespect for other people's work,* and Will was left sitting in awkward silence, wondering if she should try to recapture the conversation. It was the first thing Tarrant had said to her in *weeks* that wasn't an insult or an obnoxious attempt at correcting her. Perhaps poking muted fun at Abbeia could be a shared interest.

But before Will could chance another probe out into the abyssal depths of conversation with Tarrant, the other girl finished collecting her miniature library and bolted, leaving Will to exhale a sigh of mingled relief and disappointment. Tarrant and Sutsu headed for the canteen and Will followed—just close enough to hear the question Sutsu asked.

"How was the symposium?"

Will's eyebrows rose. What sort of symposiums was *Tarrant* attending?

Her annoyance evaporating, Tarrant gasped. "Cara, it was *amazing*! All these pillars and open squares, and real grass all over the place, just for people to sit on and talk."

"The Academy has grass?" Sutsu sounded taken aback. "For *sitting* on?"

Enthusiastically, Tarrant nodded. "And that's not even the best part. The *conversations* they were having! People just sitting around, in public, talking about Plato and Hawking and Austen—all these ancient thinkers from Old Terra. And everyone was *interested* in it all!"

"It sounds like your version of heaven." Sutsu smiled, and Will found herself in agreement, though if she'd been the one saying the words they would have been a little more barbed.

There was no doubt Tarrant would be happiest if she were surrounded by a load of people as insufferably clever as she was, so they could all sit around and pat each other on the back about how insufferably clever they were. Then again, Will herself was undoubtedly Tarrant's equal, and Tarrant didn't enjoy spending time with *her*. Perhaps Tarrant would not find the Academy to her taste after all.

"There were four doctoral candidates presenting," Tarrant burbled on happily, oblivious to Will's uncharitable thoughts. "One comparing the Fall of Rome to the Great Terran Decline in the twenty-second century, one on Jules Verne and early western hemisphere fiction's contribution to the space age, one on China's opium wars, and one on Peru's rise to power in the late twenty-first century."

"So did you decide?" Sutsu pressed, and Will sped up, straining to catch each soft word.

Luckily, Tarrant had all the volume control of a megaphone, and *her* answer was easy to hear. "Yeah. I'm pretty sure Terran history is the one."

Sutsu burst into effusive congratulations. "Paige, that's *wonderful*! I bet you'll get a doctorate—you'll be the youngest professor at the Academy!"

Will listened with growing disbelief. Terran history? *Why?* Tarrant was—Will hated to admit it, but it was true—Tarrant was like Will: a polymath, an adept in more subjects than Will cared to count. And *unlike* Will, Tarrant did not have the benefit of countless hours of private study with expensive tutors. Tarrant somehow managed to keep up, more or less, with Will Arrex herself. And she was going to take all that skill, all that potential, and throw it away on *Terran history*?

Will had studied it, of course. She read philosophy, psychology, politics, military strategy, and oratory at home with her tutors, and they all drew extensively on historical sources and case studies from Old Terra. But that was different. Will's career was fixed in place; it had been since birth. She was an Arrex, and she was being trained for power: *excelsior*. She studied the history of leadership, not history itself.

But Tarrant was not a Noble. She could go into any career, take any path. With her intellect and skill, she could be an aeronautics engineer, an astrophysicist, a geneticist like Will's own mother—anything. Why would she take all that freedom and throw it away on a dead-end subject that only looked backwards?

It was a complete waste.

The crowd of students flooding into the canteen grew thicker, and Tarrant's panegyric on the joys of the symposium and the possibility of learning Latin was lost in the roar. The tension in Will's shoulders finally eased, and she relaxed her ramrod posture by a couple of degrees. Another lunch eaten alone, another few hours of listening to material she already knew backwards and forwards; it wasn't so bad really. Anything was better than listening to Tarrant planning to fritter away the precious freedom she had been given. Freedom Will might, if she wasn't fully committed to her duty, have given *anything* to possess.

CHAPTER 2

Spoke 6, Eden Station – Year 452 – Day 312 – 13:01

A few heads turned to follow Will as she headed for her usual table, passing the queue winding back and forth in front of the food-fab distributors. She was not a new sight at school—she had been there every day for the last thirteen years—but like it or not, she was the daughter of the man who held absolute power over everyone in Spoke Six, and that made her an object of interest.

The canteen was one of the largest rooms in the spoke. From the table of four-year-olds in the corner, thronged about with carers and childminders, all the way through to the nineteen-year-olds looking like all of this was very much below them, one hundred and five students ate there together—over a full sixth of the population of the spoke.

Will's table was beside a wall, occupying a prominent but not predominant position in the room. Occasionally people would pause beside her and try to talk, but with a bit of polite disdain and a few icy pleasantries she could usually get rid of them. If they had something serious to ask, she made a point of being friendlier, and sometimes went as far as directing them to the appropriate member of her father's staff to talk to—but that was a rare occurrence. She wanted to be respected, not *available*.

Her classmates generally sat at the next table over, a decision largely made by Lysse, who enjoyed basking in the reflected glory of being Lady Arrex's acquaintance. Will didn't mind; their proximity made it easier to continue her morning pastime of listening to their chatter while appearing safely aloof.

She settled herself with a book open in front of her—a treatise on the geography of Amalthea. It was a dry read, focusing on mines in the Gaea crater where drone pilots extracted the ore, ice, and minerals it took to keep the Eden functioning. Will let the details slide past her until she reached the revelation that on Old Terra the name *Amalthea* was associated not only with Zeus's foster-mother, but with the mythical unicorn. The Greek mythology was not new to Will, but the fable of the last of the unicorns was, and she read the three paragraphs devoted to the subject with interest.

Today Lysse hovered pointedly in front of Will's table. She cleared her throat a few times, but Will studiously ignored her. She'd had her fill of Lysse for the day. It took three re-reads of the page before Lysse gave up and slammed her tray down in her usual spot beside Erntz.

When Will glanced up again, Tarrant and Sutsu were sliding on to the benches alongside the others, their standard-issue nutribars sitting square and unappetising in the centre of their plates. More depressing fare she could not imagine.

Belatedly, Will reached for her own bag. She hadn't had the chance to check what Tunis had made for her, but hopefully it was something good.

"Have you heard?" Tarrant asked the others without preamble, and Will cocked her head to listen while keeping her eyes safely lowered.

"Heard what?" Erntz asked impatiently.

"Grigor says it's going to happen in less than a *month*."

The other students stilled.

"Really?" Siln Joss asked, and they sounded frightened.

Erntz all but scratched his head: a caricature of himself. "What's in a month?"

Tarrant turned to look at him and Will could see her strangely pallid face. Like all the blood had fled from her skin. "The Lottery."

At that word, even Erntz rocked back, and Garth reached for Joss's hand.

Will hastily turned back to her lunch and opened the bag. An apple, an orange, and a pear waited within, and despite the turn the conversation had taken, she half-smiled. Fruit fresh from the orchard labs; Tunis had come through for her again.

"But the odds—they're tiny, right, Austyn?" queried Joss anxiously, turning to Garth. "Six people drawn from everyone between fifteen and twenty-five in the spoke. That's a pool of...of dozens, isn't it? Nearly a hundred people."

"Only seventy," Tarrant answered, almost absently. Like she was just responding to one more question from the professor.

Joss looked appalled. "That's less people than there are in this *room*."

The whole table looked around nervously at the packed canteen, as though the Lawkeepers were already coming to haul them away.

Glancing up at the sudden movement, Will was unfortunate enough to make eye contact with Tarrant, who glowered back at her as though Will was personally responsible for the Lottery and all it entailed.

"I suppose at least *some* people don't have to worry about it," she snarled, taking a savage bite out of her nutribar.

Will winced, pretty certain Tarrant was imagining the nutribar was her head.

Joss and Garth glanced over at Will too, but no one else took the bait.

"I just can't believe they include the *fifteen*-year-olds," Sutsu said softly.

Will found herself hoping the Lottery would at least pass over Sutsu. Always so busy worrying about other people that she never seemed to take any time to worry about herself. She was too soft for the world beyond the Eden. Well—probably all of them were. It was a very harsh world out there.

To hear Xavier Arrex tell it, the Lottery was a beautiful and necessary part of how the Eden functioned. It brought the citizens of Eden together like nothing else, he said. Once every twenty-five years, the Lottery would select thirty-six of Eden's finest youths, six from each spoke, chosen at random with only the children of the Nobles exempt. Two pilots aboard each of the eighteen Laika ships built with love and care over the preceding decades, three ships per spoke—shot out into space, soaring into the infinite abyss in search of hope and the future of Eden.

It did *sound* beautiful, when Xavier talked about it. Poetic. The glory of humanity's indomitable spirit, facing the stars and sending out the flower of its youth to bring back tidings of the healing worlds beyond the Eden. But when Will listened to her classmates, it sounded less poetic and more terrifying.

With an effort, she refocused on her lunch, rolling the apple between her palms and taking a small bite.

"But it's not likely any of us will be drawn," Joss was saying, almost pleading with the others.

"About nine percent likelihood that you'll be drawn," Tarrant answered miserably, the calculations coming automatically. "Or…or…forty-two percent that one of the six of us will be drawn."

Joss gasped audibly at the second figure. Will was taken aback, too. With sixty-plus other people in the running, she hadn't realised it would be such poor odds for her classmates.

Garth rubbed Joss's hand. "It'll be okay, Siln. Nine percent is very low odds. We'll probably all be fine. And even if—if the worst happens—people do come back."

"Maybe we're thinking about this the wrong way," Tarrant said wistfully. Almost hopefully. "Imagine if it works. If someone goes out there, and they find one of the terraformers, and it's actually worked."

Erntz grunted. "So we have a biodome or two as well as thirty-six dead kids. Big whoop."

Tarrant shook her head, curls bouncing emphatically. "But it's more than that. If we have a biodome, we can have five. If we can have five, someday five *hundred*. And then—boom!" She slapped her hands on the table and Cara flinched. "A whole *planet*. Sky. Grass. Hills that go on forever. A life without spokes. Without Recycling. Without Nobles."

There was a beat as her words sunk in. Will waited for the outrage that would surely follow the word *Noble*. Her family had given their entire lives in service to the Eden, over and over, for generation after generation. Honour, righteousness, justice: not a single Arrex had deviated from that silver-steel path that led to their predestined place among the stars. *Excelsior*. Sacrifice. The people of Spoke Six knew that, deep down. Even her classmates. Even Tarrant.

But none of them said a word.

"You don't really believe that do you, Paige?" Garth asked, and Tarrant hesitated.

Before she could answer, Joss sniffed, looking suddenly close to tears. "At least Matthias is safe. He's only thirteen."

Blotting her lips with a napkin, Will quashed the remnants of annoyance at their ingratitude and did her best to tune the conversation out. For the first time, eavesdropping was starting to feel...it didn't feel right.

"Yeah," Erntz agreed. "I'm glad that Foali and Horick are both too old. If more than one of us was up for it I'm pretty sure Mum'd have a heart attack."

Siblings. They were talking about their siblings. Will swallowed another bite of apple, trying not to feel...not jealous, no...she wasn't feeling anything. With her parents' fertility a matter of the law, she would never know what it was to have a sister or a brother. No matter how many times she aced the Parental Aptitude Test, she would never have more than one child. Would be *forced* to have that one child to ensure her line of the Arrex family continued. Each Noble family had two branches, each line limited to a single child. The Founders had decided, in their wisdom, that a profusion of Nobles might lead to dynastic wars. Only if one branch should die out was the other permitted to have two children to restore the two-branch system. There were no choices involved in being a Noble. Everything was already written.

"I just...I can't believe it's really happening," Joss said.

"It's okay," Garth repeated, chafing their hand in his, following it up with more comforts too soft for Will to hear.

Tarrant smacked her palm down again. "Let's talk about something else. Cara—"

Will couldn't follow the thread of all the separate conversations, and was conscious now that she shouldn't be trying to. An Arrex did not *eavesdrop,* and she ought to be above it. She pulled the pear out of her bag and bit into it: tangy and crisp, ripened to perfection.

It wasn't like she was proud of the habits she had acquired, but when she spent all day being aloof and unreachable, there wasn't much else to do. And usually it was interesting to hear Tarrant talking with the others like a normal person, instead of snapping like an alligator. Today had been less interesting, and more...painful.

"He'll get to see it," Tarrant said, suddenly loud enough to render herself audible again. "We'll make it happen."

Will tuned back in, unable to resist the temptation.

"How?" Sutsu replied, still as quiet as ever.

"We'll find a way," Tarrant said.

"He's getting sicker and he says it's what he wants, if it turns out he has to—if he needs to—go to Recycling...early." The last word was whispered, as though in agony.

Will was almost entirely reliant on lip-reading now, but she thought she had heard that right. Early Recycling? This was another serious conversation, then. Some elderly relative of Sutsu was very, very close to death.

"It's okay," Tarrant said soothingly. "That won't happen. He'll be fine. You'll see."

"It's such a basic thing, but there's no way I can..." Sutsu was close to tears now, wiping at both eyes with her fingers.

Tarrant's hand rubbed soothing circles on Sutsu's back and Will felt a sudden wave of irritation rising. She was sympathetic to Sutsu's plight, of course she was, but did they have to have their therapy session right *here*, where it was bothering everyone? In a second they'd be *hugging*.

"I'll talk to Papi," Tarrant promised, and Will's eyebrows rose sharply.

The more important of Tarrant's two fathers was, surprisingly, given his daughter's hatred of all things Noble, a member of Xavier's Cabinet. Grayson Tarrant, Inter-Spoke Relations Minister, was a personable man. He had earned both his Parental Qualification and his office at a startlingly young age, and there were whispers that his prodigy of a daughter might follow in his footsteps. Only, Will thought caustically, if she could be prevailed upon not to throw her life away as a Terran history doctoral candidate.

But if Tarrant was going to involve Minister Grayson, this had to be something big. What was Tarrant going to ask? Surely nothing outside the rules. Tarrant wouldn't ask her darling *papi* to skirt too close to the edge of legality.

No one could alter the Recycling deadline—everyone went when they turned eighty-five, no matter who they were. But if someone were supposed to go *early*...perhaps that nomination could be overturned, if one knew the right people. Early Recycling dates were only given out in the most serious cases, when the quality-of-life assessments were failed. If Sutsu and Tarrant were planning to fight that—well, then Minister Grayson Tarrant would have no one to turn to but Lord Xavier Arrex, First Minister of Spoke Six.

And *that* realisation was the one that made Will narrow her eyes and look directly at Tarrant, determined to catch her next words. If Tarrant was going after Will's father, asking him to alter a Recycling date during the Surveys, then Will wanted to know. He would need to be warned ahead of time.

But Tarrant, with her uncanny awareness of when exactly Will was watching her, did not speak again. Instead, her gaze snapped over to Will and they locked eyes. Her sympathetic expression morphed into a glare. "Bet *you* have a good view from your house, don't you, *Arrex*?"

The question was so totally unexpected that Will could think of nothing to say. She had anticipated an accusation of listening in, had readied her defence—*Is it my fault if you talk so loud, Tarrant?*—but this was not what she had planned for.

"What?" she asked eloquently, and the sound of her voice was enough to end the other conversations on her classmates' table as they all turned to ogle her.

"As I think you heard, Cara's grandfather is sick," said Tarrant, spite oozing from every word. "And all he wants is to look outside. At the stars."

"Oh," said Will. "Then—why doesn't he?"

Tarrant scoffed and turned to the others beside her, as though she had been proved right about something. Sutsu gave a pained whimper and buried her head in her hands.

When Tarrant turned back to Will, she spoke slowly, scornfully. "He doesn't *have* a window. None of us do. Do *any* of you guys know anyone that does?"

There was silence. One by one, the others shook their heads. Lysse flipped her hair and started to say something about her boyfriend's brother, but Tarrant cut her off abruptly.

"See? Not one of them. Cara's grandfather hasn't seen Jupiter since he was at the Academy."

"Nearly fifty years ago," Sutsu added in a whisper.

"Windows are old-money territory," Tarrant explained, as though to an idiot. "Even my papi can't afford a house with a window, and he's on a minister's salary. But I'm willing to bet that *you* have at least three windows."

There was a ripple around the table. *Three. Three windows! Bonkers.*

Tarrant fixed Will with a challenging stare. "Right?"

Guiltily, Will thought of her bedroom and its wall of glass. The panorama of stars glimmering in the distance beyond the Wheel, speckled through the sky. Nebulae of every hue spreading their tendrils across the cosmos: a view that would be breathtaking if Will hadn't seen it every day of her life. The great hall where she ate her breakfast, the office where her father delivered her lessons, starlight in his hair. She thought of the private observatory above the study, where she kept her own telescope and her astrology tutor showed her the mysteries of the universe.

"I knew it," Tarrant said triumphantly. As though possessing a window was a crime.

Finally recovering from the shock, Will felt anger beginning to bubble in her chest. Why *should* she have to apologise?

"It's hardly my fault who my ancestors were," she said, forcing a note of calm into her voice. Let Tarrant be the one to get emotional and make an ass of herself. She was so much *better* at it than Will was.

Tarrant rolled her eyes. "Of course not. Just like it's not your fault you don't have to worry about being in the Lottery. Or ever having to get a real job. Or—"

"Leave it, Paige," Garth was pulling Tarrant forcefully by the arm. "It's not worth it. And will you *stop* bringing up the—" With a nervous glance at Joss, he cut himself off. "Just drop it."

Will met Tarrant's eyes again and allowed a tiny, triumphant smirk to steal across her lips. The audience was on her side; another point scored. The aftertaste of the Lottery conversation finally faded. Victory was invariably sweet, but victory over Tarrant was always the sweetest.

CHAPTER 3

Spoke 6, Eden Station – Year 452 – Day 314 – 18:15

The vidscreen beside the bed flashed, suffusing the room with soft orange light. A series of gentle chimes sounded. A groan from the bed as the amber faded into a more subdued yellow. It was an exact replica of a summer sunrise on Old Terra, designed to wake her gently and naturally, but Will had never felt more exhausted.

The music swelled louder and louder with every note, and Will curled deeper into her pillows.

"Wilhelmina!" snapped a voice from the intercom recessed into the white wall. "Please get up *before* we are all deafened."

That was enough to dispel what remained of the fogginess in her brain. Will's pale green eyes snapped open, and she stared upward at the golden-tinted surface of her ceiling. So much for her power nap.

With a stretch and a yawn, she sat up. There was another pause as she pulled the blankets up to her chin, wrestling with the urge to snuggle back up for another hour or two. She was achingly warm, and it would be so *easy*…

The intercom sparked. "I am *leaving*, Wilhelmina."

The moment passed and Will swung her legs outward. A twenty-minute nap wasn't enough to make a dent in her bone-deep weariness, but healthy sleep schedules were for people with more leisure time than she'd ever possessed.

A tap of the vidscreen, and a section of wall retracted seamlessly to reveal a wardrobe. One more tap, and the entire wall opposite the bed split in two, peeling back to reveal infinity. The Eden was in its two-week night phase, and there was no sunlight to dim the stars' glory today. Stars and planets and Jupiter's many moons, all conducting their slow and silent dance. A thick band of black cutting across the centre of it all was the only reminder of the Eden's presence at all. The Wheel was perhaps a kilometre wide, and the view above and below its girth seemed to stretch on forever. Spoke Six was currently facing out into the empty abyss, so even the ever-present Jupiter was not in sight.

Will's eyes slid over it and skated away—the last thing she wanted was to relive the window discussion again. Two days later and Tarrant was *still* icing her out, and without her insults school was even more boring than before.

Anyway, Will was no poverty-stricken inner-spoker being treated to the sight of a window for the first time. Her focus was on her wardrobe: jumpsuits, cardigans, and dresses of every cut and style imaginable, all in the same steel-grey. The only relief from the icy Arrex hue was her school uniform—a plain iron-grey jumpsuit the same colour as the default Spoke Six uniform—and even that was just a darkened version of her family's signature shade.

But after she shucked her pyjamas and snagged a jumpsuit, Will couldn't deny that whatever designer had first chosen the colour for her distant ancestors had done their job well. This jumpsuit was a formal one, steel-grey with wide white lapels designed to hark back to the original uniform worn by Helmsman Javier Arrex. Thanks to genetic editing, every Arrex had the same trademark white-blonde hair, skin bloodless and pale—all suiting the metallic colour scheme perfectly. The only hint of colour was the eyes, flinty chips of sea-green in a world of white and grey.

One last pause to tug a comb through her hair, ensuring her parting ran straight and true down the exact centre of her skull. It didn't take much; her hair brushed her shoulders, clipped to a practical blunt edge. Again, a case of night from day with Tarrant. *Her* hair was almost waist-length, with curls throwing themselves in every direction.

With a huff of irritation, Will shook off the thought. Tarrant and her frosty silences had ruined enough of the day. There were more important things to worry about. Like her father, stewing by the intercom as he waited for her—Lord Xavier Arrex, *waiting*—and the Summit beyond, shining like the jaws of a compactor about to spring shut.

The door to the great hall slid quietly open, and Will's eyes went straight to her father, clustered with his staff in front of another vast window. He looked...anger was the wrong word for it. Such a gauche emotion would never find a place on the face of Lord Arrex. But there was a certain tightness to his jaw, a slight compression of his lips, hinting that the aide was on very thin ice indeed. As though he felt her gaze, Xavier looked up, and even that vague suggestion of feeling faded. Xavier was a firm believer in the old Arrex tenet that political strength lay in impassivity, and he never failed to set a good example.

Will carefully schooled her own face into polite neutrality as he waved away the aides. "Good evening, Wilhelmina. So gracious of you to join us at last."

Will didn't bother to correct him on the name; it was a battle she had lost too many times before. "Yes, Father."

Once or twice when she was younger she had attempted the daring sally of calling him *Dad* or *Papi*, copying what Tarrant and her other classmates called their own male parents. To other children, a father was a thing one had, not a title—but much like her efforts with her own name, it had not been successful.

"What *were* you doing?" he asked, not bothering with any further preliminaries like how she was feeling or how her day had been—things Will believed other fathers might ask their daughters.

"I was studying," lied Will easily. He had heard her alarm, but it still wasn't worth openly admitting the truth. An Arrex was many things, but lazy was not one of them.

Xavier's thin lips thinned further, and he gestured impatiently towards the door. Will hastened after him, taking care to keep her strides long. When she was eleven, he had once chastised her for *scurrying,* and the word had burned itself into her brain.

Tunis pressed a small bag of food into her hands as she passed. "I'm sure he'll settle down," she murmured sympathetically, and Will offered her a grateful smile as she slipped through the entryway after Xavier. Between her father's aides and his Cabinet, the Arrex mansion was always overflowing with people, but it sometimes seemed like Tunis was the only friendly face for miles around.

Xavier led the way out into the vast circular room beyond, Will keeping pace. The ringing of their steps against the glossy floor was joined by the familiar booted thud of their Lawkeeper honour guard falling in behind.

Will pulled in a breath: one last moment of peace before the chaos began. The great dome of the atrium arched above her, another circular window in the apex. The air was filled with the noise of water trickling in the fountain, more stars glinting in the reflecting pool beneath. As ever, Will averted her eyes from the columned door across from their own. Like bad pennies, Lauron and Loris always turned up, and Will refused to notice them even if they were there to be seen.

The tramcar was waiting, faithful as the Lawkeepers, its track a single slash of silver in the unbroken expanse of the atrium floor. The tunnel to Centre yawned beyond.

It wasn't until the doors of the tramcar sealed behind her that Xavier spoke again. "Tell me," he said, "what do you think I've been working on today?"

It was not a difficult question to answer. "The Surveys." Obviously. Nothing else had been discussed in the Arrex household for the past six months. With less than two months to go, the heat was only rising.

"It seems no one can tell me what Loris's campaign will centre around," he said, voice still as light as ever, but the tension returning to his expression. "But all my sources suggest that this is her big push."

Will leaned back in her seat as the tramcar hummed into motion. "She's been happy enough in the background for the last twelve years. Why take a stand now?"

One corner of Xavier's mouth quirked. "Happy isn't the way I would put it."

Will turned her palms upward noncommittally, the closest Xavier would tolerate to a shrug. She had never seen their elder cousin anything but delighted with her share of the Spoke Six taxes. "She certainly puts on a convincing show."

"Wouldn't you take care to do the same, if Lauron were the one in charge?"

Will pulled a face. Lauron was as much of a snake as his mother. Xavier raised an eyebrow, and Will hastily smoothed her expression.

"She's been biding her time since my father went to Recycling," Xavier went on. "And this year, she has a reason to try."

He paused meaningfully.

"Your second term as Lord Captain is coming up next year," Will drawled, trying to inject an edge of derision into the words. He was practically spoon-feeding her the answers. She was not an *idiot*.

"You will respect your elders, Wilhelmina."

"Of course, Father." Will smiled sweetly, once again the model daughter.

Xavier smiled back at her, and for a moment green eyes looked into green eyes, the subtle humour of the moment not lost on either of them.

"Yes," he said, as though the deviation from the original topic had not occurred. "She wants the captaincy."

"So she *has* a plan, but no one will tell you what it is?" Will asked sceptically. "All that suggests is that she's paying your spies better than you are."

He looked pleasantly surprised, and Will tried not to feel insulted. "A solid insight."

"I live to please."

If her words were dry, he made no sign of recognising them as such. "And do you have anything else to suggest?" He spread his hands, the fingers long and elegant as her own. "Come on, Wilhelmina. Advise me."

Pursing her lips, Will considered. This was a test, of course. With her father, everything was a test. But she had seen the frenzied discussion with his aides. This might also be an actual plea for help.

Xavier took her pause as hesitancy and prompted her again. "I could do something extravagant—free meal for everyone the night before, perhaps?"

"A little blatant, don't you think?"

He smiled. "If it works, then it doesn't matter."

"I don't know," Will replied doubtfully. "If they see through it you might send them running the other way."

Her father frowned. "You're right," he said, and Will began to suspect that this was a real discussion after all. "If I knew what Loris has up her sleeve, I could counter it. Outdo her once and for all. But until she shows her hand..."

Will sighed and nodded. "Maybe we just need to think bigger than we usually do. The average person doesn't notice good governance and orderly enforcement of the law."

For the first time, he looked a little lost. "What can I do that I don't already?"

"You've got to make a splash in their everyday lives. A few days off for everyone, or something. Free alcohol, concerts in the park. I don't know."

Xavier made a noise in his throat and turned away. The idea was unexceptional, then. One he'd already had and discarded. Will sagged a little, and then forced herself to straighten. *Get over it.* Disappointing him was nothing new. Mask intact, she turned to the window to watch the joins in the tramcar tunnel rush by.

Windows.

She had not quite grasped what a sensitive subject it was. But it made sense. Six hundred people in Spoke Six, minus those who were away at the Academy. Over two-thirds of the volume of the spoke was dedicated to factories, farms, offices, recreational spaces, and the school. That left little room for housing, crammed up at the furthest end of the spoke. The rich lived on the outside of the cylinder, just below the surface, and some valuable homes had small portholes. The wealthiest lived at the top of the spoke, where larger windows were the norm. And of all the homes she had visited with her father, all the parties and dinners, Will had only ever seen glass walls in the two Arrex mansions at the spoke's tip, one belonging to Xavier, and one—slightly smaller—to Loris.

Will let her fingers rest against the tramcar window, the glass cool beneath her touch. A view of the outside world was such an ordinary thing that she hardly noticed it. Beautiful, when you took the trouble to stop and look—but how often did she have the time to do that?

She saw Tarrant's eyes flashing, her face flushed with righteous anger. *Even my papi can't afford a house with a window, and he's on a minister's salary.*

"Father," she said suddenly, turning back to Xavier. "I've had another idea."

He raised his eyebrows.

"People at school were talking about looking outside. Apparently *none* of them have a window at home."

Xavier looked unimpressed. "And?"

"Some of these people go their whole lives without ever seeing outside. We could change that." She felt almost...guilty, for stealing Tarrant's words like that. Twisting the accusations hurled to suit her own purposes. But—no. That was foolish. Why should she feel guilty? Tarrant ought to be pleased. Here Will was, trying to implement her crazy, impractical idea. She ought to be *grateful.*

"We could change that before polling day," she added pointedly, in case he had not picked up on the obvious.

"An interesting idea." His fingertips drumming on the plush arm of his chair, Xavier considered it. "A very interesting idea."

Will was still turning the idea over in her head. "Some sort of open house? Let people into the great hall for a viewing. Or even buy a house down-spoke with a window and turn it into a public amenity. Spoke Six's smallest park."

Xavier finally rewarded her with a rare smile. "I'll discuss it with my team. Well done, Wilhelmina. I think this has some real promise."

Will beamed. "Thank you, Father."

Immediately, that slight feeling of guilt was washed away. Genuine praise from her father! Who would have guessed eavesdropping would be so productive? Her little hobby, developed as a way to fight the boredom of school, was suddenly an unexpected insight into the minds of the electorate. It was always pleasant to be justified.

A sudden rush of light from the window illuminated the tramcar: the tunnel giving way to Centre's tramcar station. The tramcar network was Eden's lifeblood, and the station was the beating heart. Tramcars hissing to a halt beside low platforms, doors swinging up to disgorge their human cargo. People flooded out from the bulky vehicles, so much larger than the sleek Arrex tramcar. Journeys from every spoke coalesced here, and people hurried in every direction to reach the line that would take them to their final destination.

Xavier and Will suffered no such indignities, of course. Instead of the usual forty seats, the Arrex tramcar contained only four, each a plush grey affair more akin to an armchair than a passenger seat. Like all six Noble families, the Arrexes had a private line leading direct from their home to Centre, where the six lines combined into a shared tunnel that ran straight to the Command Module at Centre's peak.

The tramcar slid smoothly to a halt beside a platform where three figures waited. Two wore the salt-grey uniforms of Arrex Lawkeepers, and the third a white doctor's coat. Xavier leaned forward as they approached.

The door rose, and a cloud of sweet perfume flooded the air. Eloise's yellow hair streamed behind her like a halo as she swept inside.

Xavier sprang to his feet. "Eloise, my love."

His wife beamed as she advanced on them both, and there was nothing Arrex-subtle about *her* smile. It was a hundred-watt blast of sunshine, and Will let it wash over her, knowing how brief the moment would be.

"Hello, my darlings! How was school today, Will? I do hope you didn't strangle that poor girl. What's her name? Torrent?"

"Tarrant," Will snapped, her good mood evaporating abruptly as she wished both that her mother would listen better to her impassioned late-night rantings, and that she would *not*.

"That's what I meant, darling," her mother replied easily. "Give her my best, won't you?"

"No, I certainly will not."

Eloise shrugged and breezed past her. "Oh, Xavy, I'm exhausted."

She did not look exhausted, but instantly Xavier was all concern. "What happened? Tell me."

"It was endless, my darling. Absolutely endless. There was a couple who passed all their tests, but they have *twelve percent* consanguinity. I cannot think *why* their marriage application was accepted when they're so close to the legal limit. Now I have to spend the next *week* combing through their embryos and editing away all the issues."

Outside, the two Lawkeepers saluted sharply as the tramcar hummed into motion again and left them behind.

"That's ridiculous." Xavier frowned, keeping her hand sandwiched tightly between his own. His face was animated, that icy reserve vanishing under the full force of her attention, and Will marvelled anew at the miracle of the woman who could thaw Xavier Arrex. "It's inefficient, to expect geneticists to edit so much. Their request to use both their own gametes should have been rejected. A donor would solve the issue without taking up a week of your time."

With her free hand, Eloise gestured helplessly. "Exactly. But they *are* below the legal limit. I have to grant clearance."

"Not if I lobby the Noble Council to lower the legal limit," Xavier offered. "Say nine percent? It likely wouldn't go through fast enough to affect your workload this week, but it might stop the issue from recurring."

Eloise chuckled and patted his fingers. "Oh, Xavy. Any lower than thirteen and we'd be losing a huge chunk of our available pairings. Three thousand six hundred people was considered a *small* population on Old Terra, and we have to expect edits. You can't alter the law every time I have a bad day at work, darling."

Pressing her hand in return, Xavier smiled. "I just hate to see you so tired."

Will turned back to the swift slide of the tunnel past the window as Eloise lowered her head to Xavier's shoulder. "I think I might close my eyes for a moment, my dears."

Will opened her mouth to suggest that her mother take the tramcar home again, but closed it again before the words left her lips. It was a silly suggestion; *every* Noble was present for a Summit. No matter what. But Will also knew exactly what awaited her in the viper's nest everyone politely referred to as the Command Module. A Summit was a gauntlet to be run, the reason behind all her father's constant tests. Even more so than at school, perfection was required tonight. She would be facing enemies much more serious than Tarrant. People with *actual* power.

The thought of Tarrant pulled her away from the Summit, back to the chilly silences at school. The Lottery. *I suppose at least some people don't have to worry about it,* Tarrant spat, her eyes fixed on Will and filled with hate. A forty-two percent chance one of her classmates' numbers would be drawn. Those were staggering odds. Will was disconcertingly likely to lose one of the people who had shared her classroom since she was a toddler.

And Tarrant. Suddenly, Will's blood ran a little colder. What if it were *Tarrant* whose ticket was drawn? The vision of the classroom without her presence was more vivid than the others. Will could almost see it. And it was horribly, echoingly empty. No snark. No sparring. Just...an empty seat beside her.

There were only two years of Will's schooling left before she would move to Centre for the Academy, but if Tarrant's ticket was drawn, those two years would be spent in total isolation. Apart from Lysse's hunger for advancement, the others would avoid Will as they always had. Only Tarrant's cutthroat competitive spirit had been enough to bridge the gulf of frosty silence that divided an Arrex from her lessers.

Those two years would be not just empty, but pointless too. Academic success was a given for Will. She was more intelligent than most of the adults she met, let alone the teenagers. Tarrant was the only one who had ever given her a run for her money. Without Tarrant to beat, what...what would be the point?

Irritating, bloody-minded Tarrant. If her number was drawn, her life wouldn't be the only one ruined.

The tramcar began to slow. They had almost reached Centre's peak. Will lowered her head into her hands and sighed. She needed to get her head into the game. A Summit was a serious matter, especially so close to the Biannual Approval Surveys.

"Wilhelmina!" Her father's voice was sharp enough to have her sitting bolt upright again in less than a heartbeat. "Don't *slouch*."

Almost two kilometres above the spokes, the Command Module possessed a view unparalleled on Eden, and with windows weighing heavy on her mind, even Will was forced to pause and admire the sight. Six enormous curved panes of glass displayed a full three-hundred-and-sixty-degree panorama—Eden's constant companion Amalthea on one side, Jupiter beyond. The huge sphere utterly dominated the sky, banded with stripes of ochre and vermillion, cream and white. A halo illumined its edge, hinting at the presence of the sun currently hidden behind the giant. And somewhere beyond Jupiter's bulk lurked Terra, the dead homeworld that no living human had ever seen. In the opposite direction, the great black vastness of open space, spattered by galaxies like paint thrown carelessly at a canvas.

Within, the circular hall was dominated by a huge desk, raised on a dais that curved to accentuate the throne-like chair at the centre. That was the Lord Captain's seat, and Will could still remember the heady days when it had been Xavier's, and her ten-year-old self had been permitted to sit beside him as he ruled Eden from on high.

The great windows were punctuated by six short stretches of wall, each bearing a larger-than-life portrait of the six Founders. The original Eden crew, back when the Eden was just the little seedship now enshrined in the museum wing of the Academy. As ever, Will's eyes went first to Javier Arrex, Founder and helmsman. She squared her shoulders as she glanced up at him. He looked so like her father.

Indeed, despite the intervening centuries, almost every individual in the room could be identified as a direct descendant of one of the crew in the portraits. Danis in orange, Oriel in blue, Waltek in green, Chassiron in white, Suriss in black and red; the faces as similar to the portraits as the clothing was. Genetic editing was not usually allowed for frivolous reasons, and most citizens of the Eden could only expect their children to be eligible for health edits. But as in so many other things, an exception was made for the Nobles.

Beneath the portrait of the first Lord Captain Chassiron stood the current Lord Captain Chassiron. A long plait of iron-grey hair hung down over one shoulder, her creamy brown skin set off perfectly by her white robes. Galba Chassiron was old—old enough that this was her *tenth* term as Lord Captain. Her cousin had never once challenged her for the leadership of Spoke One.

Lord Captain. The pinnacle of every Noble's ambition, the ultimate reward for years of labour and victories in the Surveys for their spoke. The title rotated between spokes every twelve months, and next year it would pass to Xavier for the second time—*if* he could keep control of Spoke Six out of Loris's grasping hands for long enough. For the second time in his twelve-year rule, he would be Lord Captain Arrex. It was a title that sounded right to Will's ears, and she knew how much he wanted it. How hard he had worked for it.

As her parents moved away in the direction of Lord Captain Chassiron, Xavier flicked a finger to signal that she was free to roam. "Careful tonight, Wilhelmina."

Other than a slight dip of her chin, Will did not respond. This close to the Surveys, she did not need the reminder. She turned instead to scan the room for a second time—focusing now on the occupants rather than the decor and the skyscape behind them.

There was Lauron, his odious blonde head flanked on either side by the ginger curls of Dalton and Dalcifer Danis. Lauron's gaze flashed up to meet hers, his lips curling in a smile that bordered on a sneer. His sallow face was like an unpleasantly accurate mirror, and Will's desire to network abruptly left her. Let Lauron be the one to grovel. Time enough later for the machinations and electioneering. The allegiances she wanted to renew first were of a closer sort.

"Will!" Someone shouted her name, startlingly loud in this room of hushed conversations and subtle insults.

She looked around to see her friends descending.

"Will, it's been *ages!*" It was Zuria who had shouted, of course. It was always Zuria who shouted.

"Speak up a little, Zu, I don't think they heard you on the Wheel." Close behind Zuria came Xanthe, both of them in Waltek green. They were as alike as sisters, with the same big black eyes and tight-curling hair bouncing across their shoulders, and like the Danis boys, one Waltek was seldom seen without the other. Not every Noble hated their cousin as much as Will did.

"Have you been avoiding us?" Zuria demanded, folding Will into an enthusiastic hug.

Will smiled. "It's only been a month!"

"We *could* meet outside of Summits, if we really wanted," a dry voice interjected. Carroway Oriel smiled down, clad in the shining peacock-blue worn by every Oriel since the Eden's founding, the light refracting from the polished skin of his shaven head as much from the iridescent material. "Even you, Will."

Will breathed easier as the four of them closed ranks. She was swimming in familiar waters now, back among her own kind. No one would scold her for possessing a window here.

"I'm sorry," she said now—words that left her lips more seldom than any others. An Arrex did not apologise lightly. "Things have been manic. I couldn't get away."

And it was not a lie. Nine hours of school, three hours of tutoring, and two hours of work with her father left time for very little else on a school-day, and the weekends were not much better. Keeping up with the polls was already eating into her sleep.

"It's alright," Xanthe said, with a slight smile. "I know things are going to be close in Spoke Six."

"Carroway came over last weekend like usual," Zuria interjected brightly. "We missed you, but it's probably better you didn't come—we went to watch the glider-racing."

"A surprisingly entertaining evening," Carroway said carelessly, with a smile at Will as he glanced down at his porta-vidscreen. "Can't think why you hate it so much."

"Because it's a sport for people like Lauron who have too much free time," Will responded automatically, the words coming without any real force behind them. Her friends chuckled, but Will zeroed in on Xanthe again. "What do you mean, it's going to be close in Spoke Six? What have you heard?"

Xanthe rolled her eyes. "Nothing, Will, I swear. Word is that Lady Loris is going to make a fight of it for once, that's all."

"Who told you that?" Will pounced. "Come on, Xanthe, I *need* to know."

Xanthe laughed. "You sound just like my dad. Biannual this and Surveys that, morning till night."

Will was about to press further, but Carroway took her arm and pulled her in the direction of the buffet table. "Come on, Will. Let's just have one night off, huh? Surely we're all a bit sick of the polls talk—even you, deep down."

With a sigh, Will let herself be towed. She was clearly outvoted, and it wasn't like he was *wrong*.

The four of them loaded up a plate each from the table groaning beneath the weight of its burden—more food than an inner-spoke family would see in a year. *Tarrant would have a fit if she saw it.* Will smiled, taking a perverse pleasure at the mental image of Tarrant's eyes bulging out of her head.

"So," Carroway said with a wicked smile as they settled themselves on a cluster of plush sofas beneath the portrait of Founder Leona Suriss, the Eden's first environmental control technician. "My dad heard from the other consorts that Ganith's getting hungry for the succession—but Lady Galba won't give up control."

Will grinned and relaxed. Carroway was the king of gossip, and he could always be relied upon to steer the conversation to other people and their misdeeds: his favourite topic.

"Of course not," Xanthe said witheringly. "That's not news, Carroway; everybody with eyes can see that. The Lord Captain won't give up anything until it's pried from her cold, dead hands."

Zuria let out a gasp of shocked laughter, and Will hastily looked around to make sure the sound had not drawn any unwanted eyes. But no one was looking, and it was *good* to be with her friends. All of them understood, instinctively. They knew what it was like to be Noble. To be set apart and watched from birth, judged for everything you did, and held to an impossible set of standards. Being with them made Will feel comparatively normal.

"I've heard something better than that, anyway." Xanthe brushed a curl back behind her ear, black eyes sparkling.

"Tell us, Xanthe!" Zuria was practically thrumming with excitement, and Carroway wasn't much better.

There was triumph in Xanthe's voice as she laid it bare. "There's a rumour Lord Captain Chassiron is planning to make an exception to the Recycling date."

Now *that* was enough to make Will's jaw drop.

"What?" Carroway and Zuria spoke over each other, both electrified by the bombshell. "An *exception*? For who?"

"Lady Wandea," Xanthe smirked. "Who else?"

Will shook her head. There was—there was no *way*. Even for a Noble's consort, even for the Noble themself, it just wasn't possible. "That can't be true."

"Can't it?" Xanthe retorted, eyes gleaming at the reaction she had elicited. "Lady Wandea is only three years away from Recycling. Why wouldn't the Lord Captain want to keep her around a little longer?"

"But she couldn't. It's the *law*."

Will's mind turned once more to Tarrant. Her promise to plead with her father. The anguish on Cara Sutsu's face when she talked about her grandfather. Presumably not even close to eighty-five, the Recycling age—not like Lady Wandea Chassiron-Hyle—and he was already staring it in the face. No, surely not even the Lord Captain could save her wife from Recycling—not after she had lived a full life and achieved the maximum lifespan. It wouldn't be *fair*.

Tarrant would have a meltdown if she had so much as an inkling that an exception for a Noble was even being *discussed*— and Will wasn't sure she'd be in the wrong, either.

Xanthe was not backing down. "And can't the Lord Captain change the law?"

"If it came to a vote," said Carroway thoughtfully. "Half the Noble Council would back her. Lord Waltek's been in her pocket for decades, and Lady Suriss will follow if she's pushed. Even Uncle Zeko and Lord Arrex would probably swing her way when it came down to the wire. She's too damn powerful to refuse."

"Daddy has *not* been *in her pocket*," hissed Xanthe, incensed. "My family makes its *own* decisions."

"Alright, alright!" Carroway held up his hands. "Not trying to start a fight."

"At least *my* father is the head of his own family," Xanthe persisted, refusing to be mollified.

Carroway shrugged. "No skin off my nose. Mum's always been perfectly willing to let Uncle Zeko do the work, and I'm happy to follow suit. There's no harm in being a backup, eh, Zuria?"

Zuria coloured, and Xanthe gave Carroway a little shove—just enough to knock him off balance, but not enough to cause a scene. "Don't tease her!"

"It *is* impossible, though," Will said, calling their attention back from the squabble. "Even someone as powerful as Lady Galba can't change *that* law, surely? I mean—" she glanced around to make sure none of the Chassirons were within earshot to hear her slander their matriarch, "—even *she's* only seven years out from Recycling."

The others stared at her, eyes wide. "Will!"

"What?"

Carroway leaned in. "You can't just *say* that. She might be old, but Lady Galba has the ears of a *bat*. My mum thinks she has the Command Module bugged."

"Then she'll hear the truth," Will snapped, too nettled now to back down. "Even a Lord Captain can't change the law just because it's *her* wife that's gotten old."

Carroway threw up his hands in surrender. "I was just saying, Will."

"I...sorry. I know." Reluctantly, Will patted him on the arm. It wasn't Carroway's fault she was on edge. It wasn't his fault her head was full of Cara Sutsu's dying grandfather—and Tarrant, of course. Always Tarrant.

CHAPTER 4

Spoke 6, Eden Station – Year 452 – Day 322 – 08:00

Breezing into the classroom a full hour before class was due to start, Will was certain that today at least she would win the race. There would be no smug little smile from Tarrant, with her books already spreading across the desk like fungi. Will would be first, settled at the desk and ready to glance up idly when Tarrant finally rushed in.

"Oh, Tarrant?" she would say, with just the right amount of careless insult to her tone. "You're finally here."

But when Will tapped the wall to open the door, the classroom was not empty. She froze for a second in the doorway, staring at them all. Despite the early hour, every single one of her classmates was here.

And something was wrong.

They huddled together, shoulders hunched. More than one face was stained with tears. And in every hand rested an identical envelope, coloured traditional Arrex grey, the colour of Spoke Six. When she saw that colour, realisation finally struck. The Lottery tickets had arrived.

"I got number thirteen," Lysse said pettishly, crumpling the paper in her hand. "Can you imagine anything unluckier than that?"

"My mum says it's a lucky number," rumbled Erntz, but from the way Lysse sneered at him, it was scant comfort.

Joss was curled up against their desk, Garth, Sutsu, and Tarrant all huddled round them.

"I can't do it. I can't. I don't want to get shot out into space to die."

"There's that spokeswoman," Garth said, but he sounded too nervous to offer any real reassurance. "Arc? Cark? Whatever her name is. She came back. The Laika pilots don't all die."

"Only most of them!" Joss snapped at him, raising their head. "Meteors, system faults, crashes—what even *are* the return rates?

My parents don't know *anyone* who sent off a friend twenty-five years ago who ever saw them again!"

"I'm sure there's plenty," Garth said weakly. "Maybe there's more in the other spokes."

"Even if you manage to get back, you're gone so long that you might as well be dead," Joss went on miserably. "Ten years, fifteen, I've heard some of the missions are. By the time you got back you'd have missed everything. No Academy, no job, no Parental Qualification. What would be left, even if you did make it home?"

No one answered them this time.

Will took a few tentative steps into the classroom. Would this be a good time to mention the window-viewing evening? Xavier's staff had almost finished the planning. There were three hundred tickets, enough for half the population of the spoke to attend if they chose to. It was all but guaranteed to be a triumph, and Will was certain nothing Loris could do would be able to match it. Most of the tickets only allowed the holder half an hour, but Will had three four-hour tickets in her pocket and three comfortable armchairs tucked away in the observatory, safely away from the crush of people in the great hall. One for Sutsu, one for her grandfather— and one for Tarrant, if she chose to come.

Perhaps it would cheer them all up. A silver lining for a gloomy day. A cautious smile edged on to Will's face as she imagined their response. Sutsu would be thrilled, of course. And Tarrant had a nice smile, when she chose to use it. It might be pleasant to have it directed Will's way for once.

She drew closer, and the others looked up at the sound of her footsteps.

Will opened her mouth, but as soon as she saw who it was, Tarrant leapt to her feet, eyes flashing, ready to defend her friends.

"Go *away*, Arrex."

Will raised her hands. "I—I just wanted to talk to you and Sutsu."

"I said leave us *alone*," Tarrant spat. "None of us want to hear from you today. This isn't something that will *ever* affect you. Go away."

Her eyes were too bright. Were those—were those unshed tears?

Will flushed. As usual, she'd chosen precisely the wrong moment. They were all too vulnerable right now. Wound too tight.

"Sorry," she mumbled, looking at the floor. The *floor!* What was she thinking? An Arrex did not look at the floor and mutter apologies. Her father would have a fit. Sharply, she looked back up, meeting Tarrant's big brown eyes. "We can talk another time," she said, more clearly.

"Good," Tarrant said fiercely. "Because none of us are in the mood for *you* right now."

Her throat working, Will swallowed. That stung. And the hurt was all the more poignant because it was so unexpected. Since when did she care what her classmates thought? She knew they weren't friends. She had spent most of her childhood trying to *ensure* that they weren't friends.

But—she hadn't thought they were enemies, either. Rivals, maybe, especially Tarrant. But with the rest she had tried to cultivate a careful neutrality. Distant and polite. So that in twenty years' time, when she was up against Lauron in the Biannual Approval Surveys, the six of them would look back on their days in school together and say—*Oh, Lady Arrex? Yes, we were in school together. She was nice enough, I suppose.* Nothing scandalous, nothing personal.

And even with Tarrant—Will thought of their antipathy as a mostly academic one. Competing since the very first day. Four-year-old Will Arrex—cleaned and scrubbed to within an inch of her life and, thanks to the rigorous preschool tutoring schedule her father had set up for her, already able to read and multiply—had expected the first day of school to be a breeze.

"You are an Arrex, and the future leader of this spoke," Xavier had said, very seriously, before Tunis escorted her to school. "You must be the best of all of them."

In the very first lesson, when the teacher had asked if anybody knew their alphabet yet, Will had confidently raised her hand. And then another hand had shot up, stretching even higher than Will's as the owner rose half out of her seat to wave it at the teacher.

"Go on, Paige," the teacher had said.

And Will's dreams of establishing herself firmly as the leader of her little cohort had crumbled as this stranger with the tangle of wild hair almost as long as she was tall rattled off the entire alphabet, *A* to *Z*. It was done without finesse, without clarity—almost without taking a single breath—but it was right, every letter. All the hours Will had spent practising with her oratory tutor, making sure her pronunciation was perfect, that she enunciated clearly enough to fill the classroom with the sound of her small voice—all wasted.

But Will had risen above it. *Excelsior.* She tried harder than ever, and she let the rivalry born that morning become the fuel that stoked her fire. Tarrant was her opponent, and much as she disliked the girl, she respected her too.

Apparently the feeling didn't run both ways.

Tarrant was looking at her as though she *hated* her. Real, personal hatred. Like it wasn't just Will's ability to actually beat her sometimes that she hated...like it was Will herself that Tarrant loathed.

And that *hurt.*

Tarrant's abhorrence ran deeper than she'd believed. Personal enemies were dangerous, and exactly the sort of thing Xavier warned Will to avoid. Those were people with a motive to damage you in the future, politically or otherwise.

An image flashed into her mind—Tarrant, wearing the charcoal sash of a Spoke Six minister, just like her father. But it was Lauron's government she served in, Lauron she stood beside. Anger bubbled up, hot and red. If Tarrant joined Lauron's government to help him bring Will down...after thirteen years of sitting beside each other every day, striving to outdo each other, few people knew Will or her limits as well as Tarrant did. If she chose to join Lauron, she would be gifting him a weapon Will could not match.

She couldn't let it happen. She could not *allow* it to happen.

Tarrant was *hers.*

That thought was incongruous enough that Will caught herself. *Calm down,* she thought, trying to imagine what her father would advise. *Disengage,* Xavier would say. *Tensions are too high. Come back later, when you're better prepared.*

Tarrant was still waiting, fists clenched, full lips thinned by how hard she was pressing them together.

Will looked into those furious brown eyes and forced the angry words away. Starting today, she had to find a way to put Paige Tarrant firmly into *her* camp—or at least restore the neutrality she had believed was there. Working against Will Arrex could not be even a *possibility* as a career option for Tarrant. In fact, Tarrant's prospective career as a Terran history professor suddenly did not seem like such a tragic waste of her abilities after all. If she was safely tucked away in the Academy for the rest of her life, there wasn't much risk of her deciding to take up a career in politics.

So Will followed Xavier's imaginary advice and retreated—not just back to her desk, but from the entire classroom, letting the door swish shut behind her.

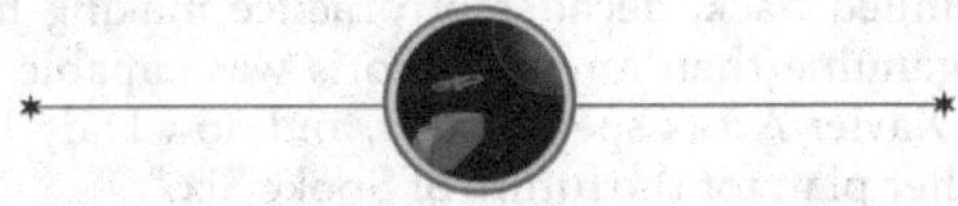

With a sigh, Will flopped onto the vast sofa and let herself stare at the ceiling. The last of her tutors was gone, and she could finally breathe. Concentrating on her lessons was a lost cause regardless: all she could think about was Tarrant and Tarrant's accusations. *None of us want to hear from you today. This isn't something that will ever affect you.* Tarrant was right. More than anything, exemption from the Lottery was what set her apart from her classmates. What set her family apart from their people.

And it was issues like that—and the resentment that stemmed from them—that would come into play in the next eight weeks. If Will wanted to save her family from humiliation, that was what she had to find a way to address.

For the first time in her life, she had no idea what to do.

When the silence stretched too deep, Will reached for the control panel concealed in the arm of the sofa, and the vidscreen taking up the entire wall opposite flickered into life. Letting the noise from the newscasters wash over her, Will lost herself in the view from the window. Jupiter and its moons dancing on in their slow, stately revolutions. A million miles away from the turmoil of the Eden, and utterly uncaring. The endless digs from Tarrant about her station and her wealth were uncomfortable, but at least they were a reminder to be grateful for what she had. To enjoy it. And it *was* beautiful here. The stars, the nebulae—the red expanse of Amalthea. It was all beautiful. If Lauron won, would he sit in this room and watch the stars? Somehow, she doubted it.

Then a word on the vidscreen caught her attention. Had that been *Arrex*?

"We're so glad you could join us here tonight, Lady Arrex," the newscaster said, and Will's blood ran cold.

The first day of the campaigning season, and Loris was on the vidscreen, televised to the entire spoke on the late-night news. It could mean only one thing: Loris was ready to play her first card.

The camera panned out, the shot widening to show Will's aunt sitting beside the newscaster, a beatific smile pasted across her pointy face. "I'm delighted to be here, Cirrus."

Cirrus smiled back, decades of practice making his attempt look more genuine than anything Loris was capable of. "We've heard Lord Xavier Arrex speak today, and now Lady Loris Arrex will lay out her plan for the future of Spoke Six."

Will's hands tightened on the fabric of the sofa cushion. She had watched her father's speech with her oratory tutor not two hours before. The jewel in the crown of the prime-time news spot, Xavier's speech had been exactly what she expected. Tradition, continuity, a safe pair of hands. An admirable performance, but the writing was uninspired. Erring too far on the side of caution, trying to avoid overpromising until Loris tipped her hand.

Loris beamed again, first at Cirrus and then at the camera. She wore a simple suit in Arrex grey. Her hair, the same white-blonde as Will's own, was pulled back into a sensible bun, and her cool green eyes were sincere.

Will glared. The woman was a *snake*.

"I am pleased to announce the beginning of my campaign against Lord Xavier Arrex," Loris said gravely. "I am confident that by this time next year, I will be First Minister of Spoke Six, and that you all will have placed your trust in me. I plan to improve all our lives through…"

Loris launched into her spiel, and Will picked up the first of the strawberries from the bowl Tunis had left. It was sliced into precise quarters. Tunis knew exactly how Will liked things. Clean, ordered, organised.

Was this all Loris had up her sleeve? Tax cuts for the businesses, tax relief for the poorest in the spoke. Will kept her eyes on Loris's face. There had to be something more. Something big and splashy to get people talking.

But Loris was picking up steam again, building to some sort of crescendo. "My cousin, Xavier Arrex, has been in power a long time. Twelve years. And his father ruled for thirty years before that. Xavier is, I'm sorry to say, sorely out of touch. He doesn't understand the people of Spoke Six, and I fear most of us are only voting for him out of habit."

Will's lips twisted in a wry smile. Loris included herself in *most of us*, though she was barred from voting along with every other Noble.

"The issue that we face today—the Lottery—is the perfect example. The flower of Spoke Six's youth, our best and brightest, are thrust into danger's way along with all of the rest. We are losing valuable personnel—our *children*—and I ask you," Loris paused, her forefinger quivering in the air. "I ask you, why should only the Arrex children be exempt?"

Strawberry halfway to her lips, Will froze. *Here it comes, the big reveal.*

Loris paused once more, and then spoke with triumphant finality. "If you vote for me in the Biannual Approval Surveys, my first act will be the introduction of a new law that allows for ten exemptions per Lottery. Four will be purchasable, and six will be scholarship exemptions, awarded based on merit. No longer will only the Noble children be exempt. Now your children can be, too."

She smiled again at the camera, and Will knew that the wicked edge to that pleasant expression was meant only for her.

"Vote for Lady Loris Arrex, and I will save your children."

Cirrus babbled his thanks, looking as excited as Loris did, and Will flicked the vidscreen off in disgust.

There it was. Loris's grand plan. Never mind that the Lottery could not be altered by one spoke. Truth didn't matter to Loris, and the people certainly didn't care about technicalities. They were sheep, desperate for a scrap of hope, and they would follow where she led. Loris could lie through her teeth and then fail to deliver once she was safely in power. Xavier was different; he had enough honour not to promise something he couldn't achieve. And if he said as much—if he said Loris was lying—she would just retort that he didn't *want* to help, and the public would love her even more for it.

And such a suggestion was bound to be popular. Absolutely guaranteed to be. Will had seen the fear on her classmates' faces. Their parents would vote for someone who promised deliverance. They would vote for someone who promised even the tiniest shred of it.

Will bit into the strawberry, and its taste flooded her tongue. Like Tarrant's hair smelled. Red and sweet and full of flavour. Had Tarrant ever eaten a real strawberry? Somehow, Will doubted it.

None of us want to hear from you today. This isn't something that will ever affect you.

The Lottery. Everything in this round of Surveys hinged on the Lottery. It was something that impacted every young person on the Eden, that every parent and relative would care deeply about. Windows, equality: every other petty concern faded into obscurity. This was the issue that would decide the Eden's next Lord Captain. Every single voter in Spoke Six had a stake in the Lottery.

Only the Arrexes moved above it all, cut off from their people. They were unique and envied for it.

Loris recognised that, and she had marked herself out as the people's champion. Xavier had to respond. But he wouldn't lie to the electorate, and either way, he couldn't just copy her idea.

Will shut her eyes and thought, fingernails digging into her temples as she chewed. Xavier couldn't just offer *more* exemptions than Loris, and he certainly couldn't offer to cancel the Lottery altogether. Not only was it impossible without unanimous support from the Noble Council, the Laikas were a vital part of Eden's lifecycle—the terraforming programmes scattered across the solar system were the key to any planetside future, and they needed to be monitored. Without the Laikas, Eden would wither away into nothing. The last gasp of a dying species from a dead world.

No, the Lottery had to be maintained.

What, then? There had to be something related to it—something that could sway public opinion away from Loris and back to Xavier.

This isn't something that will ever affect you.

Tarrant had said that.

And she had been right. The Lottery would never affect Will, unless—unless it *did*.

The idea came to her then, fully formed and crystalline in its clarity, and it was like a punch to the gut. It left Will breathless. Could she do that? Would she *dare* do that?

But it would be popular. It would be *wildly* popular, and if she could prove that Loris's promise was undeliverable, the anger at the lie combined with the nobility of Will's sacrifice would be enough to bring the voters back to Xavier.

Will let out a breath. It was audacious, ridiculous—but definitely workable. And almost guaranteed to be a success, if she could force all the disparate parts into harmony.

She was going to enter the Lottery.

Xavier would refuse, of course. He would say it was lunacy. He would say it was not behaviour befitting a Noble. And he would be right. But that was exactly why it would *work*.

If Will did this, she would forever set *her* branch of the family apart. Loris and Lauron might be Arrexes, but Xavier and Will would be the Arrexes of the people. The populace would see Will lining up with her Lottery ticket alongside all of their children, and they would love her for it.

The Surveys would be a landslide victory.

"It's a blatant lie." Xavier's voice was bubbling with barely suppressed rage. "Completely unenforceable. It's not a spoke issue. She can't change Eden-wide law like that, and she certainly won't get the Noble Council to support her idiotic idea."

"I think that's what she's banking on," Will said, through a mouthful of toast.

"Don't talk with your mouth full," he said automatically, but his heart wasn't in it. He sneered down at his vidscreen, watching Loris deliver her message over and over again. "Even if she *could* do it, it wouldn't matter until the next Lottery, when she's deeply unlikely to be in office, and couldn't impact policy—" He cut himself off, breathing heavily, and abruptly slammed his fist down onto the table. "I could wring her *neck*."

Carefully swallowing her toast before she spoke this time, Will tried for a reassuring tone. "It won't work, Father. We'll show everyone she's a liar."

"Impossible," he said bitterly. "If I call her out and explain the details, I'll bore half my watchers, and give Loris the opportunity to dismiss me as a pessimist. The people don't want hard facts. They want promises."

"We'll come up with something better, then."

"Such as what? My staff are about as useful as a shower in zero-G. They had *nothing* for me at last night's crisis briefing."

Will almost told him. The words were on the tip of her tongue. *I can save us both, Father.* But she couldn't take the chance—the risk was too great. Once the plan was in motion, she could talk him round.

"The window-viewing party next week will be a good start."

He brightened momentarily. "Yes. But one event isn't enough to win the Surveys. And after this, I don't know where to take the campaign. We had announcements planned—some corporate bonuses, a new Lawkeeper training initiative. It's not emotive enough."

Will nodded understandingly, her resolve solidifying with each word. Her family needed this. Her father needed it. She would enter the Lottery, and prove once and for all that it was *her* side of the family that understood the common man.

And besides—there was nothing quite so satisfying as the way the colour drained from Tarrant's face when she was proved wrong. Will could already picture the moment when she would slap a Lottery ticket down on the desk between them. Who would be the elitist snob *then*?

"Focus on the party for now," she said. "It'll be an opportunity for us to hear some real voter issues."

Once he headed to the Cabinet chamber Will slipped out the front door. The usual complement of Lawkeepers standing guard outside saluted. As she strode towards the waiting tramcar, Will eyed the entrance to the secondary Arrex mansion. The portico standing not quite as tall as her own; the pillars flanking the door a little less thick. A few hazy childhood memories of the inside were more of the same: a limited library, a diminutive great hall. A less generous stipend from the taxpayers of Spoke Six. Identical, but inferior.

Will looked at that doorway, and let it forge the fear within to steely certainty. She would do this for her father, for her family. She would show Loris, Lauron, Tarrant—everyone who doubted her.

They would all see what Will Arrex was made of.

With an abrupt start, the door hissed open, and a small, balding figure bustled into the room, sweating and apologising with equal profusion. "My apologies, Lord Arrex. My secretary didn't tell me you were waiting. He's a terribly scatterbrained boy, fresh out of the Academy, and he must have missed your call—" He finally looked up from his sheaf of notes, and choked on his own words.

"Not Lord Arrex, I'm afraid." Will smiled casually. "Only an emissary."

"L-Lady Arrex?" He appeared even more discomfited, and the expression was vaguely familiar. "How can I help you, my Lady?"

Will waited patiently as he squeezed his portly frame into the small space not taken up by his gigantic desk, narrowly avoiding spilling a day-old mug of tea. The disarray of papers and files was almost as bad as Tarrant's half of the table at school. A large plaque on it read *Hrue Lipson—Director of Lottery, Spoke Six*.

As Hrue Lipson fidgeted with his papers, Will regarded him with a critical eye. The Lottery programme was a strange career, demanding one year of intense activity followed by twenty-four of utter sloth. Only the Laika production team were required to provide regular output, through the slow construction of the ships. The Lottery division probably fell apart during the gaps between Lotteries—and Hrue Lipson certainly looked unprepared for the Herculean task he had been presented with.

But Will needed this little man's help, and she pasted on her friendliest smile. "Just a minor issue, Mr Lipson. It won't take too much of your time."

One of the many beads of sweat on Hrue Lipson's large forehead trickled slowly down his face to lose itself in his eyebrow. Will did her best not to follow it with her eyes.

"I—I'm always happy to assist."

She gave a little sigh and leaned forward in her hard plastic chair. "I won't beat around the bush, Mr Lipson. I want a ticket."

His weak blue eyes bulged, and he blanched even whiter. "W-what?"

"I'm here to collect my Lottery ticket."

"I'm not quite sure I grasp your meaning, Lady Arrex."

"My father has decided that it would be good for morale to make an exception to the exception for Nobles," Will explained airily. "So I will be needing a ticket number, just like all the other young people."

More beads of sweat sprang into existence, and Hrue Lipson produced a handkerchief to mop himself. "A-and Lord Arrex is requesting this? That—that *you* be entered into the Lottery?"

Maybe a firmer touch was needed. Will's nostrils flared slightly. "Must I repeat myself?"

"No, no!" He all but yelped the words. "Of course not. I just—I'm afraid I don't quite understand. Nobles are—you are *exempt*, Lady Arrex."

"And I am telling you that for this Lottery, and this one *only*,"—Will had no desire to change the law permanently—"my father wishes me to be exempted from the exemption."

Hrue was staring at her, his eyeballs protruding from their sockets in a way that gave him a permanently horrified expression. Will was no longer sure if he was shocked, or this was simply his natural appearance.

"I cannot do that, Lady Arrex," he whispered. "The law—"

"States that the children of Nobles are not *required* to enter into the Lottery, not that they are barred from doing so." Will had not come this far without doing her research. Legally, it was perfectly doable; it was just that Will was the first Noble insane enough to ask for entry.

"But your father..." He tailed off.

Will had prepared for this eventuality too. Calmly, she produced one of her father's spare porta-vidscreens from her bag and laid it on the table. A few taps of the screen, and Lord Xavier Arrex's official letterhead flickered into sight. Will scrolled down the document slowly enough for Hrue to follow, and watched his face pale as he read.

In light of our current situation...I have judged it best...Assist to the fullest extent of your abilities...Signed, Lord Xavier Arrex, First Minister of Spoke Six and Member of the Noble Council.

She had sent it to herself from the vidscreen in his office that morning. The vidscreen had unlocked itself at the sight of her face: she had full access. The Arrexes did not keep secrets from one another. Aside from this, of course.

Will kept her face impassive as Hrue tried in vain to keep his hands from trembling.

"If I may...on a personal level..." He was sweatier than ever. "This is not something you want to do, Lady Arrex."

All at once, it clicked, and Will remembered where she knew him from. The last Lottery, twenty-five years ago. Old footage replayed on the vidscreen, brave survivors disembarking. The lone returning Laika. A sharp-faced girl triumphant with tidings of the terraforming station on Io, and the doughy, damp boy behind her.

Hrue Lipson was a pilot.

"I'll decide that for myself." No, that was wrong. Too individual. He wouldn't buy it. "I mean—my father has made his decision."

"This is...it will be unprecedented. In all of Eden's history."

How this man had survived a Laika mission, Will had no idea. Living with someone so moist in low-grav had to have been hellish; the air would always be full of little beads of sweat, floating around like unpleasantly warm raindrops.

She kept her voice firm. "Nevertheless, it is what my father wants."

Hrue Lipson whimpered, but like any good bureaucrat, he knew when he was beaten. He bowed his head, and began to poke at his vidscreen.

Will sat back in her chair, satisfaction at having played the game and won warring with the sick feeling settling deep into her bones. *This isn't something that will ever affect you.* How wrong Tarrant had been.

When Will left the unfortunate man's office, there was a piece of thick, embossed card in her bag, the number printed on it burning against her skin even through all the layers of fabric.

Spoke Six Lottery, Year 452—Ticket Number 69.

CHAPTER 5

Spoke 6, Eden Station – Year 452 – Day 330 – 19:00

"Welcome, everyone. Welcome to our home."

Will stood tall at her father's side, smiling at the endless queue of people filing through the double doors. She nodded and murmured pleasantries, accepted their thanks, and shook any hand that was thrust in her direction: a pretty standard evening of canvassing. But when she turned to look further into the great hall, it was obvious that for many tonight was anything but standard. The tickets had been distributed on a random basis among the least affluent of Spoke Six's residents, and now the great hall was packed to the rafters. Fingers pointed at Jupiter's myriad moons, and smiles shone bright as the stars beyond.

"We're so glad you could join us," Will said to the latest newcomer. "Thank you for coming."

The attendees had been flooding in for the past thirty minutes, their best clothes freshly rumpled from the Lawkeepers' security searches in the atrium. Next in line was a family with two young children, who stared past Will without even seeing her—already agog at the sight of the planet they had orbited all their lives and never seen outside of a vidscreen.

Will's greeting for this group was more genuine. While the parents mumbled something self-conscious to Xavier, she bent down to face the children. "Hey, guys."

The older boy jumped and looked guiltily away from the stars to Will. "H-hello." A nudge from his parents. "I mean, good evening, Lady Arrex."

"Good evening," Will smiled. "I hope you enjoy looking. How many moons do you think you'll be able to spot?"

"There's eighty," the boy answered with the utmost sincerity.

Will's lips quirked. "And you think you'll be able to spot all eighty tonight?"

Doubt flashed across his face. "Won't we?"

"I bet you can make a good start, at least," Will reassured him. "Do you know all their names?"

He shook his head. "Nuh-uh. But Callisto is my favourite." A pause as he thought. "Do *you* know all their names?"

"No," Will fibbed, laughing a little as she did. "Or I didn't when I was your age, anyway. Callisto is visible tonight, I think. Look past Adrastea and you should be able to make it out."

A quiver of excitement ran through him. "I will!"

"And if you look *really* hard," she added, straightening back up, "you might even be able to spot Saturn! It looks more like a big star from here and you can't see the rings, but it's still lovely."

His eyes were round as saucers. "Will we be able to see Terra, too?"

Will was about to try and explain when the boy's father tugged him away. "Come on, kids. Let's go have a look and leave Lord Arrex be."

Will watched them go until Xavier's voice prompted her to turn back to her public, a camera-ready smile on her face—only to find herself staring straight down the barrel of a stun gun.

"Hello, Lady Arrex," Tarrant said, a smirk playing over her lips.

Will gaped.

Tarrant's hair tumbled loose down her back as it always did, its unruly volume surely almost as insulating as the fluffy jumpers the miners on Amalthea wore under their spacesuits. Nearly obscured beneath the curls was a lemon-coloured shirt and a tailored jumpsuit that faded from yellow to orange as it passed the flare of her hips and flowed loose over her legs. Will had never seen Tarrant dressed like this—in anything but the classic iron-grey school jumpsuit—and it was enough to leave her floundering.

She opened her mouth, and nothing came out.

Tarrant's smirk widened slightly, before transforming into a polite smile as she turned to Xavier. "Lord Arrex."

The warm shades suited her—the honey overtones to her dark curls were more obvious, and her brown eyes looked almost amber. Smiling up at Xavier like that, she didn't look like the awful know-it-all that had devoted the past decade of her life to being the bane of Will's. She looked almost...pretty.

Xavier shifted his weight, and Will came back to herself with a sharp breath. Tarrant's presence in her home should not unsettle her this much; she had *invited* her, after all. Will swallowed hard and forced herself to say something. *Anything.* "Uh—good evening—Tarrant."

"Wilhelmina," came her father's warning hiss.

Yes. Politeness. That was the name of the game this evening. Civility and hosting. Even Tarrant had thrown in a *Lady Arrex.* "I mean, good evening, *Miss* Tarrant." And then, belatedly noticing the two figures hovering behind Tarrant, "Miss Sutsu, Mr—Mr Sutsu, I assume?"

"This is my grandfather, Jin," Sutsu said, stepping forward to stand beside Tarrant. "Thank you for—for this, Lady Arrex. It means more than you know."

Sutsu's eyes were shining, and the obvious gratitude there helped Will to find her footing again. Back in her awkward tween years, her public speaking tutor had covered several modules on basic conversation, and she leaned on that familiar training now. The first step was easy: *consider your audience, and which response will land best with them.* Had Tarrant not been there she would have gone with a simple *It's nothing, really,* but she could already see the path that conversation would take. Tarrant would sneer something like *Of course it's nothing to someone as rich as you*—and from there it would devolve with horrifying swiftness into their usual mud-slinging. That wasn't something her father needed to see, let alone the camera crews circling like vultures amongst the guests.

Instead she spread her hands, palms upward, in a gesture of welcome. "I'm just glad you could come."

"Your classmates, Wilhelmina?" Xavier asked, stepping forward to retake control. "I don't suppose Miss Tarrant is a relation of Grayson Tarrant?"

Will glanced at Tarrant, who cocked a brow. Will could see the wheels turning in her mind. *Wilhelmina?* That would probably make an appearance during their next scrap.

"Yes, Lord Arrex," Tarrant confirmed. "Papi always tells me about how much he enjoys working with you."

"Grayson is a very talented man," Xavier replied. "If you're anything like him I'll wager you keep Wilhelmina on her toes."

Tarrant looked as though she was holding back a laugh as her eyes flicked to Will. "I hope so."

Pressing her lips together, Will gave them both a slightly strained smile. Xavier retained little of what she told him of her days at school, but he would probably take a dim view of the hours of effort she sunk weekly into trying to outdo Tarrant.

"These are the guests I mentioned, Father. I'm going to show them upstairs, if you don't mind."

Xavier nodded permission, his attention already transferring to the next group. "Welcome, everyone."

Jostled unceremoniously further inside by the surge of people behind them, the others looked to Will for guidance.

"Upstairs?" Tarrant asked sceptically. "Are you planning to secrete us away somewhere and have us killed? A bit much even for you, Arrex."

With Xavier out of the way, Will was finally free to return fire. "You assume you're worth the effort of an assassination plot."

"And *you* assume you know anything about what I think—" Tarrant snapped back, all the restraint she had shown in front of Xavier evaporating.

"Paige!" Sutsu's voice interjected.

She was standing beside Jin, his thin hands clutching her arm—and now that Will was looking more closely at him, she was startled to see someone slight enough to make birdlike little Sutsu look robust. Two small figures huddled together, one crumbling away as the other struggled to hold him together.

"Oji-san isn't used to the way you two talk," Sutsu insisted, and Jin coughed, a sound as dry and papery as his rumpled skin. "Can't you get along?"

Her words were addressed only to Tarrant, but Will took the reins, frustrated that she had slipped so far in front of Jin. "Of course. I've set something quieter up. This way."

Without waiting for a response, she turned and swept towards the spiral staircase, the crowd parting like water before her. Nice and smooth—no admission of wrongdoing, no apology necessary.

The others trailed behind her as she mounted the stairs. The bustle below faded once she reached the gallery, but the old man's laboured breathing became more obvious.

A whisper from Sutsu to her grandfather. "Careful, Oji-san."

"Quit your fussing, Cara—I'm old, but I'm not dead yet."

It was somehow unreal to see Will's oldest enemy transplanted from the neutral territory of the school to her own home. Her yellow jumpsuit seemed to blaze like fire against the Arrex grey: sunshine in a world of steel. Will had never seen someone who looked less like she belonged, but Tarrant carried herself with the confidence of a Noble.

Brown eyes flashed as Tarrant noticed Will watching. "Not inspiring any confidence that I was wrong on the luring us away to be murdered front, Arrex. How big does this place need to be?"

Will shrugged. The Arrex mansions—both the greater and the lesser—were more than family homes. They were limbs of the state, vital to the running of Spoke Six. Their cavernous halls housed the government and civil service. But Tarrant would never understand that, even if Will tried to explain. All she would ever see was excess and luxury.

They passed the last of Eloise's home laboratories and Will tapped the panel that would open the final door, revealing a second spiral staircase. Jin let out a dry breath at the sight of it, and Will felt another spike of guilt.

"It's shorter than the other one," she offered, in an attempt at reassurance. "And the view is much better than downstairs."

"View, you say?" Jin said, showing the first spark of real interest she had seen from him. "I can handle a few little stairs."

Re-energised, he hurried forward, leaving Sutsu and Tarrant scrambling to aid him on the steps. Will bounded after them, not wanting to miss the pay-off after all her careful arrangements.

Panting and dishevelled, the party emerged into the silver-red glow of Jupiter's light.

The observatory was kept in constant darkness, to allow for better viewing of the galaxies beyond, and Will still remembered the first time she had seen it. She came in here less than she used to, and watching the amazement dawn on her companions' faces, she felt like it hadn't been often enough.

"Ah." The word was an exhalation, a prayer. Jin was staring out at the vista, one hand fluttering up—as though if he just reached out, he might touch the stars themselves. A smile played over that wrinkled face, and his filmy eyes glittered with tears. "I'd forgotten."

Cara, clutching his other hand with both of her own, turned to Will with overflowing eyes. "Thank you, Lady Arrex. Thank you so much."

Will flushed. "Call me Will, Su—I mean, Cara. You can call me Will."

"Will, then," Cara smiled. "You don't know what this means to him."

Jin pulled sharply on her sleeve, drawing her attention back to him. "Look, Cara! The *sun.*"

Eden was four days into its latest sunrise, and the sun was visible on the curve of Jupiter's horizon—a brilliant white ball pulsing with light and power.

As grandfather and granddaughter stepped forward hand in hand, Tarrant hung back with Will—perhaps wishing, as Will did, to give them some privacy.

"I had no idea you lived like this." The words were said without rancour. Tarrant's voice held only wonder.

"Like parasites leeching off the people?" Will suggested sarcastically, ready for whatever smackdown Tarrant was trying to set up.

That earned her a snicker. "No. I knew that already. I meant with all this...beauty."

Will paused to consider. The stars quivered like living things, and Cara and Jin were silhouetted with a pale white halo. "Yes, it is beautiful."

She waited for Tarrant to add in the jibe—*You don't deserve it* or *Most people will never experience even one-tenth of what you were just handed at birth* or even a ham-fisted *Pity you're so ugly, though*—but none came. The two of them just stood, watching the Sutsu family stare out into the wilderness of the void, enthralled by the lights that danced there.

Moving slowly, Jin and Cara wove through the telescopes and machinery speckled around the darkened room, and Will heard their exclamations of delight as they found the plush armchairs and steaming teapot waiting for them. Tarrant took her seat beside the others, but Will lingered, hovering on the outskirts of a moment that did not include her.

"Is that Amalthea, there?" Cara said in a whisper. "It's so much bigger than it looks in the textbooks."

"It's different than I remember," Jin croaked. "More jagged. I think I smoothed it out in my memory."

Tarrant reached for Cara's shoulder and squeezed it. "Look. See the way the sun's shining?"

With a disbelieving little laugh, Cara reached out as though she might touch it. "Real sunlight."

Jin coughed, and the spell over Will was broken. With a horrible rush of embarrassment, she realised that she was doing it again. Eavesdropping. Listening in on conversations that weren't meant for her to hear. Abruptly, she turned to go.

But Tarrant rose to stop her—fingers hovering just centimetres above Will's arm. "You're leaving?"

"This is a political event, after all," Will said, shrugging a little weakly. "Got to go and make the rounds."

"Listen, Arrex."

Will paused on the stairs' threshold. Waiting.

"You've done a good thing here." The words were almost unwilling.

Her discomfort giving way instantly to a broad smile, Will swung back to face the other girl. "Was that *praise*, Tarrant? How unlike you."

Tarrant rolled her eyes. "Heaven forbid you just take the compliment. But yeah. I'm not afraid to admit it. For once in your life, you did something for somebody else."

"Well then, you're welcome." She gave a slight bow, playing it up with a flourish of her hand, and Tarrant snickered.

"I mean, you found out in a shitty way. Listening to us talk is weird, and you're *not* as subtle as you think you are—but at least this time you did something good with the knowledge, you know?"

"High praise."

"Yeah. Don't count on a recurrence."

"Back to normal on Monday, I assume?"

"Oh yeah. Ceasefire ends as soon as you walk through that door."

Will raised her hands. "For tonight, I surrender. See you later, Tarrant."

And as she headed back down the stairs, Will could have sworn she heard Paige Tarrant actually *giggle*.

Will paused halfway down the stairs that led to the great hall, watching the ebb and flow of the crowd below. Susurrations ran through them like the wind through a field of grass in the old videos. The room was ringing with laughter and exclamations as people pointed out different moons to one another and jockeyed for position around the waiters dispensing flutes of Xavier's prized champagne. But despite the noise, it was somehow a peaceful moment.

You've done a good thing here. If even Tarrant thought so, there was no question. An Arrex did not doubt herself. Will had been taught that from birth. But Will knew despite the honour of her family, that there was little she and her father would not do to keep power safely out of Loris's hands. Arrexes kept their word and did what was best for the spoke. More abstract concepts like *goodness* seldom entered the equation.

It had been the most backhanded of compliments, wrung from unwilling lips, but it had been true. And yes, the impact the window-viewing party would make on impressionable voters had played no small part in her decision. But she had *also* done it for Jin Sutsu, for Cara Sutsu. For Tarrant. To show them that she was more than just a Noble. That she could do something good.

An Arrex victory, by Will's internal reckoning of her little spats with Tarrant. But it wasn't like the usual victories, where the winner was the one who had the last word, knew the most, or inflicted the greatest hurt. This had been a moral victory, where Tarrant herself had been forced to concede Will's upstanding character, and that felt *sublime.*

Will wondered if she could somehow pull it off again.

"Lady Arrex!"

The powerful voice cut through the babble like a knife through butter, smooth as silk and twice as sharp. Will turned her head, a gracious smile already spreading across her features before her eyes even met his. It was time to bring the final piece into play.

"Cirrus," she said calmly, descending the last few steps with hand outstretched. "How lovely to see you."

He took the offered hand and shook it heartily. The omnipresent cameraman at his elbow zoomed in conspicuously on the interaction. The beginning of Cirrus Liana's exclusive interview with the heir apparent.

"What a novel party!" Cirrus beamed like a small child that had just been handed its first ice cream.

"You can expect more like it if my father is selected as First Minister again in the Surveys," Will said. "No one understands the citizens of Spoke Six like he does."

Cirrus nodded, subtly angling his body towards the camera instead of Will herself. "I've been asking the public what they think, and a few of them said it really *opened a window* onto a new perspective." He obviously expected her to burst out laughing.

Loris, if she were here, would be cackling like a witch. But Loris was an idiot. Will was controlled; Will was *better*. Cirrus would soon learn she was not so easily led.

"I'm glad that they feel that way." Simplest to respond as though it had been an entirely serious statement, and segue into a campaign talking point. "The importance of this matter to our citizens, particularly those who are inner-spoke, is exactly why I'm delighted to announce that next week my father Lord Arrex will be opening a new public park featuring a window. For the first six months, everyone will be welcome to attend for free. After that we'll continue to offer means-tested free tickets for our lower-income citizens. If my father becomes First Minister again, he commits to continue funding for both the park and the means-tested tickets for the next six years at least."

Taking her rejection of his joke with good grace, Cirrus peppered Will with clarifying questions until the topic of the window-viewing park was thoroughly exhausted. In truth the sad little outer-spoke flat that Xavier had purchased—at *astronomical* expense—was hardly deserving of the name *park*. It was a mere three rooms, cramped and depressingly bare now that the furniture of the previous occupant had been cleared out. But the painters Xavier had hired were putting in some murals of different forests from Old Terra, and the gardening team that looked after the larger parks thought they might be able to manage a few planters full of grass and flowers. And the truly important thing was what the third of the three rooms possessed, despite its unimpressive size: a small porthole window in the centre of the outermost wall, showing the same stars that the Arrex great hall looked out onto. The scope was not the same, and the viewing angle meant that the Wheel and Spoke Three blocked a great deal of the vista, but it was enough. It meant that anyone who didn't get one of the three hundred tickets tonight would be able to look out at the stars, and know that Lord Xavier Arrex was responsible.

It was a solid idea. Far more tangible than Loris's promise of future exemptions. But Will's real stroke of genius was yet to come. With one last nervous twitch of her fingers—the only outlet she would allow herself, her face still smooth and serene as ever—Will bared her proverbial neck to the sword. "Actually, Cirrus, I'd like to talk about the Lottery."

The crowd had left a wide circle of clear space around them, but they were not far enough away to be completely out of earshot. There were a few low rumbles, and Cirrus stilled.

"It's become the hot-button topic of the Surveys," he agreed cautiously.

"My aunt has certainly done her best to ensure it is."

The hint of contempt in her voice was enough to have him tripping out the very question she wanted.

"And how would *you* respond to the accusation that Lady Loris has done more than Lord Xavier to address the anxiety felt by voters?"

"Well, Cirrus, I would probably say that my aunt has miscalculated the extent of the First Minister's power. The Spoke Six government can't issue exemptions."

"With respect, Lady Arrex, wouldn't you say that's dodging the question?"

Cirrus's eyes glinted, and Will resisted the urge to smile. It was familiar, this dance. Cirrus had been interviewing Will on matters of policy since she was eight years old, and Xavier had stopped his intercessions between them when she was ten. Will knew exactly how to handle Cirrus Liana.

"With equal respect, Cirrus, I would say it isn't. Lady Loris Arrex has promised things she cannot deliver. Lord Xavier Arrex, in contrast, always keeps his word. Anyone who has lived in Spoke Six for the past twelve years can tell you that. Every year, everyone in Spoke Six receives a piece of real fruit for the Year Change Festival, paid for from my father's personal funds. Everyone is able to enjoy the new tennis pitches in the upper-level park. Every business has benefitted from additional government contracts from the Six-First Bill that bans the government from going out of spoke to find lower prices. Lord Xavier Arrex keeps every promise he makes."

"But to return to the issue of the Lottery..."

"I'm just working my way back to it." Will flashed the camera her most disarming smile. *I'm just a teenager, but I know better than Cirrus,* that smile said. *You and me, viewer, we're in on the joke, both of us.* "My father understands the fear our young people feel. The anxiety of their parents. But the Laika Programme is our future:

our only way of monitoring Old Terra and the terraforming projects begun by our ancestors."

Cirrus opened his mouth, but she held up her hand to stop him. She knew already what he would say—*Fine words are all very well, but...*—but these were not just fine words.

"And my father understands the pain our people feel when they are asked to send their children out into the darkness, when the Nobles do not."

Across from her, Cirrus went very still. This was not the direction he had expected her to take.

Will wondered what Tarrant would say to her at school tomorrow. Would she say that it was a good thing to do? Would she smile at Will again, that same starshine-bright smile that she had displayed in the observatory?

"That is why, despite the fact he does not have to, despite the fact he is limited to one child by law, despite the enormous personal sacrifice—my father Lord Xavier Arrex has decided, on a one-off basis..." She pulled in a breath; there was no going back once the words were said. "To enter my name into this year's Lottery."

The silence that followed was absolute. Cirrus's mouth opened and shut like a vidscreen on mute. Like a fish gasping for air. The crowd was dead silent, staring openly at Will, disbelief splashed across every face. In that vast, empty silence, Will heard a single strangled gasp and turned to see Xavier staring at her over the heads of the hundreds of strangers in their home. Their eyes met, and she saw his face turn the colour of ash.

Will smiled tightly and said it again. Just in case anyone living on the Wheel or in the Amalthea mines had happened to miss it. "So I will be participating in the Lottery process alongside everyone else."

The words hung in the air above the multitudes, blotting out the stars they had all come to see.

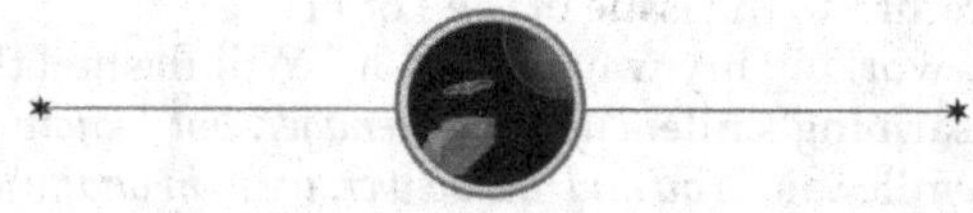

By the time the noise of the last few guests had vanished from the corridors outside, Will's ironclad belief in her plan had begun to waver. With infinite caution, she raised her hand to knock. Her fingernails dug into the soft flesh of her palm.

"Come in." The words were clipped. Curt.

The door hissed open, and Will obeyed. What else was there left to do?

Her father regarded her over the top of his vidscreen, which was flickering madly with different images. Will saw herself there, at a dozen different stages of her interview, looping and replaying.

He watched her with flat grey-green eyes as Will seated herself. Her hands felt slippery.

"Now, Wilhelmina," Xavier began, his voice low and dangerous. A predator closing in for the kill. "Would you like to explain to me what, exactly, you were thinking?"

"It's the only possible counter to Loris."

He stared. Will leaned forward, desperate to make him see the truth of it. It was the one path open to them.

"It will win us the Surveys. It means you can be Lord Captain again. I know it seems extreme, Father, but it's the right thing to do."

"The right thing to do." Xavier gave a hollow laugh and passed his hand over his eyes. "It will be an uphill climb, but we can still make all of...this...go away. Perhaps you had a little too much champagne. Perhaps you got too excited; perhaps you're still too young to be seriously involved in a political campaign. There's five years between you and Lauron, after all. Yes. With a bit of work, I can make Cirrus sell that spin."

Listening with growing horror to this infantilisation, this *dismissal* of everything she was and had worked to become, Will opened her mouth to shout a retort before thinking better of it. Xavier only offered respect to people like himself. Cool and calm, manipulation without emotional excess. She swallowed the angry words, and they burned like bile all the way down.

She produced the piece of embossed card, printed in smooth Arrex grey. It was not crumpled, like Tarrant's surely would be by now. It was pristine, and the words on it were printed in stark relief: *Spoke Six Lottery, Year 452—Ticket Number 69.* She pointed an imperious finger at it. "It's there. It's real. How are you going to make *that* go away?"

He would see, eventually, that she was right. As soon as the people saw Will in that room along with the other Lottery ticket holders, her white-blonde Arrex head right there among their own children, they would flock in droves to the Surveys office to vote for Xavier. Loris could offer only a phantasm, and Will had concrete proof that *her* side of the family was the one that cared for them most.

And Xavier would realise that this was the only way.

"Father, if you would just let me *do* this for us, I swear it wi—"

"*No!*" he bellowed, with sudden, white-hot fury that knocked Will back into her seat and left her trembling. Xavier was always so controlled, so careful. He dragged a hand across his hair. "*No,*" he repeated, a little quieter but with no less force. "You are my only child, Wilhelmina. My *only* child. I will not let you throw your life away."

"You're the one that says the Laika Programme is the future of Eden." Will crossed her arms, determined to stare him down.

Xavier met her gaze without blinking. "You don't understand." Every word was a slap to the face.

"So *explain*, Father!"

Xavier's teeth ground together with an audible *snap*. "I can't."

Disappointment rising like a tide, Will sat back in her chair. "You mean you won't."

"Whichever you prefer."

"Then I have no choice but to continue with my original plan of action." She folded her arms. He would see he was not the only one who could be immovable.

Xavier's eyes snapped back to her, and his hand came down hard on the desk. "You will obey me as the head of this family—"

"The head of this family who has been repeatedly elected as First Minister on the idea that he keeps his promises. You made a promise tonight, Father, through me. How can you withdraw now?"

Xavier was very still. Watching her.

Will smiled. She was doing exactly as he had taught her. The trap was laid, the net carefully woven. Little by little, she had drawn it tight around him, so slowly he had hardly noticed it. All that was left now was to seal it off.

"It'll cost you the Surveys. And *every* Surveys in the future. You'll be handing Loris not just one captaincy, but all of them. Even I might not recover from the stain on this family's good name. Lauron will be First Minister after his mother."

Face blank, he studied her. "Make your point, Wilhelmina."

"It's a simple choice, really." Slowly, carefully, Will let each word slip. Let the message sink in. "You choose honour and victory, or you choose disgrace and defeat. For both of us."

His thin lips stretching into a terrible, mirthless smile, Xavier looked into his daughter's eyes. "You have left me little choice, it seems."

"I'm glad you see it my way," Will said lightly. "And it will work out for the best. It's a solid plan. After all—what are the odds my ticket will actually be drawn?"

CHAPTER 6

Spoke 6, Eden Station – Year 452 – Day 344 – 10:31

"I'm heading out," Will said, rising from her place at the table. Her breakfast sat cold and congealed on the plate in front of her. Untouched for the third day running.

Xavier didn't glance up from his work. Stacks of paperwork obscured whatever food he had chosen that morning—if, indeed, he had chosen to eat at all. Appetite had become a rarity in the Arrex household.

"I'm going," repeated Will, louder this time.

"Today's the day, then?" Xavier still wasn't looking at her, and Will felt the tendons in her wrists flexing as her hands curled into fists. He *knew* what day it was.

"It was a good plan, Father," she said tightly. "It *is* a good plan. The interview I give to Cirrus today after the tickets are drawn—"

Now he looked up, those chilling green eyes flashing almost silver in his anger. "What will you say, Wilhelmina? If your ticket is drawn, what will you say?"

"I keep telling you it *won't* be," she hissed. "The odds are astronomical—"

"Far higher than you seem to think," he interrupted again, voice clipped with tightly controlled rage. "And you seem to have given *no* thought to the possibility—"

"If you were there *with* me we could put on a much better show." Will's patience snapped; let *him* see how he liked being constantly interrupted. "Father and daughter united, stable leadership for decades into the future. You know there'll be rumours if I'm alone. It makes us look weak."

"It's not usual for Nobles to attend—"

"Even when your own child is—"

"*It's not usual* for Nobles to attend anything but the final drawing of the tickets," he repeated, more forcefully. "Which I will be."

"But not with *me*."

"I can hardly sit among the ticket holders and their families."

"I'll be sat there. Why not you, too?"

Xavier sighed and ran a hand through his long hair. "Wilhelmina, the longer this conversation continues, the less it sounds like a discussion of reasoned strategy and more like the whining of a petulant child."

"I'm not—!" Will began hotly, before catching herself and starting over, voice carefully measured. "I am not whining, Father. I am *asking* you, as your co-runner in these Surveys and your heir, to accompany me and *show support* in the public eye. Loris and Lauron do everything together."

With a sigh, Xavier turned the page of the report before him. "I will be arriving at the usual time, and I will be overseeing proceedings from my usual seat. That you will not be in yours is entirely your own decision."

As if this whole thing was a whim. A fancy, and not something she had done for *him*, for them *all*. His show of disinterest was ridiculous—all the more so because her plan was *working*. Her announced participation had caused a stir, grabbed headlines across the Eden, and within Spoke Six, the polls were steadily ticking in Xavier's favour. Loris was growing desperate, throwing out more promises of tax cuts, for the workers this time and not just the companies. But it did nothing to stop the inexorable creep of the points to Xavier's side. And Will knew that it was *her* that was making the difference. Her story—a Noble selfless enough to enter herself in the Lottery—was more than enough to capture the imaginations of the people, and she was going to do her damnedest to win their hearts, too.

The last thread of her patience snapped, and she shoved her chair back with an ugly screech. "You're being *ridiculous*, Father."

"No, Wilhelmina," called Xavier from behind her. "What *I* call ridiculous is making far-reaching policy decisions on your own, risking your life, and then expecting me to fall in line."

Will's hand slammed down on the button that sealed the door to the entryway behind her, freeing her to snarl a selection of swearwords back in Xavier's direction without risk of further escalation. Worse than blind, he was *wilfully* blind. He and his team of idiots had *nothing* to counter Loris's trumped-up Lottery exemption idea. The best minds of the Academy, strategists and analysts and thinkers galore, and none of them could offer anything but the same thing Xavier had already been doing for twelve years. Could he not see that this set of Surveys was different? Loris was no longer content to roll over and let him have victory in exchange for her comfortable lifestyle. This year demanded risks, and Will had been brave enough to take those risks on her father's behalf.

He ought to be *applauding* her.

Her black mood as she stalked out of the front doors between the usual pair of Lawkeepers was not improved by the sight of Lauron hovering by the fountain.

"Good morning, cousin!" he sang out, and Will quickened her pace. Of course *today* would be the one morning he stirred before noon.

"I wanted to wish you the best of luck!" he called. "I hope you *win*!"

Will had to physically stop herself from turning on her heel and sprinting back to punch him right in his smug mouth. Wretched *Lauron*.

She ducked into the tramcar and the Lawkeepers sat opposite her. Never the same two, which was something. At least she didn't have to learn any names.

The tramcar hummed to life, and the atrium fell away behind her. She was completely, perfectly isolated.

All that mattered to Xavier was her disobedience, and Tunis had nothing to offer but confusion. *You're exempt, Lady Will. Why can't you pull out?* In desperation, Will had tried her mother. *What will we do if my number gets drawn?* A tinkling little laugh had been her only answer. *Darling, your father will never let that happen.* And that was the end of the conversation.

She was headed down to the school canteen to watch Hrue Lipson take her life into his hands and her parents didn't care at all. Xavier was still furious, and just like every other morning, Eloise wasn't even present. Will was alone, with no one but a couple of faceless Lawkeepers. Her heart thudded in time with the tramcar's pulsing engine, and anger gave way to despair.

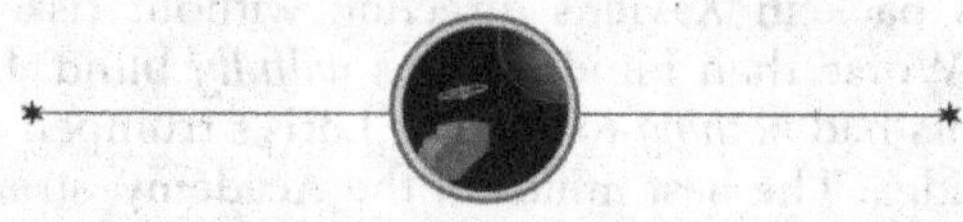

Will shifted from foot to foot, trying to keep the blood flowing in her legs. The wall at her back was a constant temptation; a few inches back and she could recline in comfort, just as the two Lawkeepers flanking her were doing. But an Arrex did not lean, was never anything less than ramrod straight.

The canteen was packed full to bursting, with families crowding into every available space not taken up by the stage and the seats for the ticket holders. Will was attracting stares, of course. But instead of curiosity and respect, the eyes on her today were cold. *You're not one of us,* they seemed to whisper. *You don't belong.*

With a deep breath, Will centred her gaze above them all, on the line where the wall met the ceiling. They didn't matter. Today was only the first step on the path she had chosen for herself. At the end of it lay victory, glory, Lauron ground into the dirt and Tarrant smiling again, acknowledging that Will had done something *good*.

But before that reward there was a gauntlet to be run. The Lottery was real. It was happening. Six numbers waiting to be drawn. Sixty-eight other ticket holders in this room. The seventieth would never come—Lauron was as exempt as Will ought to have been, and unlike her, he would never waive his rights. But aside from him, every youth in Spoke Six was present. The oldest were back from the dorm towns in Centre, the rest released from classes for the day—all the way down to the fifteen-year-olds, clumped in a corner and looking horribly young.

A movement by the doors: Cirrus entering with his camera crew. Will caught his eye and ran a hand over her silk-smooth hair as he made a beeline for her. No matter what state her personal feelings were in, the Surveys would always come first.

Cirrus was practically frothing at the mouth. "Lady Arrex! What a pleasure to see you here this morning, and in such an *unusual* role. Could we trouble you for a comment?"

"Of course." Will gave him a tolerant smile, as though it was her obliging him and not the other way round.

"I'm sure all our viewers will join me in wishing you good luck in today's draw—or rather, *bad* luck. After all, we hope that your number *doesn't* come up, eh?" And Cirrus chortled complacently at his own joke, as though it hadn't been made a thousand times in every iteration of the Lottery.

But Will smiled a little wider, more than happy to indulge him. "Absolutely, Cirrus." She could afford to smile at any number of recycled jokes. This was the moment her entire Lottery gambit had been geared towards. The risk she was taking was immense, but so would be the pay-off.

Cirrus extended the microphone towards her, and Will wasted no time launching into the spiel she had practised in front of the mirror the night before. The time might have been better spent sleeping, but a foggy brain and dark shadows under her eyes were nothing when the Surveys were on the line.

"Like all of my fellow Lottery entrants," she began, looking directly into the camera, expression grave, "I'm a little nervous this morning."

I'm one of you: that was the key message. *I'm one of you, and I understand your heartache. Vote for me, vote for my father, and we will fix everything.*

She pulled in a breath, and her expression changed to one of steely determination. "But I believe in the vision Lord Xavier Arrex has for Spoke Six's future, and I will stand alongside my classmates—your children—to face the Lottery like everyone else."

Cirrus looked as though he were about to interject, but Will steamed on. She had no need for banter this morning, only a microphone into which to deposit her speech.

"My aunt Loris Arrex wants to rule simply for the sake of ruling—she doesn't care about the Eden or about its people. My father *does*." She drew herself up, shoulders squaring, as she built towards her crescendo. "And once the Lottery is over, and we turn our attention to the Biannual Approval Surveys, I want you to remember where Lord Xavier Arrex's only child was this morning. Remember that I was *here*, while my cousin—" and she gestured in what she hoped was an eloquent manner, fanning her fingers out almost despairingly, "while my cousin was not."

There was a beat of silence after she closed her mouth, and it was a comfort to know that her words had managed to reach even Cirrus. There was the proof, if she had needed any, that her speech would hit home with viewers. The Lottery was an event with pathos unmatched by any other, and she had been right to make it the field of battle. Unwilling to risk himself, Lauron had never even left his castle, and the war was all but won.

Will bid Cirrus and his audience farewell, and made her way back to her spot by the wall. All that remained was the unpleasantness of the Lottery draw—and then it would be over. The odds were in her favour. She would be back home tonight, safe in the knowledge that Xavier's victory was guaranteed. Merely having entered the Lottery would win as much public sympathy as if she had been sentenced to pilot a Laika herself.

She saw the doors beyond her bodyguards open once more. The last group of stragglers entered, and Will's blood ran a little colder when she saw her own classmates. Lysse, walking tall as always. Erntz, Garth, and Joss behind her. Cara at the back, her black eyes huge in her thin face. Behind her came a familiar cloud of dark hair, bouncing with every step its owner took.

Tarrant.

Wearing yellow again. Seeing her in colours other than grey was still weird. Tarrant's eyes were flashing fire as she glared out from behind Cara—as though she would attack anyone who dared approach her pale little friend. Will glanced sideways at her two nameless grey escorts and wished with all her heart for an ally of her own.

But the sight of Tarrant gave Will some much-needed clarity, and she shook off the flash of melancholy. She was here to save her father and her family, to best Loris and Lauron, and—and to prove that she was more than the spoiled rich girl Tarrant made her out to be. She was here to play this silly little game and *win*.

Her gaze raking across the room, Tarrant's eyes finally landed on Will, and her mouth fell open. Her face paled, and Will tried and failed to decipher the expression there. Was Tarrant shocked? Angry? But before she could figure it out—before she could even move—

"Arrex!" Tarrant's voice cut through the rumble of muttered conversations.

She advanced on Will with such fury that all doubt about her reaction vanished. Raw hatred sparked from her every pore, and anticipation flooded through Will. Cirrus was dealt with, the speech was made, and with the Lottery draw looming, a sparring match with Tarrant sounded perfect. A little distraction was exactly what she needed.

"Nice to see you, Tarrant," she said, pleasantly enough. With campaign season at its peak and school on break for the Lottery, Will had not laid eyes on the other girl since the party, and it was easy to see that Tarrant had meant every word of her promise that their ceasefire would not hold.

"What the hell are you doing here, Arrex?"

Tarrant came to a halt only a short distance from Will, the finer curls of her hair illuminated by the harsh lights, surrounding her in a fiery halo. Will's two guards moved to intercept her, but Will jerked her head at them in annoyance. It wasn't like *Tarrant* was going to hurt her.

"Same as you, I'd imagine." Will struggled not to let her smirk widen into a grin. It felt good to get back to normal.

"This area's for ticket holders *only*."

"Haven't you turned on your vidscreen any time in the last fortnight?" With no small feeling of triumph, Will whipped out her ticket. Number sixty-nine, plain as day.

"I didn't think you'd have the guts to actually show." With a snarl, Tarrant snatched it from her hand. "You have *got* to be kidding me. You're trying to—to *what*, slum it with the rest of us paupers? Pull out at the last minute and say it was all a big joke to make us feel better? Or did you just pay them to rig it?"

"Funny," Will replied, with no humour in her tone, "coming from the daughter of one minister to another. Really reminds me how much of a pauper *you* are."

"Don't play that game with me. I *had* to be here." Tarrant pointed a finger at Will, trembling with fury. "Tell me the truth. This is a publicity stunt."

Brilliant. Of course Tarrant would land right on the money with her very first guess.

Will kept her face impassive. "Of course not."

But the wheel had started rolling, and there was no slowing Tarrant now. "This—this is just part of the game, isn't it? Your *stupid* elections."

Will did her best to look morally superior. "They're polls, actually. And no. This is real."

Tarrant stepped closer, her finger now jabbing directly into Will's collarbone. "How dare you? How dare you come down here and play-act like you're part of this, when *we* are putting our actual lives on the line?"

Will's Lawkeepers started forward again, but she waved them off. *Idiots.*

"I'm not acting, Tarrant. If you think I am, perhaps you need to reconsider your prejudices."

"*My* prejudices? *Mine*?"

Tarrant was about to truly boil over. It was only a matter of time before she started shouting or genuinely attempting to cause a scene, and with Tarrant, Will didn't fully trust herself not to rise to the bait. It was time to wrap this up.

"By the way, I brought these for you. And Sutsu." Will thrust three tickets into Tarrant's hand.

Disarmed momentarily, the other girl glanced down at them, eyes skimming uncomprehendingly over the text. "Season tickets...? What?"

But by the time she looked up, Will was already sauntering away, a broad smile on her face. "To the new window-viewing park, courtesy of the *prejudiced* Arrex family."

Game, set, and *match*.

"Oh, *thank* you," Tarrant hissed, and Will halted. "For stooping to dispense largesse again. Marie Antoinette would be proud."

"Yes," Will said drily. "Because doing *this* is all very 'let them eat cake' of me, isn't it? I'm really enjoying the spectacle from the top of my ivory tower."

She had hoped to shock Tarrant with proof of her own knowledge of the obscure period—show her that history wasn't something only *she* had heard of—but Tarrant didn't even seem to notice the reference.

She was almost shaking with rage, stalking closer with every word. "You know as well as I do that this is all fake. There's no way in hell your number is coming up, and once you're done slumming it down here with us you'll retreat right back up your stupid tower—"

"This is not *fake*—"

"And you'll never come down again!"

Both of them paused, breath heaving, almost nose to nose, eyes narrowed in fury. Will could see the tiny flecks of amber in the brown of Tarrant's irises. Somewhere in the back of her mind, beyond the fury, a small, cold voice took note and catalogued the detail. *I never noticed those before.*

The thought was enough to drive her back to reality, to notice their raised voices, the attention they were surely already drawing. She needed to end this. Now.

Turning abruptly on her heel, Will burst into motion, eyes fixed firmly on the one empty seat left in the front row. While it wouldn't be pleasant to get such an intimate view of Hrue and his slippery forehead, it would be in clear view of the cameras. An ideal spot for close-ups.

But there were footsteps, and when Will turned Tarrant was there—stomping along behind with her eyes fixed on the chair Will was aiming for.

Will's teeth came together. *Really?* How was it possible for one human body to contain so much pettiness?

Well, at least they were no longer shouting. And it wasn't like she was about to let Tarrant win. Will upped her pace, but Tarrant was picking up speed, and Will had to focus if she wanted to beat her.

The chair was almost upon them. Will swerved left, Tarrant in hot pursuit. Stretching out her arm as she rounded the end of the aisle, clipping her hip painfully hard on the final chair, Will clapped her hand down on the back of the empty seat. Not even a heartbeat had passed before Tarrant's hand slammed down beside hers, pulling the whole chair over towards her.

"Find your own seat," Tarrant growled, and Will felt something uncoiling within her chest. Not violence, not quite—but close.

With deliberation, Will tightened her hold on the chair. What gave *Tarrant* the right to make unilateral demands? She should be sitting with her snotty friends, anyway. Will was the one who needed this seat.

Tarrant glared at her, chest still heaving from her run.

"Sorry," Will said, as lightly as she could. "This one's taken."

"Oh, I see. So this chair's *yours*, is it?"

"Yes." Will had never met anyone who pushed the careful composure of her public-facing mask as far as Tarrant did. She managed the careless smile she was aiming for, but it was harder than it should have been.

It was stupid—Will was fully aware of how juvenile they were being—but she wasn't about to surrender. Not to Tarrant. Not now.

Tarrant's hair was practically vibrating with the force of her anger. "Don't you ever get tired?"

Idly, Will flipped her free hand over to study her nails. "*I* didn't run that hard, Tarrant."

A scoff. "I mean tired of everything being *yours*. Everything you could ever dream of has been yours since the moment you crawled out of your crib." She paused. "And now this stupid chair, too. Just to round out your collection."

Will scowled. "I'm getting really tired of you throwing my family in my face, Tarrant. I *earn* what I have."

Hadn't she proven that? She was *here*, wasn't she?

If people hadn't been staring before, they were definitely staring now. A Noble entering the Lottery, and now she was making a scene. Will felt the eyes on her and began to regret not just giving Tarrant the seat.

"But still you come in here, where you weren't forced to be, unlike the rest of us. And now everything here has to be yours, too." Tarrant smiled, and it was a vicious smile. "Like I said—don't you get tired of it?"

Will hesitated. She didn't want to let Tarrant win—but this was their second showdown in as many minutes. She needed to put a lid on this, or before the Lottery numbers were even drawn she'd be on the news for brawling in public. And that would be the death knell for Xavier's campaign. A Noble stooping to violence—all the Lottery tickets in the world wouldn't be enough to help her then.

With a sigh, she removed her hand from the chair. "Sometimes it does get a little tiring, I suppose. So I'll let you have this one."

Triumph flared in Tarrant's eyes, and Will glided a few steps to the next row back, tossing one last parting shot over her shoulder.

"I hope you enjoy my cast-offs."

"I hope *you* enjoy being beaten at your own game," Tarrant shot back, quick as a whip-crack.

Her pleasure in having the last word withering and dying, Will ground her teeth together and threw herself into her new seat.

Stupid bloody *Tarrant*.

A Lottery official appeared on stage, and ripples of awareness spread through the crowd, the clusters breaking up as they all turned to face the stage. Will followed suit, shooing her twin shadows away to stand behind her.

The Lottery official muttered something into the microphone about the presence of Lord Xavier Arrex, Lady Loris Arrex, her consort Lady Wythe Arrex-Sandison, Lord Lauron Arrex, and—a pause here—Lady Will Arrex as well. Lady Eloise Arrex-Kal sent her regrets, because of course she did. Will had not expected anything else.

Will watched as her extended family filed in, Xavier holding himself apart from the rest with studied disdain. He would not meet her eyes—only gazed out over the crowd. Solemn and grave, just as the Lottery demanded. Always the perfect statesman.

It left a bitter taste in her mouth, and it was with relief that Will let her attention slide back to Tarrant. Her little court was rallied around her again, and others in the front row had shuffled down for them. The warm flush of battle hadn't yet faded from Will's limbs, and the sight of the familiar honeyed curls was reassuring in a way that the presence of her father was not. But watching the way those curls fanned out over Cara's shoulder as Tarrant leaned her head against her friend's, watching Garth put a reassuring arm around them both—even the old game of watching Tarrant soured. They had one another to lean on. Who did *Will* have? No friends, no family. Only the two silent figures to her left and right, both clad in identical salt-grey.

It wasn't fair. It wasn't *right*. She had gone to all that effort, just for Tarrant and her stupid friend and her stupid grandfather—alright, Cara and Jin were very pleasant people, but *still*. She had expended *enormous* amounts of Arrex capital to not only throw a party, but to purchase a permanent location where Jin Sutsu could go and view the stars to his heart's content.

And did Tarrant appreciate it? Did she even say *one* word of thanks? Of course not. Will couldn't even get a *chair* for her troubles. She was ending this occasion exactly as she had begun it: alone.

Finally, Xavier stood. He spoke a few words of solemn welcome, and Will let her body run on autopilot. Expression engaged, head moving every now and then to indicate agreement. But no one clapped. No one even attempted a pretence of interest.

As Xavier returned to his place, conspicuous between the two empty seats for his wife and daughter, Will's eyes moved slowly over the crowd. Her gaze caught on a little boy—presumably one of the fifteen-year-olds, though he didn't look much over twelve—as he began to weep. It was more sobering than anything else she had seen so far, and for the first time, Will thought she might come to regret this vast gamble she had made.

She had been playing tug of war with Tarrant over a seat. It *felt* just like school, where all she had to worry about was their usual point-scoring and one-upmanship. But this wasn't a game. This was life and death.

Hrue Lipson crept on to the stage, moister than ever beneath the bright lights, mopping at his forehead with a handkerchief.

"W-welcome, everyone." His eyes flicked to Will. "Welcome to the Spoke Six Lottery."

An answering murmur ran through the young people, and Hrue Lipson flinched as though he had been slapped.

"There are sixty-eight—I-I mean sixty-*nine* ticket holders."

Another ripple, as people turned to peer at Will. Jutting her chin upward, she met every gaze that she could. She was a Noble. Let them look. She was used to scrutiny.

"You...six of you will be chosen at random to begin training as Laika pilots." As Hrue got into his flow, he stood a little taller, evidently taking comfort in the well-rehearsed speech. "As is traditional, we're using a true random number generator based on current levels of cosmic radiation, which are constantly, immutably random. The decay of..."

His voice receded into a dull monotone, and Will turned back to watch Tarrant out of the corner of her eye. She already knew the details of the Lottery selection and the way the coding worked. She had found a first-edition copy of the handbook on it in the Arrex library at home and read it the night before. Like most of the Eden, in four centuries the Lottery had changed very little. There was no reason to alter what functioned perfectly.

Not like Tarrant, a person in constant flux, her moods a shifting sea that always left Will struggling to catch up. The other night at the window-viewing party she had seemed almost *friendly*. And now things were back to ground zero, without even the familiar rapport of their academic sparring to fall back on. Will was never quite sure where she stood. Not with Tarrant.

Hrue finished stuttering out the information that would determine the lives of the people before him, and the crowd was frozen. Crumpled tickets were clutched in hands, heads were bowed.

Hrue coughed loudly into the microphone, causing a screech of feedback that echoed horribly in the empty air of the canteen, and tapped the vidscreen to call forth the first name of the damned.

"...Grigor Yon."

The boy who answered the summons was one whom Will recognised vaguely from school. He was in the year above, and sometimes hovered on the periphery of Tarrant's friendship group. Will had never seen Grigor Yon anything but casual and self-assured, but as he stumbled towards the stage he looked close to tears—turning from side to side as though someone in the audience might still save him.

"Jasper Ware."

The second unfortunate was another boy, another inmate of Will's school. Two years above her this time, one of the much-vaunted Johann's classmates. Jasper hardly seemed to understand what had happened to him. He sat very still, only roused at last by a helpful neighbour pushing him to his feet.

Infinitesimally, Will felt the tension in her muscles begin to ease. Two down, four to go. With every name read out, her own risk was lowered. Not to mention that of her classmates. By Monday she would be safely back in school where she belonged, with nothing more serious to worry about than besting Tarrant in the upcoming chemistry exam.

Then Hrue called out the third name.

"Cara Sutsu."

The words took a second to permeate. When they finally did, Will's first thought was one of disbelief. *No. Surely not.*

Not *Cara.*

Uncaring now if she was noticed, Will craned her neck to see past her classmates to Tarrant, whose face was ashen. Cara stood with the jerky, lifeless motions of a robot and walked mechanically towards the stage. Tarrant half-rose, reaching after her, but Siln pulled her back down. The four of them—Tarrant, Siln, Garth, and Erntz—they just *stared* as their friend walked towards her death. Helpless.

Will had watched the tapes from the last Lottery. Twenty-five years ago. She had been too focused on the younger versions of her father and grandfather to pay attention to the six young people who were selected. They had seemed distant figures to her then. Already history.

Now it was all too real. Cara was gone, as good as dead, and her quiet voice would never be heard in their classroom again. And Will herself might be next.

"Maddox Harding."

Will felt no relief as the next stranger took her place beside Cara on the stage. There were still two more names to be called. And as desperately sorry as she felt for Cara, there was a dread that ran deeper. If the next name called was her own—*Your father will never let that happen*—could anyone save her?

"Firni Evans."

Another gasp of horror, another frightened teen. Another set of weeping parents.

Hrue pressed the screen again to generate one last number, one last name. Will watched that plump finger flatten against the screen, the flesh soft and pink as an earthworm's, and marvelled that sixty-nine lives—her own amongst them—lay in the palm of that moist little hand.

And—and what if Cara's fate was not the final horror of the day? There was more at risk than just Will herself. What if the Lottery took *Tarrant*, too?

Will had looked forward to the coming return to normalcy with such excitement. Squabbles with Tarrant, petty little victories and defeats, listening from the edges to the conversations at lunchtime. But that status quo would now never exist again. Cara was gone, ripped away in one horrible sweep. Hrue had been aboard a Laika and lived to tell the tale, but not all those chosen would manage the same feat.

And with Cara gone, Tarrant would not be happy. She would not want to spend her time in the familiar old contests with Will. She would be the same as she was right now: pale, frightened, her liquid brown eyes huge and haunted.

Tarrant would be *miserable*, and Will would never again have the competitor she had come to rely on so heavily. Without Cara, Tarrant would—

"W-Will...Lady Will Arrex."

Hrue's voice reverberated over and over, the microphone catching its own shadow in a slowly dying wave of noise. The words did not at first *seem* like words. Just meaningless sounds.

There was a distant ringing noise. A high-pitched whine like the rotors of a drone. Will could hear it, but it sounded far away. Echoing down an impossibly long tunnel. This wasn't real, Will decided. Couldn't be real. Things like this didn't happen.

But heads were turning, mouths opening in disbelief, and even her stoic Lawkeepers were looking at her, aghast. And before Will fully knew what she was doing, she was rising to her feet. They had called her. The fates had called her, and she was doomed.

As though moving through a dream—a *nightmare*—Will drifted towards the stage, coming to a halt beside the other children. The other walking dead. Ghosts, just like her. Still present, but already gone.

Hrue Lipson's jaws were opening and closing, his complexion whiter than milk, but somehow Will could not hear a word he said. Other voices were echoing in her mind, dozens of them at once, tumbling over and under one another like ice cubes falling into a glass.

There's no way in hell your number is coming up.

Darling, your father will never let that happen.

And once you're done slumming it down here with us you'll retreat right back up your stupid tower and you'll never come down again.

At last, Xavier met her gaze, and Will saw in his face the death of all they had worked for.

I will not let you throw your life away.

As Will turned back to face the audience, her eyes went automatically to Tarrant, who was staring at her with the same stricken look with which she had regarded Cara. They locked eyes, and for one terrible, endless moment that terrified expression was all Will could see.

This isn't something that will ever affect you.

Tarrant had said that. It seemed a long time ago, now. Will had determined that she would prove Tarrant wrong, as she had so often before. She would *make* it affect her. But despite her resolution—despite the fact she had done the impossible—somehow, deep down, she had still believed Tarrant. That it could never quite touch her as it could touch the others.

This isn't something that will ever affect you.

How wrong they had both been.

In all her plotting, in all her planning, she had never genuinely believed that this moment would come to pass. But...but somehow, incomprehensibly, counter to all the laws of the universe as Will knew them...somehow, it had.

And *everything* had gone wrong.

CHAPTER 7

Spoke 6, Eden Station – Year 452 – Day 344 – 19:31

Pressing her forehead against the cool surface of the window, Will watched as the crowds were swallowed up by the darkness of the tramcar tunnel. All she wanted was to be *home*. To shut the door on the outside world and just...tune it all out, for once in her life. To forget about the polls and the ratings and the damn Surveys—and now the Lottery. It was just...too much. Too much coming at her all at once.

When, finally, the vast expanse of the atrium had been traversed and Tunis had been dodged, when Will had finally shut and locked her bedroom door, and then shut and locked her bathroom door, and then finally shut the shower cubicle door as well, when she had maximised the number of closed doors between her and the outside world, the evidence of her many failures, Will slumped against the white plastic wall and wept.

The vidscreen on the shower wall was brimming with messages, of course. Zuria, noisy as ever—*You're being crazy, Will!*—and Xanthe's more pointed brand of critique: *You didn't think this through. You're going to get yourself killed. Or mess up the exemption for the rest of us.*

Carroway was less outspoken, but the few messages she received from him were brimming with incomprehension. *Why did you bother? I know you don't intend to actually go, but the risk-reward ratio doesn't add up.*

Will didn't know what she *intended* to do; she had entered the Lottery in order to win the Surveys, and that was it. And while it was one thing for Tarrant to accuse her of being there for trauma tourism or whatever crazy opinion she'd spouted, it was quite another thing to hear the same from Carroway. And not even in the *form* of an accusation—like it was a given that she would find a way to weasel out of it.

There was the usual drivel from Lauron: *I hope your campaign is going as well as mine, Cousin. Good luck with being shot into the sun, by the way. Want to join me for a race tonight? I imagine you'll need all the practice you can get piloting spaceships.*

Clenching her jaw almost hard enough to hurt, Will thrust the message off the vidscreen. Fucking Lauron. He had no mind of his own, no originality—no skill at anything besides *needling*. His mother was exactly the same. If the two of them somehow got into power they wouldn't have the faintest idea what to do—twenty years spent critiquing someone else was poor preparation for actual leadership. The Lottery exemptions had been the ace up their sleeve, and now that Will had countered it, the only way they could think to handle it was cheap shots at her. Well, they would be disappointed. Will Arrex would not rise to their bait. She was...she was *winning*, and that was what mattered.

But the message that resonated the loudest was the one that did not come. Nothing from Xavier. Nothing from Eloise. Nothing, though every vidscreen on the Eden must be blaring the news on a loop. A Noble losing the Lottery. A Noble going aboard a Laika.

And try as she might, Will couldn't escape the image of Tarrant's friends, huddled up around Cara. Loving each other and being loved. Will watched Tarrant, and she wished that she had...well, something like that.

It was galling.

She snarled, and for want of any other channel to pour her frustration into, she hammered a fist into the vidscreen. Instantly, water poured down over her head, and Will gasped, caught off guard. She was still fully clothed.

Somehow, in a painfully unfunny way, it was a little funny. A tiny bit. Half laughing, half sobbing, Will shucked her clothes and let the water course over her bare skin. Every inch of it as pale as ice. She dialled the temperature up almost to its maximum and watched that bone-white skin turn slowly, painfully red.

Forget Tarrant. Forget her. There were bigger things to worry about. Like Lauron and the Surveys and the fatal Lottery ticket sitting in her room.

The discomfort of the heat served its purpose. Burning away the confusion and the emotion just as surely as it did the tears, redirecting her focus. Wreathed in steam, Will considered. There had to be a different way of looking at this. A way to put a more positive spin on it. She was in danger, yes, but nothing was settled yet. Nothing was over. The water was scalding, and Will turned the dial higher again, air hissing through her teeth as the burning droplets scalded her lobster-red skin.

When Will emerged, mist billowing around her like a cape, her pale skin flushed a violent crimson, she knew one thing for certain. She was going to Lauron's stupid race tonight, and she was going to grind him and everyone else into dust.

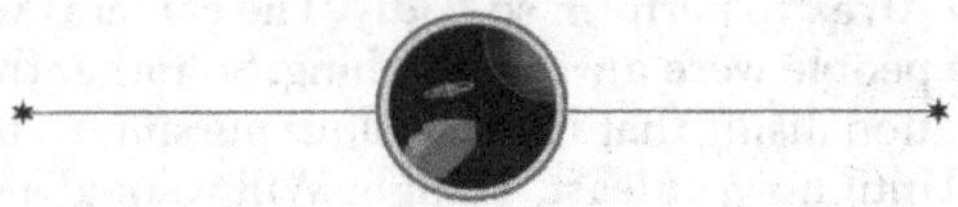

The Arrex tramcar hissed to a halt, and Will rolled her neck, wincing as it cracked.

This isn't something that will ever affect you.

What a joke.

The door of the tramcar rose up, and a wall of noise forced its way in, engulfing Will before she even rose from her seat. Coloured lights flickered in time with the pounding beat. Five years had passed since she last flew, but the glider racetrack had not changed at all. Someone screeched with laughter, their voice climbing higher even than the music. Will winced at the sound.

This isn't something that will ever affect you.

It hadn't been—not until Will inserted herself right into the middle of it. Transformed from disinterested spectator to participant. Cocooned herself in the whole mess until she burst out again in her new form: victim.

Unwilling to dwell on it any longer, she quickened her step. The room was packed to bursting, dominated by a bar that stretched the full length of one wall, staffed by an army of bartenders doling out drinks by the dozen. Obscured by the bobbing heads of dancers who had mistaken the observation deck for a nightclub was a door, the neon words *PILOTS ONLY* blazing above it.

Vidscreens and windows of equal size alternated on the walls. The windows displayed a peaceful view of the Wheel's vast width with Spoke One and Spoke Two stretching back towards Centre, the darkness of space beyond. The vidscreens showed close-ups of various glider ships while a wildly excited Cirrus rhapsodised about the abilities of their pilots.

If she were to try and get close enough to make out the sound from the speakers over the hubbub of the partygoers, she knew she'd hear her own skill quantified. It would not be a favourable analysis. The last time Will had flown, she had been twelve: a loss so resounding that she had vowed never to get behind the controls of a glider again. It had only been a hobby, but it wasn't—it wasn't *right*, for an Arrex to perform so badly. The cameras were always on her. The people were always watching. So rather than fail, she gave it up, rationalising that such frivolous pursuits were better left to Lauron. Until now, at least. Tonight Will wanted a distraction, and she was damn well going to get it.

And, whispered an ominous little voice at the back of her mind, Lauron was probably right that she needed the flight practice. If the worst happened and there was no way out, she didn't want her first trip outside the Eden in five years to be when she was forcibly shot out of a centrifuge at thousands of kilometres an hour.

Will threaded her way through the press of people, smiling and nodding with steely determination whenever anyone stared. The Lottery and its terrible result were omnipresent, but it didn't matter. Her focus would remain on the Surveys. Everything was still going according to plan. She just had to keep her eyes on the prize.

She was almost within reach of the pilots' door when she spotted a familiar face. Dark skin shimmering almost violet beneath the flickering neon lights, his teeth flashing as he laughed. Relief coursing through her, Will swerved around a knot of people to reach him. Here at last was her chance to feel a little of the camaraderie that Tarrant's friends offered one another. She was already smiling when she tapped him on the shoulder. "Did you come to watch me, Carroway?"

He turned, startled, but on seeing her his face cleared. "Absolutely. You're being an idiot, but I wouldn't miss a chance to cheer you on."

Suddenly feeling wonderfully normal, Will snorted. "Thanks."

Carroway ran a hand over his shining skull, as though smoothing non-existent hairs back into place. "I just wanted to make sure we were still...you know. You didn't really reply to my last message."

"Oh." Time seemed strange today. Stretched and distorted. That message in the bathroom felt like months ago now. "No—we're fine."

And to her mild surprise, Will found that she meant it. What good was it holding a grudge against the few friends she possessed? She was no longer sure why she had ever expected them to understand. It was a measure too extreme for them. They were confused, even angry, in Xanthe's case. Will no longer had the energy to hold it against them. They would come around eventually, or they wouldn't. What did it matter?

That fleeting impression of normalcy was already vanishing.

Carroway's easy smile flowered into being again, and Will did her best to mirror it.

"You'd better get going, though. Only ten minutes till launch."

Again, it hardly mattered. Nothing seemed to anymore. Will headed for the pilots' door, Carroway and everything else receding into the distance.

But there was another dimly familiar figure leaning against the doorframe. Dandelion-fluff curls and flared trousers the colour of poppies.

"Good luck out there, Arrex."

At the sound of her voice the world rushed back in. Tarrant was here, dressed too fancy, her eyes big and haunted. Her best friend was doomed, but Tarrant was *here*, hobnobbing with the rich people she claimed to despise. For the first time since Hrue Lipson called her name, Will felt something other than numb. A twisting in her gut. Something like disgust.

"Why the hell aren't you with Cara?" she hissed, and Tarrant reared back in shock. Silhouetted against Jupiter's red light, she looked completely alien.

"What?"

"Is everything you pretend to believe in a lie, or just all the stuff about wasting money on parties that could feed hungry inner-spoke children?"

"Cara's with her grandfather. Papi had to come for work, and I...I heard you were competing." Tarrant's expression shifted again, into something stupid and sheeplike. Soft. Like she actually had the nerve to look at Will Arrex and pity her. "I wanted to say—"

Rage turned Will's vision white. "Save it." Tarrant had been ready to slap her at the Lottery draw today, but now she wanted to play nice. No way. Will wanted the fight. There was a gnawing hunger deep in her belly, and the only thing that would satisfy was Tarrant showing her claws. "Whatever it is, I don't care."

Tarrant finally seemed to get the message, and the warmth faded. Her lips curled up in something like her usual mocking smile and she placed one hand on her hip. "Am I not allowed to wish you luck?"

Resting her weight on one leg to mirror Tarrant's casual posture, Will attempted to summon her cruellest smirk. It felt wrong—wobbly—but an Arrex did not feel fear, did not feel anything that made her weak, and so Will ignored it. "You never have before."

Shaking back her hair, Tarrant laughed. It, too, sounded wobbly. "Well, this time is different."

Her blouse was blue tonight, clashing horribly with the red trousers. The colour was too cool to really suit her—Will preferred the yellow-orange jumpsuit—but the effect was still...nice. It must be pleasant, not to have a family colour. To be able to wear anything, whether it worked for your complexion or not.

"How?"

"You'll need every scrap of luck you can get." Tarrant's smile suddenly had an edge, and Will felt Tarrant drawing close to whatever elaborate insult she'd been setting up. The punchline was almost upon them, and at last, they were back to normal.

The chaos receded, and just for a second the two of them were alone together, suspended among the stars, cut off from everything and everyone.

"Why's that?" Will asked, playing along. Even if the end result was a brutal slapdown, she wanted to see what it was Tarrant had made all this effort for.

"I don't think this is really your sort of thing," Tarrant said primly. "Glider-racing takes quick reflexes, and the last time an Arrex displayed those was when Javier Arrex replied to the job offer for seedship navigator. Ever since then you've all just stagnated in place, like rich little algae vats."

The only response Will could muster was a snort. It felt wonderfully, blessedly familiar. "Been saving that one a long time, have you, Tarrant?"

Tarrant turned puce, and Will grinned, certain that she had hit the nail on the head. *Thought so.*

Hell, Tarrant had probably heard Will was racing and dropped everything to schlep all the way out to the Wheel just to insult her.

It was gratifying to know that she was living rent-free in Tarrant's head.

"Thanks for the good wishes, Tarrant," she snickered. "But I'm afraid I've got a race to win."

A hint of that previous sadness resurfacing, Tarrant smiled. "Looking forward to seeing you try. Knowing your usual talk-to-talent ratio, you'll crash into a spoke five seconds in—and then all my problems will be solved!"

With a slight effort, Will laughed and waved goodbye. "I can always count on you to lift my spirits."

And despite the dark cloud still looming overhead, she did somehow feel a little lighter as she walked away. Tarrant had been...almost nice, once she swallowed that insulting display of pity. Like she had been at the window-viewing party.

Re-energised, Will took the steps down into the hangar three at a time. Once upon a time she would have paused to marvel at the gigantic room, larger than almost any other on the Eden. A space big enough for the dozens of gliders to line up in front of the double-layered airlock doors that opened onto empty space.

There was no time for contemplation now.

Will beelined for the familiar Arrex-grey outline in the distance. The floor beneath her feet thrummed with energy. She was walking atop the Wheel itself, the source of all the Eden's power. Gliders of every colour were scattered around, racers suiting up and strapping in. Somewhere among them would be a glider in the same steel-grey as Will's, embellished with the stylised white flames that were Lauron's trademark. Will looked neither left nor right, not wanting to see him, but she could feel his presence polluting the air like mould spores.

The technician waiting beside her glider had been well-briefed; he wasted no time in handing her a helmet and suit, both freshly manufactured. Her old ones would no longer have fitted, Will supposed. She donned both as quickly as she could, muscle memory rearing its head as she clicked buckles and zips into place. Her helmet was the final piece of the puzzle, and the seal hissed as it took effect: a safeguard in case her glider's cockpit should fail.

Like her new suit, the glider shone, all sleek and steel. Someone on her father's staff had kept it updated, and Will felt a brief flash of gratitude as the suit pressurised, clamping tight against her skin. She didn't even want to imagine the way the race would have gone if she'd tried to fly a glider five years behind every other pilot's.

"Two minutes, racers!" called a distant voice over the tannoy.

The already-rapid activity in the hangar became frenzied. There was no time to think about anything else, and that was exactly what Will wanted. She vaulted up onto the wing of her little craft—as fragile and slender as a paper plane—before dropping into the seat. The cockpit was narrow, barely wide enough for her to move her elbows, and a dizzying array of lights blinked at her from the dash. The controls had been familiar, once, when she was a child convinced that glider-racing was the biggest thrill to be had on the Eden. To be outside the station's protective silver walls had been exhilarating: to see the stars close enough almost to touch.

Now all that familiarity had been lost, along with the joy.

She ran her hands over the joystick, touched the buttons. The primer she had flipped through on the tramcar ride over no longer felt like enough.

The technician gestured to one of the switches and Will hesitated a fraction of a second before flipping it. Instantaneously, the hood of the cockpit lowered and snapped into place with a hiss of air identical to the one her helmet had given. The technician sprang down from the wing of the glider and bolted towards the storage bays, along with every other non-pilot still in the hangar.

The same tinny voice read out a countdown over the intercom system, an alarm shrieked, and then just like that, the airlocks ground themselves open. The inner doors and then the outer, and then the air was rushing out of the hangar and Will's paper plane was hurled forward by an enormous, spiteful child, her body forced back into the seat.

It was dreamlike—unreal. And as Will's flimsy little ship was dragged forward into the void, the remnants of life that the fight with Tarrant had offered faded. All she could feel was empty.

The next time this happens, I won't be coming back. The thought echoed in her mind in a voice that was not wholly her own, and Will tried to master herself, to fight the fugue.

The glider was tumbling, spiralling in the rush of air spilled out into the vacuum, and all around Will the more seasoned pilots were sparking their engines up and zipping away towards the Wheel's surface. Only Will was still in freefall, and if she didn't fix the situation soon it would worsen exponentially. Without the Wheel to anchor her, she might fall forever.

Come on. React.

With an effort, she forced the blood back into her hands and clenched her fingers on the joystick.

She heaved it downward, at the same time flicking the switch on her engines. Fuel was very limited in the featherweight gliders, but if ever there was a need to use some of her reserve, it was now.

Her boosters spat blue fire, and a new force pressed Will down against the cushions. Jetting back towards safety, Will activated her mag-lev and the attraction of the Wheel's titanium composite was enough to do the rest.

Her glider slammed back down, stopping only a few metres above the Wheel's surface, and she flipped the mag-lev switch again to accelerate the propulsion loops. Instantly, the glider lurched forward, and Will was back on course, chasing the laggards at the rear of the group.

It was a spectacle, the glider launch. Silly and wasteful—a whole cargo bay's equivalent of oxygen lost at once—but it was nothing if not indicative of glider-racing as a whole. If Will were Lord Captain she would have put a stop to the frivolity, to the needless expense; but she was not Lord Captain, and the drama of the gliders being dragged out into space, the confusion and the collisions—those were judged more valuable. The masses needed their vidscreen content, after all.

She could see Lauron up ahead now, his grey and white wings standing out among the riot of colours. He was well ahead. Zipping up the Wheel towards Spoke Two, manoeuvring deftly through the pack.

Will gritted her teeth and shoved the joystick forward as she gave chase.

It was coming back to her now. The way the glider handled. The way the segments of the Wheel slid past underneath, dozens of them gone in the blink of an eye.

A few boosts from her engines had her skirting the edges of the rearmost bunch—staying nice and safe in the centre of the Wheel's breadth. She'd had enough near-death experiences for one day.

Will jetted forward, flicking her mag-lev from *go* to *follow*, latching on to the slipstream of the closest pilot. She hung on just long enough to slow him down with the weight of two gliders...and then back to *go* and another blast of blue fire from the engines shot her past, leaving him raging in her wake.

Skipping from one rival to another, Will worked her way through the pack, marvelling at her luck. Perhaps things were finally looking up.

Like a river on Old Terra, the racers split into two multicoloured ribbons as they sped past Spoke Two. Bunched together in the narrow lanes to either side of the spoke's base, they jockeyed for position and Will flipped between them to gain some considerable ground. Ruthless driving, reckless driving. Locking on to one, then another, then another, dragging herself forward by the power of her glider's mag-lev alone. It was a new thing, this *follow* setting, and only the most expensive ships had it. Luckily, expense was not a concern for an Arrex.

Glancing up as she passed beneath the thin spire that would bulk out further up to become the spoke proper, Will caught her first true glimpse of the stars.

Bisected as always by the far side of the Wheel, space splayed out on either side of the black strip like the wings of some incomprehensibly vast, impossibly beautiful butterfly. Spangled with a thousand points of light and Jupiter looming on one side, it was beautiful. Breathtakingly so.

If Will was doomed to die out there...well. At least she would die surrounded by beauty.

Something slammed into her from the left and Will snarled out an expletive, her attention rudely dragged away from contemplation of the infinite. A red glider emblazoned with acid-green lightning bolts and its pilot's callsign—*Hot Thunder*, for crying out loud—splashed in neon pink over the whole mess. The pilot, reflections flickering wildly across his helmet, offered her a mocking salute, and Will hissed in fury as she kicked her engines on and left him in her dust.

Spokes Three and Four whizzed by in a blur and Will edged her way closer to Lauron. Progress was tortuously slow, and he was still unchallenged. Secure on his throne as leader of the race.

But Will was nothing if not determined, and the Arrex glider was sleek and beautiful. It combined the very latest featherweight design with cutting-edge engines powerful enough to blow a hole through a meteorite, and mag-lev strong enough to make those engines almost redundant.

Hopping from one slipstream to another, ruthlessly cannibalising the momentum of others to feed her own, Will gained on her quarry. It was almost enough to drive everything else out of her head. Even the Lottery. Even Tarrant and her ugly pity. Spoke Five screamed past, and only four gliders were left between her and Lauron.

She looked ahead to Spoke Six, and right at the end of it she could see the distant glimmer of yellow lights streaming from the Arrex mansion.

Somewhere up there Tunis would be preparing dinner. Xavier would be closeted with his staff, planning campaigns and speeches. Eloise's tramcar might be pulling up in the atrium. Her family were up there, their lives going on as normal. Will's Lottery bombshell had shaken them, but they were still committed to their mission. Win the Surveys. That was what mattered. Everything else was just a part of that one overriding goal. Her family were up there, doing their parts. And she was out here doing hers. They were counting on her, and Will did not intend to let them down.

She jackknifed around the edge of Spoke Six, coming close enough to see the little dints and dings in the metal of the spire connecting it to the Wheel. Engines roaring, she sliced through the yellow outline of the Arrex mansion lights and soared into the home stretch.

There was the hangar, a little nub of imperfection on the perfectly smooth Wheel. Only Spoke One was left between the glider and its goal. The other pilots had fallen away, mere shadows in the rearview vidscreen built into Will's dashboard, and she paid them no mind. Her entire being was focused on the grey ship up ahead, streaked with tacky white flames.

I'm coming for you, cousin. She flipped the switch to light her engines and pressed her foot flat to the floor, no longer caring about preserving her limited fuel stocks. It was all or nothing now.

The flames roared in the soundless vacuum, and Will imagined she could feel their heat on the back of her neck. It was working. Slowly, slowly, she was gaining on him. She was edging alongside. He looked over at her and she saw hatred twist his features, but she kept her foot down.

She was going to win.

But Lauron had her up against the edge as they sped towards the tip of Spoke One. Even through the shields of cockpit and helmet, the grin on his face was visible, feral in its intensity. He wanted that victory. He was willing to risk anything to get it. And Will had to choose—keep jostling for position or play it safe and fall back.

It was then that Tarrant popped back into her head—at precisely the wrong moment, as she so often did. *Don't you ever get tired of everything being yours?*

This was dangerous. Too dangerous. Will had already laid her life on the line once today, and she hadn't yet begun to pay the price. And glider-racing was risky: stray too close to the edge and you run the chance of slipping off and jetting out into empty space. Without the Wheel to anchor the glider's mag-lev, the engine was pretty much powerless. There were retrieval ships, but there was always the risk that they wouldn't reach the glider in time—or that a little stray asteroid would reach you first. And that was without even mentioning the humiliation of having been the idiot to fall off the track.

Tarrant was right, in a way. Will didn't have to win everything, and even the Lottery wasn't enough to make her want to risk dying during a pathetic glider race. With a groan, Will cut her engines and watched Lauron zip away into the lead, his laughter ringing in her ears despite the lack of radio contact. He vanished into the gaping jaws of the hangar and was swallowed up by the brilliant white of the lights.

As she crossed the finish line in a distant second, Will braked hard and taxied across the hangar to come to a stop as far from Lauron's glider as she could. It was somehow a strangely anticlimactic end to the fury of their race. Will had expected fanfares, confetti. Champagne spilling from bottles.

All that would come, of course—but not until the airlocks were safely sealed behind the last racer. Until then the pilots would wait in their sealed pods, alone with their jubilation or humiliation.

Her thundering pulse beginning to slow, Will finally allowed herself to take a breath. The oxygen flooding down her throat was almost painful in its sweetness. It was over. For the first time in years she had braved the world beyond the Eden. A feat which ninety-nine in a hundred of Eden's citizens would never accomplish. Will had done it before and she had done it again— *And, please*, she added internally, hopelessly, *let that be the last time. A silly little race. Don't make me do it for real.*

The other pilots were returning, straggling in one by one, and Will's panting breaths came more evenly. Gradually, the fear faded and rational thought returned. She had come close to winning. It would have been wonderful to show Lauron who was the better pilot as well as the better politician—but it wasn't worth her life.

The airlock doors resealed, and Lauron leapt from his glider, the hangar ringing with his exultant crows. Still lingering in her pilot's seat, Will thought of Tarrant. Perhaps she'd left: gone back to Cara's after all. Trying to console where no consolation could ever be enough.

And the thought of Cara brought everything crashing back in.

Lauron's minions were already surrounding him, bearing drinks and Arrex banners to drape over his shoulders. No one waited by Will's glider, no friends to console her for this or the larger loss. Carroway was upstairs, but Will had never wanted to see him less.

When he saw Will finally emerge from her cockpit, Lauron shoved through his posse, a huge grin plastered across his face. "Cousin!"

He said it like it was the friendliest, most natural greeting in the world. As though the word wasn't seething with hate bubbling just below the surface.

Will ignored him, dropping heavily to the ground beside her technician. "Call my tramcar," Will said. "I'm not going to the bar. Tell them to send it to the cargo bay."

Behind her, the whoops of Lauron's friends echoed through the cavernous room.

CHAPTER 8

Spoke Six, Eden Station – Year 452 – Day 346 – 08:00

When Will finally saw him again, after the race, Xavier's detachment had given way to the fury of a titan. He would not allow this to happen. For a Noble to risk her life on a Laika was unthinkable. Will was irreplaceable. The Lottery would be redrawn, he vowed. Another ticket would be produced, another number. Another child condemned, another family ruined, *anything*—but Will would be spared.

In vain his aides reasoned with him about the impossibility of it all. There would be riots, they whispered, faces long and drawn. He would lose the Surveys, and the captaincy too, and any chance at regaining them for the rest of his life.

He was implacable. His daughter would not be sacrificed. His power and his captaincy were nothing without an heir, *his* heir, his daughter.

In cold rage he swept from the house, off to seek the support of the Noble Council, to secure the intervention of Lord Captain Galba Chassiron herself. She who would fain change the law to save her own wife would surely waive it to save his daughter.

With quiet despair Will awaited his return, accepting the tears and embraces of a horrified Eloise returned early from the lab for the first time in years. With waning hope she listened for his step in the entryway, and with silent acceptance she saw the misery in his face when he finally appeared. It had been a failure. Even for a Noble, even for Xavier Arrex, the law was the law, and the Lord Captain would not bend even before an unbending man.

Will Arrex's ticket had been drawn, and into the Laikas she must go. Without even the luxury of tears Will understood this, and attempted to resign herself to it. She had, after all, entered herself into the Lottery. No one had done this *to* her. It was all her own mistake: all her own fault. Better to concentrate on what was left to her, than to rail against what had happened. Better to cling to these precious few hours remaining.

The last weekend was a beautiful lie.

For the first time in living memory there were no tutors, no aides or meetings or embryos awaiting genetic screening in the labs upstairs. Even campaigning was suspended.

It was just the three of them. Will, Xavier, and Eloise. Shoulder to shoulder on the sofa, Will sandwiched between her parents as they watched a movie together. A game of golf in the great hall. Kisses pressed into her hair, Eloise's yellow-blonde mixing with her daughter's platinum white. Table tennis. Chess with her mother while her father cheered them both on. Tunis bringing snacks, endless snacks, her old eyes bright with tears. Even a trip to a restaurant—no photographers, just a whole restaurant that Xavier had emptied so they could be alone.

Will knew better than to ask her father if one of his aides had planned these final moments, but she wondered. They were almost too perfect, delivered one at a time like photographs framed in impossibly expensive wood from pruned orchard branches. Pure gold for the Surveys if only Cirrus and his crew had been present to document them.

Will understood that her parents were trying. She saw it in every carefully curated activity, every halting breath when they tried to express the things they did not have the words for. Xavier watched Will unceasingly, a predator's gaze as he offered up one gift after another, but even he could not quite mask the stink of fear. Again and again, Eloise tried to say what Xavier couldn't. Each time she failed, never quite coming to the point and falling back into brittle smiles and frantic cheer. Will played her part and did her best to feign happiness for them. Their time was short, and she would not muddy the waters with the emotions roiling inside her. Best to leave the truth, whatever it might be, safely unspoken.

A lifetime of family memories compressed into two days, the kind of activities Will had always imagined Tarrant and her parents doing. She thought it hurt more because it was so sweet: the taste of what might have been. A life they could have had.

But it wasn't...it didn't feel *real*. Nothing did. A mirage, the fleeting flicker of a hologram over the cold and hard reality: when the weekend ended, Will would leave. The Training Centre waited for her.

And all too soon, Sunday night arrived. Tunis brought Will a parcel, large and square and ominous. With Eloise clutching her shoulders like a drowning woman, Will opened it to reveal a Laika jumpsuit in the same iron-grey as the standard school uniforms. It bore a large number six on the breast, but instead of the usual second six on the arm there was only the Laika logo. A little ship alone on the vast swathe of material.

The fabric was different too. Coarse, tight-woven and hard-wearing, designed for long use. Tailored close to the body to allow a spacesuit to be worn on top. Will didn't know how they could have gotten her measurements, but evidently, they had. There were flaps and zips in all the spots that the spacesuit would need to attach to her body, but other than that it was one smooth sheet of dark grey, fastening all the way up to the chin. There would be no room for an undershirt beneath this jumpsuit; no way even Tarrant could unbutton a few centimetres to show a touch of individuality.

There would be no school tomorrow. No race to be earliest, no smug little smile from Tarrant with her books already scattered across the entire desk. No Tarrant at all. Not ever again. That realisation hurt more than Will had expected.

But there was one relief, at least. Will would never have to see Tarrant wearing one of these jumpsuits. She was safe here with their remaining classmates, and she would go to the Academy and study Terran history for the rest of her life.

And maybe, without Will to plague her, she would be happy.

Will shook herself and folded the jumpsuit back into its box. That was not a healthy train of thought. She would return, give or take five years or so. And she would find Tarrant in her cushy office at the Academy and pick up plaguing her right where she left off.

Everything could still work out fine.

It *could*.

Sleep came, though Will fought to stave it off as long as she could. Monday morning dawned, the lights flicking on when the timer kicked in. Will stirred, and beside her on the sofa Eloise did too. Xavier was at the far end of the gargantuan piece of furniture, his face twisted in uneasy sleep and his smooth blonde hair the most unkempt Will had ever seen it.

"I think it's time, Mum."

"Yes, my darling. I think it is." Eloise's voice was too fragile and too calm all at once.

"We'll still see each other." *Surely we will.* Launch day was almost two months away, but how long would the training be? Will didn't know. She hadn't looked into it. She had been so sure that it wouldn't be her who was picked.

"Of course we will."

But Will couldn't shake the feeling that they were both lying to one another.

She'd expected Xavier to make a fuss when the time came for her to leave. But after they ate a silent breakfast together, Tunis weeping into the milk as she poured it, after Will robed herself in the stiff grey jumpsuit and faced him at the door—all he did was squeeze her shoulder, just once.

"I know you'll be a worthy Arrex, Wilhelmina. Even there."

She swallowed as she looked up into his eyes, a mirror of her own. "You aren't going to...try again?"

Resignation might have come, but that didn't mean she had altogether given up. She knew as well as he did that it would be political suicide—if not *outright* suicide and the spark for a rebellion—to pull out at this stage. The Noble Council had withdrawn any chance of aid. Will was on her own.

But she couldn't help *hoping*.

He offered her a bitter smile. "We've come this far down the path you chose, Wilhelmina. We might as well go a little further."

"I suppose so."

He looked away and said the obvious. "The Surveys are too close now for us to do anything else." Then he gestured, and Tunis produced a parcel for him to pass to Will. "But I do have something for you."

Will opened it and shook out the grey fabric inside. A Laika jumpsuit, just like the other—but a better cut, the material infinitely softer and more breathable. Not the standard-issue Spoke Six iron-grey, but the safe, familiar Arrex steel.

Xavier offered her a thin smile. "No daughter of mine will go into that cesspit dressed like a commoner."

Will's throat was tight, and she took his hand in her own. Not quite a handshake, not quite holding it. "Thank you, Father."

Then with a quick hug for Tunis and a brief, *I'll see you soon, my darling,* from Eloise, it was over. Will was out of the door, an honour guard of Lawkeepers saluting her on every side as she crossed the atrium to the platform where the tramcar waited. Behind her, the door to her home still stood open, her parents terribly small within it.

She didn't look back until she was shielded by the tramcar's darkened windows. They didn't wave, and nor did she. They were Arrexes, they were Nobles. They did not wave. And—this wasn't goodbye. They would see each other again. With unblinking eyes, Will watched them until the tunnel swallowed her whole.

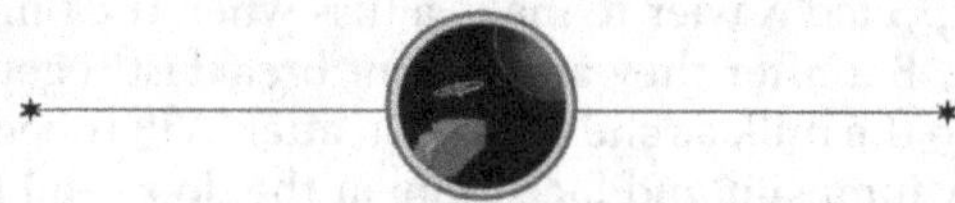

Will looked at the little room that was to be her home for the next seven weeks, and felt horror rising deep in the pit of her stomach. It was small, smaller than her *bathroom* at home—and the size was supposed to simulate the living conditions on the Laikas themselves.

How could they expect her to spend the rest of her life in a room no bigger than a bathroom?

Leaving her bags in the hallway to deal with later, Will stepped inside. Upon further investigation, what she had thought was one room was actually *four*, subdivided to the point of lunacy. Three doors led off the cramped set of living quarters. Squeezed into the main space was a two-seater sofa facing a vidscreen, a kitchenette, and a table with two chairs shoved right up against the wall. Also, incongruously, an exercise bike, wedged between the stove and the sofa. The first door led to a hideous attempt at a waste disposal unit and bathroom combined. It was less than a meter squared, where the entire floor served as the shower tray. Will was disgusted—was she expected to shower *while sitting on the toilet*? What was going *on*?

The final two doors at the room's rear turned out to lead to two identical and minuscule bedrooms, each containing little more than a single bed and a few dwarf-sized cupboards.

Staring into the left-hand bedroom, Will shook her head. She wasn't a materialistic person, but to be given a bedroom less than half the size of her *bed* at home—it beggared belief.

There were no windows. Of course.

Will sat on the bed and listened to the other new arrivals trickling in as the tramcars pulled up at the station beyond the heavy containment doors. She expected exclamations of horror at the accommodations, but all she heard was how nice the rooms were. How clean. How spacious. *Spacious?* Were they joking?

She almost wished Tarrant were here—she would have an absolute field day if she could watch Will be confronted with the evidence that she was far richer than she'd ever realised. Maybe her malicious glee would be enough to distract Will from her own sense of hopelessness.

She drifted back to the shower room, morbidly fascinated by it, and was horrified anew when she found it ran only cold water and turned itself off automatically after two minutes. How did people *cope* without baths? It was inhumane.

A rustle and a bang from the corridor outside. "Dammit, who left all this stuff here?"

A girl burst through the outer door, dark hair swinging wildly as she struggled with her own bags before dumping them in the entryway—blocking the door and any hope Will might have had of escape.

Frozen, Will stared. Despite the fact the room had two of everything—two chairs, two beds—its size was such that Will had somehow not connected the dots to understand that she would be expected to *share* it with someone.

The girl was clattering her suitcases about now, piling them together and kicking the bottom one to get it out of her way. All without showing any hint of noticing Will at all.

Finally, she looked up and made eye contact with Will, and then she, too, froze.

"Shit," gasped the girl, and Will felt that yes, that about summed the situation up.

There was a pause.

"Hello," Will said stiffly.

"You're her," the girl said, eyebrows climbing out of sight beneath that heavy fringe. "The Noble."

Will pressed her lips together into an approximation of a smile. "I'm Lady Will Arrex." It felt pretentious to introduce herself by her title, but given that this girl clearly understood who she was and had chosen not to use the proper forms of address, perhaps a reminder was needed.

The girl looked her in the eye with a confidence that Will felt was beginning to border on insolence and shrugged. "Duh."

Her smile well on its way to becoming a grimace, Will tapped her fingers against her leg. *Control, control. I deal with Tarrant every day. I grew up with* Lauron. *I can handle this.*

"I'm buddies with Nic," the girl offered finally, by way of explanation. "My dad and his were at the Academy together. Roommates." She gave Will a wonky grin. "Like us, I guess."

Will tried to put the pieces together. Nic, Nic...did she mean Nico *Chassiron*?

"You're from Spoke One, then?" she hazarded a guess.

The girl's thick black eyebrows disappeared again as a look of surprise came over her face. "You mean you don't recognise me?" She laughed. "Weird. I'm so used to everyone knowing. Panset Pall, of the Spoke One Palls. You *must* have heard of us."

Will paused. That did ring a bell, a very faint one. "The algae famers?"

Panset smiled, thoroughly satisfied. "That's the one. Biggest vats on the Eden."

"Right," Will said slowly. Well, she was in for a rough time of it if this girl was her roommate. Her family's wealth and her father's friendship with a Chassiron consort seemed to have given her the impression she was a Noble herself.

"I race a lot," Panset said brightly, utterly oblivious to any misgivings Will might have. "Saw you lose to Lauron the other night. Must've stung. I've gone up against him a few times, but I beat him three outta four."

"Yes," Will said tightly. "Well, I've had losses that stung worse." Like the Lottery, to name one example. Or the roommate draw she must have lost in order to end up with Panset.

"I bet," agreed Panset. "Like the Surveys, right? My money's on Lauron. I know *I'd* vote for him over you."

Will glanced over her shoulder at her tiny bedroom, which suddenly looked a whole lot more inviting. It had a door. One she could shut right in Panset's dreadful face.

"I like how he thinks the higher-ranking non-Nobles should be exempt," Panset explained, clearly completely comfortable carrying the conversation solo. "Makes sense to me."

Entirely occupied edging back towards the left-hand bedroom, Will did her best to ignore the contents of Panset's words and restricted herself to a polite nod or two. She was almost there.

"And obviously," Panset said carelessly, pushing past Will to flop down on the bed, the door still open wide, "he's hot, your cousin."

Will's lip curled. Was this girl incapable of keeping any thoughts, no matter how inappropriate, to herself? For all that she was from one of the richest families on Eden, she behaved worse than the most illiterate inner-spoker Will had ever seen.

"Don't suppose you could get me an intro?" Panset asked, still squinting at the ceiling, and then, looking back up, "Wipe the judgement off your face, Princess. We're all about to die; why shouldn't I have a bit of fun first?"

Frustrated at having been so easy to read, Will tried to modulate her voice when she answered. "I'm not used to hearing people talk about him like that."

Panset snickered. "Must not have been around many people, then. Everyone I know thinks Lauron Arrex is hot." With a critical eye, she considered Will. "No one really says that about you, though."

This time Will did not trouble to keep the outrage off her face.

"I don't know why," continued Panset, with no qualms at all. "You look exactly the same. I guess pointy and brooding just doesn't work as well for a girl."

Will was almost trembling with fury. "You'd be arrested if anyone heard you talking like this in Spoke Six."

Clearly surprised, Panset sat back up. "Arrested? Are you serious?"

"Don't speak to me like that," Will snapped. *Or better yet, don't speak to me at all.*

Panset clambered to her feet and crossed her arms over her chest. "You think I'm not being respectful enough, Princess?"

Will's fists clenched, but she didn't reply. No one had *ever* treated her like this. Not even Tarrant. Hatred was infinitely easier to handle than disrespect.

And that thought was another reminder that while Tarrant would be back in school today, sitting at their desk, Will would not be there beside her. No, she was stuck here with Panset, and no doubt a bevy of similarly awful people. Undergoing their 'training' together in preparation for the day they'd be cast out of the Eden forever.

Her fingernails dug deeper into her palms, ten tiny crescents of pain.

"I'd be arrested in Spoke One, too," Panset said lightly, walking closer. "For not calling you Lady Arrex or bowing or whatever. But here's the deal, Princess." And here she smiled. "We're beyond the reach of the law now. There's nothing left to punish us with."

"Are you *threatening* me?" It would be a short one-way trip to jail, if so. Panset might still be going to space, but she didn't have to receive her training here in Centre. Distance learning would be just as effective.

To Will's shock, Panset actually began to laugh. And not an unkind laugh—just the laugh of somebody who had heard something truly amusing.

"Obviously not." She wiped a tear from one corner of her eye. Whether it was real or just another part of the act, Will couldn't tell. "I'm just saying I'm not gonna be bowing and scraping. You're going on the Laikas same as me. You're not special."

"Do whatever you want," Will snapped, drawing back. *Just leave me alone.*

"Thanks," laughed Panset, but it was still without rancour. "Now, do you want a hand carrying all those bags in? Guess Nobles don't know how to pack light, huh?"

"No, thank you," Will answered stiffly. It was tempting to drop the pretence at politeness—but just because Panset behaved like an animal, it didn't mean everyone had to.

Panset shrugged and Will headed back outside into the corridor. She looked at the heap of bags, and then drifted on to the next room. Inside she found a serious-looking girl bending over a textbook on spaceship design, and in the small bedroom to the rear, the most familiar face of all.

Cara.

She was seated beside a very young boy, her arm around his thin shoulders, and Will wondered at first if he was some sort of relative of Cara's, come to see her off. But that was impossible—they had all been shuttled in alone, no parents or siblings allowed.

But surely that boy wasn't a day over twelve. He *couldn't* be a Lottery winner.

He was crying, quiet sobs shaking his thin shoulders, and Will was about to withdraw when Cara looked up and saw her.

"Hi, Lady Arrex." Her voice was as tremulous and quiet as always, and all Will could see was the look on Tarrant's face as she watched her best friend being led away.

I'll look after her for you, Tarrant, she promised suddenly, the thought taking her aback with its intensity. But on reflection—it made sense. Tarrant would be looking after Jin for Cara's sake. She was probably with him right now. Well, she would be once school was done, at least. She would look after Jin for the rest of his life, all for Cara. Tarrant was that sort of person. She would do selfless things for her friends. Maybe, for Tarrant, whom Will would likely now never see again—maybe Will could do a selfless thing too.

Besides, it would be a relief to have someone to talk to who was not Panset.

"It's Will, remember," she murmured, stepping into the room and walking past the girl with the textbook. "Who's this?"

"This is Thune," said Cara softly, rubbing the tear-stained boy's shoulder.

Thune sniffed hard and held out a wobbly hand for her to shake. "Thune Sisparia, f-from Spoke Three."

"And that's my roommate Loysa," Cara added, gesturing to the girl on the sofa.

"Nice to meet you, Thune," replied Will gently, electing to ignore Loysa for now, given that she still hadn't looked up from her rocket textbook.

With a watery smile, Thune muttered something vaguely polite back in Will's direction, and she gingerly seated herself beside him on the bed. He was even smaller up close, and she was struck again with just how young he looked. Surely he couldn't be fifteen? The Lottery didn't pull in just young people, but also *actual* children.

"There you are, Princess," called a strident voice from the doorway, and Will gritted her teeth. She was getting tired of that little nickname already. "I was starting to worry you'd ditched me!"

"Hi." Will's voice was flat. Panset was, in her way, as persistent as Lysse was. And twice as annoying.

Panset bounced in. "Introduce me!"

Pausing long enough to push the very outer limits of politeness, Will gestured. "This is Cara and Thune. And that's Loysa."

"Hi." Loysa waved an absent hand without looking up from the textbook.

"Hey, Thune!" Panset shouldered past and crouched down, flashing a million-watt smile at the little boy. Despite herself, Will was slightly amused at how irrepressible Panset seemed. Her bounciness might be fatalistic, but at least she was still bouncing.

"You sure you're old enough to be here, bud? My little brother's eleven and you don't look much older."

Thune crumpled back against Cara, who patted his hand soothingly, though she looked close to despair herself.

"Hey, hey, I didn't mean to upset you," Panset said, dropping heavily onto the bed between Will and Thune, almost ejecting Will from the tiny room altogether.

"I want my mum," Thune said, very quietly. His eyes were watering. "I want to go home."

"You'll be okay," Panset answered reassuringly. "We can look out for each other, you and me, huh, bud?"

Thune just bowed his head. Like the weight of it was too much for him to hold up anymore. Cara and Panset pressed close on either side of him, like surrogate parents.

Finding herself unexpectedly deserted, Will tried to make conversation with Loysa, who remained stooped over her textbook. From what little she said, Will gathered that Loysa was a student at the Academy, well into her thesis on photodynamics and drone design—and, most shockingly, she had actually *wanted* to win the Lottery.

"Laika pilots are the only spacefarers the Eden produces," she said, when Will pushed her. "It's the biggest frontier left for us. Why wouldn't I want to be a part of it?"

Because it means almost certain death, maybe?

Once Thune was calmer, they ventured out to explore. Other hollow-eyed teens hunched on beds or wandered past in silence; Eden's thirty-six sacrificial lambs. The range of their new quarters was alarmingly limited: a simulation hall, a canteen-classroom hybrid, and the single corridor lined with eighteen shared suites. The interior doors hissed open readily enough, but when Panset rattled the handles of the doors that led back to the tramcars, they remained stubbornly locked, and everyone quieted at the reminder.

Prisoners.

"They probably keep them locked all the time," Panset said, and this time the energy had left her voice. "Stop us getting any big ideas."

Will glanced at Thune: huddled against Cara, he looked close to tears again.

"Where could we go?" Cara asked hopelessly. "There's nowhere to hide on the Eden."

"I'd bet you could find somewhere, if you were desperate," replied Panset, unfazed. "And in a few weeks, most of us are going to be desperate."

"Oh, can't you guys just stop it?" Loysa interjected.

They all turned to her.

She coloured. "We're lucky. We have the chance to go out there and do something *real* for humanity. We're going to see the terraformers. Some of us are going to see *Earth*."

For a moment Will let herself give in to it, to the wonder in Loysa's voice. She imagined that little blue-green speck as the earliest videos showed it, before it was blasted and scoured and turned to desert. It would be wonderful, to see that. Even if only once.

"Most of us are gonna die, though." Panset did not let the moment last.

That was enough to shatter what little remained of Thune's composure, and he dissolved into tears.

"I'm sorry, bud," Panset said, instantly contrite. "I didn't mean it like that."

Will hung back as Panset and Cara led Thune away. Suddenly, she'd had her fill of socialising. But then the door opened, and Will whirled. Surely her father hadn't somehow managed to—?

No. It was a member of staff, robed in the same dull brown as all the others. She let the door shut again, the dull click that let Will know, once again, what it was to be a prisoner—and then she called out a name. "Cara Sutsu? I'm looking for a Cara Sutsu?"

Heads poked out of doorways. People stared.

Leaving Thune with Panset, Cara scurried back down the corridor and presented herself. "I'm Cara."

"Come with me, please."

The brown-clothed woman brushed past Will as though she wasn't there, Cara trailing in her wake. The door slammed closed behind them. Less than a day after entering, Cara had left the Laika complex.

There was a flurry of activity as people scrambled to speculate what it might mean. Was Cara somehow in trouble already? Had she been arrested? As their guesses grew more wild, Will's anxiety began to spike. *Just* as she had made that promise to Tarrant—in her own head, at least—Cara was removed. What did it mean?

When the others lost interest and drifted away to bed, Will remained, leaning against the wall by the outer doors. Waiting for Cara to reappear.

An hour passed. Three. Five. Will waited, but Cara Sutsu did not return.

When the door finally clunked open again, Will started awake, glancing at her watch. Nearly three in the morning. Cara had been gone all night.

But as she opened her mouth to ask a question—*Are you okay*—the words died on her lips.

Because the girl before her was not Cara, pale and wan.

Facing her was Paige Tarrant, hair tumbling in disarray down over her shoulders, tangling in the strap of the bag she held on her shoulder. Will gaped. What was Tarrant doing here? Why was Cara gone—and *Tarrant* roaming the halls in her place?

Staring back at her, Tarrant looked just as displeased as Will was.

Scrambling upright, Will pointed a finger at Tarrant, and was surprised to see it shaking. "What the hell are you doing? Only Lottery winners are allowed in here." As she said the words, she was aware of the symmetry—hadn't Tarrant once said almost those very same words to her? *This area's for ticket holders only.*

Tarrant showed no such awareness, only an intransigent, dull anger. "Well, I am one now."

"*What?*"

"I swapped."

"Swapped? What do you mean? You can't *swap*."

"Well, I have. I swapped with Cara. So I'm...I guess I'm a Lottery winner now."

"Tarrant—why the *fuck* would you do that?"

Her armour crumbling with an abruptness that shocked Will more than any of the previous revelations, Tarrant stared at her, eyes huge. "I—it's—it was Cara. She has a *family*. She's the main earner. Her grandfather can't work, and he'd have to report to Recycling ten years ahead of schedule if she left. My...*my* parents are young. They'll be fine." She blinked hard, her eyes suspiciously bright. "They might even make it back into the Child Eligibility Pool if I'm gone."

Will stared, utterly at a loss. "Tarrant—you *cannot* be serious. You *volunteered* to join the Laika Programme?"

Suddenly defensive, Tarrant folded her arms. "Wouldn't you have done the same if it was your friend?"

Will didn't need to think about her answer. She knew with absolute certainty that if somehow Xanthe or Carroway had been selected, and she had the chance to take their place—she would not have done it. It wasn't ignoble, or selfish. It was just the truth. She wouldn't have done it.

She didn't respond aloud, but Tarrant could clearly see the answer on her face. She gave a small, hollow laugh and turned away. "Not everyone thinks like you, Arrex."

With nothing more to say, Tarrant vanished into what had been Cara's room, and Will slowly, reluctantly, retreated to her own. She couldn't get her head around it. Tarrant had been *safe*. She had gone through the Lottery process, and her number had not come up. She was completely safe, and she had given it all up for Cara.

Possibly even given up her *life*.

Will lay in bed and listened to Panset snoring softly, and did not close her eyes even for a second. Tarrant was here. Tarrant was *here*, doomed to die just like Will. To be shot out into space and likely never be heard of again. She would never make it to the Academy, never study Terran history. Never write a dissertation on why the European Union fell or something equally trite. She would be gone.

Tarrant was here, to take the place of Cara—whom Will had truly pitied. She hadn't deserved to be on a Laika.

Why, then, was Will even *more* afraid now that it was Tarrant who was facing the same fate?

CHAPTER 9

After three hours spent tossing and turning, Will rose and headed out. Breakfast was apparently meant to be prepared in the kitchenette and eaten with your roommate, and she had no desire to wait around for Panset. She walked the length of the corridor once, twice, and then did a lap of the simulation room. No holograms yet. Just a big white room, echoing with the lonely sound of her footsteps.

Classes would begin today. Nine until six in the evening, just like school. So when her watch told her it was almost seven in the morning, Will decided to head into the classroom. An hour before she usually arrived, but her new prison was too limited to offer any other options.

She settled herself at a desk in the front row, the one on the far right. The same seat she'd always occupied in the old classroom on Spoke Six. She'd wondered if Cara would sit with her, but now Tarrant had come to take her place. And she certainly would not want to sit beside Will—not when there were thirty-four others to choose from.

Everything was so familiar. So achingly close to the life Will had left behind. Classmates, school, now even Tarrant. And yet it was all wrong. The room was huge: a classroom for forty, not seven. There would be no real lessons, only a crash course on piloting a spaceship, the bare minimum needed before they were thrown out into the void less than eight weeks from today. No bright future at the Academy. There was no future left at all.

Will put her head down on her arms, cushioning it against the desk, and let herself drift away.

Sleep didn't come, but strange half-waking dreams swirled around her. Tarrant was there, snarling. *This isn't something that will ever affect you.* Her hair crackled with electricity, barely restrained lightning. Cara was behind her, holding Jin up as he collapsed. *Wouldn't you have done the same if it was your friend?* Tarrant laughed, and laughed, and she wouldn't stop laughing, even as the sound of it cut into Will like a blade. *You wouldn't, would you? Selfish, selfish, selfi—*

The hiss of a door made Will start upright, breathing hard. Someone was standing in the doorway, looking towards the back of the room, not the right-hand side where Will sat. For a moment Will was afraid it was Panset, come to hunt her down and tell her all about how *hot* her cousin was—but then she saw the familiar halo of wild hair, and she exhaled.

Tarrant might be the stuff of her nightmares, but she was also a welcome touch of normalcy right now.

"Morning, Tarrant."

At the sound of her voice Tarrant whipped round, eyes wide. Her gaze fastened on Will and she relaxed into her usual expression of annoyance. She didn't speak, but Will could practically see the thoughts flickering across her face. *Of course you'd be here. Of course I don't get even a second alone to prepare.*

Will smiled weakly. "I thought about letting you have the early win this morning—but then I thought, why break the habit of a lifetime?"

It was a risky manoeuvre: acknowledging that not only had this always been a game, but also that Will intended to keep playing it. Still, why not hold on to it? In this strange new world, they had little enough left to cling to.

She watched for Tarrant's reaction, and finally the other girl gave her a wan, exhausted smile. Wove through the desks and—to Will's shock—dropped into the seat beside her. The desk shook. As ever, Tarrant moved with all the grace of a sack of potatoes.

But Will let the opportunity for an insult slip by.

Tarrant repeated her shrug, that same tired smile still in place. "Like you said. Why break the habit of a lifetime?"

A smile spreading over her own face, Will looked back at her notebook, open to an empty page. Of her own free will, Tarrant had chosen to sit next to her. Miracles were still possible.

She wanted to say something, to make some response...but Tarrant was always touchy, prone to snapping, and Will didn't want to jeopardise the fragile ceasefire. Besides, she looked so weary. Like she was only a few hard knocks away from total collapse. She had done a terrible, wonderful thing. To sacrifice your whole life, to save a friend—best to let Tarrant rest. She needed it.

The minutes stretched on, and Will savoured each one. Before all of this, their rivalry had been the closest Will had come to a friendship at school—not that Tarrant's poisonous glares had been particularly close to friendship, but still. For Tarrant it was different. She had been the possessor of real friends. Here, though, she was alone. Just like Will. Maybe sitting together could be a good thing for them both.

One by one, the other students filed in, and slowly the classroom filled. Will winced when Panset appeared, dreading the introductions she might be forced to make—imagine if Tarrant actually struck up a *friendship* with Panset. Will had watched her interact with morons like Lysse and Erntz every day for years and never seem to resent their presence. But thankfully Tarrant was too out of it to notice anyone in particular, and Panset was absorbed babysitting Thune.

Finally, at nine on the dot, a teacher materialised. A weaselly woman clad in the same mud-brown as all the other Laika staff Will had seen lurking around, only a white armband marking her out as a higher rank. This time Will had no trouble placing the familiar face. This was the sharp-faced girl from the old recordings, aged a couple of decades and more sour-looking than ever. Like her co-pilot Hrue Lipson, Professor Clark had boarded a Laika and lived to tell the tale.

"This," the professor said, clearly savouring the moment, "is the Laika."

In front of every student, vidscreens sparked into light simultaneously, each displaying a 3D image of a blunt-nosed little ship. A single minuscule porthole to show the world beyond the cockpit. The Laika was a vehicle built for function above all else. Speed and beauty took a back seat to pure survival.

"The living quarters are small, only one-third of the ship's volume. The rest is engines, fuel tanks, and life-support systems." The diagram on the vidscreen bisected, showing a cutaway. "The studio flats you are currently staying in are designed to simulate what life on the Laika will be like for you and your co-pilot."

Will swallowed. The idea of spending what little life remained to her in a tiny box with a stranger—unless, oh god, was it supposed to be *Panset*? Now *there* was a thought even less pleasant than the Laika itself.

Beside Will, Tarrant leaned in to look at the vidscreen before raising a hand. "Will we be taught how to maintain the life-support systems?"

Professor Clark's pointy nose twitched. "No, you'll have no need of that. The Laika pilot modules are fully sealed off from the ship's mechanics, which are almost fully automated. It might be fairer to call you passengers than pilots."

"Why are we being sent, then?" muttered someone from the classroom's rear. Will half smiled before she caught herself. Her fellow pilots were wasting no time becoming as disillusioned as she felt.

Only Tarrant spoke loud enough to force an answer. "Why include the human element at all?"

A barely suppressed sigh from Professor Clark. She could not ignore the question when it was asked at a proper volume, right to her face. "Radio signal. The distances involved are vast, and humanity is now fully localised to Eden and Amalthea. We don't have the satellite network our ancestors did. Your role will be to respond to crises the pre-programmed route can't take into account, to investigate once the destination is reached, et cetera." Professor Clark gestured, eager to move on, and the display on the vidscreen changed. "We will be sending missions to eighteen sites."

Bright white circles marked the destinations—four to different moons on the far side of Jupiter, one to Uranus's moon Oberon, seven to various locations on Mars and its moons, one to Mercury's dark side, one to Saturn's moon Titan, and four to different points on Venus.

"Why these sites in particular?" Tarrant was not letting up.

Another rodent-like flare of the nostrils. "Before and during the Last War, the ancients on Old Terra sent out a variety of automated terraforming equipment. Different mega-nations and corporations used different technologies, so we have no way of knowing what stage the various sites are at. Collated intelligence from Old Terra at the time of Eden's founding suggest roughly three hundred possibilities, so we send out Laikas to those locations in rotation, in hopes of an update."

Will exchanged a glance with Tarrant—how strange it was, to be on the same side for a change—and knew she was thinking it too. If humanity's only chance at ever leaving the Eden was to go in person and investigate *every* potential site, without certainty of making it home even if the news was good...it didn't bode well for humanity in the long term. With the help of raw materials from Amalthea, the Eden was self-sustaining, but the almost religious hope that someday humans would again walk planetside was a lot more distant than most people believed. No wonder the truth wasn't revealed to any but the Noble Council and those selected to die for that same slim hope.

Another hand went up. Loysa, this time. "Excuse me, Professor, but these schematics—they aren't very detailed. Will we be given access to the full blueprints before launch?"

She looked confident, as though she expected nothing but an instant agreement, so when Professor Clark replied in the negative, she crossed her arms.

"Surely it's important to understand our ships fully," Loysa insisted. "Maybe it would cut down on the failure rate. It's strange that it's so high. Long-distance space travel was something the ancients solved a long time ago."

"She's not wrong," muttered Tarrant.

Unsure if the remark was addressed to her or not, Will didn't hazard an answer.

Professor Clark's lips thinned. "Loysa, is it? I'll ask if a copy can be made available to you. That's all I can do."

Her expression dissatisfied, Loysa sat back in her seat.

"Rest assured that five hundred years of experts have perfected the design of the Laika as far as it can be perfected," Professor Clark said, with an air of finality and a smile that didn't reach her eyes. "The simple fact of the matter is that space travel outside the Eden is incredibly dangerous. That is why we are all so incredibly grateful to you, and the sacrifice you are making." She paused, looked from one face to another, trying to connect with each of them. It was an old trick, one of the very first Will's oratory tutor had given her, and Professor Clark did not do it half so well as five-year-old Will. "You are doing a heroic thing, pilots. When you return you will be given guaranteed housing and employment within the Laika Programme."

Will wrinkled her nose. *And exactly how many do return?*

Little was known about the exact Laika pilot survival rates. Launches only came around once every twenty-five years, and public records were hazy. Survivors in the plural were always mentioned, but the statistics themselves were a closely guarded secret, shared only with the Noble Council and senior Laika

Programme staff. Still, the general shape of the numbers was obvious enough. Occasionally, three or four years after a launch, a ship might limp back into port, just as Professor Clark and Hrue Lipson had done. The pilots were celebrated as heroes for a month or two and then quietly pensioned off into comfortable jobs in Centre. The Noble Council seemed firmly of the opinion that any returnees were an unexpected boon rather than a matter of course. And prior to the events of the last few days Will had never had any reason to disagree with that. Only now that she was one of the terminal did she begin to wonder what exactly her chances might be.

The room was silent. Professor Clark's smile became more genuine, gratified at the opportunity to continue her lesson uninterrupted. "Missions will be randomly allocated, and each Laika is designed for a maximum five-year trip."

"*Five* years?"

"That isn't fair!"

"God, I hope I get the Jupiter mission. You'd be home in a year, right?"

Will's head was reeling—she felt like there had barely been time to respond to each bombshell before the next had been dropped. Randomised missions might be a bad thing, they might not, but she was no longer sure how to tell. She was still trying to get over Tarrant's presence, their apparent truce, the fact that they were *both going to die*, along with everyone else in this room. What did any of this information *matter* in the light of that single fact?

"You will, however, be able to choose your co-pilot." Professor Clark smiled like her offer was the height of generosity. "You have two weeks before the decision, so use the time to get to know your fellow Laika pilots."

Will glanced over her shoulder as the others immediately began to look around for prospective co-pilots. Panset was smiling reassuringly down at Thune, Loysa was motioning to another boy. It was the oldest chestnut out there—a basic popularity contest. Had Will still been at school, it would have been a lost cause. She'd held herself too aloof for too long. The best she might have been able to hope for was someone weak enough to order about.

But here, things were different. Will was surrounded by strangers. It was only her second day, and she'd already managed to make a few almost-friends. Not that she would *want* to spend years of her life with Loysa, Thune, or—heaven forbid—Panset. Particularly if those were her final years.

Will cast a sidelong glance at Tarrant. She would likely go with Loysa. They were roommates already, and Loysa seemed intelligent and kind. It was a pity. Five years—or less than five, followed by a grisly end—in space with Tarrant did sound hellish, but perhaps it would have been a little *less* hellish than with any of these other baboons. At least Tarrant had a brain.

As Professor Clark chuntered on in her explanation, Will sighed and rested her chin in her hands. It was going to be a long two months. The future was not promising, and for the first time in her life, Will found herself powerless to change it.

There was a lump in her throat, too big to swallow past. Will coughed as discreetly as she could, trying to ease the discomfort while painfully conscious of the drumbeat rhythm of her pulse. It was unsettling, approaching those double doors and already feeling the relief of release, yet knowing her reprieve would last only a few hours.

It was also unsettling the way Tarrant somehow knew exactly when Will was on her way out. If looks could kill, Will would be dead fifty times over. She drew her shoulders a little higher, tensing under the weight of Tarrant's glare, and did her best to mimic Xavier's smooth gliding step.

Technically, life in the Laika Training Centre was meant to be lived in seclusion, without visits to the outside world. Family and friends were welcome for two-hour visitation periods on Monday, Wednesday, and Friday, and there was a free-for-all on Saturday where guests were permitted to remain all day if they wanted. But the nascent pilots were not allowed to leave. The doors to the Training Centre had closed behind them on that very first day, and they would stay that way until launch.

But twelve days in and Will's presence as a Noble was still a grey area: murky and bewildering to Professor Clark and her staff, who reported directly to the Noble Council and Xavier. The public would not accept her unilateral withdrawal from the Laika Programme, but they would not balk at a little special treatment. That was normal for Nobles. Under the circumstances, Will thought it was *more* than warranted.

And so it was that despite the locked doors, Will was granted permission to attend an evening of campaign events and the latest Summit. All she had to do was brave the Cerberus that guarded the gates.

"Must be nice," Tarrant hissed, not even troubling to lower her voice, "to be rich enough to come and go whenever you want. Must be nice to be a *tourist*."

It grew harder to swallow the anger that rose unbidden each time Tarrant started slinging insults. She didn't understand. It was nothing to do with money. If poverty was the barrier keeping them here, Panset wouldn't have stayed longer than a single hour. No, Will left for the simple reason that she had *other* responsibilities. The sacrifice she was going to be forced to make on the Eden's behalf was only one of the crosses she had to bear. Her other was one that she had carried since childhood: the burden of leadership. She had a spoke to look after, and the Biannual Approval Surveys were only a few weeks away.

But Tarrant had never understood what it meant to be a Noble. All she saw were the most obvious aspects: the hereditary power, the privilege. She would never be willing to grasp that—for the Nobles who took their duties seriously—there was much more to it. They were shepherds, stewards. But reasoning with Tarrant on this particular topic was impossible. She would have stormed away before Will could finish the first sentence of her explanation.

So Will settled for lifting one shoulder in a half-shrug and offering Tarrant her most dashing smirk. "Careful, Tarrant. You keep following me around and I'll start to think you're obsessed with me."

This was a dig that had never yet failed to elicit a strangled squeak of fury and a hasty departure. It was all terribly satisfying, and left Will with no less pleasant a glow than it used to at school. She felt positively relaxed as she strolled out through the doors. The staff member who had escorted her this far turned back, and her old friends the Lawkeepers snapped to attention and fell in on either side of her.

"Anything new?" she asked.

"Lord Arrex will meet with you after Cabinet today," replied the Lawkeeper to her left.

The one to her right placed a porta-vidscreen into her outstretched hand. They were not permitted within the bounds of the Laika Training Centre, and the vidscreens in the classroom and the bedrooms were limited to an internal network. Will could only suppose that Professor Clark did not want the misery in which the pilots lived to become public knowledge. If she'd been the one in charge, she probably would have done the same thing.

She opened her messages and scanned the contents. Commiserations from Xanthe and Zuria. Nothing from Carroway. A few paragraphs from her father, updating her on what had changed in the campaign, the data from the latest polls. Xavier was now well ahead of Loris, to Will's relief. At least her horrible fate was having an impact on the hearts of Spoke Six.

The journey to Spoke Six was mercifully short, making Will glad again of the private rails. Before half an hour had passed, she was seating herself on an overstuffed sofa designed more for aesthetics than comfort and putting on her mask for the cameras.

"Welcome, Lady Arrex." Cirrus was overflowing with geniality. He knew which way the polls were swinging, and he was as effusive in his praise of Will as the rest of Spoke Six. Her humility, her condescension, her great sacrifice. Sixty-three percent of the population was predicted to vote her way right now, and some polls suggested approval was still climbing.

Giving him a beatific smile, Will folded her hands in her lap. "It's a pleasure to be here."

"I appreciate your presence all the more," here Cirrus assumed a more sombre expression, "because the last couple of weeks have been so tumultuous for you."

"Yes." Will allowed the smile to fade from her own face. "That's why I'm so glad to visit you, Cirrus. It's lovely to get a break." It was a fine line to walk. Too much emotion and she would seem weak—but the image of a scared girl torn from her home was too powerful not to use. It would resonate right now, with five families besides her own missing a child.

Cirrus pouted in commiseration. "I think I can speak for all of Spoke Six when I say how very proud we are of you, Lady Arrex."

"That's so kind of you." Will did her best to combine *humble* and *competent* into a single expression. "All I want to do is serve my spoke. That's what my father taught me to do."

It wasn't the most subtle segue, but just like that, the conversation was turned back to the most pertinent issue—Xavier and why he deserved the people's vote.

He gave her a sage dip of the head and let her talk for a minute, but Cirrus was not prepared to let her steer the interview entirely. "I've heard some rumours, Lady Arrex. People are saying there's a possibility you won't be flying."

Will looked him dead in the eyes. *People? You mean Loris.* But she kept her smile steady, and nodded thoughtfully, like it was a question worth answering. "Whoever told you that has their facts wrong. Lord Xavier Arrex keeps his word, and I keep mine. I entered the Lottery, and I'll abide by the law just like everyone else." *It isn't like I have any other option.*

More questions followed: Cirrus put on a show of grilling her, but Will could tell that the interview was over. She had conquered.

Her second tramcar ride was a mere ten minutes in length. Cirrus's studio was in the upper echelons of the spoke, and the Arrex mansion was at the peak. As she headed for her room, hugging a watery-eyed Tunis as she passed, Will scanned the latest figures from her father's aides. The primetime interview, right after dinner—she sucked in a triumphant breath. If the Surveys took place tomorrow, an astounding *seventy-one percent* would vote for Xavier Arrex over Loris Arrex.

Will sat back on her bed with a sigh and smiled the weary smile of a job well done.

The mattress was softer than a dream. It was pleasure verging nearly on pain to lie back on it and feel herself sink—to spread-eagle her arms and legs and still not come close to touching the edges. So different from the rock-hard bed she endured in the Training Centre.

She might have shut her eyes—just for a moment—but the hiss of the door pulled her back.

"You did well."

His tone was warm, but Will kept her eyes fixed on the stars beyond her window. It had only been twelve days away from them, but—how small and miserable her room in the Training Centre seemed in comparison. Until she had lost it, Will had not realised just how much she valued the solitude and the beauty of this place.

"Thank you, Father," was all she said.

"Only an hour until the Summit." The words were hesitant. Strange to hear that tone, almost deferential, coming from the mouth of Xavier Arrex.

She nodded. "I know."

"Are you ready?"

For the first time in her life, it was a question and not a command. Her attendance had never been negotiable before. She was a Noble, and Nobles attended Summits. Every single one. But things had changed too much for her to pretend that life could continue to run along the same well-worn tracks as before.

"I don't think so, Father. Not tonight."

He gave her a small, sad smile, and crossed the room to press his hand to her shoulder—perhaps the closest two Arrexes aware of their own dignity could come to a real hug. Will's throat tightened, and she wished she had the courage to embrace him properly.

But then he was moving away again, the moment past. The door opened, and with one last inscrutable glance he was gone.

Will stared out at Amalthea, at its red-hued mountains and valleys, at the distant blots of the different mining sites. How small the changes humanity had made were when viewed from a distance. Five hundred years of intensive strip mining reduced to a few specks on Amalthea's surface. How small her own problems were, in the grand scale of things. What was one life to an ecosystem like the Eden?

Yet from her own small, flawed little perspective, how *huge* it all was. All her plans, all her dreams...all of them punctuated by one single, brutal full stop. No, Will could not go to the Summit. She could not face the questions, the pretended sympathy. The wound was still raw. She would rather go back down to the Training Centre and let Tarrant rip into her than suffer through Xanthe and Carroway pretending to empathise. Tarrant at least was like Will: facing down the same monster.

Will sighed and stood up, leaving the cloud-softness of her bed and the gentle light of the stars behind. They were mere memories now. She did not belong here. Her place was down in the lowest bowels of the Eden. Safely out of sight with the other condemned.

CHAPTER 10

Centre, Eden Station – Year 452 – Day 360 – 12:45

So far as distracting people from impending death went, choosing co-pilots was the perfect pastime. The first two weeks in the Training Centre had been a mess of vetting, infighting, and behaviour so desperately cliquey that Will felt like she was back in the early days of school. Everyone trying so *frantically* to secure a friendship for themselves, while leaving those they disliked out in the cold.

The final decision was made by blind ballot, a system as needlessly convoluted as everything else about the Lottery and the Laika Programme. You wrote your name down on a slip of paper, along with the name of your chosen partner, and you hoped they had written down the same. Then Professor Clark would balance out the numbers, pair any odd people left over with one another, and that was it. You knew who you would be spending the remainder of your life with—all five years of it.

When the moment came, Will hesitated for a long time after writing down the words *Will Arrex*.

"Lady Arrex?" A brown-clad staff member hovered in the doorway. "There's a visitor waiting in the hall."

Hope flashed like lightning in the heart of a storm. *Father*. She shoved her chair back and headed for the door at a speed right on the border of what Xavier would consider dignified. Perhaps he'd finally found a solution—though what it could be, Will could not imagine. If he'd actually made the trip down to the Training Centre it had to be something big.

But as she burst into the hallway, Will stumbled to a halt. The figure waiting for her was about a foot too short, and instead of silky hair bound back into a braid, an eggshell-smooth scalp shone beneath the florescent lights.

As she approached, Hrue Lipson put on his most ingratiating smile, and it took all Will's years of training to keep the disappointment off her face.

"Lady Arrex," he greeted her, and she answered with the barest incline of her head. The more time she spent down here, the more hollow that title rang. Was she still the same person she had been in the starry world above?

"How can I help you?" She had no idea what he wanted, but the sooner she could get rid of him, the better.

"I know the co-pilot selection is tomorrow," Hrue began, and Will narrowed her eyes.

She had not seen this man since the day he called out her name and ruined her life. What was her co-pilot to him?

"I just wanted to say...I've been where you are. And the choice..." Hrue gleamed like a billiard ball beneath the lights, eyes wide and frightened. Finally he seemed to steel himself and plunged onward. "The most important choice you have left is your co-pilot. You need to make sure you choose someone...practical. You're in a unique position: I think *your* chances are good, but you still need to make the right decision. Someone who understands the way things are."

"My *chances*?" Will repeated, feeling her scalp prickle. "With what? The missions are random."

The unspoken follow-up hung in the air between them. *Aren't they?*

Hrue flushed. "Y-yes, of course! What I meant to say is you need someone who you can get along with for the entire duration. Someone *biddable*."

He looked almost desperate, and Will realised with a sinking feeling that this wretched little man was trying to *help* her. He thought her chances were good—whatever that meant—and he was trying his best to give her an edge. To save her.

Biddable. Is that what he had been, as a teen? Had sweaty Hrue Lipson been malleable enough to make the Laika leadership pick him out for an easier, more survivable mission?

"Hrue!" Professor Clark's voice was sharp as a razor, and Hrue flinched as though she had slapped him.

Will turned to face her, eyebrows raised. Laika pilot or not, she was still a Noble, and some consideration was due.

"I didn't believe Morris when he told me you were here, Hrue," Professor Clark said, her tone turning more careful. "It's always wonderful to see you, but you know *your* work ends with the Lottery. You should be relaxing now, not running down here to visit me."

"I'm sorry, Karis," Hrue whispered, pale and frightened, and for the first time Will felt something closer to compassion than disgust. "I wasn't trying to intrude."

"Nevertheless," Professor Clark said stiffly. How had these two spent *years* together on a ship the size of one of the dorm rooms? They acted like Lord Captain and minion. "The Noble Council won't be happy."

Will's ears pricked up at that. Why on earth would her father and his friends be unhappy that Hrue had attempted to aid her?

"I'll go," Hrue agreed meekly. *Someone biddable.* "I'm sorry, Karis. Really."

Professor Clark ushered him to the door, scanned her pass, and Hrue fled—throwing Will one last wide-eyed glance as he vanished. It was a mystery; if everything was already set in stone, it shouldn't matter who she chose as co-pilot or how malleable that person was. Will watched the door slam shut behind her would-be saviour, sealing her in once more, and her head began to pound.

Slowly, Will returned to her scrap of paper, to the decision that deep down, she'd already made. *Someone biddable.* If Cara had not been replaced, she would have chosen Cara. Not because of what Hrue said. From a sense of duty, perhaps, to Tarrant or to the sweet girl who had only wanted to save her grandfather. An attempt to protect her, even while knowing Cara would probably be trying her best to protect Thune or someone else. But Cara was gone, and there was only one person here Will would ever want to select, biddable or not. Only one name she would ever consider, though the holder of that name would never consider *her*. There was only one possible choice, unless she wanted to leave it blank—submit herself to the vagaries of fate or Professor Clark, both of whom she had equally little faith in.

In the end, she did not leave it blank. She wrote it down, that name.

She made the only possible choice.

Hands fisted at her sides, Will stared into those brown eyes, deep and dark and flecked with little beads of amber. *Like a pile of shit with corn still in it,* a crude corner of her mind whispered, always ready with an insult. *Like stars,* whispered another part. Her breath was coming too hard, and she shoved the thoughts about those stupid bloody *eyes* far away.

"Why?" she demanded, her voice too loud in the crowded classroom.

"Why what?" snapped Tarrant, volleying it back quick as a tennis player returning a serve.

Quashing the instinctive reply of *Isn't it obvious, you fucking idiot,* Will forced the words out. "*Why* did you pick me?" Spelling it out nice and slow, like she was talking to a very young child. That always got Tarrant's back up, and right now Will wanted that anger. She wanted to feel the flames against her skin.

"Why did you pick *me*?" Tarrant folded her arms, one eyebrow raised, a challenge in every facet of her being—

And just like that, Will's fury vanished. Tarrant was not afraid of her. She met Will blow for blow, and just like Will, she would never back down. They were enemies, but unlike all the rest, Tarrant was an enemy you could *respect*.

Besides, being on the receiving end of a challenging look from Tarrant was the closest thing to coming home Will had left.

Admitting surrender with an abruptness that surprised even herself, she snorted. "Fair enough."

Spreading her arms wider in a loose-limbed shrug, Tarrant quirked one corner of her mouth up in what was almost a smile. "Well, can you imagine going into space with any of these people?"

A glance around at the others was enough to answer the question. "No. They're all idiots."

Tarrant laughed and her cheeks reddened slightly. "You know, I think that's the first time in our lives that you've ever admitted that I'm *not* an idiot."

The vidscreens on their desks had pinged in synchrony, everyone's at once. A message notification from Professor Clark, containing nothing but a flat statement as to the identity of their co-pilot. Delivered with all of Clark's usual tact and grace, right before a mealtime, where all the disappointments and drama would be played out in front of everyone. Will was almost *certain* it was deliberate. Another distraction. But even so, she hadn't been able to resist the fury that coursed through her. Bad enough that *she* had no other option, and had humiliated herself by writing down that name. But *Tarrant,* with all her sparkle, all those friends and everything that Will had always lacked—how could Tarrant be reduced to choosing her nemesis? Will had planned it all out: Tarrant would choose someone sensible, and if she asked who Will had selected, Will would only smirk. She would leave Tarrant wondering forever, and the last laugh would be hers. Now Will's grand, futile gesture was ruined, because Tarrant had chosen her too. It was—it was ridiculous. It was too much.

But Tarrant had disarmed her again, and the anger was ebbing from Will's veins, leaving only a strange mellow feeling.

"Why didn't you choose Loysa?" asked Will, after a heartbeat of quiet.

A brief look of surprise from Tarrant, her thick eyebrows rising. "Loysa?" When Will failed to elaborate, she continued, "Loysa's doing this as a *career* move, Arrex. Interplanetary travel is her life goal; she wants a specialist with her, not a schoolgirl."

"Who did she choose, then?"

"Lain, I think. The arboriculturist. He didn't want to be here, not like she did, but he's the only one with a career she thinks is relevant, and he's as competent as she is. There was never a chance she'd pick me over him, no matter how much she likes me."

"Oh," Will said. "Right."

It was unusual that Loysa believed she would actually return. Will—and everyone else here, she was pretty sure—had chosen solely on the basis of the person she would hate to spend the last five years of her life with the least.

"Plus, like I said," that little quirk at the corner of Tarrant's mouth was back, "I couldn't really imagine going into space with anyone else."

That started a warm glow in the pit of Will's belly, spreading up her spine like a caress. Was Tarrant being *nice*? It felt...it felt surprisingly good. Maybe this was what it was like. Having a real friend. A genuine friend, not just a fellow Noble to share your woes with. Hastily, she turned back to her lunch, shaking her hair forward across her face to conceal the colour there. She was pleased that her grudging respect for Tarrant was mutual, that was all. No big deal. And Tarrant certainly didn't need to see the evidence.

Panset vanished, and was replaced by Tarrant, five strings of fairy lights, and a great many books—her family must be shipping them to her by the boatload. Will watched in dismay as her minimalistic living quarters were transformed into a library, but by the time all the fairy lights were up, she would have been lying if she said she hated the changes. They were small and useless, yes, but they somehow added a touch of warmth to the utilitarian space. A little light in a dark place.

Training continued, the same routine as always. Breakfast with your co-pilot, classes, lunch, training sims with the holos, dinner, and then back to the dorms. Little by little, the two of them fell into a routine. Will rose early to use the exercise bike, maybe do a lap of the simulation room if she felt energetic, and was usually finishing her breakfast by the time Tarrant emerged, bleary and tousle-headed. If Will had thought Tarrant's hair was wild before, that was *nothing* compared to how it looked when she woke up in the morning.

Will slept early while Tarrant lingered over her books and cocoa, reading late into the night. Will was never sure what exactly she was researching, but fresh books arrived every day. Will's parcels were the same as before. Lessons from her tutors, terse missives from her father, a rare note from Eloise, and creature comforts sent by Tunis to ease her stay. Shampoos, scented candles, novels—and fruit by the bushel. Grapes, pears, oranges, apples, strawberries, raspberries, blueberries. Anything Tunis could get her hands on, without any of the pretence at frugality she had maintained before. Now that Will was incarcerated it seemed budget was no longer a concern.

It was nearly a full week of living with Tarrant before Will plucked up the courage to disrupt that carefully maintained timetable, sharing a space without intersecting.

"Hey," she tried, mouth dry.

No response from Tarrant, who was like the walking dead at this hour.

"Hey!" Will raised her voice, shifting her weight awkwardly against the hard seat of the chair. "You want some porridge?"

Pausing in her stumbling path towards the shower, Tarrant turned to stare at her. "Porridge?"

Flipping her bowl to show its contents, Will attempted a winning smile. "It's got pears in."

That seemed to be enough to penetrate the fog of sleep. Folding her arms across her chest, Tarrant came alive, her eyes alight with suspicion. "What's going on?"

Slowly, Will lowered the bowl. "What do you mean?"

"Arrex, we've known each other thirteen years, and this is the closest we've ever come to civility. Ever."

"Aren't I allowed to offer you porridge?"

Tarrant cocked an eyebrow. "Before we moved in here I think you'd have rather shot yourself in the face with a stun gun than offer me anything—let alone your precious fruit."

Now Will crossed her own arms. "That's not fair."

"Isn't it? *Would* you have given me some?"

"I mean—maybe." Will was struggling not to sound defensive and was aware that she was failing. "You never asked!"

"I remember what used to happen when Lysse asked you."

"Well, *Lysse* was annoying."

"And you didn't find *me* annoying?"

Will sighed. There were few people as annoying as Tarrant was—but she still might have shared her fruit if *Tarrant* had asked. If she'd chosen to sit next to her in the canteen of her own free will, rather than as part of an assigned seating plan in class. "It was a different sort of annoying."

With a toss of her head, Tarrant turned away. "You would *not* have shared."

"I would too—" Will began hotly, and then stopped. They could keep this up all day. "Look, do you want some porridge or not?"

"Fine." Tarrant flopped down into the other chair. "Give."

With a victorious smirk, Will slid the second bowl across to her.

Before she'd even swallowed the first bite Tarrant was groaning in delight. "God, it's been months since I've had pear. Have you been eating this every day?"

"Of course."

"We're supposed to be living off the reconstituted rations from the food-fab, you know." Tarrant's voice took on her familiar preachy tone.

Making a face, Will shook her head. "I'll go as long as I can before I eat recycled shit, thank you."

Sticking her tongue out in return, Tarrant helped herself to another few spoonfuls, humming in pleasure with every one of them. "Privileged ass."

Though there was no sting in the words, Will felt that a roll of her eyes was warranted. What a relief it was to be able to eat breakfast and not worry about her facial expressions. Being accused of being indecorous was a thing of the past now. Tarrant didn't care. She was ten times as theatrical as Will was.

"*You* wouldn't know, of course, but *most people* have to live off the food-fab rations their whole lives—"

"Can't we ever just have a conversation without you telling me what a crime being a Noble is?"

Folding her arms, Tarrant began to glower. "Sure, when something comes up that your insane privilege isn't relevant to." The spoon, still in her hand, was getting porridge on the sleeve of her pyjamas, but she didn't seem to notice.

"If you're really as forward-thinking as you claim, wouldn't you be willing to have a normal debate, without always banging on about my *insane* privilege?"

Tarrant huffed. "Only you would be privileged enough to think that your privilege isn't a factor."

"Ugh," Will groaned. "Can't you just *eat* the pear?"

"Not until you understand why it's wrong that we should have pear when no one else does."

Tarrant put her nose in the air, and Will suddenly found herself struggling with the overwhelming urge to reach over and flick it. Not enough to hurt, of course. Just enough to annoy, to snap Tarrant out of her silly self-righteous rant. Maybe to make her laugh, and then Will could laugh too, and they could enjoy their breakfast together.

"Look," she said, in her most reasonable voice, the one she developed aged nine when Tunis tried to debate her into eating *all* of her vegetables—*Yes, Lady Will, even the asparagus.* "Look, if I promise to buy enough pear that *everyone* gets some this weekend, will you just shut up and let yourself enjoy it?"

Sticking her tongue out—still half-coated in pear and porridge—Tarrant assented with very poor grace. The two of them ate the remainder of their cold porridge in companionable silence, and Will thought that perhaps it tasted even better than it would have done hot.

"I want to wish you all a happy Year Change Festival," Professor Clark said, raising her glass. "I'm so glad we are all able to celebrate it together."

A scattering of applause answered her, but there wasn't much heart in it. Almost three weeks into training and spirits were lower than ever. The clinking of cutlery resumed, and Will let out a long, slow breath. She eyed the rapidly cooling meal before her. At home she would have had a premium LabGro steak, roasted to perfection, ringed with every kind of vegetable Tunis could get her hands on. The main course was preceded by salads and soups, and followed up with sorbet and meringues. The whole table would be piled high with the fruits of Tunis's labour: vast dishes to share and divide alongside hors d'oeuvres served small enough to be eaten in a single bite.

The sad offering on her plate now—a meat-flavoured nutribar accompanied by a few withered peas—was less than appetising.

The festivities would be going ahead as usual this year, up at the apex of Spoke Six, but Will would not be playing a part. Her father's key allies would assemble, cameras would flash—but without the excuse of the Summit, no exception could be made, and Will would stay in her cell like a good little prisoner. There were political upsides, of course: her absence would enable Xavier to pull a long face and talk about the terrible sacrifices he was willing to make for Spoke Six, even on this most special of days.

She understood the reasoning. It made *sense*, and she would see Xavier later in the evening, when he finally crossed the threshold of the Training Centre for the first time. But these rational thoughts did not make the nutribar any less disgusting, or the canteen less bleak.

The paper lanterns hanging in the great hall at home were all a metre or more in diameter, suspended from the double-height ceiling like miniature planets and glowing every colour under the sun. They were spectacular, of course, but Will's favourites were those tucked away in the observatory, painted to resemble Io, Europa, Ganymede, and Callisto. Seeing those four little paper moons hanging in the dark always made her feel like the holiday had really begun.

The paltry few lanterns dotted around the Training Centre canteen were barely worthy of the name. Crumpled, miserable little balls of paper no bigger than a fist, flickering feebly and dimmer than Tarrant's fairy lights.

And the worst of it was that not everyone seemed to realise that there were better things out there than this. When Thune first saw the decorations, he actually smiled.

"Look, Panset!" he chirped. "There's so many of them!"

"Don't you do lanterns at home?" Panset asked with amused tolerance.

"We usually only have a couple," Thune answered, and Will suffered the depressing realisation that no matter how bad she felt, she could always feel *worse*.

After forcing a few mouthfuls down her throat, Will drifted towards the simulation room. Xavier would be settling into his seat in the Arrex tramcar sometime in the next quarter of an hour, but perhaps she could catch him before he left and say hello to Tunis and Eloise at the same time.

"Where are you headed, Arrex?" Tarrant's voice called after her.

"Telecall with my father," Will answered, slowing her pace. "Didn't Clark say we could use the vidscreens any time today?"

Tarrant nodded. "I spoke to my dads this morning. See you back in the room, then?"

Mutely, Will nodded. As nice as the fragile peace with Tarrant was—they hadn't had a blowout fight since the night Tarrant arrived—it was little comfort today. It was the Year Change Festival, and all Will wanted was to be *home*.

Watching the endless file of other parents and siblings in and out of those barred doors on visitation days, Will had tentatively requested an afternoon with her parents. But there were meetings and interviews and campaign events. There were always a thousand reasons why not. On top of the day-to-day governance of Spoke Six, there was little time to spare for the long ride down to the Training Centre.

Still, the Surveys must come first. They always did.

It had taken the largest holiday of the year to persuade Xavier to finally agree. The media would be paying more attention than ever, and the shots of a grieving parent visiting his confined child were too good to miss.

Tarrant's parents came to visit *her* three times a week. Will learned to recognise the smile and the lightening of Tarrant's step that heralded their coming, and always made herself scarce. It wasn't anything personal. Xavier was prioritising, that was all. It was good strategy, and the polls reflected the impact they were both making. And today at least, she would see her father in person. The closest approximation of home possible under the circumstances.

The simulation room was as large and echoey as ever. Will selected the vidscreen furthest from the others and dragged it a little further away for good measure. Once she had logged in, she clicked the icon for Xavier and leaned back in her chair, trying to dispel the tension that had accumulated in her shoulders. It had been an awful day and a worse month, but miracles were always possible: maybe talking to her parents would make her feel a little better.

That hope died a sudden and violent death when Tunis answered the call.

"Lady Will!" Tunis's face lit up, all her wrinkles folding into and over one another as she beamed out of the screen at Will.

"Tunis?" Too late, Will realised how confused she sounded. How disappointed. "I mean—I mean happy Year Change Festival, Tunis. But...why are you answering Father's telecalls?"

"The party's running over." The smile on Tunis's face faded, replaced by something much worse. Pity. "He says...he says he's finally making progress with the unions, and he can't cut it short. He asked me to tell you how sorry he is."

Not only was he dodging her calls, he wasn't coming at all. It was like a knife to the gut. This visit had been scheduled for *weeks*.

"The unions? Which ones?" The Factory Workers' Union, the Agricultural Workers, even the Students' Association. With every name Will felt her stomach twist. The unions were *big* voter blocs, but—"We planned those meetings *together*. He said he'd loop me in for them." How could he move ahead without her?

"I'm so sorry, Lady Will." There were actual tears in Tunis's eyes.

Will's own eyes had never felt drier.

The worst part was that she could see the logic in it. If she had been in her father's place, advised by his media team, she would have done exactly the same thing. A father forced to skip his Year Change Festival visit to his only daughter was too emotive an opportunity to waste. Xavier Arrex, a paragon among Nobles, working through the holidays. Duty before family. *Excelsior*.

"Right," she said, and then, more firmly, "right. What about Mum?"

Tunis wilted. "I'm afraid she's—"

"Upstairs in the lab," Will finished for her. "Don't know why I asked."

"She had an urgent request from the clinic," Tunis pleaded. "It was a couple who—"

Will held up her hand, fingers spread. "I don't care, Tunis." Suddenly, she felt almost unbelievably weary.

Surreptitiously, Tunis wiped her eyes. "How about a nice long chat, just the two of us? I'm not blood-related, so they won't let me down there, but we can—"

Before even really stopping to consider the offer, Will shook her head. "No, that's okay, Tunis. I—I wouldn't have been able to stay long even if Father was free. It's...very busy here."

Tunis sniffled and smoothed her already-smooth hair back into place. "If...if you're sure. But if you ever want to talk, you just call me, okay? Any time."

Will attempted a smile, but it failed to launch. The one person who acted like a real parent called her *Lady Will* and was paid to love her. "Thanks, Tunis. I appreciate it."

"Happy Year Change Festival!" Tunis sang, trying to inject some levity back into her voice.

Mumbling an indistinct response, Will ended the telecall. The simulation room was very quiet all of a sudden. She pulled in a shaky breath, and almost laid her head down flat on the desk. No.

No. An Arrex did not fall apart in public. They didn't fall apart ever—but *certainly* not in public.

Will ripped the headphones off with such violence that she nearly knocked over the chair, and plunged towards the doors. The hallway to her room was endless, thronged with visiting families and trainee pilots in the coloured jumpsuits of their various spokes, the doors to the rooms standing open as they came and went. Some of the gloom seemed to have lifted with Professor Clark's departure. There were even a few snatches of song drifting out from open doors. Will did not stop to listen. All she wanted— all she needed—was to shut the door of her meagre excuse for a room and be *alone.*

But the door to her room stood open, and leaning against the wall outside were Tarrant and a man who looked uncannily like her. Not Grayson Tarrant, the minister Will knew distantly. The other father, then. Of course *Tarrant* would be surrounded by her loving family. The Year Change Festival was a time for family.

Just not for Will's.

"How's your dad's party going?" Tarrant said, smiling in a way that was almost friendly. "Papi's up there, but Daddy came down to see me instead. Do you want to—"

"Excuse me," Will growled, pushing her way past them, *desperate* for them not to see the tears prickling in her eyes.

Tarrant's eyes widened, but whether it was in hurt or anger Will didn't hang around to find out. She slammed the door to her tiny bedroom and pressed against it, shoulders heaving, breath shuddering. In the world above, her family were moving on. And she was entombed here, her sacrifice complete. A dead girl walking.

Forgotten.

Alone.

CHAPTER 11

"Apparently all Lain's taking is vodka." Tarrant giggled as she said it, and Will joined in.

It wasn't really very funny, a boy wasting his entire ten kilograms of personal effects allowance on alcohol with which to numb his pain—but there was nothing really left to do but laugh. It was either find the humour in *some* of the horror they were facing, or go insane.

"What are you going to take?" Will was still undecided. Alcohol was proving a popular ask, along with luxury food items and different gaming devices. She supposed she could do worse than take ten kilograms of porridge and pears. Their breakfast of choice had become almost a tradition.

"Books, I suppose," Tarrant said, taking a sip of her tea. "And notebooks. Pens."

Will laughed. "Is that it?" How very *Tarrant*, that she would want only her textbooks to carry into the afterlife with her.

Tarrant shrugged. "We'll need plenty of entertainment. Anything's better than thinking about what will actually be happening."

"And books are the only form of entertainment high-minded enough for you?"

Will's tone had been teasing, but Tarrant grew sober. "I mean—I suppose I'd take some movies, if I could get some. But they take a lot of memory. Won't fit on a porta-vidscreen."

"Can't you just get a hard drive?"

Tarrant looked at her as though she were stupid. "Remember what I said about your *insane* privilege?"

Will flushed. "Oh."

Will was just reaching for the notepad that lay beside her own cup of tea, ready to jot down another request for Tunis, when a noise from the vidscreen caught her attention.

"And now a word from Lord Zeko Oriel."

Carroway's uncle? What on earth was the First Minister of Spoke Three doing on the Spoke Six news?

"How about you, Arrex?" Tarrant asked, but Will shushed her, focused on the vidscreen.

"I'm so pleased to be here in Spoke Six," Zeko said. "It's been too long since I visited."

"Spoke Six is a wonderful place for a trip," Cirrus agreed. "There are some marvellous new restaurants up-spoke. Piccolo won *Lavender Magazine*'s Fine Dining Award last year."

Zeko ignored Cirrus's attempts at pleasantries, and Will felt the first pinpricks of foreboding. This was no ordinary media appearance.

"Our two great spokes have always been closely linked, and if Lady Loris Arrex becomes First Minister for Spoke Six, those ties will become even stronger."

Will's blood ran cold.

"Lady Arrex plans to open new manufacturing plants on the Spoke Three model, meaning more jobs for Spoke Six, more trade between our spokes, and prosperity for us all."

Was Zeko Oriel, head of the Oriel family, really *endorsing* Loris on live television? What the hell was he thinking? The Noble Council would—

"That is why," Zeko said firmly, cutting off Will's panicked train of thought, "I am supporting Lady Loris Arrex in this year's Biannual Approval Surveys."

Will bolted to her feet, took a single step towards the vidscreen, as though she could somehow reach Lord Oriel. Like she could stop him. But his words kept flowing, his deep voice rich as molasses. So like Carroway's.

He paused, just to let his message sink in, and then added one final blow. "If I were a resident of this fine spoke, I would vote for her."

"What the *fuck*?" Will whispered, staring at the screen. "What the fuck?"

Cirrus reappeared and began to stammer out some other headline, and Will was still paralysed. Nobles were impartial. Nobles did not meddle in each other's spokes. It wasn't done. It didn't *happen*. Especially not now, a mere week before the Surveys. Three weeks before launch day, the price Will would pay for her hubris. Not now, after all she had given up.

This was betrayal, hot and acidic.

The two sides of the Arrex family were rivals, but Carroway and his mother were different. They were Zeko Oriel's flunkies, and they knew his plans. Carroway was in this up to his neck. He was complicit. He was the closest thing Will had to a friend in the outside world, and he hadn't even warned her.

Tarrant leaned across the table. "Are you alright, Will?"

Will was so focused on the vidscreen, on Zeko Oriel's smug fucking face as he shook Cirrus's hand and exited stage left, that she barely noted the dropping of the surname. "Yeah, I'm just *fine*, Tarrant. I'm bloody *brilliant*."

Tarrant's voice cooled, the concern fading into nothing. "Sorry I asked."

Rather than answer, Will swung away from the vidscreen and headed for the door.

Tarrant followed. "Where are you going, Arrex? We've got flight training today."

"Noble business trumps this little farce, I'm afraid," Will snarled without looking back. "I have an Oriel to deal with."

"Arrex! You can't just *bail* on me!"

Will didn't answer. Just stalked from the room.

"Arrex!"

With Tarrant's enraged shouts still ringing out behind her, Will strode down the corridor. Just outside those locked gates were her Lawkeepers. Waiting for her here as faithfully as they once had outside the Arrex mansion. All her old power, just out of reach. They would have a porta-vidscreen for her, a tramcar, anything she wanted. But those doors were still locked, and Will was trapped on the wrong side.

Will stopped short and turned on her heel, fists curled tight at her sides. She knew exactly how she would have done it if she had been free. One little ride to Spoke Three and Carroway and all his answers would be at her mercy.

Now, though…she was going to have to get creative.

A glimpse of a muddy brown jumpsuit, and Will lashed out. Her hand fastened on a collar, and she hauled the unfortunate staff member to her, fingers of her free hand already outstretched. "Your porta-vidscreen. Now."

He blanched. "L-Lady Arrex, we're not supposed to—"

"Now."

With trembling fingers, he offered it, and she snatched it from his grasp. She entered Carroway's details, the private line, and hammered in the password it demanded. No answer. He didn't pick up, and Will's confusion and anger turned into a terrible pounding in her head. To *fury.*

"What the fuck is this, Carroway?" she spat into the speaker. "What is going on with your uncle? You'd better have an explanation for me or I swear to *god* I will murder you myself. And—how *dare* you decline my call? Like I don't know your porta-vidscreen is fucking *glued* to your hand!"

She stabbed at the button to hang up. So Carroway wanted to avoid her? Well, *fine.* If he wanted to play this little game, Will would show him just how well she could bend the rules.

The skinny staff member was still hovering nervously. "M-my porta-vidscreen, Lady Arrex…"

With a sigh of disgust, Will shoved it into his hands. She didn't need him following her around or getting Professor Clark involved. There were other avenues still open to her.

Will prowled into the simulation room and stared witheringly at a miserable-looking boy speaking to his mother until he fled. A small part of her considered feeling guilty, but the urge passed. There was no time for false scruples. This was an emergency.

She slid into the seat the boy had vacated and entered her credentials again. Xavier picked up on the first ring.

If Will were someone else, she might feel hurt that her father had cancelled their Year Change Festival visit, yet picked up immediately when there was a campaign problem. Viciously, she pushed that stray thought down. *Later.* It could wait.

"Father," she said crisply. "You saw?"

"I saw." Xavier's voice was icy. She could see the anger in the tightness of the skin around his eyes, the slightest divot in that smooth, opaque brow.

"I have a request. I'm afraid it's somewhat...unorthodox."

Interest kindled in those dead eyes. "Go on, Wilhelmina."

"I need access to Carroway. In person. He's dodging my calls."

"What good would that do?"

"The most important aspect of crisis management: usable intel."

Xavier smiled, a cold and perfect reflection of Will herself. "I see. You think you can get to the truth of it?"

Will flexed her jaw. "When we're face to face, he'll cave."

For what felt like the first time in a long time, her father did not second-guess her. He simply nodded. "I can pull some strings. It will ruffle Lord Oriel's feathers, but after this debacle I'm not averse to a little ruffling. The Noble Council won't protest, and I'll handle the Clark woman."

"It will need to be public," Will warned him. "An invitation he can't refuse."

Xavier did not smile, but the cool fury emanating from Will's screen seemed to ease a little. He was pleased with her plan. "We'll need to pick our time carefully."

Will smiled wide enough for both of them. "I know exactly when."

The risk was low: just subtle enough not to be an instant Survey-risking story. The key was to threaten Carroway's dignity just as much as her own. Make the force involved into a secret he wanted to keep too.

Will spread her net wide and waited for her prey.

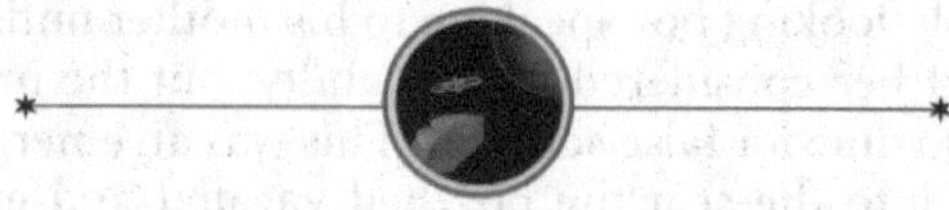

Will exhaled. The noise echoed in the empty simulation room. She paced, and circled, and watched the hours tick down on her watch. She had no interest in attending class today—not when something *real* was finally happening.

Despite the scheduled training, Professor Clark and her other students did not appear. Perhaps the scrawny underling had reported the situation; perhaps Xavier had delivered his promised assistance. Either way, Clark had chosen, in this one instance, not to cross Will. A wise decision. Will had played along perfectly, she had done her part and obeyed the rules—but everyone had their limits, and this was hers.

It seemed to take an age. Aeons passed. Will sat on the edge of a sim cube at the centre of the room, every muscle in her body drawn tight and tense. Her stomach rumbled; she ignored it. The same image kept turning over and over in her head, thrumming in time with the pulse that beat in her temple. Carroway's uncle up onscreen, breaking every unwritten law that governed Noble conduct, and doing it with Carroway's consent. Will ground her teeth together so hard it hurt. She would make them regret it.

At last the hour came. Classes in all of Eden's schools ended at six. Cara and the other Spoke Six students would be shovelling their textbooks into their bags and hurrying home, leaving behind them empty desks to match the one where Will and Tarrant should be.

The familiar scene would be mirrored across every spoke, and Will could picture the school in Spoke Three with perfect clarity. Deep blue jumpsuits replacing Spoke Six's iron-grey, hordes of students rushing through the corridors in just the same way. The same small bubble of silence and space that Will knew well surrounding the school's only Noble: Carroway Oriel. Outside the school's doors his two Lawkeepers would be waiting, clad in a paler shade of blue. Carroway would be heading towards them, but if Xavier had kept his word—and an Arrex always kept his word—eight helmeted figures in Spoke Six salt-grey were already marching through the school corridors.

Access through the maintenance passages was a closely guarded privilege, but today of all days Xavier was ready to throw his weight around. Carroway would emerge from the school and head to the station, same as always—but this time, the Arrex tramcar would receive him instead of the Oriel one. There would be no chance for the Spoke Three Lawkeepers to call for backup. It would all be over before Carroway had time even to reach for his porta-vidscreen.

Will curled her lip in an approximation of a smile, small and vindictive. She would show him what happened when you crossed an Arrex.

Six-thirty, long enough for the journey to Centre. Will's stomach was cramping now; in their room, Tarrant would be eating one of her disgusting nutribars. Seven. Any minute now.

Faint noise beyond the simulation room doors. Will's head snapped up at the familiar sound of Lawkeeper boots tromping in the corridor. She straightened, legs apart and stance confident in the epicentre of the huge white room.

Let the reckoning begin.

Carroway and his escort burst into the room. Eight Lawkeepers in Will's own grey and a measly two in Carroway's blue, their expressions panicked.

"Lovely place you've got here, Will," Carroway growled, his cutting tone belied by his rumpled clothes and the way the Spoke Three Lawkeepers were hemmed in by their Spoke Six counterparts.

The legendary Oriel gall at work; he ought to be grovelling at her feet, and instead he was trying to condescend.

Will raised her chin and strove to match his tone. "I'm *so* glad I can finally host you."

"How could I refuse an invitation from the martyr Noble?" he asked bitterly. "It would have caused even more of a scene than you already forced on me."

"Perhaps if you answered your porta-vidscreen," suggested Will, and Carroway finally deflated, sinking down onto the white sim cube she indicated as his chair.

"Ugh. But to come for me at *school*, in front of everyone. Was it *really* necessary?"

Will folded her arms. "You tell me."

Carroway's porta-vidscreen pinged and his fingers went to it reflexively before he caught himself.

"Well," Will said, her voice dripping with sarcasm. "Looks like you didn't lose it, after all."

His two Lawkeepers took up position behind him, looking as uncomfortable as he did. Will felt the shadows of her own fall across her as she sat, heard the metallic shift of the stun guns they carried in their hands. She let a smile spread over her face. Fear was not her favourite choice of weapon, but she knew how to wield it when she had to.

"My uncle knows I'm down here," he said at once. "I told him."

"I imagine the entire Noble Council knows," Will replied calmly. "You're here to visit your good friend Will, with Lord Arrex's full knowledge and approval."

Carroway glowered, but his bravado faded.

Will shifted, snakelike. She was only just getting started. "You obviously know what this is about. Care to explain?"

For the first time, Carroway met her eyes, his mahogany skin turning bloodless. Will felt a faint but undeniable edge of triumph beneath her anger. It was always pleasant when the opponent felt themselves to be the guilty party. It made victory that much easier.

"Look, Will," Carroway began, and then stopped. "What Uncle Zeke said—" He cut off again.

He wasn't even *trying* to pretend that it had been as much of a surprise to him as to her.

"What the hell is your family thinking?" Will kept her tone calm, but made no attempt to soften her words. "This is an act of war."

Carroway attempted a conciliatory smile, but it died halfway onto his face. "Will, you of all people know how difficult cousins are to control—"

"Don't *bullshit* me," Will hissed, her patience evaporating. "Your mother is lazy as shit and so are you. You're flunkies. If Zeko did something, you're backing him."

"Will!" Rearing back a little, Carroway looked almost shocked at how she was speaking to him.

Like he *cared*. He had cut off all pretence at friendship when he failed to warn her of whatever plot his vile uncle had hatched.

"The truth, Carroway," Will snapped. "Now."

Carroway made one last effort to control the situation. "I could have walked away, you know. It would have been dramatic, but I didn't have to engage with your little army here. I came down here because I *wanted* to explain."

Will scoffed. How utterly typical. He avoided the confrontation at every possible chance, and when she finally forced him he tried to take the credit for himself. Magnanimous Carroway, coming down here to—to what? All he was doing so far was prevaricating.

She wanted to scream, she wanted to shake him, but she channelled all that rage down and away until all that remained was cold Arrex perfection. She tapped a finger against her leg. "Explain what, exactly?"

Come on, Carroway, she willed him. *Admit it.*

Carroway ran a hand over the smooth skin of his scalp. Freshly shaven and impeccably groomed as always.

"*Tell* me," she insisted. Just how illegal was it to order one's Lawkeeper to use a stun gun on another Noble? Probably better not to find out. No one liked a meddler, but even Xavier could not work miracles, and the Noble Council's tolerance would only stretch so far.

He threw his hands up in despair. "Fine! Fine. Look—the family, we've...entered an alliance with Loris."

That much was obvious. "But *why*? Why meddle in my Surveys? You *know* how hard I've worked." He knew what she had *sacrificed*.

"I just—it's just—we agreed to support her, and—"

Almost against her will, her hands fisted. "Carroway, you are making *zero* fucking sense and I suggest you start trying, or I'm going to—"

"You don't *get* it!"

She slammed her palm down onto the cube she sat on. "Then *explain*."

He flinched, but steeled himself. "It's—I—Will, I'm *engaged*."

Engaged? Will stared at him with utter incomprehension. "What does that have to do with anything?"

"I—I—it's who I'm engaged to."

"And who might that be? Because unless it's my stupid fucking aunt herself, I can't see why—" she froze, taking in the expression on Carroway's face. "Oh."

"Right," he said softly.

The fight suddenly left Will's body. This was worse than even her most unhinged theories. "Lauron."

He was silent.

"You—you're engaged to Lauron? My moron of a cousin Lauron Arrex?"

Carroway could no longer meet her eyes. "Yes."

"And...and what, Zeko is in support?"

"Yes." He paused. A glance upwards, almost—almost bashful—and then finally began to talk properly. "He wasn't, at first. It wasn't until my mum promised to stop contesting the Surveys at all that he said he'd allow it. His support for Loris was part of the deal."

It was—*staggering*. His hubris. His sheer fucking *selfishness*. For the sake of Carroway's stupid little crush and a couple of manufacturing plants, his family had stomped all over the unwritten rules that governed Noble conduct.

"So you bargained away *my* spoke as part of your little deal? You screwed over *my* family, messed with our Surveys, our spoke—just because you want to bang Lauron?"

He flinched. "I wouldn't put it like that."

"Why not? It's the truth."

"I'm in *love!*"

Will scoffed. "Is *he?*"

Carroway drew himself up. "Yes. Lauron loves me."

"That idiot only loves himself, Carroway. If you can't see that you're a lot less intelligent than I thought."

Now his lower lip was quivering. She was hurting him. *Good.*

"You don't know him."

"Oh yes, *you* know him much better, I'm sure. I couldn't possibly know my own cousin."

"You're estranged, you don't—you don't understand him."

"I understand him just fine, Carroway. We're estranged because we're *exactly the same*. We're Arrexes. He'll do anything to get his mother the captaincy—just like I'd do anything for my father. He'll tell you anything you want to hear."

"You're lying!" He was on his feet, trembling all over, staring into her eyes. Almost pleading with her.

Will had never seen Carroway so close to actually *caring* about something in her life, but she would show no mercy. Just as he had shown none to her.

"I'm not. Lauron doesn't even *like* boys, Carroway. He doesn't look twice at enbies, let alone men. I've never seen him date anyone but the prettiest girls he can get his hands on."

"You're wrong, Will!" Carroway's hands were clenched into fists, the veins ridged along the back. He was shaking. "You two have always hated each other, and you've—"

"He's a sneaking, duplicitous little liar, and he's using you."

"He loves me," Carroway insisted.

Shaking her head, Will finally began to view him less with anger and more with pity. "He's got you right where he wants you."

Carroway slumped back down, the tension leaving his limbs. "You're supposed to be my friend, Will. Can't you...be happy for me?"

Will leaned forward. "I *am* your friend."

Or she had been once, at any rate. And aside from her white-hot *rage* that Carroway would betray her like this—would offer up *her* spoke to Lauron on the altar of his love—she did feel for him.

He was going to get his heart broken.

Idiot.

"How is it even going to work, Carroway?"

"What do you mean?"

"Even if I'm wrong, and Lauron likes boys enough for this marriage to function, what then? Is your child going to be an Oriel or an Arrex? You can only have one. Whose heir will they be?"

"I don't care about that stuff."

"You *have* to, Carroway. You're a Noble. You have a duty to your people." She paused. "And even if you don't care, Lauron certainly does."

He shrugged. "Then I'll be the one to give it up. Maybe they'll let Hisha have two, and they can be the next-gen Oriels. God knows she's gagging for motherhood."

Will was staggered. "You'd give up your birthright for him? Your spoke?"

He snorted. "Everyone knows I never had a chance against Hisha, Will. I'm not her equal." He dropped his gaze. "And...honestly...all I want is him."

Letting out a breath, Will shook her head. He was a lost cause.

Carroway was staring up at her again, suddenly oddly vulnerable. "Do you...hate me, Will?"

She met his eyes squarely. *Did* she hate him? She pitied him, certainly, but maybe there was a little hate in there, too. He did it to win his heart's desire, but he had still betrayed her.

Her mouth tugged up at one corner, a parody of a smile. "Did you even come to that race to see me? Or was it Lauron?"

He hung his head. The answer was obvious.

Will's pity vanished. "You've been planning this for weeks, then. While I've been trying to—to make it through the day—when you *knew* how hard it's been for me. I've been risking my life, Carroway, and you've been—you've been feeding all my secrets straight to him!"

She had spoken to Carroway little enough since the Lottery began, but even *that* made more sense now. Instead of messaging her or Xanthe or literally *anyone on the Eden,* he had been messaging *Lauron.*

He turned his face to the wall, raising his hands to shield his eyes. "Leave me alone, Will. You've had your say. Now leave me alone."

"Gladly." Will got to her feet, her breathing still coming slightly too fast. She looked down at him, and her face twisted in disgust. "You won't make it to the wedding, Carroway. And when he lets you down, I hope you remember what you gave up for him. I hope you remember that I warned you."

He rose stiffly. Trying to keep his face impassive, but his face was still tear-stained and he'd never been able to match Will's control. "If you've *quite* finished."

"Oh, I have." Will looked past him to the Lawkeepers. "Call Lord Oriel's tramcar. We're done."

Carroway Oriel was *dead* to her.

He rose to his feet, breathing hard, and all but ran from the room. Will flicked her fingers towards the door to signal release to her own Lawkeepers. As they retreated, Will wondered just how many of her fellow pilots were lining the corridors, watching this latest episode of her life play out. How much had Tarrant heard? Did it even matter?

Finally alone again, Will dropped her head into her hands. The feeling of victory she had anticipated—the dopamine hit she used to chase every time she went up against Tarrant at school—was absent. She had the truth, but she didn't feel vindicated. All she felt was exhausted. Suddenly all Will wanted was to go home. To curl up in bed and let the balm of Tarrant's soothing, quiet presence wash over her. Tarrant always knew when to stay silent and let Will rest—*wait*. Wait.

It was only then that Will realised that when she thought of *home*, she no longer pictured the glass-walled great hall beyond the atrium so similar to this one. She no longer pictured late-night meetings with her father and fleeting, treasured moments with her mother. When Will shut her eyes and imagined the feeling of coming home, she saw a beaten-down table and chairs where Tarrant waited with two bowls of oaty mush. Sarcasm and peaceful sniping at one another. Home.

With a sinking feeling in the pit of her stomach, Will realised that the closest and most meaningful personal connection she had left was with Tarrant. *Tarrant.* Of all the people in the world.

Will laughed, but it was more of a sob. It was like a bad joke.

"Arrex?"

"Leave me alone."

It had worked the first time, but this time the door opened to reveal Tarrant, standing in her checkered pyjamas, hair in disarray, lapel freshly stained with toothpaste. "You doing okay, Arrex?"

Will gave her a listless shrug.

Cautiously, Tarrant came to seat herself on the floor beside Will's bed. "You ran off so fast you didn't even finish your tea. I thought the sky was falling."

Will gave only a noncommittal grunt in answer.

"Do you want to talk about it?"

Did she want to explain exactly how much it hurt that the person she once would have called her closest friend had turned against her?

"No. Not at all."

But even that was not enough to repulse Tarrant, and she maintained her seat.

"I know how hard it is to miss your family. Your friends. I…I cry myself to sleep most nights." Tarrant's voice was raw. Vulnerable.

It made Will want to cry too. That Tarrant should be trusting *her* with this—it was *painful*. That they had been ripped away from everything and everyone else, and Tarrant was now forced to confide in Will, of all people.

"So I know how you must be feeling." Tarrant was still earnest. Still trying to bridge the divide between them. Just as she had done when her father was there. As Will had done with the porridge. "And I want you to know that…I'm here for you, I guess. We can talk about it. It's awful, not being able to go home. I miss my papi and my dad so much, but we just have to remember that they'll still be rooting for us, even when—"

"Tarrant—"

"Even when we're out there, they'll be right here waiting for us when we get home."

"Tarrant."

Finally, she stopped.

"Just…just don't."

There would be no one waiting for *Will* when the mission ended—and that was *if* she didn't die during the course of it. Her friends…well, what friends? Her parents would be given special permission to have a normally illegal second child, and it would happen, despite Xavier's insistence on her place as his heir. Will would be replaced, and no one would miss her. It would be as though she had never existed.

But Tarrant didn't get it, not yet. She still had *hope*.

"Don't what?"

Will had meant *Don't try to make me feel better,* but now she shrugged. The second meaning worked just as well. None of them cared about her, so she would have to cease caring for them. Simple. Mathematical. "Don't miss them. They're not worth it. Turn it off."

Tarrant regarded her with an inscrutable expression. "I can't turn off my *feelings*."

Will only shrugged again, unwilling to say more. Tarrant might not want to admit it, but friendship was a pack of lies. No one *really* valued their friends. No one was unwilling, when it came down to it, to betray them. Even Tarrant's friendship with Cara—for all of Tarrant's sacrifice, the street only ran one way. Cara hadn't demurred or refused. Tarrant had offered her a hand to lift her from the pit, and Cara had all but bitten it off in her haste to escape. She had dragged Tarrant down in her stead and abandoned her there.

With perhaps the single exception of Tarrant—an over-earnest idiot who took everything literally—no one ever really *meant* any of their promises.

And family was no better. Xavier, Eloise—they, too, were content to let Will rot down here. No telecalls, no commiseration. Not even on the Year Change Festival. Even Tarrant's darling papi hadn't come. Both of them had been hurled down here to die, left with no one but their bitterest rival for company and support.

If Tarrant believed the people she loved actually loved *her*, she was living a lie.

There was a long stretch of silence, and then finally Tarrant heaved herself to her feet. Will stared fixedly at the wall behind Tarrant's legs. She had been right. Even the infallible Tarrant was admitting defeat, now.

Everyone left her.

But Tarrant did not stir. Instead, she held out her hand. "Come on, Arrex. You don't want to talk: fine. Let's go watch a movie. Being alone isn't going to do you any good."

Will looked up into Tarrant's liquid eyes, flecked with starlight, and her breath hitched. Everyone had left her, but Tarrant had not. Not yet. Their partnership was a forced one, born of their mutual bondage, but—but Tarrant had been *kind*. She had drawn from *Will* a kindness she hadn't known she possessed.

She was an over-earnest idiot, that much was true, but she was still...Tarrant. Still frighteningly smart. Still sharp and waspish and prickly. Still loyal.

Will swallowed hard, and then she surrendered. Tarrant led the way through to the living room, and Will flopped down on the sofa beside her as the vidscreen sparked to life.

The film Tarrant put on was some twenty-second-century epic about the life of a queen of Egypt and her marriage to a Roman. Exactly the sort of historic garbage Will would have expected from her nemesis, but it wasn't so bad. Kind of funny, in a distant way. Tarrant was in raptures from the sight of the first doric column, and professed flagrant disbelief that Will had never heard of Cleopatra.

But Will could not bring herself to enter into the gentle exchange of banter with the other girl. Not tonight. Tarrant eventually gave up the effort, and they watched in silence. The warmth of Tarrant's shoulder against Will's was...nice. For a second she felt a little less alone.

But as the credits rolled on the dying queen dressed in golden robes, clutching an asp to her breast, Will sighed. Cleopatra had been abandoned, too; Caesar and Marc Anthony proved to be as false as each other. Betrayal really was a universal human truth. At least Cleopatra had the sense to know when she was beaten. She went to her death with dignity—perhaps the best fate that Will could now hope for.

As the music swelled, Tarrant's eyes flickered over Will's face, narrowing slightly. The colour seemed almost to shift and darken—perhaps just a trick of the light, or perhaps something more.

"I think perhaps it would be easier if I *didn't* love them," she murmured, voice low.

Eyebrows raised, Will turned to face her more fully. Just because *she* had espoused a perspective of healthy nihilism didn't mean she wanted to hear *Tarrant* do so. Tarrant was supposed to have everything Will did not: friends, community, a loving family.

And despite her misery, several hours on the sofa with Tarrant's warmth beside her had worked its magic. She was feeling...not better, but not *worse*. She didn't want to return to their previous topic of conversation, but she didn't know how to reject it.

"Surely you don't mean that?"

Tarrant shrugged. "If I just...didn't care...well, I wouldn't be here, would I?"

"I suppose not," Will said slowly, willing to concede the point.

"If I were..." Tarrant's eyes moved away, back to her own hands. "If I were more like you."

Will went very still. "Like me?"

As though she was only now realising what she said, Tarrant stiffened. "Well, I mean—you know what I mean."

"No," replied Will rigidly. "Please do explain, though."

Registering the change in her tone, Tarrant crossed her arms defensively. "You don't—you *don't* care as much. You're always on your own. You want it that way, right?"

Pulling sharply away, Will turned her shoulder to the other girl. "You have *no* idea what my life is like, Tarrant."

Tarrant scowled. "How else would you explain it?"

"I'm here because I made the mistake of loving people. Just like you. If you were half as understanding as you pretend to be you'd understand *that*."

Tarrant opened her mouth to respond, but Will wasn't going to wait around to hear it. She climbed to her feet, almost dragging herself away from the warmth of Tarrant's arm against her own, and slammed her fist down on the button to close the door to her room.

And it was only then, after one last betrayal on a day full of them, that Will Arrex finally began to cry.

A new day dawned, merciless and unforgiving. Will paced in the kitchen before deciding on porridge with not only diced pear, but raspberries and strawberries as well, with honey and sugar stirred in. Last night had ended on a sour note, and in the cold light of morning she was forced to admit they couldn't leave it that way.

Tarrant had been cruel, and so had Will. For better or worse, they were a team now. And the prospect of living out the remainder of her life without the hope of even the last pseudo-companion left to her was a very bleak one indeed.

She said nothing as Tarrant groped her way from bed to bathroom. Living with Tarrant had taught her that it was no use trying to discuss anything before Tarrant had blasted herself in the face with the hottest water she could find, which here in the Training Centre was not very hot.

When Tarrant emerged, Will was ready with a perfectly timed bowl of hot porridge. "I made it fancy this morning," she said, hoping for an armistice.

"Save it, Arrex." Tarrant was already headed for the door.

Will swallowed her disappointment and followed. Another day of training lay ahead. The simulation room waited, a new array of blocks scattered across its huge area like the abandoned toys of a gigantic toddler.

The knowledge that the blocks making up the ground and terrain could move even as you walked on them did not help. The simulation room was an endless sandbox on an infinite scale. One in which she and Tarrant might wander forever, lost, if not for the built-in safeguard of being able to remove the VR equipment at any time.

After launch day, there would be no VR equipment left to remove. It would all be real.

Putting on the spacesuit was an old habit now, and Will moved with increasing confidence as she went through the motions of hooking up zippers and tubes to the corresponding parts of her jumpsuit. This, at least, was within her abilities. It had been daunting the first time she tried it, but given that it was pretty much the only aspect of the ship that would not be automated, cleaning and maintaining the spacesuits had made up a fair chunk of their training.

The nose tube delivering her oxygen was the final step. By the time the whole ensemble was in place, the weight was noticeable. Will was glad again for the higher-quality jumpsuit her father had given her, soft and breathable against her skin. The others in their rougher clothes would be sweating up a storm. Poor Tarrant.

Not that Tarrant, confidently donning her VR gloves, looked as though she was uncomfortable. Will had always thought of Tarrant as...bookish? At school she was always buried beneath piles of paper covered in her own abominable writing, and Will had assumed she was something of a nerd. But living with Tarrant had proven that beneath that fluffy hair lurked surprisingly high stamina, able to carry her for miles on the exercise bike. Often with a book balanced on the handlebars, of course. Maybe carrying thirty textbooks around every day had actually given her muscle.

The transformation was completed when Tarrant seized her great mane of hair in both hands and swept it back from her face. The bun was gigantic, obviously, but her face was completely exposed. No curls hanging down, covering her from head to hips. No softness left. Just a hard-faced girl with fire in her eyes, sliding the VR goggles into place. The fish-bowl helmet followed, and then Tarrant was fully armoured.

She turned her head in Will's direction, eyes hidden by the goggles but the meaning clear enough. Will was taking too long.

For all that *Tarrant* was the one who had accused Will of being incapable of love, she was certainly determined not to forgive. Typical: no one could hold a grudge like Tarrant.

Hastily, Will pulled on her gloves. It wasn't *her* fault Tarrant had distracted her. Standing there posing like an actor auditioning for the role of warlord. And putting her hair back? Will had never seen Tarrant's hair tied back in her *life*. Even in physical education at school she had insisted on it being loose, coils bouncing like springs with every step she took.

Will snuck another glance. It was like looking at another person. Tarrant looked so...so much older. It showed her cheekbones, the unexpected curve of her neck, the skin spattered with the same freckles as her face. It was a harsh sort of beauty, like the androgynous models that glowered from vidscreen adverts for fashion designers, but it was still there.

Tarrant began to tap her foot, and Will got the hint. She snapped her goggles into place and slotted her helmet on, and then straightened.

They ran through the holo without much fanfare. A simple trip to a simulated biodome on a minor moon orbiting Saturn. Tarrant kept things frosty, but they cooperated same as always, checking oxygen levels and pH levels in a series of exercises that had become routine.

Professor Clark clearly didn't want them getting comfortable, because Will heard the creaking of metal and barely managed to drag Tarrant out of the way of the steel girder that slammed into the floor mere inches from where they had been standing.

Both of them stood rooted to the spot, panting. Will's fingers were locked into claws on Tarrant's arm and she could feel the pulse hammering even through the spacesuit. It all looked so damn *real*. Will would never have expected to have wished that she spent *more* time indulging in holos. Maybe if she'd been more like Lauron and frittered away her time gaming, she wouldn't feel so freaked out right now.

"Thanks, Arrex," Tarrant said, very quietly, and just like that the ice was broken.

Will swallowed. Reached up to pull her goggles off, bringing herself safely back to the real world. "We make a pretty good team, huh?"

"For two people who loathe each other, sure." Tarrant's words were harsh, but her tone was light. Almost joking.

Will's breath came a little easier. This was familiar ground. Safe again, trading blows with her co-pilot. "I don't loathe you."

"Oh?"

"No. I think you're an annoying try-hard, but I don't *loathe* you."

"And that right there? That's why I loathe *you*."

Cocking her head, Will tried for a devilish smile. It only came out a little wobbly. "I'm charming, Tarrant."

The counter was instant. "Who told you that? The tutors your daddy pays to teach you how to be likeable?"

Will's smile wilted. It had in fact been her public speaking tutor who had assured her she had mastered the craft of sparkling conversation.

Tarrant cackled. "I *knew* it."

CHAPTER 12

Centre, Eden Station – Year 453 – Day 8 – 20:45

"Not to toot my own horn," remarked Tarrant with false modesty, "but I am an incredible cook."

Will chuckled; it was still surprising to see this more relaxed side of Tarrant. She rose and began to clear the table. Tarrant stacked the plates for her, and Will wondered if she would have believed it if a year ago someone had told her they would be working together, even on as small a task as this.

"We probably shouldn't keep doing this, though." Tarrant's voice grew subdued as Will turned away to the sink.

In slight alarm, Will looked back at her. "Doing what?" If Tarrant was about to announce that their fragile new peace was at an end, she—she didn't know what she'd do.

"The cooking," Tarrant answered, and Will sagged in relief. "We can't have food like this on the ship. We're meant to be getting used to the food-fab bars."

Grimacing into her dishwater, Will passed her a plate to dry. "We've still got three weeks left till launch. I can't say I'm keen to start eating that garbage before I have to."

"It'll only make it harder to transition," Tarrant said, but there was little conviction in her tone, and she didn't press the point.

When the washing-up was complete, they retreated to the sofa to choose the evening's film. Tarrant always claimed to be shocked by how little Will had seen, or as she liked to call it, Will's *philistinism*. Will just laughed. Outside of the annual family viewing of the Javier Arrex biopic, she had possessed precious little time for leisure.

And constrained as her new life was, there was something deliciously *decadent* in just...doing nothing. Will had always lived a tightly scheduled existence. Here, after her hard work and painstaking preparation for her future were rendered useless by the simple fact that she no longer *had* a future...here, she could stop.

Silver linings, she supposed.

"Have you ever heard of fantasy?" Tarrant asked now, and Will snorted.

"Like what *you* do when you go into your room and think about a big strapping textbook with a six-pack?"

"Oh, ha *ha*, very funny. You been sitting on that one a long time?"

"No," lied Will, who had come up with the insult three days ago while in the bathroom.

"Not that sort of fantasy, anyway," Tarrant continued, with an air of long-suffering forbearance. "I'm talking about the entertainment genre that was popular from the twentieth to the twenty-second century. It's all about magical non-human races doing quests, but it's usually just an allegory for the issues of the period transplanted into a new setting. Like they'll address racism by using orcs and elves."

"That sounds *exhaustingly* preachy." And therefore exactly the sort of content Tarrant would adore. "What's an orc?"

"A big green man with tusks."

"And an elf?"

"A thin blonde man with pointy ears."

"Tarrant, this sounds dreadful."

But Tarrant was already pulling the film up. And sure enough, there was a large green man and a small pale man, their respective armies ranged behind them as they glared into one another's eyes.

"Ruination of Yesterday?" Will asked, her voice dripping with scepticism. "Even the title is..."

"What?" snapped Tarrant, now beginning to sound cross. "Epic? Majestic? Sweeping in its breadth and heartbreaking in its narrative intensity?"

"I was going to say overdramatic." But Will knew when the battle had been lost, and she flopped back onto the sofa. *"Fine."*

"Just wait for the waterfall scene," Tarrant said happily. "When Urgam and Raenerillor realise their true feelings—it makes all the build-up worth it."

With trepidation, Will peered up at the green man's gigantic battleaxe. "Just how much build-up are we talking?" It had taken a whopping *four hours* for Cleopatra to finally embrace her asp. While it *had* been a good distraction from the Carroway issue, with hindsight Will felt that the same effect could perhaps have been achieved with two or three hours less.

"Exactly the right amount," replied Tarrant, with infinite satisfaction. "And if you like it, we can watch *Ruination of Tomorrow* next."

"There's *sequels*?"

"Yes. Eight."

And then Tarrant flumped down beside her, delivering that increasingly familiar hit of dopamine with the simple fact of her proximity, her presence, her *warmth*, and Will surrendered to her fate.

"Fine."

Ninety minutes later, when Raenerillor was delivering a beautiful, high-flung speech to his band of leaf-armoured archers as they prepared to mount a suicidal charge at first light into the very heart of Urgam's horde, Will was clutching a pillow, transfixed.

"I told you you'd love it," Tarrant said smugly.

"Shhh," Will said, clapping a hand over Tarrant's mouth. "Let the elf finish."

Beneath her fingers, she felt Tarrant's lips curve in a smile, and it was a sensation so distracting that she snatched her hand away again, ruffling an errant curl in the process. Her fingers smelled of strawberries. The scent still lingered in her nostrils for the rest of the night, sickly and cloying without being *altogether* repugnant.

She was six minutes behind schedule.

For once in her life, Will would have welcomed the sight of Tarrant hovering like a spectre beside the doors, glowering for all she was worth. All the old acid would be back in her eyes, and Will would almost relish the burn of it against her skin. *Noble*, Tarrant would say, before the porridge and the changes, the word like dirt in her mouth.

But the hour was early, with a full morning of preparation and refinement of pre-written materials ahead, and Tarrant was still fast asleep. Will had lain there for an hour or two, watching the minutes tick down on her watch, listening to the soft strains of Tarrant's breath through the wall. Tarrant was still an irritating little swot, but...that noise had been comforting, in a strange sort of way. So comforting, in fact, that after a sleepless night she had finally started to drift off, and now she was six minutes late. Unacceptable at the best of times, but on today of all days—Will's jaw tensed. She was getting lazy, and an Arrex was not lazy. Never mind that the even sound of Tarrant's breathing had been soothing, had made Will feel a little less alone. She could not let herself slip any further off track.

No, this morning Tarrant was not the one waiting for Will in front of those locked doors. As had been arranged, there was a figure in brown waiting by the doors to let Will out, but the second skinny shape slumped against the wall wore Spoke One off-white.

Panset Pall.

Will gritted her teeth as she drew nearer. This was all Tarrant's fault. If Will had stuck to the timetable...ugh. Six minutes could have made all the difference in the world. Maybe she could have slipped away without anyone seeing her at all. But no, Tarrant even had to *sleep* noisily, shoving herself into everybody's faces, making a song and dance of how peaceful she was, how sweet her dreams. Now Will was late, and Panset Pall stood between her and where she needed to be.

Panset was resting her head against her hand, face obscured. With a brief flash of hope that maybe she was dozing, Will quickened her pace further and gestured at the brown-clothed staff member to open up. Maybe she could escape unnoticed. Even at the best of times, conversation with Panset was strained, and this was *not* a good time.

But through the thick black fringe, Panset's eyes gleamed, and the slim hope of escaping undetected was lost. "Hello, stranger."

Panset's long legs uncurled, blocking the way to the twitchy-looking young man with the access card that would release Will from this hellhole. Was it the same man who had unwillingly surrendered his porta-vidscreen to her when she called Carroway? Will dismissed the question; it hardly mattered now, and she was seven minutes late already.

Stretching her arms for good measure, Panset grinned up at her, her stance as wide as a repellent little insect with no meat on her bones could humanly be.

Reluctantly, Will summoned a smile. "Hi, Panset."

"Where are you sneaking off to at this time of night, Princess?"

"Nowhere," Will said, trying to sound imperious. Like someone even Panset wouldn't question.

That tone might have worked on someone weaker, but it slid off Panset's armour-plated hide like water. "Come on, you're clearly headed *somewhere.*"

"Just to stretch my legs."

Panset's expression grew sharper, and she rose to block Will's path properly. "The Surveys are over. You should be confined to quarters like the rest of us."

"What business of it is yours?" Will snapped, impatience bubbling to the surface. Why should she be forced to justify herself to a nobody algae farmer?

"I know what day it is," Panset said, prowling a little closer. "I'm not stupid. Your aunt is right, *Lady* Will. Why should you get special treatment?"

"I'm in a hurry, Panset," Will replied, with as much hauteur as she could muster. This conversation should have been over two minutes ago; should never have progressed beyond *hi.*

"My mum has always said it doesn't make sense that the Nobles never change," Panset went on, almost conversationally, and Will stiffened. "To keep the same six families in power forever, just because they happened to be the first idiots onto the seedship. When there are other families just as old, just as well-respected."

For a moment, Will was stunned into silence. These were dangerous words. Seditious words. Even Tarrant had never ventured this far.

Despite her shock, her eyes flicked back to her watch again. Eight minutes.

"The Founders were Terra's most skilled scientists and leaders," she said, which was the barest response she thought she could give. It was high time to make an exit. "Anyway, I really should go."

Panset sneered. "You're not taking Paige? You two seem so close. I wonder if she knows you're being let out again. Maybe I'll pop round for breakfast and tell her, hm?"

It felt wrong to hear the name Will had never used on Panset's lips. Profane, somehow. Only Tarrant's friends deserved to use that name.

"It's funny," Panset went on. "I thought for certain you'd be bored with each other by now."

Panset was needling, Will realised. She hadn't received the reaction she wanted from the subject of Nobles, so she moved on to a point she thought was more vulnerable. It was almost laughable. As though Will would ever rise to the bait, when the bait was Tarrant—a person Will had devoted more time to insulting than anyone else on the Eden. A person who did not matter to Will in the least.

And that Panset had the temerity to suggest that *Tarrant* was boring? Indignation pulsed in Will's veins. Tarrant, with her vast well of knowledge, and her stupid peaceful breathing. Tarrant, with her strange, unexpected flashes of sympathy.

"No," she answered stiffly. "She isn't boring."

"Not like you, eh?"

Will thought of herself as a cold creature. Passionless. She solved things with words and logic. But she had never wanted to punch someone even a tenth as much as she wanted to punch Panset Pall right now, and she had grown up with Paige Tarrant.

Tarrant's method of attack was somehow a lot less *nasty*.

With difficulty, Will controlled herself. She was now *thirteen* minutes late. Panset was not an enemy worthy of her efforts. Will had better things to do. Her spoke was waiting.

"Excuse me, Panset," she said firmly, in the same voice she had developed with her oratory tutor to quell journalists asking too many intrusive personal questions. A voice designed to make the listener feel as small as possible.

As though sensing defeat, Panset's narrowed eyes flickered between Will and the hovering Laika Programme lackey. "They aren't seriously letting you out, are they? Why should *you* get to go?"

"Pardon me." Will pushed past.

Panset drew herself up. "You'll be late for class if you're not careful, Princess."

"Like I care." Will could no longer summon the energy to fight. A far greater foe awaited her, and for all that Panset puffed out her fur, she was nothing but small fry.

The doors opened. The world swallowed Will whole, and she was once more her father's daughter. The Lawkeepers saluted, and it was unbearably easy to let herself slide back into the familiar old grooves, a machine finally running right once more. She smiled crisply, her father's smile, and led the way towards the tramcar.

"Come on," she said, her voice steady and smooth. "It's a big day."

Fourteen minutes behind schedule, but she knew what would follow, every second of the rest of the day.

To be back on autopilot was almost a relief. The freedom her prison offered was terrifying. No rules, no schedules, no interviews or cabinet meetings. Nothing to contribute at all but the occasional remote offering to their campaign, and her sheer existence as a Noble condemned to the Laika Programme. The rest of her time was her own, and that was too much.

There was none of that here. Only numbers. Only requirements that must be fulfilled. Obstacles to overcome, enemies to defeat. That was...familiar. That was safe.

Internally, Will let herself drift. She had tried. She had done her very best. She'd plotted, and schemed, and worked. She'd fought off the terrible fugue of peace Tarrant had somehow lulled her into, and made it this far.

What more could she do?

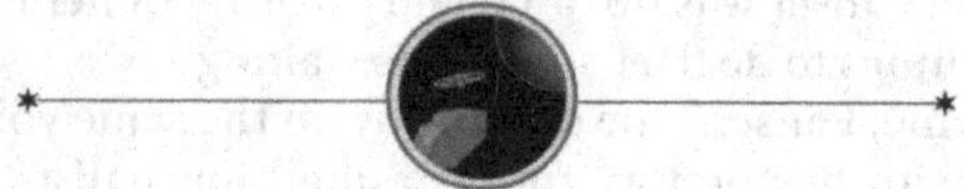

"And the winner of the four-fifty-three Spoke Six Biannual Approval Surveys is..."

As the words dripped from the announcer's lips, the world seemed to move in slow motion. Will stared at him blankly. *Willing* it to be the right name that he said next.

"...Lord Xavier Arrex, with a majority of..."

Her father stood ramrod straight, his head held high.

"...Fifty-six percent of the vote..."

Loris and Lauron exchanged a look, Loris dark and Lauron despairing, and Xavier strode past them both to grasp the announcer by his hand and address the crowd.

"I want to thank you all for your support. You can be sure that your confidence is not misplaced..."

It was the second of two speeches he and Will had prepared. The other was for the second possibility: a gracious admission of defeat and a promise to hold Loris accountable in two years' time.

They had won. They had *won*. It didn't feel real. It was more like a dream. The ultimate victory, placed gently into the palm of her hand, shining and golden. But it felt too light for the weight the metal should hold, and when she turned it over, she realised it was hollow.

"...and please believe me when I say that I will strive to make *your* life better."

Will blinked and came back to herself as Xavier finished his speech. She was supposed to be participating. Hastily, she moved forward to stand at her father's side, a small smile painted across her lips. Together they waved at the cheering crowd, and then in an instant it was over.

Will followed at her father's elbow, stopping when he stopped, smiling when he smiled, thanking their aides and campaigners with a mechanical precision. Squeeze the hand tight, just for a moment, to show sincerity. Pressure even across all the fingers, but not too hard. No need to be aggressive.

It wasn't until the door closed behind them in his office and he turned to her that she started to regain her presence of mind. It was the closest approximation of a grin she'd ever seen on his face.

"Now we can turn our attention to the legalities. Loris lied to the spoke, and we can..." He was racing ahead, already moving on to the next step.

Her focus slipping again, Will let his words wash over her. A tide of nonsense and noise.

"And what about the Oriels?"

Will glanced up. "Hm?"

"We're due a little retribution, aren't we? I think the Noble Council will agree to punish Lord Zeko. A tariff or two, and the Oriels won't cross us again."

He was still smiling, expecting her to share in his delight, but Will couldn't feel a thing.

"Yes," she said absently.

Xavier ran a hand over his already-smooth hair. "You're right; I'm getting ahead of myself. All of that will come in due course. For now, let's focus on this."

Will waited while he poured out two drinks.

"Well done, Wilhelmina." He pushed her shoulder gently, and she dropped obediently into a chair and accepted the drink he put into her hand. When she sipped it, the bubbles danced and popped on her tongue. Lemon and raspberries. "I couldn't have done it without you."

He looked at her with unconcealed pride, and dimly, Will was aware that she ought to be enjoying this. That this was a moment to be treasured. She had succeeded, and her father was proud of her.

"Thank you," she said finally.

"I was worried how it would go: your first big campaign. But you have a real aptitude for this." He took a satisfied sip. "And it feels good to outmanoeuvre Loris and that odious boy of hers, doesn't it?"

She nodded numbly. Even Carroway's machinations had failed before the weight of a Noble child sacrificed on the same altar as every other. The prize was hers. The polls were over. Only two weeks left aboard the Eden. Nothing beyond but the Laika ships, the blackness of space, no one but Tarrant at her side. It was the thought of Tarrant that finally steadied her a little. They had training this evening, postponed until after Will would be back from the results announcement. She couldn't be vague and fuzzy *then*—any lapses and Tarrant would rip her apart.

"I didn't see the logic at first," he raised his glass, "but I admit it: your Lottery move was a stroke of genius."

"Yes," Will said numbly. "I'm just...glad it's over. I can concentrate on launch day now."

He laughed, as though she had told some particularly amusing joke. "Launch day? Come now, Wilhelmina."

Will stared at him, uncomprehending. "What?"

He spread his hands. Like it was obvious. "We played the game and won. You can pull out now and be proud of what you've done."

It was—it was the last thing she had expected him to say. Pull out? Her ticket had been drawn. Her number was up. There was no coming back from that.

"How?" It was the only question she could think to ask.

He waved his glass. "Ill health, perhaps. A sudden sickness. A deterioration in your fitness. If we absolutely have to, an injury."

Will gaped at him.

Misinterpreting her silence, he patted her hand reassuringly. "But it shouldn't come to that. No one will question us. Not now."

Will thought of Tarrant—who sacrificed everything to help Cara and her grandfather, a man she barely even knew. Who chose her, *Will*, to brave the depths of space beside her.

She could not leave Tarrant to do it alone.

Will shook her head, a flat denial. "I can't back out now. You think the people will allow that?"

"Of course you can. I'm the First Minister of Spoke Six; next year I'll be Lord Captain. They'll allow whatever I say they will."

"And you think they'll forget it in two years' time? You'll make the situation worse than ever. Loris will win."

"The news cycle is far shorter than two years, Wilhelmina. They'll get over it."

"They won't. You saw what it was like when you talked about rerunning the Lottery."

Xavier's pale green eyes locked on to hers, and suddenly he was deadly serious. "Wilhelmina—if you go, what is any of this for?"

"What do you mean?" Will didn't feel that any of this political manoeuvring had been for her sake.

"We've been over this. You're my heir." Her father spoke slowly, as though to an idiot. "If I don't have an heir everything passes to Lauron in a few years regardless of our victory today."

"I'll come back," Will promised, with a confidence she did not feel.

Xavier looked ashen. His skin, always pale, was now the colour of exposed bone. "And if you don't?"

Will swallowed. "Then I suppose you can have another child."

He scoffed. "Your mother and I are far too old. And you aren't replaceable."

Once, it would have warmed her heart to hear that from him. Now, she just felt numb.

"It doesn't matter," she said finally. "It doesn't matter, because I *will* come back."

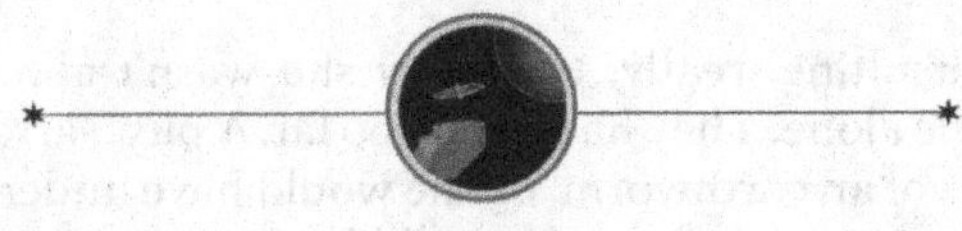

"Congratulations. I heard the news."

"Yeah." Will still felt too flat to summon a smile. She had worn it out performing for the cameras.

"And...what comes next?" Tarrant was obviously dancing around something.

"I go to bed, hopefully." Will was too exhausted to wring whatever it was out of her. "If my stupid roommate will get out of the way and let me."

Tarrant sprang back as though scalded. "Sorry."

Will set her hand on her door, and it hissed open. Before she could step through, she heard Tarrant pull in another breath and she paused wearily. "Just spit it out."

"You're not...you're not moving out?"

"Where the fuck would I go?" Will snapped. It wasn't like there were any spare beds in the Training Centre, and she had less than zero inclination to change her co-pilot now. No matter how annoying she could be.

And then the full meaning of Tarrant's question sank in, and Will turned back. *Oh.* Tarrant was asking exactly what Xavier had asked. Now that the Surveys were over, would Will prove herself a hypocrite and go back on her word?

Maybe that was even the explanation for Panset's bizarre attempt to waylay her: a fit of jealousy at Will's perceived escape.

Why did none of them *believe* her when she committed to something?

She met Tarrant's eyes squarely and watched the other girl fidget with a strand of hair, twisting it anxiously in both hands.

"Where the fuck would I go?" Will repeated, her tone harsher now. If Tarrant wanted to accuse her of something, let her come out and *say* it.

"I—nowhere, I guess," Tarrant said, and the strand of hair fell from her fingers, free again. A small smile crept over her lips, and Will almost felt the urge to smile back at her.

Almost.

It was insulting, really. *Obviously* she wasn't about to leave Tarrant to die alone. They had come too far. A pity Tarrant had the social graces of an earthworm, or she would have understood that. For all her massive intellect, she could be dumb as a rock.

"If that's all, then," Will said, the fatigue creeping back into her voice. "Can I go to bed now?"

"Oh—yes, sorry," blurted Tarrant, still grinning like a moron. "Sorry."

Will collapsed face down onto her bed. Screw propriety, screw boundaries and the appearance of strength. She was exhausted, and it wasn't like Tarrant was going to tell anyone. They were in this together now.

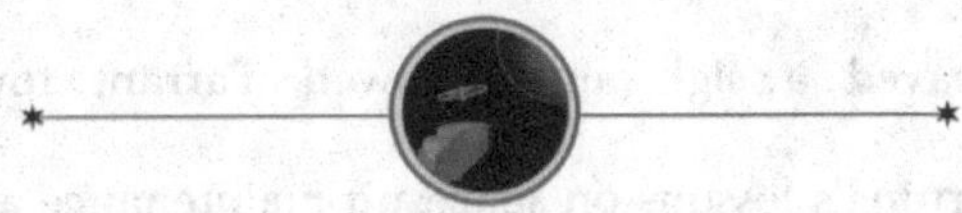

Tarrant paused with a spoonful of porridge dangling delicately between two fingers. "By the way—who are you taking to the launch party?"

Will looked up, startled. "We don't just go with our co-pilots?"

Eyes widening, Tarrant's spoon wavered for a moment, caught between balance and gravity. "Oh—I—I didn't think you'd want to—I said I'd go with Cara."

"With *Cara*?"

"Well—yes. She asked me."

"Why?" Will knew she was being rude, but she couldn't help it.

"Because she's my friend and she wants to say goodbye? God, maybe because she wants to *dance* with me?" Annoyance was fast becoming anger on Tarrant's face, and she dropped her spoon into the bowl with a clunk. "Why wouldn't she want to go with me?"

The image of Tarrant and Cara swaying in each other's arms was enough to banish what was left of Will's patience. "I don't know! But you could have asked me who I'm going with first."

"I *am* asking you!"

"Yeah, after you've already made plans with someone else." It was irrational, to be so frustrated about this, but the words just kept coming.

There was a sudden, taut silence. "Did *you* want us to go together?"

Finally remembering herself, Will leaned back in her chair and snorted. "Get over yourself, Tarrant."

Tarrant shoved her chair back and stormed away. The door slammed shut behind her.

Almost immediately, Will regretted what she had said. The party was a sham put on for the families the night before launch. Designed to make everybody feel fuzzy and warm about sending a load of untrained teenagers off to their deaths.

But it would be the last time Will ever saw her parents. Perhaps the last time she ever saw anyone. It would be a nightmare, at the very best, and she could hardly imagine facing it without Tarrant by her side.

Will heaved a sigh and followed Tarrant towards the classroom.

The morning's lessons on spacesuit maintenance and how to change air filters on the Laika ships didn't allow for much discussion, and it wasn't until lunchtime that Will managed to pin Tarrant down for another attempt.

"About this morning."

The other girl tossed her head, every inch the imperious Tarrant of old. Able to deflect meteorites with the strength of her self-righteousness. "What about it?"

"Look, I may have...phrased it poorly. Hear me out."

With a contemptuous sniff, Tarrant crossed her arms. "I'm listening."

"I know you want to go with Cara," she started. "I just..."

But was it fair, to guilt Tarrant into this? She would be spending more than enough time with Will *after* launch. And it might be nice to watch her reunite one last time with her friends. Like old times at school, partaking without participating. To see Tarrant just be purely, uncomplicatedly happy.

No, it wasn't fair to bully Tarrant into going with her. But...but she *wanted* it. Was that so bad? They would have *fun* together. And Cara would still attend. The pilots got as many guests as they asked for, and Tarrant could have her whole friendship group there regardless of who she took as her date. The only difference was that this time—this time Will would be inside that circle, instead of hovering on the edges.

A flash of dimples. "I'm not sure your question has fully loaded, Arrex."

Will tugged a hand through her hair. "All I was trying to say was...yes. I want to go together."

"I don't think I heard that right."

Another sigh. Sometimes Will felt like she did more sighing than ordinary breathing when she was around Tarrant. "You heard me, Tarrant."

"Let me get this straight." Tarrant fanned her hand in the air. "You, the mighty Will Arrex, want to go to the launch party with me? *Together*?"

Her face flushing, it was Will's turn to glare down at her nails. "Not *together* together."

"Really? This is a real question, and not, like, a practical joke?"

Heart sinking, Will waited. It was a ridiculous idea. Of course it was. What had she been thinking? Of course Tarrant would never want to go with *her*, the cellmate she was going to be forced to spend the next five years with. She would want to spend time with everyone else, anyone else, rather than begin their solitary confinement a moment before she had to. And Tarrant didn't fight with *Cara* the way she fought with Will.

"Forget it," she snapped, rising to her feet. She didn't have to stay here and wait to be rejected.

She stalked to the canteen door, hand extended towards the button that would open it, when a hand grabbed her wrist.

Will froze.

There it was. Skin on skin. Just a couple of Tarrant's fingers brushing against her, where the uniform didn't quite stretch all the way down to her palm. Just a couple of fingers, but enough to send a bizarre tingling coursing up and down her spine, enough to narrow her whole worldview down to just those few millimetres of skin that Tarrant was touching.

Exactly like when she touched Tarrant's face, that night they watched the first of the ridiculous orc films. Her hand on Tarrant's mouth, feeling her lips move.

She didn't dare look over her shoulder. God knew what her face was doing right now.

"Hang on," said Tarrant. "I never said *no*, did I?"

Hope surged, enormous and unreasonable, through Will's breast. Her heart lifted, the tightness around her lungs receded. A wild overreaction, a small voice in the back of her mind whispered, to a potential ally accepting an arrangement that suited them both.

"And I can see," Tarrant went on, carefully, "that it might be...fun."

"Exactly," Will said, forcing the word out, still focused on the silk-soft feel of Tarrant's skin against hers.

She risked a glance over her shoulder and saw those rich brown eyes, unnervingly close, and her eyes flicked down to Tarrant's lips. Full, and soft, and—

Whoa there.

This was *Tarrant*.

With sudden swiftness, Will wrenched her wrist free of Tarrant's grip. It was just like the movie nights. God only knew how many three-hour piles of fantasy garbage she'd sat through, just for the sake of Tarrant's warmth against her side.

It was getting disturbingly hard to keep her priorities straight when Tarrant was touching her. She needed to get it under control. She was—she just needed to remember that she was *stuck* with Tarrant. That she didn't *like* her. She was an odious, insufferable know-it-all who had hated Will from childhood for the crime of having been born slightly richer than herself. They had to work together, that was all. And any other thoughts were just—silly daydreams. Hormones run amok.

"You can come with us," Tarrant continued, those keen eyes still scrutinising Will's face, "but we're going to need to work on that."

Will pulled in a breath and pushed her hair roughly back. The strange heat of Tarrant's touch still lingered, and it was all she could feel. "Work on what, exactly?"

"Cara isn't going to believe I ditched her for you if I can't even touch you without you pulling back like I'm made of literal faeces," said Tarrant, a slight edge to her voice. "And my parents are not going to be calm and happy about my future if it looks like we're going to murder each other as soon as the ships launch."

Half-closing her eyes, Will tried to dispel the tension in her shoulders. Tarrant was right—for once. Xavier was already skirting the edges of a breakdown; if he thought Will would be unhappy on her voyage she had no idea what he would do. "That's...a good point."

"I think it would be a good start if you could look at me without sneering," Tarrant laughed, the cloud of anger lifting as suddenly as it had appeared. "We'll need to practise."

"Fine," Will countered, rubbing her arm. It tingled as though it had been burned. "If *you* can practise being *polite*."

Rewarding her with a mocking, courtly bow, Tarrant just kept laughing. "No problem at all, Lady Arrex."

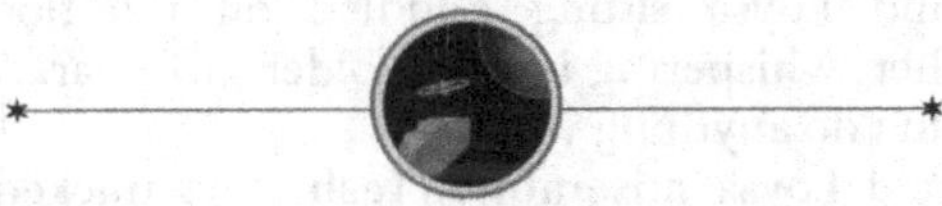

They were woken the next morning by a scream.

It was loud and long and piercing, and so full of loss as to rend the soul. Will bolted out of bed and sprinted to the door, her first thought that something terrible had happened to Tarrant.

But Tarrant came tearing out of her room, eyes wide and hair wild. "What's happened?"

They both burst out into the hallway together, to find a crowd of frightened young pilots already milling around.

"What is it?" Tarrant demanded of anyone that would listen.

There was a disturbance up at the far end of the hall, where the classroom was. A small pack of brown-robed figures dashing in and out, calling for Professor Clark, for a doctor, for one another. The students waited, silent and fearful, to see what fresh horror would descend.

When, finally, one of the staff emerged from the classroom, leading Loysa by the hand, it seemed almost like an anticlimax. She looked fine—apart from the way she kept her head bowed. As though there was a great weight upon her shoulders.

And then a second group followed, this time carrying something between them. An object wrapped in a sheet. Someone gasped. Will blinked, trying to focus. There was...there was something sticking out from the sheet. An arm, clad in the dull black uniform of Spoke Four. The fingers protruding from the sleeve were long and graceful. An artist's fingers.

It was Thune who broke the silence. Poor little Thune, who said in the voice of an old man, "Isn't that Lain?"

The pilots stood at the doors to their rooms, huddled in their pairs, deadly quiet as he was carried past. Loysa stood alone in her own doorway. White as a ghost with tears still trickling down her cheeks.

When it was over, and the brown-clothed staff had carried the sheet that concealed poor Lain through the outer doors, Loysa turned on her heel and retreated into her room.

Tarrant darted after her, and with only a moment's hesitation, Will followed.

She found Loysa sitting huddled on the floor, Tarrant embracing her, whispering into the older girl's ear. "It's not, it's not. You didn't do anything wrong."

"It is," said Loysa miserably. Fresh tears tracked their way down her cheeks. "I know it is."

"That's ridiculous, Loysa." The grief on Tarrant's face turned into sad, sweet sympathy. "It's not your fault he made this choice."

Neither of them seemed to have noticed Will, but it was only then that she finally understood. Lain had...he had killed himself.

Loysa sniffed, coughed. Wiped ineffectually at her eyes. "I told him—we'd been talking about some—some issues I thought the Laikas might have."

"Issues?" Tarrant kept her voice soft, and Will drew closer, wanting to hear whatever was coming next.

Loysa sniffed hard, the image of the studious, unemotional girl shattered for good. "It was the schematics Professor Clark gave me. My work's in mining drones, but even I can see that they don't make sense. The fuel tanks just aren't big enough."

"And Lain?"

"I *told* him about it," whispered Loysa. "I told him...I told him that I thought we wouldn't reach the end of the journey with that level of fuel, let alone get home again."

A soft exhalation from Tarrant. The wind knocked out of her. "Oh."

Classes were cancelled for the day. Everything was cancelled for the day. Lain was gone, long since returned to his family and the cold embrace of Recycling. But the void he left behind pulsed, dark and angry like a wound, growing bigger with every passing hour.

And—and—the worst thing was, had Lain's decision been such a crazy one? He and Loysa had stumbled onto some sort of hidden truth, something that reduced their chances of survival even further. Staring down the barrel of launch day, with only one week left, Lain chose another way out. It was awful, it was terrifying, and—and somehow it didn't surprise Will at all.

CHAPTER 13

Centre, Eden Station – Year 453 – Day 30 – 19:00

Inhaling deeply, Will paused at the open doors of the simulation room. Transformed tonight as it had so often been transformed—but this time, no VR goggles were necessary. Instead of empty white space, the room was full to bursting and alive with colour. Lanterns and paper streamers hung from the ceiling, scattering rainbow shadows over the dance floor. In the centre of each table blossomed creamy bouquets of potato flowers and carrot flowers fresh from the SoilGro beds. It was...unexpectedly lovely.

Familiar faces were everywhere. Her parents, her old classmates, Cirrus orbited by his cameras like Jupiter by its moons. Carroway, radiant in peacock-blue, beaming as he clung to Lauron, who turned his face away. For once, Will found herself perfectly in accordance with her cousin.

Tarrant was across the room, glimpses of her visible through a knot of their classmates. Her sunshine-yellow dress was like a beacon, white underskirt puffing out around her legs, her hair a dark counterpoint behind her. Will could almost smell again the scent of strawberries, so constant these days.

Her own gown was sleeker, in the obligatory Arrex steel-grey, of course. The exact sort of outfit she had worn to a thousand functions, a hundred parties. But this time there was one difference—a single flare of colour, nails painted yellow to match Tarrant's dress. *Want some?* The question had been so casual, delivered offhand as she finished painting her own fingers the same shade. She had to have known what she was asking; Nobles wore their family colour, end of story. But she'd left the bottle on the table as she slipped out to meet her friends, and Will sat down and stared at that small yellow crack in the fabric of her universe. Remembering that glorious jumpsuit Tarrant had worn to the window-viewing party, and how wistful she'd felt, thinking of what it might be like to wear colours other than her family's. To have the freedom Tarrant did.

She unscrewed the lid and dipped the brush into the paint.

The Laika Programme was a cruel punctuation mark to Will's dreams. She knew what tomorrow would bring, but…it had given her things, too. It had given her this little spark of colour in her life. It had given her this hint of friendship.

Will forged herself once more into a thing of steel and silver, and stepped forward. *Excelsior.*

Heads turned, of course. The Lottery's only Noble, brought down low enough to risk her life alongside the common folk. Will felt the weight of those stares on her, and she straightened her spine. She had nothing to be ashamed of.

Her father made eye contact and tilted his head. A summons. Will extended a forefinger. *In a minute.* She refocused on Tarrant. They were attending together. Or rather—Tarrant was attending with Cara and her friends, but Will was invited, and she *would* be included. For Xavier, for Tarrant's parents and friends, they needed to showcase their teamwork. Childhood rivalry was past, and calm cooperation had replaced it. They were co-pilots, and in a few years, they would be back.

But as she got closer, her determination ebbed, until she was awkwardly hovering on the edge, just as she had always done.

"Hi, guys," she said at last, as bravely as she could. This was almost more nerve-wracking than her first Cabinet meeting had been. At least everyone there was *obligated* to be kind.

Heads swivelled. A cautious chorus of "Hi, Lady Arrex," greeted her.

"Arrex," Tarrant said happily, hauling Will firmly into the circle. "Finally!"

Siln Joss was the first to extend their hand. "Hey. We were all…pretty surprised when we heard you two were co-pilots."

Austyn Garth gave a little laugh. "*I* wasn't."

Everyone chuckled, and then, finally, the ice was broken. Tarrant resumed a long and involved narrative about the training sims they had been subjected to. Will laughed in the right places, concentrating more on the way Tarrant's friends were looking at her, at the way Tarrant's eyes shone with happiness, revelling in the chance to actually be a *part* of the conversation instead of a covert listener.

Just as Tarrant reached the saga of the steel girder, Will saw her father eyeing her more pointedly, unwilling to be put off any longer. She leaned over to Tarrant. "I'll be right back."

Pausing in her story, Tarrant nodded hesitantly. "See you later, then?"

Will saw their classmates exchanging glances and squared her shoulders in response. "We shouldn't waste all that *practice*, Tarrant."

Tarrant caught her tone and quirked a corner of her mouth. "Of course not, Arrex."

As Will retreated, she heard Erntz's loud voice ringing out over the crowd.

"I thought you *hated* her, Paige!"

The small smile of genuine amusement on Will's face faded fast as she waded through the crowd towards Xavier, fending off greetings and congratulations on the Surveys from every side— each one tinged with a shade of pity that she was beginning to resent. Dozens of different well-wishers descended, swarming like the locusts Cleopatra had failed to drive away from the fields of the starving kingdom she inherited from her father in Tarrant's miserable film.

Even Panset was prowling past, and she offered Will a hemlock grin, poisonous as her personality. "Enjoying the party, Princess?"

Will kept her mask in place. "Of course."

"Makes you see things differently, doesn't it?" Panset said, turning with her. "Lain going. Knowing we'll be going soon too."

Offering another strained nod to some unfortunate pilot's uncle, bubbling with enthusiasm at being face to face with a real Noble, Will pushed past. "We're all going to miss him."

"Funny," Panset snarled from behind her. "I don't remember you ever talking to him."

With difficulty, Will controlled herself. Held back the response that flowed easy as water to her fingers. *If you followed Lain, who'd miss you?* Panset was not worth the effort it took to fight her.

When she finally reached her father, he offered her a polished public smile of his own. "You look lovely, Wilhelmina."

"Thank you."

He led the way towards the room's edge, where the sim room cubes were functioning as seating. "I heard about the Spoke Four boy. Did you know him well?"

"Not well," Will said, glancing across the room to where Loysa sat, slumped against the wall. "But I knew him."

"Then I'm sorry for your loss."

"Father—" she paused, trying to word it right.

"Yes, Wilhelmina?"

"Lain and Loysa thought they'd discovered something. About the Laikas' fuel tanks."

He went very still.

"Do you—is there anything I ought to know, Father?"

"Wilhelmina, I—" Xavier suddenly looked very old. "Just tell me—are you *certain* that you're set on this? It isn't like choosing a job, or a subject to study at the Academy. Getting on board those ships isn't something that can be undone. Once you're outside of Eden's walls, I can't help you."

Will swallowed. She looked at Tarrant, talking with Cara and Austyn. Even now, it was not too late. She could still leave all this behind her. Close the door on this dark chapter of her life and pretend it was all just a bad dream. Xavier could still protect her— as he had planned, an injury would be enough of an excuse. For the price of a scar or two, Will would be free.

She would live.

She looked again at Tarrant, that cloud of hair floating over the yellow dress that floated too.

She would live, and Tarrant would die.

As though he sensed her decision, Xavier edged forward, his expression almost pleading. "It's not too late."

But it *was* too late, and Will shook her head. "Why didn't you just—" she choked the question off before she could finish it. *If you wanted to save me, why didn't you just make certain my number didn't come up?* But that wasn't something she wanted to say. It wasn't brave. She hadn't wanted special treatment—that had been the whole point.

But Xavier knew exactly what she meant, and his face twisted in a bitter smile. "The Laika Programme is Centre, not Spoke Six. It's protected from regional tampering. Not even the Lord Captain could have done it."

Will dipped her head in acknowledgement. Pushed out the words from between lips that were still half-unwilling. "It doesn't matter. This...happened. And an Arrex keeps her word, right?"

Disappointment flashed across his features before his usual glacial calm reasserted itself. "If you're set on it, if you're certain, do one thing for me."

"What?"

"Make sure you get Laika Fifteen."

Will blinked. Of all the possible requests he could have made, she could not have predicted this one. What could it matter which ship she entered? The whole point was that it was randomised.

"Why?"

"The programme is centralised, but ship production is local. I've...made some modifications." He seemed unwilling to elaborate.

"What sort of modifications?"

"For your comfort, let's say. Just make sure you get it."

"Father, I don't understand—"

"Wilhelmina." His voice grew sharp. "I have humoured you in *everything*. Will you please humour me in this one thing?"

Will bowed her head. What did it matter? She would die the same whichever ship she was in. "Yes, Father."

"There are no problems with the Laika ships," he said at last. "I expect your friend was just...mistaken."

He looked into her eyes, meeting her gaze squarely, nothing held back, and Will felt the doubt ebbing away. Loysa was still only a student, after all. Not even one specialising in spaceship design. She had gotten the wrong impression, and Lain had made his own choice. The Noble Council knew the truth, and Xavier would never lie to her. Not on her very last night.

Would he?

"Yes, Father," she said at last, both reassured and fully aware that she wanted more than anything to *be* reassured. To cling to whatever promises he could give her.

Tarrant grinned. "Finally! I thought you'd ditched me."

Will thought of Xavier's offer. If Tarrant knew how close she was to the truth...

But giving voice to that thought would only hurt them both, so she limited herself to a simple smile and apology.

As the two of them skirted the dance floor, drifting towards the drinks table, Tarrant passed on her own miserable tidings. Jin Sutsu's Recycling date had been set.

"Makes me sick I won't even be here to help Cara through it." She gave a sad little laugh. "She actually asked me if I thought it was too late to swap back."

For a second, Will was distracted from her own tragedy. Cara Sutsu was a girl that didn't deserve the hand she had been dealt—and the one time she had met him, Jin Sutsu had been kind. "What do you mean, to swap back?"

"She thought that now the date was certain, I—I might *regret* it." Tarrant looked like she might vomit. "She thought I'd want her to go with you instead."

The prospect was horrifying—Tarrant was going to run out on her, after all she had sacrificed. After she had stayed in this nightmare process *only* for Tarrant. After her father had offered her the same option, and she had refused him. For Tarrant.

"What did you say?" She attempted a casual tone, but it came out as more of a croak.

Tarrant gave her a narrow-eyed look. The sort that said *Why even ask that?*

"No, obviously."

Obviously. That word cut Will to the core. Of course. Of *course* Tarrant had not hesitated. Not like Will had hesitated. She was too loyal for that. Too unselfish. Will felt like she might vomit. She had very nearly said yes to Xavier's offer. She would have doomed Tarrant to the same fate as poor Loysa. Dying alone and unloved. Forsaken by everyone.

"I...I'm not feeling too good. I think I need to go." Without waiting for an answer, she pulled away. She needed to get somewhere quiet, away from the cameras and the watching eyes. She needed to be alone.

"Arrex, wait. What about the plan?"

Will was frozen for a moment.

"Come on, Will," Tarrant said, and Will could see a hand reaching for her shoulder, the nails so carefully painted in the same shade of yellow as her own. "We were going to hang out with everyone, remember? There's going to be dancing later. Stay. Tell me what's wrong."

She wrenched herself away before those fingers, those loyal unselfish *better* fingers, could touch her. "I need to *go*."

And then she broke away, all but running as she neared the door. Leaving Paige Tarrant standing, hand outstretched, on the dance floor behind her.

Will drifted alone for what seemed like aeons. Twisting and turning in place, with no sense of movement no matter how hard she struggled. She tried to call out, and found to her horror that she had no voice at all. The blackness took her words and swallowed them whole.

She jerked awake, gasping for breath and reaching out with desperate hands for something—anything—to save her.

The darkness of her coffin-sized bedroom pressed in close, swallowing the half-spoken plea.

Waiting for her racing heart to slow, Will looked at her watch. Only ten hours till launch. Only ten hours until life as she had known it would end.

Flopping back down, Will stared into the shadows and wondered. Could she have done it? Could she have walked away from the strange new life she was building with the girl she'd once believed her worst enemy? From the death they'd agreed they would share?

It would be easy, to retreat into the embrace of her family, the comfort of her old life. Waking up in her room full of stars, basking in her scalding-hot shower. Trekking from school to tutors to Cabinet and back again, drinking in all the knowledge she could, readying herself for her move to the Academy and the next step into her glorious Arrex future.

She could leave, right now. Even at this critical juncture, she knew that her father would save her. One message, one *I've changed my mind*, and he would storm down to Centre with all the forces of Spoke Six at his back. He would save her, and damn the consequences.

So yes, Will could leave. It was within her capabilities. But *could* she? And if she did, would she be able stop herself from coming back again?

It was a fantasy.

A brief flash of lunacy before the storm that was about to break. Will could no more leave than any of the rest. Her ticket had been drawn, her number was up. She was one of them, now. Tethers stronger than blood bound her to these people. Honour, Arrex honour. What it meant to be Noble, in the truest sense of the word. And...and Tarrant, of course. There was always Tarrant. The strongest tie of all.

No. She could not leave. If it had ever been an option, it had long since ceased to be one.

Pushing the blankets away, Will left her little bed for the last time. She found Tarrant seated on the sofa, staring into space. "Hey."

It took a moment, but finally Tarrant seemed to see her. "Hi."

"Couldn't sleep?"

"No."

"Me neither."

Tarrant curled up her outstretched legs, and Will flopped down beside her.

"I still don't fully get why you came here," she said, and Tarrant raised her eyebrows. "You didn't have to."

"Nor did you."

"It was for Cara, right?"

"I did it for her, yeah."

Inexplicable disappointment flooded through Will like a tide. "But not just for her."

"No?" replied Will with what she hoped was indifference.

"For you, too."

And if even one sliver of doubt had been left in Will's breast, that was enough to extinguish it forever. Tarrant had come here to die with her. To die *for her*, as well as Cara.

What was there left to do, but for her to stay and die for Tarrant, too?

Part II
EXCELSIOR

CHAPTER 14

Centre, Eden Station – Year 453 – Day 31 – 11:00

One last breakfast. Silent as the grave. Porridge that stuck in the craw. Fresh pears that tasted like nothing. One last look around their room. The walls were bare now, stripped of their fairy lights. The fruit bowl was still full, like they would be back in time for dinner. Will watched Tarrant run her fingers over the spines of the books that hadn't made it into her baggage allowance, and she slipped an apple into one pocket and a tangerine into the other.

One last taste of home.

The buzzer sounded, and the pilots filed out of their rooms. Bunched together, acting on instinct: safety in numbers. Will saw Tarrant reaching for Loysa, and she put her own hand on Thune's shoulder. A little kindness would cost her nothing now.

They all squashed into a single tramcar branded with Centre's zero motif. The first time in Will's life she'd ever travelled in a public tramcar—and it was not at all like the Arrex version. Forty seats instead of six, and no plush grey velvet or Lawkeeper escorts. Just hard plastic that bit into the flesh, and neighbours pressed too close. Everyone frightened and silent.

The Eden's orbital mass accelerator waited for them at the very bottom of Centre, directly beneath the Laika Training Centre. As the tramcars dropped, Will thought about those strange Old Terran legends. A subterranean world populated by the souls of the damned. Looking around at the ashen faces of her companions, the terror in their eyes, she could almost believe it. The Laikas were their ferries, and they were about to begin their one-way voyage across the Styx.

The tramcar door slid open all too soon, and somewhere at the back a girl began to cry. Thune was already sobbing, his face buried in Panset's shoulder. Over his head, Panset stared with icy accusation at Will. There was nothing she could do. There was nothing any of them could do.

Along the corridor that led to the mass accelerator, a line of parents waited to bid the pilots goodbye. Lawkeepers in the colours of every spoke hovered at the edges, stun guns at their hips. In case anyone got any last-minute escape ideas. And through it all, cameramen circled like sharks, capturing everything—every tearful goodbye, every shaking child—all diced and prepared and served on a silver platter to a salivating public.

The herd splintered as everyone sought out their own relatives. With a faltering heart and a blank face, Will approached her father. Eyes were still on her, and she would, at the very least, be remembered well. If this was truly the end, she would die like an Arrex.

Xavier reached out and pressed her hand between both of his own. "Remember, Wilhelmina. Laika Fifteen."

Her resignation and despair evaporating, Will almost snatched her hand away from him, but caught herself. Was that all he had to say to her, after the way he had ruined the launch party? But it was not his fault he no longer knew her—perhaps had never known her. There was no use in parting angry.

"I'm sorry, Father," she said.

After all, she was not the only one losing everything today. Xavier's legacy was his life. He had put seventeen years of work into the product that was his daughter Wilhelmina, and she was throwing it all away.

A long pause, and then he gave her a very small smile. "I can't say I would have carried it to this extent, but I...understand following through on your promises. We are Arrexes, after all."

It was a struggle, but she managed to return his smile.

"Goodbye, Father."

She almost wished he would reach out and hug her. Almost. But Cirrus was there, and the cameras were on them, and the Arrex dignity was between them, stronger than any wall.

"Goodbye, Wilhelmina."

Eloise pulled Will into a flowery embrace, littered with tears. It was as fleeting as her presence in Will's life had always been, but Will could no longer be bothered to resent her.

Perhaps, in her way, Eloise had loved her. Or maybe it was just too hard to love a child whose future was fully mapped out before they were even conceived, who would look nothing like you. To be a mere incubator for the long and ponderous history of the Arrex family. Will would never know. Whatever the truth, soon Eloise would have to carry a second Arrex scion. A replacement child with silver-blonde hair and hard green eyes, ready for Xavier's lessons.

Tarrant was still sandwiched in between her fathers, three dark heads clustered close together, and Will had to wait, pretending that she was unaffected. That she did not want to collapse into a puddle of tears at the sight of that beautifully ordinary familial love.

But finally, even Tarrant was forced to let go, and her papi and her dad watched as their daughter returned to Will. It was Minister Grayson who had the colour and the set of Tarrant's eyes, but it was Carr who had their expression. He looked at Will, looked into her soul with those same deep-seeing eyes, and she saw the plea in them. *Take care of my daughter.*

Slowly, carefully, she lowered her chin the barest fraction of an inch. *I will.*

And then Tarrant was back at her side, and there were no more excuses. As reluctantly as the other pilots, they moved forward, following the trickle as it swelled into a current. The first airlock door slid open. The Laika pilots drifted in, dragging their feet, looking back at their families. Only Will did not turn her head.

It took a long time for all of them to make their way into the airlock. Will wondered if some would do more than hesitate—if they would flee. But the Lawkeepers loomed with the full force of the law behind them: prison and early Recycling. Whatever route they chose, the life of those selected in the Lottery was destined to be short. No one ran.

The first door closed, and there was a hiss as the air depressurised slightly. Then the second airlock opened, and the vast centrifuge was revealed.

Eighteen ships waited on eighteen sets of rails leading to eighteen doors. Once they had boarded, the mass accelerator would start to spin, and when terminal velocity was reached, the doors would open and eighteen silver ships would be flung out in eighteen different directions. Eighteen Laikas on which the pilots would live and die. All of them identical in every way but for the numbers painted on their sides.

Each ship had its own mission, pre-programmed in. To Oberon, Mars, Mercury, Titan, Venus, and the far side of Jupiter.

Missions between one and four years long, with success or failure dependent on the whims of fortune. Nothing was preassigned to the pilots, and the question of which mission you got—where you would likely die—was essentially just dumb luck.

Timidly, the pilots stepped forward. Drifting uncertainly towards different ships. Heading towards lucky numbers, hunches, choosing something purely because something had to be chosen. *Remember, Wilhelmina. Laika Fifteen.* It was the very last thing her father had said to her. Would *ever* say to her. *Do one thing for me. Make sure you get Laika Fifteen.*

Will grabbed Tarrant's sleeve and began to run.

They broke out ahead of the pack, making straight for number fifteen, and it started a stampede. Suddenly everyone was running. Will was hauling Tarrant bodily along, and she could hear pounding footsteps behind them. She turned her head: Panset. *Of course.*

"Come on," she snarled at Tarrant, who huffed in indignation.

"Why are we *running*? It doesn't—matter—*god*, will you stop *pulling* me?"

"We have to get to number fifteen!" Will ground out, not troubling to look back a second time. "Shut up and *run*."

But Panset was fast, *too* fast, and they were losing ground.

Pulling savagely on Tarrant's sleeve, Will dropped into a dead sprint, her legs pumping like pistons. Her father, flawed as he was, wanted her on Laika Fifteen, and on Laika Fifteen she would *be*. Her feet rang like hammers on the metal floor. The gangplank was almost in reach, dropping down from an aperture high on the ship's side. They were within touching distance.

Panset ran like an athlete, with form and talent that Will would not have been able to match even if she had kept up her old fitness regime. And as it was, with weeks of losing condition, staved off with only a few desultory jogs around the sim room—she didn't have a chance.

And Panset was alongside her now—feet pounding, fingers curled into fists. Her dark hair flew like a victory banner, and when she glanced across at Will there was triumph in her eyes.

She began to pull ahead.

It was a decision made in a split second. The work of an instant. *She was not about to lose to Panset Pall.* Will took the only recourse left to her. She dropped Tarrant's sleeve and feinted left, slapping her foot down squarely in Panset's path.

The other girl went down like a sack of rocks. Her chin hit the ground with an audible *clack*, and Thune finally caught up, his voice high and panicky. "Pans! Are you okay?"

With a hiss of victory, Will burst into motion again, pushing Tarrant up the gangplank ahead of her. Laika Fifteen was *theirs*.

"Did you—did you *trip* Panset?"

"No," replied Will, instinctively knowing that it was best to fudge the truth. Emotions were too high today for any real honesty. "I just stumbled."

Luckily, Tarrant did not seem inclined to question it. "Why were we even running for this ship?"

"Fifteen was Javier Arrex's lucky number." It was as good a reason as any other she could come up with, and she knew Tarrant would buy it.

The other girl snorted. "I should have known."

They paused at the top of the gangplank, looking into the open doorway. A dark aperture, an empty eye socket in a skull picked clean. Will shivered. The last few stragglers reached the remaining ships and climbed up. Panset was among them, leaning heavily on Thune and shooting one last furious look at Will over her shoulder. A few drones began to shuttle out the pilots' baggage, and the inner door of the airlock slid shut.

The Eden was closed to them now. There would be no going back.

They stood at the doors of the ships, seventeen pairs and one girl alone. Thirty-five of Eden's children, united in that one moment in their fear and their regret as they looked back at their families. Their home.

As she searched the blurry figures behind the airlock glass for her parents, Will felt Tarrant's fingers twining with her own. There was no electricity this time. No heart-pounding mixture of fear and excitement. Just...comfort.

"Laika pilots." Professor Clark's voice. "Please enter your ships. The mass accelerator will begin to turn soon."

Will looked at Tarrant. Tarrant looked at Will, those tiny flecks of amber-yellow dancing in her eyes as Tarrant in her yellow dress should have danced at the launch party.

And then, side by side, they stooped to enter Laika Fifteen.

The gangplank led to a passageway so narrow that Will had to twist sideways to fit through.

Behind her, the announcement continued.

"In T-minus ninety seconds, the Laika ships will self-seal, and the mass accelerator will begin to turn."

Will looked back to where Tarrant was silhouetted against the light. Beyond those lights were her parents. Spoke Six. *Home.* Will felt as though she would vomit.

"I think we have to go in," Tarrant whispered. Her voice was barely audible.

How could they expect the pilots to willingly enter? If they'd thrown Will fighting onto the ship it would somehow have been less barbaric. But the threats were all oblique, veiled, and the pretence at free will was maintained all the way to the end.

But I did *choose this. I was the only one who did.*

She had been the one to start this ball rolling. That day in Hrue Lipson's office, when she told the first lie. There was no one to blame but herself.

Will strained, trying to see the airlock. Maybe—maybe Xavier would burst through it. Any second now. A dozen Lawkeepers would be enough. A dozen Lawkeepers to overpower the Laika staff and rescue her. The Lawkeepers from the other spokes wouldn't dare open fire against them. And Xavier would pull her from the Laika, and she would drag Tarrant along with her. And then—and they would both be saved.

"T-minus seventy seconds until the Laika doors seal," droned Professor Clark's disembodied voice.

Face twisting in anguish, Tarrant reached for her. "Will."

It's too late.

Will bowed her head and forced herself onward. As the light from the mass accelerator chamber faded, the feeling of claustrophobia grew. The corridor was not long, but the way it *felt*—the horror of how Will imagined Recycling might feel, of passing down the throat of some monstrous creature as it swallowed her whole. The walls seemed to press against her ribcage from both sides, burying her alive.

When she finally emerged, she was shaking from head to foot. She stumbled forward, blinking in the new light, and bashed into something hard and plastic that moved as she hit it. Rubbing her nose, Will stepped around the offending object, pressing against the wall to do so.

It was a gyroscope. A plastic wheel eight foot in diameter, fixed to the wall by a steel hub. An exercise bike identical to the one from their room in the Training Centre sat beside it, a punching bag, and a small shelf of weights and elastics.

The door opened into Laika Fifteen's home gym. It was so banal that Will suddenly had to choke back a laugh. This was her hell, then. Her Tartarus. A shitty little room with a home gym in the corner.

Tarrant was banging her way down the corridor behind her, and Will was forced to squeeze past the wheel and out into the main living space. Just like in the Training Centre, there was a kitchen in one corner, a table and chairs, a sofa, a vidscreen, a poky bathroom, and the two identical bedrooms—more cupboards than rooms, really. Other than the porthole in one wall, the only difference was a sealed door in the far left corner beside the kitchen. There had been no such door in the old room. Tarrant seemed little inclined to investigate; instead, she sagged against the sofa's arm, looking as though she might collapse at any minute. Though she felt little different, Will forced herself over to the door. Anything was better than succumbing to the despair clawing at the edges of her mind.

The cubicle behind the door did not offer much in the way of distraction. It held two swivel chairs and an L-shaped desk dotted with buttons in a layout Will recognised from the training sims. This was the control room, where they were supposed to pilot the ship during emergencies. The vidscreens lining the walls above the dashboard displayed the feeds from the cameras outside. And in a little less than fifty seconds, those screens and the tiny porthole in the room outside would be the only way Will could view the world beyond her prison.

She sank into one of the chairs, staring up at the vidscreens and the final preparations underway outside the ship. Time seemed to stretch, and Will had the terrible presentiment that this was what her future was. Eternity in this one little room, without end.

Both of them flinched when a drone appeared in the doorway and began to disgorge a series of grey packages in a heap in the room's centre, each swathed in edible, biodegradable plastic. Their baggage allowance, delivered right on schedule.

"T-minus thirty seconds until the Laika doors seal." Professor Clark's voice was loud within the enclosed space.

When the drone retreated down the passageway, wheels buzzing against the metal, both Will and Tarrant followed it. Peering over Tarrant's shoulder at the square of light outside the ship, Will wondered again if anyone would try to make a run for it. Was it better to risk being smushed against the inside of the orbital mass accelerator, or to embrace the uncertain life expectancy of a Laika pilot? Not much of a choice.

And while she was still turning the question over in her mind, the wall of the gym and the exterior door moved simultaneously, hissing closed on invisible tracks. With one final buzz of metal welding into place, Laika Fifteen fastened itself so completely it was like no door had ever existed. The last trace of her former life, gone.

Professor Clark announced, with audible satisfaction, "The doors to all eighteen Laikas have sealed, and the launch will now begin."

As the last hints of a doorway in the wall vanished, Will exchanged one mute glance with Tarrant. If a small, pathetic part of Will had dared to hope that Tarrant's hand would find its way into hers once more, she was disappointed. She returned to the control room alone as Tarrant retreated to the sofa.

The launch bay was changing. Vents opened, the air seeming to shiver as the oxygen was pulled from the room. A far cry from the dramatic launch of the glider-racers. There would be no waste here.

As Will watched, the pale blue light of the airlock glass began to move left as the floor rotated right. She glanced over her shoulder at Tarrant, lying back with one arm thrown over her eyes. Shutting it all out. In here everything was calm. But out there, the mass accelerator was already spinning, building up its charge.

The airlock passed by again and again, whipping by without even a heartbeat's space between, and then blurred into a single blue streak. And it all took place in a silence so absolute it was eerie.

Will wondered if her father would miss her. Tarrant's parents, too. Cara and her grandfather. What were the feelings of everyone across Spoke Six, across Eden, as they watched their children laid down upon the sacrificial altar? If she had not been one of them, if Tarrant had not, would Will have cared?

"Eden wishes you the best of luck on your missions, Laika pilots," said Professor Clark into the quietness of the room, and Will flinched at the sudden noise. "You go with our hopes and our thanks."

Eighteen pairs of outer doors clanged open, the atmosphere vented, and in that same great rush, so were the Laikas.

If Will had not already been in the control room, staring at the vidscreens, she might not have noticed. Apparently no expense had been spared on the Laika's internal gravity generators. There was a humming and a slight shivering, but that was all.

And even staring up at the vidscreens that lined the control room's walls, even seeing it play out before her, Will wanted to think that it was all some elaborate trick. Faked, somehow. That the ship was still docked in the mass accelerator, and soon Professor Clark would appear onscreen and announce it had all been a joke.

But this was real.

The void gaped before her, unspeakably huge. Will was a worm, an amoeba. A little speck of dust in the face of its immeasurable size. It was beautiful, yes, a billion suns burning in unison—but it was a cold, uncaring beauty. And on every side of Laika Fifteen hung other little silver specks, marring the unbroken majesty of the galaxy. Eighteen Laikas, hurled out from the Eden's underbelly. Eighteen sets of blue thrusters igniting, jetting the children away from everything they had ever known.

The Eden was directly behind them. A perfect wheel displayed against the umber backdrop of Amalthea and Jupiter beyond. A view of the station Will had never seen before outside of camera drones.

"Tarrant," she called. "We're out. You should come look."

It'll be your last chance.

Slowly, very slowly, Tarrant turned her head, curls quivering as they dragged across the fabric of the sofa. Her expression was strangely blank.

She joined Will in the swivel chairs, and the two of them sat before the desk of useless controls. The navigational system took care of everything, and there was nothing to do but watch the Eden dwindle behind them. The seventeen ships ringed around the Eden grew smaller, too. The Laika pilots were being separated, step by step.

The radio fizzed. "Laika Fifteen, this is Command at Eden." Another crackle. "Laika Fifteen, Pilots Tarrant and—a-and *Arrex*. Do you copy?"

Tarrant lunged for the radio, fumbling it in her haste. "We copy, Eden!"

"All the data from your launch looks good, Laika Fifteen. No issues and you're bang on course." It was not a voice Will knew. Someone from the deeper recesses of the Laika Programme, who did not work face to face with the pilots. Perhaps even another pilot: someone who had survived this themselves, twenty-five or fifty years ago. There was no way of knowing. "You will be going to—let's see—Deimos, Mars's smaller moon."

With a significant look, Tarrant raised her eyebrows at Will, but Will could offer no reply other than a shrug. He could have said Pluto itself, for all the difference it could have made. If they somehow reached their destination *without* dying, they had to repeat the whole journey all over again—and they were to accomplish this impossible feat with no one but each other and the little tin can they were rattling around in. It was a pipe dream.

"Records suggest that a colony was planned in the south pole, where there's plenty of shelter from the solar flares. So you'll be setting down there, checking things out, and then heading back. Simple and straightforward like the training sims." If he was trying to be reassuring, it was falling flat.

"We copy, Eden," Tarrant replied at last. Nothing more.

"You'll be out of Eden's range in a few days, but until then you're welcome to contact Command with any questions, or just to talk. We understand it will be a difficult time for you, and we've got staff in post twenty-four-seven. Your families have clearance to come in and talk to you once a day. Shall I log a request for you both?"

Tarrant glanced at Will for confirmation, and Will nodded. It was nice, in a distant sort of way, that she had not spoken to her father for absolutely the last time. But it didn't change much. She would never see Xavier again.

"Yes, please."

"Copy. As a final note, you can also use your radios to talk to the other Laikas," Command added. "You'll be in range of some of them for a bit longer than you will the Eden, but it's not an exact science."

This time even Tarrant did not respond, and Command signed off. There was nothing to say. They were doomed. What commiseration could some little jobsworth back in Centre give?

"Will?" Tarrant said carefully, once the last crackle from the radio had died.

"Mm?"

"You never said why you ran off."

"Ah." Will paused. "You mean at the launch party?"

"Yes."

"Just…nerves, I suppose. My father was…he was disappointed in me. It was a lot."

"Disappointed?" Disdain dripped from Tarrant's voice. It was almost strange to have it directed at someone else. "You're as much a hero as any of us are."

"We're heroes?" Will did not feel especially heroic. Just… frightened.

Tarrant squared her shoulders. "We're dying for our world. That's what heroes did in the Old Terran movies."

"It's not the life Father wanted for me."

And then Tarrant turned to her, eyes blazing, and squeezed her arm so hard it almost hurt. "It's the first thing you ever did on your own, without him. The…the most decent thing you've ever done."

Tears sprang into Will's eyes, but she tried to play it off, attempted a laugh. "You were going to say the *only* decent thing I've ever done, weren't you?"

Tarrant laughed too, and her eyes were glistening as well. "Maybe."

The laughter faded, and the two of them sat beside each other in the pilots' chairs, watching the Eden dwindling into nothingness on the vidscreen.

Watching everything fade away.

CHAPTER 15

Laika 15 – Day 5 – 21:10

"I love you, Paige. Never forget how much we both love you." Carr's voice broke, and Will heard Tarrant stifle a sob as well. "We'll be waiting right here when you come back. We'll think of you every minute of every day. You won't be out there alone. Not really."

Tarrant began to cry in earnest, and Will retreated to her room. This was one conversation on which she could not eavesdrop.

Her own goodbyes seemed somewhat...flat, in comparison.

"We'll see you soon, darling," said Eloise, as though Will were going on a holiday to another spoke. "I hope you have a...a *wonderful* time."

If there were any true feeling beneath the bright falseness of that voice, Will could not find it.

Xavier made her wait until he was done with a Cabinet meeting. And when his final message came, it was as cold and remote as Neptune. "I know you'll come home to us, Wilhelmina. I'm certain of it." There was no room for emotion there. No room for Will.

Will sat on the edge of her seat and stared at the radio transceiver. It was featureless. An emotionless blank. Exactly like an Arrex.

"Father," she said, and the word was almost a plea. *Give me something. Anything.*

"Excelsior, Wilhelmina," he replied, lifeless as the dead homeworld. "Make me proud."

Will felt something nameless and horrible surging in her breast, and she cut the call.

There it was. The end of everything. Her coffin was nailed shut.

Mechanically, Will rose. She remembered Tarrant's tears, the stormy protestations of love. Tarrant lived her life at the centre of a maelstrom, and Will wished she could feel the wind whipping through her hair. She wished she could feel anything.

Carefully, she opened the door. Hopefully Tarrant would already be asleep, or reading a book. A reading Tarrant was as dead to the world as an unconscious one. And all Will wanted now was to be alone.

But when she stepped into the main room, the sight that met her eyes drove all thoughts of solitude from her head. The room was bathed in a kaleidoscope of colour, transforming the oppressive little space into something entirely new. Every colour under the sun refracting from the white walls like stars. Will stood frozen, trying to work out what she was seeing.

It was the fairy lights, she realised at last. Fairy lights covered with coloured paper to make them into a rainbow. And there on the sofa, bathed in multicoloured light, sat Tarrant, nose in a book. Her hair was looped in wild tangles over the sofa arm, spilling down almost to the floor, its honey-brown length lit with a soft rainbow of light, the bright orbs landing like butterflies on the curls, the cushions, on Tarrant herself.

As Will stared in wonder at the transformed space, Tarrant looked up. Cocked a brow at her. Gave her a small, sardonic smile. "Cat got your tongue?"

It was a lifeline—the familiar tone of challenge, the oldest of habits. Will caught on to it with relief, and hauled herself out of the fathomless freezing ocean and back to reality. "Tarrant, what *is* all this?"

"Think of it as a peace offering."

Despite herself, despite her misery, Will felt a smile began to creep across her face. "A peace offering?"

"Like porridge," Tarrant suggested with a grin. "I know…I know your Year Change Festival wasn't great. Amongst other things also not being great. And I thought maybe we could both use a redo."

Leaning against the doorframe, Will felt her misery and anger begin to ease. Tarrant was a nightmare when she wanted to be— but Will was also beginning to see the side of Tarrant once reserved for their classmates. Despite all her flaws, Tarrant was a wonderful friend.

"I talked to Papi earlier." Tarrant's breath hitched, but she did not add *for the last* time. "My family always cuddles up with a film on bad days. I thought maybe we could give it a try."

With every passing second Xavier and his wintry farewell shrank into irrelevance. Will's eyebrows climbed. "I'm not planning on *cuddling* you, Tarrant."

Tarrant flushed beetroot. "No, I didn't mean—!" Her words came out in a garbled squawk, and Will couldn't help the laugh that escaped her lips.

The best part of being almost-friends with Tarrant was how easy it still was to make her rise to the bait.

At the sound of the laugh, Tarrant relaxed slightly and stuck her tongue out at Will. It was small and pointed and very pink, and what remained of Will's foul mood faded entirely. Her father could not reach her here, not anymore. Hidden among stacks of books and the comforting scent of paper, with rainbow fairy lights glittering everywhere she looked and pear porridge waiting in the fridge for the morning—here she was safe.

She crossed to the sofa and flopped down beside Tarrant. Films were Tarrant's answer to bad days; good to know. Made their first movie night about the ancient Terran queen take on a new meaning. "Alright, then. What are we watching?"

For a few moments, Tarrant looked taken aback. "Oh—I mean—just like that? You actually want to?"

"You asked me, didn't you?"

"Yeah, but I just thought—" Tarrant cut herself off and shook her head. "I expected more of a brutal rejection, I suppose. Thought you'd go off and sulk for a while."

Will shrugged. "Not even I have it in me all the time. Come on. What are we watching?"

"Ooh, it's one of my favourites." Tarrant pointed at the screen, which showed a stern-looking man in a crown superimposed over a blazing Terran sunset. "*El Final de Todas las Cosas!* It's all about Ferdinand XIX of Spain."

Will laughed again. Like a bad dream, the last of the shadow Xavier had cast dissipated. "Did you really just say *XIX*? Why not just say Ferdinand the nineteenth?"

"How else would people know it's Roman numerals?" Tarrant said defensively. "The Old Terrans used the *Roman* numbering system for their monarchs. It wouldn't be *accurate* to just say *nineteen.*"

"Fine, fine," Will waved her hands, too amused to argue the point further. "What does Ferdinand *XIX* do?"

Tarrant beamed. "Well, when Albrecht of Berlin makes his move on Brussels, Ferdinand tries to stop the mega-nation treaty, but he—wait, how much do you know about twenty-fourth-century Europe?"

Will sniggered. "Like most people, literally nothing."

Tarrant took it on the chin and just rolled her eyes. "Then anything else I tell you is a spoiler. I'll just say it's about the fall of Spain and the rise of Europea, and leave it there."

Will stuck her tongue out—a habit she had picked up from Tarrant. Childish and crude, but terribly satisfying. "Ugh. It's always empires and wars with you. Haven't we got anything a bit happier?"

"What, is the mighty Will Arrex afraid to watch a film that might make her *think*?"

"No, obviously not—I just think reality is miserable enough."

"Well, maybe we could..." Tarrant looked so disappointed that Will had no choice but to relent.

"Alright, alright. *Fine.* We'll watch *La Miseria de Todas las Cosas.*"

Another laugh from Tarrant. "Just because I don't speak a billion languages doesn't mean I didn't see what you did there."

But she pressed play on the vidscreen, and leaned back, an expression of contentment on her face.

Tarrant was in her element, mouthing the words along with the rugged man on the yellow-hued grasslands of Old Terra. The ship's sofa was smaller than the one in the Training Centre. Too small for two people, really, and it pushed Will closer to Tarrant than she would have chosen to sit. But despite the empty space surrounding them, Laika Fifteen was warm, and Tarrant's shoulder was warmer still where it pressed against her own.

If you had asked Will two months ago who she was closest to, she would have said, without hesitation, her father. How strange it was, then, that he let her leave him with so little love.

And yet Tarrant, Paige Tarrant, Will's scourge and rival since time immemorial, realised it and took steps to remedy it.

The world seemed to be turning upside down, and Will actually quite liked it.

Slowly but surely, Will relaxed into the cushions. Ferdinand waged his futile war against Albrecht of Berlin, and Tarrant's huge brown eyes drank in every detail, every line of dialogue. Will watched Tarrant watch the fall of Spain, and she thought that so far as do-overs went, it hadn't been a bad Year Change Festival after all.

"Arrex," someone hissed.

"Mmph," Will said, eloquently, groping for the button that would shut down the golden lights and the chiming.

Her hand met something soft.

"*Arrex!*"

Will jerked upright, yanking back her hand from where it had landed on Tarrant's leg. "Get off me!"

"You get off *me!*" Tarrant said, outraged. "You've been snoring on me for forty-five minutes!"

Heat rushed into Will's cheeks. "Then why the hell didn't you wake me up forty-five minutes ago?"

Tarrant turned scarlet too and took cover behind a cushion from the sofa, holding it between them like a shield. "Don't pin this on *me!*"

"I'm going to bed." Will scrambled to her feet, getting herself a safe distance away. Comfort or no comfort, *nothing* was worth this humiliation.

"Me too."

Both of them bolted—Tarrant for the bathroom, Will for her bed—and Will threw herself face down and pretended with all her might to be safely asleep. She'd behaved like an idiot. Showing her weakness, engaging with the silly little attempt at a Year Change Festival, and then actually falling asleep on *Tarrant*. There was only so much embarrassment one human soul could bear.

A pause. A scuffle. A whisper. "Arrex?"

Oh, god. "What?" Will mumbled, muffled by her pillow.

"Well," said Tarrant hesitantly. "I've been thinking."

"Great," replied Will. "You want a trophy?"

"*And,*" went on Tarrant, doing a valiant job of pretending she hadn't heard, "I think, that since we're co-pilots—since we're, you know, movie night buddies or—or whatever—"

Will hadn't heard her stutter this much in years. And *movie night buddies?* What?

"I think that we maybe ought to call each other by our first names," Tarrant said at last, blurting the words out in one hurried exhalation. "So—you know—you can call me Paige. If you want. Will."

The last word was an awkward addendum, but the sound of it was enough of a shock to Will's ears that she sat up and looked over at Tarrant once more. Tarrant was huddling behind the doorframe, still clutching her stupid cushion.

As their eyes met, Tarrant flushed.

"Really?" asked Will, sceptically. She had never been anything to Tarrant but *Arrex*, the word delivered in the tone of utmost distaste as punctuation for whatever insult was being hurled her way at the time. Like it was a synonym for *rich asshole*.

"Yes, really." Tarrant turned a brighter shade of puce and almost stamped her foot. "It's not like there's anyone *else* left to call me by my actual name. Why would I bother lying? We're too old for practical jokes!"

"Okay, okay." Will raised one hand to ward off the noise. "Then, Paige?"

The taste of the word was strange on her tongue. Like a new food, sweet and spicy all at once. *Delicious.*

"Y-yes, Will?"

"Please get out of my room and let me sleep, *Paige*."

"Ugh!" This time Tarrant *did* stamp her foot, and hurled the cushion for good measure. "You're the worst!"

"Shut the door on your way out!" Will called, and pulled the cushion over her face to create some blessed darkness.

Every morning was a series of routines, and Will tried to stretch out each one as far as she could. Savouring them as she tried to fill the empty hours. Anything to keep herself from going back to the control room, where the vidscreens showed Jupiter receding into the distance.

She rose early, ran on the gyroscope until every muscle burned, and staggered back to the kitchen to make porridge for Tarrant. Their little tradition was safe for now: most of Will's baggage allowance was freeze-dried pears. A silly thing to have fixated on, but Will was glad. The smallest, silliest things were lifelines now.

Tarrant...*Paige* had opted for books, of course. It was mind-boggling, how many paperbacks one could cram into ten kilograms when one really wanted to. A few strings of fairy lights were strung overhead. Tunis had contributed a hard drive with three yottabytes of movies. It waited by the living room vidscreen, loaded with the Old Terran classics Paige was obsessed with.

Will added some water to the hot pears, and they began to crackle as the moisture returned.

The scent of pears was enough to permeate even the thick fog of Tarrant's rest. She emerged, rumpled and yawning, just in time to accept her hot bowl from Will. "You made such a racket on the gyroscope."

Will just smiled. "Looks like you went back to sleep fine."

"Torture," Paige said without a hint of irony.

"If I can sleep through it at one in the morning, you can sleep through it at seven."

Paige snickered, and Will took a deep breath. *It's not like there's anyone else left to call me by my actual name. It's not like there's anyone else left, full stop.* Paige had made an effort for Will: the paper hanging down from the fairy lights was proof enough of that. It was time she made an effort too.

"Paige," she said, summoning all her courage. "Look at this."

She pulled the last plastic-wrapped package out from beneath the table. Pushed it into Paige's hands.

"Is that a *present*?" Paige demanded. "You've never given me a present in your entire life!"

Will smiled. A stroke of genius, and well worth the hefty chunk of her baggage allowance it had cost. A pear sapling fresh from the orchard, soil and a UV light to go with it. Even more than the porridge, it was a stupid thing to bring. But she hadn't been able to resist the possibility of tasting fresh fruit again. Of giving Paige the chance to do the same.

"Oh my god," Paige whispered, and Will braced herself for the inevitable diatribe on the ridiculous expense of purchasing an actual *sapling* from the government—but it never came.

The two of them worked together to set up their miniature orchard, giving up a full half of their tiny kitchen table to the pot and lashing the light to the cupboards above. The smile on Paige's face as she looked down at those hopeful little leaves was almost enough to make Will forget the situation they were in. Almost.

Paige glanced across, and must have seen the edge of melancholy on Will's face, because she planted her hands on her hips and grinned. "We should give it a name."

Diverted despite herself, Will smiled back. "Any suggestions?" She wanted to see what name Paige would suggest. Probably something ridiculous from Old Terran history—something along the lines of Cleopatra or Jesus or Cíxǐ Tàihòu.

But Paige was not yet willing to commit herself; she only laughed. "Anything so long as it's not Excelsior."

That pulled a corresponding snicker from Will. "I wouldn't do that to you."

Paige fingered the smallest of the leaves, not yet fully unfurled from its bud. "How about Arthur?"

The name rang a very dim bell. Whoever Arthur had been, he hadn't featured in the political and oratorical fields Will's education focused on. "This is one of your ridiculously obscure Old Terran things, right?"

A little laugh. "Not *that* obscure. He was a mythical king who was supposed to go into a magical sleep and return when the world needed him most."

It was not a subtle metaphor. "Like the terraformers."

"Exactly." Paige gave her a bright smile. It was still weird sometimes, this whole *civil conversation* thing she and Tarrant were now capable of.

"It's a good name," she said, turning back to the tree. Maybe it was a sign. Maybe, like King Arthur, the terraforming colonies were only sleeping, and not already dead.

On the sixth day, they passed out of the radio range of Eden. The voice of Command crackled one last time, and then fell silent.

There was nothing to do but stick to that same familiar routine. Eat breakfast together. Exercise. Monitor what little output the instruments and the vidscreens presented to them. And, of course, watch Jupiter shrink and shrink and shrink.

They exchanged a few words with those Laikas that were in range, and Will tried to find what little comfort was possible in the knowledge that everyone was as downcast as she and Paige were.

And then on the ninth day, they passed out of radio range of the final Laika. It was Loysa, en route to Mercury's dark side aboard Laika Three, and entirely alone.

"You can do it, Loysa," Paige said, clinging to the microphone like it was the last thread of her reason. "Don't give up. You have to *promise* me you won't give up."

"I don't know if I can promise anything anymore," came Loysa's distorted reply.

Paige's face twisted in pain, and Will moved closer to the radio and the girl before it, as though she could somehow make this easier.

"Lain wouldn't want you to give up!"

The response was a long time in coming. "...Lain gave up."

"Remember how much you want to see it all," pled Paige. "You want to *discover* things, Loysa. You're going to do that. You're going to *Mercury!*" She was trying so hard to inject positive emotion into her tone—to give Loysa some of the excitement that neither of them felt.

This time, there was no reply at all. Loysa was gone.

They had known the company would not last; even those other Laikas headed for Mars would be taking very different routes to reduce the risk of multiple ships being wiped out at the same time. But it was a horrible reality, to call out and be answered only by silence.

Paige waited by the radio for four hours before she gave up, and Will waited with her, sitting on the floor just behind Paige's chair. Finally, she reached out and rested a hand lightly on Paige's back. Touching those impossibly soft curls again, watching her fingers sink into them.

She said nothing, but she didn't need to. Paige dissolved quietly into despair, putting her head down flat against the radio console, but she let Will touch her, and Will would not have moved for all the captaincies on Eden.

It was just the two of them now. After even their fellow condemned were gone, Will was left with no one but Paige.

CHAPTER 16

Laika 15 – Day 8 – 09:45

Parry. Riposte. Remise. Guard again. Will gritted her teeth in frustration and wished she'd had room enough for a practice sabre. Her form was slipping; she could *feel* it.

"What on earth are you doing?"

Dropping her stance, Will crossed her arms defensively. "It's *my* gym time."

"You were making a lot of weird shuffling noises," Paige said, as though *that* was a reasonable defence. "I wondered if you were dancing."

Will scoffed. "Fencing. I don't *dance*, Tarrant."

Paige laughed. "Oh, I know. You stormed off from the launch party—probably the last party we're ever going to make it to, by the way—without joining us for a single one."

"You were going to dance?" More importantly, Will had been invited to join?

"We all danced. It was a *party*, Arrex." Tarrant rolled her eyes. "What did you think was going to happen there?"

"I don't know," said Will, who had attended hundreds of high-society parties over the years and spent them engaged exclusively in political discussions without ever once setting foot on a dance floor. "Talking? Does anyone actually *dance* at these things?"

"Since you missed out," said Paige, suddenly dropping the cloak of her old imperious self and lapsing back into a smile, "let's try again."

"You want to dance here?" Will said, looking sceptically at the confines of the ship. At the furniture bolted or moulded into the floor.

"Need a minute to catch your breath?" Paige said, grinning. "In fact, are you sure you're actually fit enough to dance?"

Will bridled. "Obviously I am." She thrust her chin up. Dancing. How hard could it be? Placing her hand on Tarrant's hip, trying not to pay attention to the heat of it beneath her fingers, Will summoned up the ghosts of her old lessons. "I assume you don't know how to waltz, so we'll start simple—"

Tarrant reared back. "You assume wrong."

Pausing, Will looked at her. "*You* waltz?"

"Of course I do." She tossed her curls. "My dad is the Inter-Spoke Relations Minister. You think I could attend any of those snooty functions without knowing how to dance?"

Will had never *seen* Tarrant at any of said functions, but she didn't exactly frequent the *dancing* part of the parties. But, if Tarrant had been there, then that meant...had she somehow missed a pre-Lottery opportunity of getting to know Paige? Perhaps, if she had known...things could have been different.

"Okay," she replied, finally. Pulled them both into position. "I'll lead, then."

"No, you won't. *I'll* lead."

Will glowered, and Paige dimpled.

"What? I was taught that way. If you lead I'll only end up tripping you up. I'd bet any amount of credits that your fancy lessons taught you both ways."

Faster than the striking viper that had almost killed Ferdinand XIX's daughter in that ridiculous movie, Tarrant moved Will's hand from her waist to her shoulder. Towed her out into the larger room. Then she placed her fingers—slender, strong, ridged with calluses from gripping her pen too tightly—on Will's hip.

Like electricity. Exactly the same sensation as before. Without even the excuse of skin-to-skin contact this time, those same sparks flew. While Will was still struggling to adjust, Paige stepped sharply forward, sweeping her into a turn. Tugged off balance, Will stumbled, and was forced to rely on Paige's grip to keep her upright. She saw Paige suppress a grin, and annoyance flared hot in her chest.

Instinctively, she braced herself to pull, to wrest back control, but then—those words were still echoing in her mind. *Probably the last party we're ever going to make it to.* And the undercurrent of sadness she had seen there was enough to make her grit her teeth and yield. Move *with* her partner instead of resisting.

As soon as she made the decision, suddenly it became easy. All at once it flowed, and she could follow Paige effortlessly, matching her step for step. As one, they glided around the room. The world melted away. There was no Laika. There were no empty beds back in the Eden, pulsating with the grief and pain of those left behind. There was just Will and Paige, rivals and friends in equal measure, spinning together in unison.

Just as Will was beginning to grow comfortable, Paige released her waist and slid her other hand down her arm to tangle their fingers together. Letting Will spiral out into a spin before pulling her back in. Smiling that half-sardonic, half-genuine smile that she reserved for Will alone.

And Will, idiot that she was, couldn't help but smile back. Will Arrex dancing round the room in the arms of Paige Tarrant. Who would believe it?

"You're not *quite* as bad as I expected," she said, attempting a debonair smile.

"Honestly, I thought you'd be better," replied the other girl, and Will stiffened for a second before she saw the laughter dancing in Paige's eyes.

"At least I didn't look at you like you're faeces." She giggled again, and again the bizarre nature of the situation struck her. Will Arrex, *giggling*.

Paige laughed too. "Progress."

They turned once more, smooth as fencing partners—Will supposed they *had* been duelling all their lives—and then Paige came gently to a halt.

"Look," she said, pointing to the porthole.

Will followed the gesture. She had focused on the vidscreens so far, preferring to look back at the Eden rather than at the blackness ahead. But now there was a speck of white in the dark. Just a pinprick, wavering gently in place as the Laika rotated. But it was there. A star.

"A window of your own at last, Tarrant," Will answered drily, trying to cover the quaver in her voice. "You've made it."

"Shut up, Arrex," Tarrant replied, but there was no sting to it.

Will realised with a start that they had stopped moving, but Tarrant's hands were still on her. That her own arms were still wrapped halfway around Tarrant's neck, half-buried in curls softer than cloud.

Paige saw the movements of her eyes and seemed to come to the same conclusion: both of them dropped their hands, almost jumping away from each other.

"I guess you *can* dance, then," Will said. Why did it feel like there was something in her throat, making it hard to swallow?

Slowly, Paige nodded. "But...I don't think either of us are perfect, to be honest."

"No," Will agreed, with a strange sensation of relief. "I suppose we'd better do some more practice. To stop us getting rusty."

"Good idea," said Paige. "Same time tomorrow, then?"

"Yes." Will nodded, her cheeks far too warm for comfort. "Same time tomorrow."

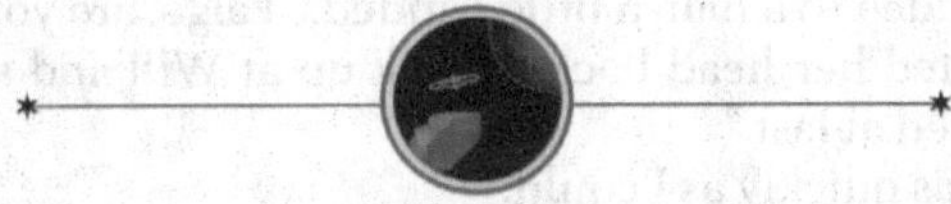

Another faint speck of light, far off in the distance. Will strained to make it out; her eyes would not adjust. But little by little the void in which she hung began to brighten. Closer the light came, and closer still, until the black became charcoal, then pewter. And finally, dim shapes appeared. Grassy knolls, bushes, trees.

She was in...a forest. Was that the word? An Old Terran biome lost to history in the Last War.

The very last of the darkness faded, and Will climbed gingerly to her feet. How *strange*. It could not have been more different from the smooth white halls of the Eden. All was rough-edged and chaotic, a riot of colour.

It was unexpectedly beautiful.

"Will!"

Someone was shouting her name. She spun in a circle, searching for the source of the noise.

The cry came again, more distant this time. "Will!"

That was Paige's voice.

Will didn't stop to think about it any further. She just ran. She loped through the trees, her strides eating up the ground beneath her feet. Despite the seemingly endless space, the lack of walls and corridors, the motion was surprisingly easy, and she grew more confident the further she went. The forest was a rich one: dozens of different species growing together, leaves intermingling in the canopy overhead.

"Paige?" she called.

"Will!" It was fainter now.

Altering her course to follow the sound, Will sped up.

The sound of running water met her ears, and all at once the grassy earth beneath her feet ran out—dropping abruptly away into a waterfall. The water, a clear, crystalline blue, hurried over the edge and tumbled ten metres down into a sparkling pool at the base of the falls.

And in that pool stood Paige, up to her waist in the water. Curls hanging heavy over her shoulders as water ran in rivulets from their tips.

Will skidded to a halt, a little winded. "Paige, are you alright?"

Paige tilted her head back to look up at Will and smiled. "So you've arrived at last."

"I came as quickly as I could."

"Not quickly enough." Despite her earlier shouting, Paige seemed calm now, and Will began to relax as well.

She stepped forward off the cliff edge and hopped down from boulder to boulder. Getting a little closer with every jump. "Why, are you in a hurry?"

Paige smiled, but it was without humour. "Always."

"You summoned me here," Will said, her phrasing oddly formal even to her own ears. "Say what you have to say."

Paige smirked, her chin tilting lower as she followed Will's descent. "We've been enemies for a long time, you and I."

"We have." Will landed with a splash in the pool. The water was shockingly cold, enough to knock the air from her lungs. She pulled in a sharp breath and started to wade towards Paige.

"And yet...somehow, I don't hate you."

The water flowed over her hips, lapping the base of her ribs as she neared the pool's centre. "I don't hate you so much anymore, either."

Paige came to meet her. Curls floated like seaweed on the water behind her. They halted inches away from each other. Will looked at the moisture beading on Paige's skin, in the flyaway strands of hair. Watched it glitter like diamonds as it caught the light.

"We're natural enemies," whispered Paige, her voice dropping into a whisper. Low, almost sensual.

"I know," murmured Will, taking another step closer. All but hypnotised by those amber-flecked eyes.

Paige mirrored her movements exactly, stepping forward until Will could see the pulse beating in her throat, count the freckles on her cheeks. She could reach out and touch her, if she wanted to. She could do so much more than touch her.

Her throat bobbing, Paige swallowed hard. "My people and yours have been at war for millennia."

And that was the first thing that felt really *wrong*. Will narrowed her eyes. It was a...weird thing to say. Unless Paige meant—Nobles and commoners, somehow? *War* was hardly an accurate description.

But nevertheless, her mouth opened, and she heard her own voice say, "The children of Elvendale have long cursed the name of Urgam Ulfsson."

It was then that Will realised she was repeating, word for word, Raenerillor's lines. Raenerillor the bloody elf from *Ruination of Yesterday*.

Will looked anew at Paige, and focused for the first time on her clothes. Instead of the usual iron-grey Spoke Six uniform, she was wearing—Will squinted, and they finally swam into focus—leather armour with rough homespun cloth beneath. The only iron-grey thing in sight was the gigantic battleaxe on her back.

With a sense of foreboding, Will looked down at her own body, and found without surprise that she was clad head to toe in leafy armour.

She *was* Raenerillor. And Tarrant was Urgam, apparently.

And this was the waterfall scene, and they were about to—

Bloody hell.

With a ragged gasp of horror, Will started upright. She patted at her body—the usual icy grey jumpsuit. Not a leaf in sight.

Had she been about to *kiss* Tarrant in that dream?

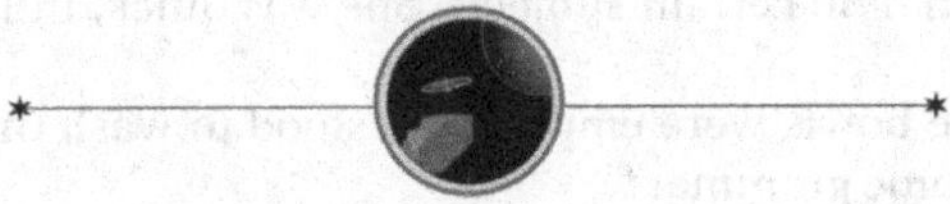

"Now. Focus. *Quid est temperatus?*"

"*Fervens es,*" replied Paige, confidently enough.

"*Fervens est.* When the subject is *he* or *she* or *it*, it's always *est. Es* is pretty much just for 'you' statements. *Ille est gentil, tu es gentil.* Right?"

"*Sic, sic.*"

"*Et si diu relinquimus, quid erit temperatura?*"

Paige grinned impishly and put her hand to her forehead in a mock swoon. *"Propter te polenta frigida est!"*

"Etiam! Mirabile!" Will offered her student a high five. "You can probably drop the *tu*, though. Latin likes to leave out the pronouns most of the time."

Paige groaned and shook her head. "The vocab is easy compared to the stupid declensions."

"I know." Will nodded, not without sympathy. She remembered the frustration when she was young, fighting back tears so her tutor would not see. "But isn't it worth it to be able to insult me in multiple languages? Anyway, *nunc ad polentan revertamur.*"

Paige rolled her eyes. "I don't see why we began with porridge."

"Because on this ship, every day begins with porridge," Will said primly. *"Nunc, Paige, quid est temperatus?"*

Paige dipped an experimental fingertip into her bowl. *"Non nimium calidum, non nimium frigidum.* But that won't be the case if we don't eat soon."

The Latin lessons had begun when Paige slapped down a copy of Julius Caesar's *Gallic Wars* on the table. "Right. You speak Latin, like a good little Noble. I need to speak Latin if I'm going to study Terran history once we're back. So you're going to teach me."

Will had raised her eyebrows—*How do you even know we're going to make it back?*—but she saw the determination in those eyes and the question remained unspoken. Tarrant was not giving up, and Will could not ask her to do so.

Less than four days in and Paige was already nearly conversational on certain subjects. She was quick. Intimidatingly so.

Once the bowls were empty, Will stood to wash them. "Want to go over some grammar?"

"No, I've had enough for this morning." Paige stood up, stretched out her arms. "Think I'm going to go for a run."

Will nodded and rolled her neck, listening to the vertebrae crackle.

Paige padded away in the direction of her bedroom and rummaged for her gym clothes, shucking her standard-issue jumpsuit without even closing the door. Flinching at the sight of the first brown shoulder, Will averted her eyes, trying to tamp down the furious rush of blood in her veins, praying Tarrant hadn't spotted her looking. Why hadn't she shut the bloody *door*?

She tried to busy herself with the two emptied bowls—but the thump of the jumpsuit fabric on the floor called her back as surely as a siren's song, and she saw—she saw—the rise of the white undershirt over the smooth expanse of skin, dotted with the ever-present freckles. Pulling higher, revealing the slight bulge of the stomach and the flare of the hips, and higher, the beginning of the ribcage, the—

And Will looked away.

It was getting harder and harder to ignore whatever this was.

Sure, she had always been able to admit that Paige was attractive, objectively. But even Panset Pall was *objectively* attractive, and Will had certainly never wanted to do anything with *her*.

But the more she got to know Tarrant—fierce, angry, blazingly intelligent, sweet, self-sacrificing Tarrant—the harder it became to deny it.

There was something there.

With blissful ignorance, Paige emerged from her room clad in a fresh undershirt and shorts, and headed for the gym.

Heart in her mouth, Will watched her go. Paige learned with a speed that was frightening. Her passion was infectious; she fascinated because she found the world fascinating. She could open a book about dusty Old Terran nonsense and show you gemstones. She could take a centuries-old movie that ought to have been absolute trash—green men romancing their little blonde rivals—and she could make Will see the magic in it. She made Will *furious*, but she made her laugh, too. She was sanctimonious and overly opinionated, but she was also electrifying and exciting. Through Paige's eyes, Will sometimes caught glimpses of a new world. A world where anything seemed possible.

Yes, there was something there. Regrettably.

Ugh. Will knew she just needed to stop *dwelling* on it. Constantly obsessing over it wasn't going to do anything but make it worse.

But it wasn't like there was anything else to *do* in this cursed little box.

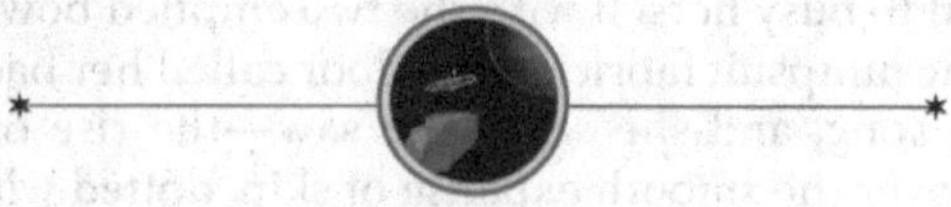

"Come *on*, Paige. Let's have a game."

Will tapped the vidscreen on the table in front of her to bring up the board, but Paige only grunted, nose deep in a book.

"Or Othello, if you don't feel like chess," Will offered gallantly. She was bored stiff, and she *needed* some company. She would play pretty much anything at this point.

Another grunt. A page turned.

"Yutnori? Drafts? Weiqi? Glider-Racer Champion?" Will hurled out suggestions at a rate that she *knew* would be annoying, but she was past caring.

Everything she could humanly think of doing, every means of passing the time, she had done. Taken a shower, gone for a run, struggled through some calculus lessons—teaching herself entirely unaided was a nightmare—a session with the weights, three chapters of a dog-eared textbook on the life of Genghis Khan stolen from Paige, a practice oration session to keep her hand in, and finally getting on the bike and cycling until her legs were limp as noodles. And all that was just today. In the past twenty-one days she had explored every possibility her brain could drum up.

The boredom was going to drive her insane before the sixth week of their journey was over.

"Mahjong, Monopoly, Afrikan Tähti...are any of these jumping out at you?" Will continued to scroll through the vidscreen's games menu. "Towerbend, Snakes and Ladders..."

Paige did not seem even to hear her this time.

At this stage, Will would have settled for a staring contest. Anything, *anything*, to look into the eyes of another human being and have a conversation.

Though Paige Tarrant possessed many excellent qualities, when she was not engaged in direct competition or fangirling over ancient films from Old Terra, she was a giant bookworm. Zero conversational skills once she had an open page in front of her. Will had spent a great deal of time the past few weeks mulling over Paige's unexpected kindness, loyalty, and—lately—attractiveness, but there were still an awful lot of *flaws* hiding beneath that big bushy head of hair.

"Alright, we'll compromise," said Will, with infinite generosity. "How about Dacii si Romanii? You must love that, right? It's about *Rome*."

Paige did not look up, but there was a certain tightness around her eyes now.

Will knew she should stop needling, but she couldn't help herself. Even a fight was better than more of the same *nothing*. It was intolerable, to talk and talk to the one companion you possessed, and never receive any response. Sometimes, when Paige ignored her, Will was seized with a deep, existential dread that she had ceased to exist at all.

"How about..." She was nearing the end of the options menu. "Uh, Sugoroku? Or Komikan? I'll even let you be the puma."

And that was what finally did it. Will could almost hear the last thread of Paige's patience finally snapping. Her head whipped up, eyes bright with irritation. "*God*, Will, can you not leave me alone for *one* minute?"

Seeing that contempt, Will's own temper flared, hot and ugly. Paige was sick of her, and she was suddenly, violently sick of Paige. "I'm *so* sorry. It must be awful to be stuck with me. You *poor* thing."

Paige huffed. "Now that you mention it, yeah, it's pretty awful sometimes."

Will slapped her hands down on the table. "If I'm so unbearable, why did you choose me as your partner?"

"Why did I—you're seriously asking this *now*?" Tarrant stared at her from over the top of her book.

The rush of anger was like endorphins. The thrill of something actually *happening*. Her heart pounding with a fierce, exultant delight, Will glared. "Yes. When else should I ask?"

With a huff, Paige shook out her halo of curls. "I don't want to talk about it, Arrex."

Even in her anger, Will could not help noticing the light hitting the different loops and whorls of that hair, and remembering how soft it had felt beneath her fingers.

She shoved that urge down, pushed it firmly away. This was an *argument*. Fighting was what she and Tarrant did best. They would both be happier after the storm broke and the tension was gone.

"What else have we got to talk about?" she demanded. "What else have we got to do? We have to talk about *something* or we're just going to sit here until our oxygen runs out!"

"Look, Will, I don't want to do this. Not now." Paige's eyes were already inching back towards her book.

Seeing the danger, Will took a sharp step forward, pulling Paige's focus back to her. "Why the hell not?"

Paige snarled under her breath and threw her book down onto the sofa with uncharacteristic violence. "You're like...like a dog with a bone!"

Finally, Will paused. "Like what?"

"It's...it was a saying." Paige was already calming herself again, reaching out for the book to make sure it had suffered no damage. "Europea and Meso-Americania, mostly. It means that you don't let things *drop*."

"Fine," Will shrugged. "So I'm a dog with a bone. I've been called worse things. But come on. Tell me why you picked me."

Paige took a moment to compose herself, placing her book back down more gently this time. "I...chose you as my partner for the same reason I swapped with Cara."

A complete non-answer. Will exhaled. She wouldn't be fobbed off, not now. "You swapped to save Cara. I know that."

The look Paige gave her was almost pitying. "You honestly think that's it?"

Will was almost ready to scream. "You told me that it was for Cara *and* me. But I have no idea what that means. How many times do I have to ask before you'll tell me?"

"If you don't get it now you're an absolute *moron*."

With a snarl of frustration, Will pounded a fist into her own thigh. "Whatever it is, just spit it out, Tarrant."

"It *means* I thought—I don't know, I thought maybe even someone as prickly and up her own *ass* as you didn't deserve to go through this alone." Paige's voice was growing louder and louder with every word. "I guess I thought I was the closest thing you had to—to *someone*—and I wanted to be there for you." By the time the tirade had finished, Tarrant was nearly crying. Tears shone in her eyes, making them luminous, and her breath was coming too fast.

"Why?" Will demanded, advancing on Tarrant. So close she could feel the other girl's anger like a physical force. "Why do you *care*?"

Tarrant planted both hands on her shoulders and shoved her away. "Because I care about *you!*"

Will was left stunned and silent. Confronted with something so utterly beyond what she had expected—what she had prepared responses for—all of her years of debating with Tarrant were suddenly useless. She had no idea what to say.

The moment stretched and stretched, taut as a bowstring from one of Tarrant's ridiculous fantasy films, until finally it snapped. Will took the only recourse left to her. Obeyed the oldest instinct she had. Will turned her back on Paige, and fled.

She bolted the length of the ship—a short enough distance, thank goodness—and hurtled into the safety of her own cubicle. She turned to close the door, fingers trembling, and locked eyes with Paige, who was still staring at her in mute, furious grief. Will's breath caught in her throat, but she didn't stop. It cost her everything she had left, but she managed to close the door. To shut Paige out.

When it was done, she leaned against the closed door for a long time, the plastic cold against her face. She listened, but despite the paper-thin walls, she heard nothing.

With the benefit of space, of a little breathing room, it began to sink in what she had just done. Dug and dug until Paige finally snapped. She'd confessed—Will hardly knew what. She had confessed *something*, and Will had responded by shutting the door in her face.

Paige was her co-pilot, her one companion in their exile. The only person in Will's life right now. But before that, hadn't she—hadn't she *already* been the only one in Will's life who really mattered? It was Paige who Will had measured herself against. It was Paige who Will had watched without ceasing. Listening to every word she said to her friends, picking up each one and turning it over in her mind like it was something precious, something to be analysed and remembered.

Will flopped down on her bed and faced the wall. The wall no thicker than cardboard, lighter than air, behind which Paige slept every night. Less than a heartbeat away.

Will lay on her bed and tried to re-evaluate the past twelve years of her life.

There *was* something there. It was undeniable. Something more than the competition she had been so hyperfixated on.

Fascination, certainly. Respect, too. And now something else, this indefinable *more* that had appeared over the past few weeks. Or perhaps it had always been there, just beneath the surface, and she was only now beginning to realise it.

In many ways, Paige had always been the only one that counted.

CHAPTER 17

Laika 15 – Day 21 – 22:18

The hours stretched, and Will remained within the safety of her room. The silence from outside gave way to the clatter of the gyroscope's wheel. Will stayed curled up on the bed, knees to her chest, thoughts drifting in circles.

Tarrant, once an enemy, had become a friend. And then…an ally, more important than any of the friends Will had left behind. The sole trusted face in a sea of traitors. Watching Paige and celebrating victory or defeat in their little skirmishes had long been an outlet in a life devoid of any others. Her eyes narrowed in irritation, her full lips compressing in furious rage, those had been points to be scored. Seeing her laugh with the others at lunchtime had been different. A bitterer taste. But now those smiles were shared with Will, too. Somehow, Paige had seen fit to promote her from the rank of hated to tolerated—and now, to some hazy realm above even that.

She had leaned against Will. She had relied on her. She had *chosen* her, of all the other pilots.

And Will had chosen her too.

The noise of the gyroscope was followed in due course by the pattering of water from the bathroom. When finally quiet reigned once more, Will wondered if Paige would knock on her door.

Come on, Arrex, let's talk this out, she'd say.

And Will would say—she would say—she had no idea what she would say.

I think maybe my obsession with you ran a little deeper than I thought.

I think maybe I always liked you.

She was trapped in a little box with Paige Tarrant, flying thousands of miles further from home with every day that passed, and yet the gulf between the two of them felt wider even than the distance they had covered together.

What was she supposed to say? What were the right words to choose? There was no tutor here to coach her for this test. No team of staff for her to fall back on. If she failed here, the failure would be hers and hers alone.

It was almost midnight when Will finally opened the door again.

Paige swung to face her, hair still clinging damp around her face.

Will waited, but she said nothing.

"So." Will cleared her throat. "Sorry for...you know. That."

A slight incline of the head was her only answer.

"I...we never had any dinner. Want me to cook?"

Paige regarded her with a flat stare. Will deflated. There would be no simple return to normalcy. Paige wanted it all laid out there, out in the open, and Will would have no choice but to comply.

"About before...I..."

"Well?"

Sometimes conversations with Tarrant were like a fencing duel, thrusts and parries flying back and forth almost faster than Will could keep track of. Other times they were more like chess, with careful deliberation before every move. This discussion was one of the latter, and Will knew that she had to weigh her words with care. There could be no untruths here.

"I came here for you, too," she said at last.

Paige raised an eyebrow.

"I only entered the Lottery because you gave me the idea. You said it wouldn't ever affect me. So I thought—well, screw Tarrant, right? I'll show her I'm not the posh little Noble she thinks I am."

Her icy control finally broken, Paige gave a weak little laugh. "Yeah, that sounds about right."

"I thought I hated you," Will said, a little miserably. "I thought that for so long."

"Me too," replied Paige, and then for a long time neither of them spoke a word.

Will wondered if she should reach out. Touch Paige on the arm, the shoulder, the fingers perhaps. Interlace their fingers as they had on the gangplank, so long ago now. Forge themselves once more into a team. Ready to take on the world, or at least one measly little Laika.

Before she could summon the nerve, Paige broke the silence. "Entering the Lottery was about winning the Surveys, though, right?"

"Oh, yeah," answered Will, caught off guard. "Completely. But sticking it to you was an extra little bit of spice. And following through...being *good*. That was all you."

Paige snickered, for real this time, and Will joined in. The stalemate was finally over. The breach was healed.

"What do you want for dinner?" Paige asked suddenly, and Will relaxed fully. Normality had returned in full force.

"How about cubed and fried?" she suggested. The nutribars never changed, but at least the presentation could be altered.

"Sure."

And the two of them went to work, chopping and dicing, sprinkling in the odd dash of their limited spice reserve. Taking it slowly as they did with everything, here in the finite little universe where time was the only resource they had in abundance. And if their fingers met once or twice on the chopping board, or if their eyes met over the frying pan...well, what was so wrong with that?

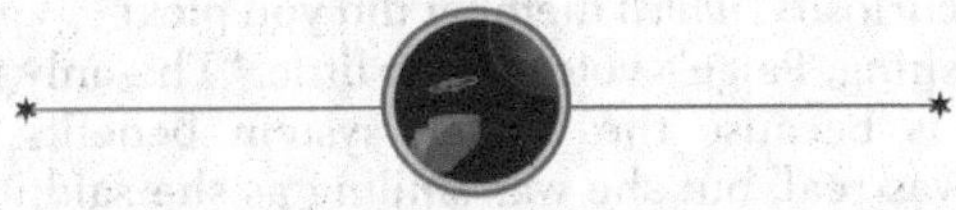

Once that initial step of realisation had taken place, Will found it difficult to hold back. There had been some fundamental block in her mind, a trace of the old *Arrex vs Tarrant* still lingering on. The last frayed thread of a once mighty cable that held back the tide of Paige-related emotion. But now, at long last, the floodgates were open, and Will was utterly helpless.

She grinned like an idiot at Paige over their porridge. She smirked like a moron as Paige cycled on the exercise bike. She even smiled when the door to her room was closed at night—the only time they were apart.

"So you never *hated* me, right?" she asked for what was probably the seventh time.

"No," said Paige, with enduring good humour, twisting a dishcloth over the mug in her hands as she dried it. "I didn't *hate* you. It was a respectful sort of loathing."

Will swilled a fork through the suds and gave it another scrub. "You were the only one at school I ever took seriously. The only one with any brains."

Paige attempted to glower, but Will didn't miss the hint of red in her cheeks. "A compliment doesn't count if you put down other people while you're giving it."

"You were the best out of them, then," Will amended easily. She could afford to be magnanimous now. "They're good people. Especially Cara. But you were my favourite."

The red was no longer a hint; vermillion blossomed like a flower, just beneath the surface. "Cara's a wonderful person," said Paige, hastily turning away to the cupboard where the mugs were stored.

"She is. And I was wondering," she added, feeling particularly daring, "who your family voted for in the Surveys?"

Paige sighed. "It's not much of a vote when it's picking one member of a hereditary plutocrat family versus a different member of the same hereditary plutocrat family."

"It's the world we live in." Will's voice was light. She was almost certain she knew the answer, but she wanted to hear Paige say it. "But out of curiosity, *which* member did you pick?"

Eyes flashing, Paige's voice rose a little. "The only reason you don't care is because the broken system benefits you." The sentiment was real, but she was smiling as she said it. And Will thought that maybe, if it was *Paige* who was campaigning for political reform, maybe even an Arrex could be induced to change her views.

"Come on, Paige. Throw me a bone." She reached out and brushed her hand against Paige's arm. Very light, very cautious. But undeniably real. Undeniably there.

The words had been calculated to disarm just as much as the touch had. As far as winning points with Tarrant went, there was nothing that could beat throwing in an Old Terran idiom. And it worked; Paige laughed. And Will felt the same sweet rush of endorphins that had been her goal and her reward for the past week. It was shocking how liberating it was. How joyous. To *choose* the person you were living for, instead of serving those you were born to.

It had been an eight-day high, and Will had not yet come back down from the first wave of it.

Paige was still chuckling. "You've been studying!"

"I *do* listen."

"We voted..." and then Paige paused, to drag out the suspense.

"Come on," pled Will.

"For you, obviously!"

And then Paige reached into the bowl of water and splashed her, and Will shrieked in surprise and delight and launched a counter-attack. And the droplets flew through that little cabin like rainbow rain, refracting just as beautifully as Year Change Festival fairy lights covered with coloured paper.

Paige was laughing, water speckling her hair like jewels, and as Will looked at her, her heart twisted in her chest.

And every fleeting glance, every tentative touch—it all seemed to push her further and further down that path. Will could feel herself changing. Unfurling, little by little, into something different—the underlying structure remaining the same, but the edges blurring, sharp points softening.

It was strange, to be discovering something so new at the very end of her life.

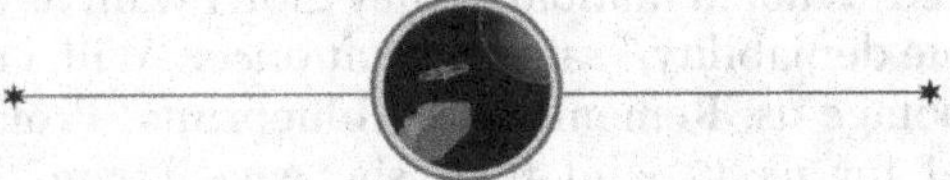

"I'm *working* on it," snapped Paige.

Will huffed. That was no news at all. *"And?"*

"Still on the stupid loading screen." Paige stabbed at the vidscreen with a forefinger. Nothing changed. The loading wheel continued its slow, stately revolutions, utterly indifferent to their sufferings.

"It's been loading since *yesterday*," Will retorted. "I thought this junk was meant to be state of the art. How has it taken twenty-four hours?"

"How should I know?" The other girl sounded almost petulant. "Probably the Noble Council cut the computer department's funding or something. Take it up with your dad."

Choosing to let that jibe pass her by, Will peered at her screen. They had been checking in on the control room vidscreens every half hour since their session the morning prior, and still the loading wheel rotated. It had been a very long day, and tempers were fraying. Despite her snappishness, Paige didn't mean it—or not *much*, anyway.

"The system says everything is fine. The sensors are all working, and the computer is apparently in perfect condition." She leaned forward. The task manager informed her that the onboard computer was dealing with a dozen things concurrently with no lag at all—everything from course corrections to the latest load of laundry—and the only thing to suffer was the loading of the detailed pilot's manual. And *detailed* as it might be, with tech even halfway as good as anything on the Eden, it should have been loaded in a minute or less.

The Laika systems were supposed to be the best Eden had to offer. So what was going wrong?

"It's like they just locked us out," she muttered, mostly to herself.

Beside her, Paige shot bolt upright. "That's it," she said suddenly. "They didn't give us access. That's what it has to be."

Will sighed. It hadn't been a serious comment, but Paige was becoming paranoid. "Why would they even bother putting a file on here called 'detailed manual' if they didn't want us to have it?"

"Plausible deniability," said Paige at once. "Will, I swear, they *want* to sabotage us. Remember the blueprints? Professor Clark prevaricated for *weeks*, and then she gave Loysa that pile of manure, and Lain—"

Her words choked themselves off, but Will understood perfectly. There was no need to say any more.

"But," she replied, endeavouring to make her voice as gentle as she could, "the Laika Programme is so *public*. It gets huge amounts of funding from every spoke. Everyone knows it's our best shot at a long-term solution. Why would they sabotage it?"

"They're sending *children* instead of actual experts," Paige argued. "And they barely trained us at all—just stuck us in simulations and spoon-fed us enough information to keep us quiet."

"They can't afford to waste working adults on something with such a high casualty rate," Will said flatly. It was blunt almost to the point of being cruel, but Paige would listen to nothing else, and Will didn't want this conspiracy theory to take root in her head. It would do neither of them any good. "Thirty-six people every twenty-five years is too many. But when it's kids it's not so bad. The parents can just...have more." And her own throat tightened, as she thought of another little blonde head resting on her own pillow. A new Arrex to bear the weight of that long legacy.

Shaking her head firmly, Paige tapped her fingers against her leg in a nervous rhythm. "I think Loysa was right. The casualty rate *shouldn't* be so high."

"Five hundred years in a space station with a population of three thousand hasn't exactly done wonders for humanity's progress," answered Will, who had listened to thousands of lectures from Xavier on the importance of not allowing the Eden to backslide—in terms of population, education, or anything else. "We've maintained the standard of living we had before the evacuation, but we haven't gone far beyond. You know that."

"They literally travelled through space to get to Amalthea. How can we have lost *that* tech?"

"You heard Professor Clark same as I did." Will shrugged. "Lots of things were lost in the Last War. All the terraforming stuff. Why not space travel, too? Maybe the seedship was the last one."

Her fingers increasing in tempo, Paige turned the full force of her frown on Will. "Why are you always so uncritical? You just accept whatever they tell you!"

"I don't," retorted Will. "I just don't see the point in second-guessing everything when there's *nothing* we can do."

Paige snorted derisively. "Or it's just because you benefit from—"

"Oh, would you drop it?" Will growled, real annoyance surfacing at last. "I'm here on the stupid Laika with you, aren't I? Proof of my privilege, right there!"

"Fine." Paige subsided. "But don't you think there are just a *few* too many problems? I mean, other than Professor Clark, not *one* returned pilot came to talk to us during training. How weird is that? People come back, and they go 'work in the Laika Programme', but *do* they?"

Will forced herself to speak calmly. "There's no point questioning every tiny thing. We can't fix it from out here."

"Maybe. But if we're...you know, *doomed*...don't you want to know the truth?"

Raising one shoulder in half a shrug, Will shook her head. "Of course I do. But wanting it isn't going to get us anywhere."

You had to accept your fate, or you'd drive yourself insane fighting it. Somewhere along the way down the corridor that led to the Laika's cabin, Will had realised that.

As she sagged back in her seat the rhythmic motion of Paige's hand finally stilled. "I suppose so." She gave the underside of the desk an ill-natured kick with one foot. "But the *least* they could do is give us access to the pilot's manual."

Cautiously, Will reached out. Placed her hand very lightly on Paige's arm. And where once Paige might have slapped Will's hand away or stormed off, she half-smiled, and leaned into the touch. Something inside Will swelled up, and her eyes prickled. She'd made Paige feel better; she'd done something *real*. She had made a difference.

"Why don't we," and here Will paused, casting about for a suitable change of subject, something they could actually *do*, "why don't we go over the mission statement again?"

A heavy sigh from Paige in response. "Because we already did that three times."

"It can't hurt to do it again, right?"

"I guess not."

Paige's enthusiasm was lacking, but it was enough. Will clicked through the files on the third vidscreen, leaving the loading wheel still spinning in solitary splendour on the second, and pulled the mission statement up.

The file had unlocked on launch day, but Will's focus had been on other things. Making the most of her last chance for radio contact with her parents. Unpacking, adjusting. And then—Paige, of course. The biggest distraction of the lot.

But well over a month had passed, and no stray asteroid or engine failure had come for them. They were still alive. Despite the odds, and despite Will's own misgivings, life continued. This was their new reality, and it was time they started to deal with it.

So the new routine of spending the morning in the control room had begun. Trawling through the files, trying to round out the scanty education they had received in the Training Centre.

Will pulled in a breath and then tapped the icon on the vidscreen. A now familiar video popped up, along with a string of documents that arranged themselves along the bottom of the screen, ready to be enlarged.

"Year Four-Five-Three Laika Programme, Laika Fifteen, destination Deimos of Mars."

The voice was male. Dispassionate, almost robotic in its delivery. Not one Will knew.

"Deimos is Mars's smaller moon. It has a radius of six kilometres and no atmosphere. The Deimos terraforming module was launched by Paudhe, a corporation funded by the Oceaniasian government. They favoured the total conversion model over the more standard biodome."

At this, the fourth time of listening, the words and their order were more than familiar. Even the stilted voice of the speaker— the drawn-out vowels, the clipped consonants.

"The plans that we inherited from the Oceaniasians suggest that the aim was to use a miniaturised inverse Dyson Sphere: solar panels on the exterior, a breathable atmosphere on the interior. According to the blueprints, the construction robots will have spent the first century building the sphere using materials from the regolith, and the following century cultivating the surface with plant life. The moon ought to be in a mature state now, ready for settlers."

The now well-known litany continued, and Will brought up a few of the different documents. A route plan, with a blinking dot to signal their approximate location. An ancient blueprint with the Paudhe logo at the top. A fact sheet on Deimos itself.

Swiping to pull the latter across to her own vidscreen, Paige began to scroll.

"The gravity is three thousand times less than the Terran gravity we use on Eden."

Will attempted to imagine existing in gravity like that, and failed. "Time to crack out the steel-soled boots, I suppose."

"And the escape velocity..." Paige giggled. "Will, if there's no sphere and we jump, there's a non-zero chance we just end up drifting through space."

Will wrinkled her nose. "Why on earth would they pick this place to terraform?"

"It was during the Last War." Paige shrugged. "Scattershot approach. They were sending these automated operations everywhere they could."

The robotic-voiced man was still talking, but Will had heard it all before. There was nothing new in the final ten minutes of the recording.

With one last glance at the loading pilot's manual, Paige stretched and stood. "You want first go on the gyroscope?"

"Nah. I was thinking I might rewatch *Ruination of Ereyesterday* this morning."

Paige screwed her face up. "Ugh. The prequels are the *worst* ones."

"I like the stuff about elf society. Sue me."

"Why don't we compromise and watch *Ruination's Nychthemeron*? You can't go wrong with the grand finale to the whole franchise."

That was no compromise. "*Paige*. It's just a four-hour battle scene."

"Ugh." Paige rolled her eyes. "Then *I'll* take first go on the gyroscope and you can go and empathise with the rich little elves in their ivory towers."

She flounced from the room. Will sniggered and followed, glancing at the porthole as she passed. The view was unchanged: the absolute darkness of space, punctuated only by faint stars floating slowly past like minnows in a stream.

"Look," Paige said, voice dropping to a whisper. As though she was speaking of something sacred. "A new leaf."

As they leaned in together to look at the tiny green bud, their cheeks were almost touching.

"Imagine what spring would be like on Terra," Paige murmured. Her breath was warm against Will's skin.

"The parks on the Eden..." Will suggested, but Paige shook her head. One of her curls, dislodged by the motion, brushed Will's neck, and goosebumps rose in its wake.

"It wouldn't be like seeing a hydroponics lab come into season, or even the trees in the parks. On Terra...you'd see a whole *planet* bloom at once."

Will tried to imagine it. The worlds she had seen on the vidscreen, in the sim room, the forest from her dream. None of it could compare to seeing something with your own eyes. Touching it with your own fingers, as she could touch Arthur's minuscule offering. A small fragment of spring, even here in the Laika. Well worth the sacrifice of her baggage allowance.

"We might," she said. "Who knows what we'll find at the terraformer?"

For once, she left the *if we get there* unsaid.

Paige's smile kindled brighter with fresh hope, and Will grinned back. Just like Arthur, Paige was a little ray of spring, too.

CHAPTER 18

Laika 15 – Day 52 – 16:21

Will was flicking through episodes of an old Spoke Two comedy show and Paige was lifting weights in the gym when the vidscreen went white. At first Will's only feeling was one of annoyance. Stupid thing, glitching in the middle of a sketch. Then came a pang of fear—if the vidscreen broke only seven weeks in, what would they *do* for the next four years? How would they stay sane?

And then came a voice—familiar, but electrifying in this context. "Laika pilots."

Staring at the vidscreen, Will answered despite her disbelief. "Professor Clark?"

Paige came skidding out of the gym, eyes wild. "How is she— we're *thousands* of miles out of range!"

"Laika pilots, please stand by for a video message from Command."

Will sat up straighter, and Paige crept to her side, both of them silenced by this new twist. A broadcast—or a recording, for surely no broadcast could reach them here—nearly two months after launch day? It made no sense. What new information could be shared here that could not be shared before?

The screen flickered again, and a heavily bearded man appeared onscreen. He wore the same shade of brown sported by all Laika Programme staff, but his face was not a familiar one. Nor were the clothes themselves quite right. The lapels of his jumpsuit were oddly wide, with red and white accents at their edges. His hair, too, was outlandish. Swept up and back from his face in complicated braids with more red and white fabric woven into them. Will stared at him as he looked gravely into the camera, and tried to think who he could be. Surely anyone with such a bizarre sense of fashion would be well known. And why would Professor Clark delegate her broadcast to someone else? The woman was a control freak. None of this made any sense.

"Hello, Laika pilots," the man said, and his accent was not that of the Eden; he sounded more like a character from an Old Terran period drama. "I am afraid that I have bad news for you."

Will exchanged an apprehensive glance with Paige.

"I will be blunt; there is not sufficient fuel for you to return home."

Her mouth gaping in a silent protest, Will started up from the sofa. *What?*

"There will be no return journey."

Surely she had misheard. Surely.

And then the man opened his mouth again, and the words fell so thick and fast from his lips that Will was left reeling.

"The ancients were masters of spacecraft, but their terraforming tools were still theoretical. The training you received was, regrettably, fiction. There is nothing to investigate. No sites to monitor. The Laika Programme is an effort in social cohesion, designed to provide a focus for the Eden."

No. *No.* Will sat in silence, wrestling with it, sinking beneath this horrible new truth. Loysa had been right. Lain had been *right.*

"Your fuel will run out within the next two hours, but as promised, your life-support systems will be sufficient to support you for a period of up to five years." He spoke so calmly. Like he was discussing crop yields or tramcar wait times. "We hope you will appreciate this extra time given to you."

All those simulations, the training, the lessons. All of it a lie. A pretence so that the pilots would not sound the alarm before launch.

An exercise in social cohesion. What did that even mean? Hope, Will supposed. Scraps of it drip-fed into the mouth of the starving Eden: a *someday*, just enough of a promise to keep a leaky ship afloat.

"Please know that we are sorry, Laika pilots. We hope you can accept what we ask of you for the good of the Eden, and make peace with it. Go softly into the night, and take with you our thanks."

The vidscreen flickered again, and the comedy show was back, the actors' mouths frozen on pause, jaws gaping wide in strange, unnatural laughter. Will's breath was wheezing in her chest.

He said he was *sorry*.

The Laika wasn't just a box. Not even a simple prison cell.

It was a grave.

"It can't be true," protested Will, a strange sound in that long silence. "It doesn't make *sense*."

Paige's voice was flat. Frighteningly so. "Really? Makes perfect sense to me."

Finally, for the first time since Professor Clark's words had intruded, Will looked across at Paige. Her face was as blank as her voice had been.

"But—it was all so *detailed*. The Oceaniasians, the sphere. Paudhe. Why would they *bother* making all of that up?"

Lifting one shoulder and letting it fall again, Paige averted her eyes. "You've got plenty of time to perfect your story when you don't have any actual missions to plan."

"But why—"

"*I* don't know, do I?" Paige flared up at last. "In case any of the parents ask where their kids are going. In case the media asks. In case *we* asked. There are a million reasons why it's better to string out the lie for as long as possible."

Letting her head fall into her hands, Will tried to hold back the wave of despair that threatened to engulf her. It was *cruel*. To think that they had done this, for hundreds of years. Lied and killed and lied again. The people of Eden had handed over their children as sacrifices over and over, secure in the knowledge that it was for the good of all. For their future.

And all of it had been false.

"There were survivors," she whispered, weak as water. Hrue Lipson. Professor Clark. She'd seen the footage of them leaving their ship with her own eyes.

"Faked," Paige said harshly.

"Maybe," Will whispered, struggling now, "we should try radioing for help?"

"What would be the point?"

Will wasn't used to being the voice of hope. She was the cynic. Paige was the idealist. The one who had so much love to give that she would love anything, even Old Terran nonsense everyone else had forgotten. But now the roles had reversed, and Will had no idea what to do.

Paige gave a little laugh. There was no humour in the sound. "Did you see his clothes?"

"What?"

"His *clothes*. No one dresses like that." Paige hammered her fist into the cushion. "How *old* was that fucking video?"

Will stilled.

"They—they didn't even have the decency to record us a new video. They've been using the same one for god knows how long. *Centuries*."

And this time, Will had no answer at all.

There was no hope. No bright future. No chance that humans would again walk through meadows and forests and look up at a blue sky above them.

They would dwell in the Eden forever, and every twenty-five years thirty-six hopeful children would have their lives cut short. And it would be that way—bleak and hopeless and empty— forever.

And Will and Paige would be slaughtered, along with all the rest. Left with nothing but a pitiful five years and the *thanks* of their murderers as a parting gift.

The silence fell like mist from the sprinklers in the orchards, and it hung heavy over them. Will tried to give Paige space, but when dinner time came she found the other girl in the gym, sitting in the bottom of the gyroscope, pushing herself idly back and forth.

Will leaned against the wall and slid slowly down until she was sitting at the gyroscope's side. "It's been two hours."

"Hm." Paige barely responded.

"The engines are...they're still going, Paige." Will had been watching the readings in the control room. Despite the words of the ancient man in the video, the axe had not yet fallen. Laika Fifteen was still on course. Was it possible it was a hoax? Some sort of sick test? Will had no idea.

Paige raised a hand to shade her eyes, hiding her expression. "Give it a while. We'll be drifting for a long time. Why rush to start?" She was trying to be funny, but her voice was so hollow it made Will feel sick.

Will tensed her jaw. She could go back to the vidscreens, keep on watching—but Paige clearly wanted to close the door on the control room, and Will was in no mood to fight. "Paige...you can talk to me, you know. Are you...okay?"

Paige shrugged, as though the answer didn't matter. "Loysa was right." She stopped there, but the unsaid second half of the sentence hung in the air between them. *And so was Lain.* Better a quick death than a lingering one. "I was wondering if you knew," Paige said, with the same tone of almost carefree detachment.

Nihilism, Will supposed. If she could find a little of that within herself right now, that accusation might hurt less. "If I *knew*?"

"About...all this."

Sharply, Will pulled away from the gyroscope, increasing the distance between them by a factor of three. "You really think I'd let all this happen if I knew?"

"No," Paige said slowly. "No, doesn't make sense that you'd sign yourself up if you knew."

Will's lungs contracted. "That's not what I asked."

For the first time, Paige looked up and met her eyes. Seemed to realise, finally, the accusation she had so casually dropped. "Oh— Will, I didn't mean—obviously I know that you wouldn't have let this happen to anyone, if you knew."

With a weak smile, Will tried to wave it away like it hadn't hurt. It was a horrible suspicion, but maybe it was a fair one. There was clearly a conspiracy aboard the Eden, and *someone* must know.

There was a pause, and then Paige broke the quiet, her thoughts clearly running along a similar track. "Do you think your father knows?"

Instinctively, Will stiffened and opened her mouth to deny it, to snap out something vehement and cutting that would wound Paige, teach her not to doubt *Xavier Arrex*—but then she stopped. She thought of her father's horror when she decided to enter the Lottery. His attempts to dissuade her, even after her ticket had been drawn.

Getting on board those ships isn't something that can be undone. Once you're outside of Eden's walls, I can't help you.

Could she say with absolute, ironclad certainty, that he had not known? Could she look Paige in the eyes and make that promise?

The fight went out of her and she slumped back against the gyroscope's edge. "Honestly, I have no idea. If *anyone* knows, it has to be the Noble Council, right? The Laika staff can't have acted on their own for all these years."

Paige nodded, accepting the confirmation of her own thoughts.

Will tried to imagine her father, cold and callous, sitting alongside the men and women she had known all her life, and condemning thirty-six children to death. She tried to imagine Xavier participating in that, approving of it, and all the while keeping the terrible secret locked inside him. Keeping it from everyone, even her.

She tried to imagine it, and she failed. How could he be evil? He was her *father*. Xavier was a good man. He served his spoke loyally, unceasingly. He worked late into the night, planning out the future that was best for all of them, slaving without relief to bring that future into being.

She dropped her head into her hands again and rubbed her temples, pushing almost hard enough to hurt. Xavier would not knowingly send children out to die. It just wasn't possible. And yet if the other members of the Noble Council knew, how could he not?

She didn't want to think about this any longer. There had to be something else. A distraction.

"So," she said, a little desperately, casting about her for a subject. Paige looked at her, waiting, and Will's grasping mind finally found something on which to fasten. "Paige, tell me—tell me what you'd have done, if this hadn't happened?"

"How do you mean?"

"I mean, Terran history at the Academy, right? Then what? What comes next for the great Paige Tarrant?"

There was safety in pretending. In burying your head in the sand, just for a little while.

Tarrant giggled, small and subdued. "I don't know. I never thought too far beyond that. Just very abstract stuff. I could do a doctorate, become a professor. Or maybe I'd write some new history books. Maybe do a bit of campaigning work: make you corrupt Nobles pull up your socks."

A laugh slipped between Will's lips. "Yeah, I always thought it'd be politics."

"You made predictions for me, huh?"

"Sure. There wasn't a whole lot else to do at school." She tossed her head, assumed the mantle of her old arrogance. "I don't know if you ever noticed, but I was a *long* way ahead of the rest of you."

"What about you, then? What was the glorious Arrex heir going to do with her life?"

Palms upward, Will spread her hands. "There's not really a choice for people like me."

"That's rich." Paige scoffed. "Not as rich as *you*, of course—"

"Oh, ha ha, *good* one—"

"But still pretty rich. You had nothing *but* choice. Every option was open to you."

"Not really. I had to be a Noble. There's no other career I could have."

"There are a thousand kinds of Noble. You could be a pro racer, like your *cousin*." Paige pulled a face as she said the word, and Will thought she had never liked the other girl so much. "You could be a philanthropist, a politician, a teacher, literally anything! No one is going to say no to whatever a Noble wants to occupy their time with."

"That's the thing, though. It's all just...hobbies. The *real* part of being a Noble, the only real career, is the politics of it. The leadership. We're...we're supposed to be like stewards. We're meant to look after everyone. And sure, some Nobles don't. They have other hobbies, like teaching or giving money to charity or whatever." *Or marrying into other people's spokes,* she added silently. *Like bloody Carroway.* "But they're just...shirking the actual job. What the Nobles were set up to do."

Paige was studying her closely, a look of faint surprise on her own face. "You really believe that, don't you?"

Bristling a little, Will shook out her hair. "Why shouldn't I? It's true."

Paige shrugged again. It wasn't just a shrug that said she didn't know. It was a shrug that said she didn't *care.* An uncharacteristic gesture that was becoming all too common. Will was so used to seeing Paige put *too* much feeling into things. Seeing her just...*stop*...was weird.

"I guess I always sort of thought you were a bit more of the rich asshole sort. Priding yourself on being better than the rest of us." She attempted a grin. "Never knew there were any principles hiding under all that money."

It stung a little, more than it should have, but Will did her best to laugh along. "Well, either way. Doesn't matter anymore, does it?

"No." Paige's expression turned pensive again. "Now neither of us will ever achieve anything we wanted to."

"No."

Slowly, Paige nodded. "Fuck it, right? Fuck everything."

"Yeah. Fuck it."

And as Will said those words, she looked at Paige's eyes, so vast and sad with their little star-flecks of amber, and she took the message into her heart. *Fuck it all.* What did *anything* matter, now? What was there left to lose?

When you were doomed to die, you might as well live in the time you had left. You might as well do everything you wanted to do before your inevitable demise.

Every single thing you wanted. No matter how insane it was.

And suddenly, boldly, Will stretched out a hand and placed it against Paige's cheek. Paige looked up, startled, her breath coming out between her lips in a rushed exhale. Will stared into her eyes, and completely froze.

They held that position for a long time—too long—but Will was powerless. It was all very well saying *fuck it* and deciding to live out your most secret, long-repressed fantasies, but when it actually came down to it—

And then Paige Tarrant kissed her.

Warmth. That was her first impression. Just like when Tarrant's shoulder brushed hers during their movie nights, but *more*. Warmth and softness and the sweet, sweet scent of strawberries. And then, as one, their mouths opened, lips parted, and all was delicious, wet, beautiful starlight.

Behind her half-open eyelids, Will saw fireworks. Explosions and volcanoes and glorious galaxies of stars bursting into being, painting indescribable patterns against the darkness.

Paige's arms slipped around her, at first gentle and then more urgent, and Will clung to her—the only solid thing in a world of chaos. She leaned into Paige, leaned into the girl she had hated and loved in equal measure for so long, and she blossomed beneath her touch.

Her fingers tangled in Paige's hair, and Paige's hands were on her back, pulling her closer, closer. Her teeth grazed Will's lower lip, and Will wasn't sure whether she wanted to sing or scream. Then Paige's fingertips skimmed her jaw, and all other thought vanished.

When it was over, when the fire receded into mere embers, Will pulled back, eyes searching Paige's face.

She looked...careful. Like she wasn't sure what had just happened. Will understood. It all seemed a bit unreal to her, too. Perhaps in a moment, they'd both wake up, safe back in their beds on opposite sides of the wall.

Paige gave a shaky laugh. "You sound a bit out of breath, Arrex."

Will finally caught the sound of her own breath, rushing in and out of her mouth almost fast enough to keep pace with her racing heart.

She swallowed. A jibe. A half-hearted one, sure, but a Tarrant flinging insults was a familiar one. A Tarrant she knew how to deal with. "Yeah. Well—I was on the bike earlier. It's probably that."

Paige laughed, and the sound was like music. "Right."

She leaned her forehead against Will's, and Will looked anxiously into those big brown eyes, too close to see clearly. "Are you...was it...?"

Paige gave her a shaky smile. "Yeah. I'm okay."

"Do you want to—" Will cut herself off. What a *stupid* thing to ask! Of course Paige wouldn't—

Paige was kissing her.

Just like before, the pressure from her lips was sweet and gentle. Just like before, her eyes were fluttering closed. And just like before, Will was instantly, utterly, lost in the moment—in the feel of Paige's skin on hers, the soft and subtle fire that burned between them. That had always burned between them. But now, instead of being directed to hurt and scorch, the fire simmered and hummed, building their heat to a thrumming intensity that made Will's head spin with the sheer power of it.

When they pulled apart for the second time, both of them panting now, Will stared into those eyes. Brighter than stars, softer than silk. Rich and smooth as chocolate.

Will could fall in love with those eyes.

She stared deep into Paige's soul, and she dove down, and lost herself.

CHAPTER 19

Laika 15 – Day 55 – 06:57

They went on kissing. It was nice. Why should they not? The final boundary was shattered, and there was nothing left to keep them apart.

It did not surprise Will, then, that about three days after the very first kiss, she woke up in Tarrant's room, the fairy lights twinkling overhead. Tarrant lay beside her, curls in wild disarray, her expression mirroring Will's own. Not surprise, not exactly. Perplexed, perhaps, at how they had gone from deskmates barely on speaking terms to...whatever this was. But not surprised.

Will had never possessed much emotion; her life was too regulated for that. The one thing that she always had emotion for—that she suffered from an excess of emotion for—was Tarrant. Annoyance, anger, grudging admiration, a strange fierce loyalty. Tarrant had always drawn from Will what no one else could. Now she was challenging Will again. Will was being taken on a journey, but she was no longer unwilling.

They lay side by side in contented confusion, and with a smile on her face, Will let herself drift back to sleep.

Mostly, life went on as it had done before. Outside, the stars still inched past, and sometimes Will thought she could feel the engines thrumming as their course adjusted. She didn't investigate. The door to the control room stayed safely shut, the way Paige wanted it.

The two of them settled into a new equilibrium. Will would bring Paige breakfast in bed, now, and Paige would smile the slow, sweet smile that had once been reserved for her closest friends. They shared their dried pear, they watered Arthur. They exercised and read and played chess, and watched countless Old Terran movies. Will liked the romances—they fit with her new mood, especially the ones where the two lovers started the story hating one another—while Paige liked the ones that dealt with the rise and fall of empires.

And sometimes, over the books or in the middle of a film, there was kissing. It was delightful, to lose herself in another. To unlearn the habits of a lifetime and turn them instead into a gentler, sweeter version. To reroute those thoughts into the channels that they were perhaps meant to have run all along.

The engines, the five-year deadline...everything seemed to fade into irrelevancy. It was terrifying, of course, but in the grand scheme of things, what did it matter? They had boarded the Laika expecting never to return, and their fears had been confirmed. It made no difference in the end.

At the very darkest point of the night, in the witching hour when there was no illumination but the vidscreen's flickering light and Paige was sleeping through another brainless romance movie, Will watched the play of colours across Paige's skin and felt her heart beating fit to burst. Sometimes she thought perhaps she would have given up those eighty-five years on the Eden in exchange for five with Page, even if she had known from the start that five was all they would get.

There was very little, she mused in those secret moments, as she lay with her arms curled about the other girl, her fingers tangled in that impossibly soft hair, there was *very* little she would not give up for Paige's sake.

"Hey, Paige." Will said the words for the sixth time, peering from her seat on the sofa to the gym, where she could just see Paige's left hand, freckled brown fingers curved over the handle of the exercise bike. It was a spark that never dimmed, knowing that Will could now *touch* that hand. That she could look into those eyes and find, not anger, but *affection*.

"Will you stop *bothering* me?"

But there was no real vitriol in the words, and Will only laughed.

"If you were doing anything more engaging than cycling I wouldn't mind watching, but as it is…" It was a lie, of course. An insult without any sting, born of habit more than anything else. There was nothing Tarrant could do that Will would mind watching.

Paige laughed again and emerged from the gym, rubbing at the back of her neck with a towel. "Well, then, what do you want?"

Will looked at Paige, and she considered. What did she want? In the short term—well, she wanted to talk to Paige. To bask in her company, to soak in the rays of her attention. She wanted to see if—maybe—Paige would want to kiss her again.

And in the long term?

The rush of emotion that thought brought on was terrifying, and Will clamped down on it immediately, turning it off like she would a tap. No—never mind about the long term. Today was enough.

"It's funny, isn't it?"

"What is?" Paige was still distracted, heading for the laundry chute in the corner that, when full, would clean and sterilise everything within it and return it for the next use.

"All of this. I've only ever shown you the worst parts of me. And…" she gestured. *And this happened anyway.*

Paige frowned. "You didn't—it wasn't the *worst* parts of you, Will."

"No? All that…crazy competition?" Her voice sounded small even to her own ears. "I was…I was cruel."

She knew what she wanted to hear in response. Vehement denial, protestations of adoration. She wanted Paige to tell her she was wrong.

But the silence stretched, and Paige's response was hesitant.

"When we were kids, you were…"

Will braced herself. Here it came. *You were a bully. A psychopath. A cold, unfeeling bitch.*

But Paige was smiling. "You were what I measured myself against. You were always so sure of everything. I knew that if I was keeping pace with you, I was on track."

Letting out the breath she hadn't realised she was holding, Will returned the smile. "I thought you hated me."

Paige giggled. "Well—I did. I hated the way you knew *everything* ahead of time. I was so sure you were cheating."

Will deflated. *There it is.* "Ah."

Taking her hand, Paige squeezed her fingers. "But you pushed me to do better. If you hadn't been in our class, I wouldn't have tried nearly as hard."

Shaking her head, Will nudged Paige's shoulder. "You never did anything half-heartedly in your life, Tarrant." She drew herself up a little, reassured. "And I wasn't cheating, by the way. I would *never* cheat." Not only because it was against her principles, but also because she did not *need* to.

Paige elbowed her back. "Throwing obscene amounts of money at a problem still counts as cheating in my book, *Arrex*."

Opening her mouth to snap back, Will caught herself before the words could come out. They were falling back into an old argument, here, but things were different now. Will was different.

"I hated you too, you know," she said instead, injecting a smile into her voice to remove the bite from the words. Best to turn the topic away from their ancient *Nobles-and-their-inherent-evilness* debate. "The way you kept up so easily, when I put so much work into being the best. It was my whole life."

"I know." Paige rolled her eyes, and it was a gesture so familiar that Will couldn't help a snigger.

"And your friends, too. I was so jealous that you had real friends."

"They could have been your friends as well."

A little despondently, Will nodded. She knew that. It had been her that erected the wall dividing herself from the non-Nobles. And now it was too late. She would never see Cara or any of the others again, and they would believe her a monster till the day she died. They would pity Paige for being sent with her.

"I was this close, sometimes, to inviting you to come and sit with us." Paige held up a thumb and forefinger, only millimetres apart. "But then you'd do something horrible, or stare at me all through lunchtime like I was dirt on your shoe, and the idea would just go *poof*."

She laughed, and Will tried to laugh too, but it rang hollow. They were cutting the meat too close to the bone, here. She knew she had been awful. She knew she had done reprehensible things. There was no way to change any of them now. A lifetime of regrets to squash into the five years she had left.

"I thought maybe if I distracted you then your marks would drop," she joked, though it was an effort. "Never really seemed to work though."

Paige's big brown eyes rolled again. "As if I'd let something so petty get to me."

Petty. Again, there it was. The ugly truth. Their time together had softened them, but Paige's original feelings—perhaps, Will thought with dread, they were her *true* feelings—still kept rearing their head.

The realisation, when it hit Will, had come like a lightning bolt, a searing flash that left behind a thousand smaller truths that smouldered in her mind like embers, waiting to blaze back into life. The truth of her feelings for Paige: that perhaps the passion she felt for the other girl was not hate at all. Perhaps it was something more.

And Will had understood, when that lightning flashed like a distant storm on Jupiter, that the *more* was the truth of it. For her, the *more* was reality, and the mask of hatred had been the lie.

She had accepted that. Sunk into the raging tide of her feelings for Paige, let them carry her away.

But for Paige…Will could not shake the doubt that perhaps for Paige it was the opposite. Maybe for her the hatred had been real, and it was their current state that was the lie. A pleasant fiction to cushion the brutal reality of the Laika.

And now that persistent feeling was growing louder. The nagging doubt that deep down, perhaps Paige did not actually like her very much at all.

Several days of their strange new normal had passed before Paige finally suggested that they take another look in the control room. The slow, steady hum of the engines had not ceased, though their fuel should have long since run out. Despite the promise of the man in the video, they were not yet drifting.

Will had been determined not to push her luck, but the release from limbo was like a physical weight lifting from her shoulders, and she all but sprinted to the sealed door.

The readings were the same as before. The cameras confirmed it, and stars were still scrolling slowly past the porthole. Their rockets were firing. They were still on course for Mars.

"I just don't understand it," Paige said, for the seventieth time.

"Nor do I." Will sighed. She had grown complacent, wrapped in the bubble of Paige's avoidance, and being pulled back out of it was disorienting. Why were they being offered shreds of hope *now*, when they had finally made the decision to give up and be happy with what they had?

"Do you think the sensors and the cameras are still set up to sell the story to us?" Paige chewed at her lower lip. "We could be a few hundred miles from the Eden and never know it. I've not felt anything but the engines since the mass accelerator."

"It's a good thing you haven't," replied Will, who wanted more than anything to go back out into the portion of the ship that felt like home, and maybe bury her hands in Paige's curls again. Maybe trace her fingers over that silk-soft skin. "If we felt anything in here, odds are it would be an asteroid taking a chunk out of the ship and pulling all the air out."

Paige shuddered.

"Come on," Will pressed. "Let's go and watch *Ruination's Centiday* or something. I don't think there's much point worrying what's real and what isn't. It's all out of our control."

Paige brightened. "I thought you didn't like the sequels."

"But you do."

And that was enough.

"You swear this isn't just another history thing?" Will pressed, reaching out a hand to brush against the back of Paige's leg.

"I thought you'd *like* the one about Vlad the Impaler," Paige insisted. "He falls in love with Justina! That's romance, isn't it? Exactly what you requested."

Will rolled her eyes. "For about five minutes, in between all the enormous battle scenes. And what about that one with all the robots and priests and crap? *That* had no romance at all, when you swore it did."

"One of the robots fell in love with one of the priests," retorted Paige, with just as much snottiness as she used to employ in their old classroom arguments.

"For about five minutes, in between *all the enormous battle scenes!*"

"Anyway, the narrative focus in *Robots vs Priests: Gears and God* isn't on their love so much as on the emergence of L-Four-Six's consciousness."

"Then why did you *swear* it was a feel-good comedy? Honestly."

"Alright, alright!" Paige rocked back on her heels and pulled up the hard drive's files on the vidscreen. "Well, you'll like *this* one, I swear. No battles at all."

A harrumph answered her. "That's what you always say."

Paige placed her hand on her heart, eyes laughing. "Will, I promise that *Soft Blows the Breeze* has zero battles."

"For someone who is ethically opposed to all forms of violence and thinks that stun guns are a tool of oppression, you sure love watching empires violently crumble." Will folded her arms in mock-sternness.

"It's *history*," Paige replied grandly. "How can you not love it? Anyway, *Soft Blows the Breeze* isn't about empires crumbling. It's a musical. They sing everything. This time you actually *will* love it."

She was clicking rapidly through the file-tree, getting to the right folder, when suddenly she paused.

"Huh."

There was something in her voice that made Will sit up and take notice. "What is it?"

"There's a file that wasn't here yesterday."

Will scrambled over the sofa cushions to drop to the floor beside the other girl. "How can that be possible?"

"I have no idea." Paige pointed a finger, and Will looked at the little icon on the screen.

A video file, ten minutes long, entitled *To my daughter.*

And there in the thumbnail, pixelated but undeniably himself, was that...?

"Isn't that your dad?"

"Yes."

Soft Blows the Breeze was nothing in the face of this.

There was a long, pregnant pause. Then they both spoke at once.

"What do you think—"

"Maybe it's—"

They both stopped. Will gestured for Paige to go first.

"What *is* it?"

"Tunis got me the film library, so maybe—maybe Father put some sort of message on there." Will's throat was suddenly tight at the thought of it. "A last goodbye."

Paige nodded slowly, and then she clicked the icon. Together, they moved slowly to the sofa and sank down onto it, eyes fixed on the vidscreen.

The image flickered, and then Xavier was there, sitting in his office, the backdrop of stars behind him. The lump in Will's throat became a boulder. *Father.* Everything in the shot was so painfully familiar. The chair she used to spin on as a toddler. The glass wall she pressed her nose against while he taught her the names of constellations and moons. The sharply angled cheekbones and silky white-blonde hair that were a reflection of her own. The flinty green eyes that only softened for Eloise and Will herself.

"Father," she whispered, and as though he had heard her, he responded.

"Wilhelmina, if you're hearing this it means that things went well and you secured Laika Fifteen."

Will heard Paige pull in a breath, but she didn't look across. No, she was fixated on Xavier, drinking in the sight of him, the parent she had thought was lost to her forever.

Xavier cleared his throat. "I hope you are holding up well. As well as can be expected under the circumstances. You must have been very unhappy after receiving the scheduled communication from Laika Command yesterday."

Beside her, Will felt Paige go rigid. The recordings of Professor Clark and her predecessor had played twelve days before. Had this file appeared on their hard drive then, tucked away unassumingly amongst the hundreds of films?

"I'm afraid I have some difficult things to tell you." He cleared his throat. "I had hoped to reveal them to you gradually, when you were older, but we will make do."

Will's heart sank.

"You know now that the public perception of our situation is not altogether accurate. The Eden is not a holding pattern to be maintained while the terraformers work. The Eden is...everything. It is all we have. Terra is dead, and at the time of the final evacuation there were no terraforming technologies close to what the population of Eden believes we possess. *Everything* our Founders possessed went into building the Eden. We can maintain it, but we cannot transform a planet. We cannot create a new homeworld or repair the old one. We never could."

The words were like a punch to the gut. Somehow, hearing it from Xavier himself made it more real. Not only that, but—he had *known*. He had known all along what Will was getting herself into, and still he had not saved her.

"Creating a second Eden might be possible—*maybe*, with the outputs of perhaps two hundred years' work and the uninterrupted efforts of every soul on board. But once it was created that would be it. Just the Eden, duplicated. So the Noble Council judged it better to let the people believe in a way out. The original purpose of the Laikas was to monitor Terra, and for years, we watched. The seas dried up. Life died out. There's nothing left but fire and desert. The air isn't breathable anymore. So we...stopped. We stopped diverting more than a third of our materials and power to interstellar transport production, and we invested in the Eden instead. Our standard of living has never been higher, our population has never been better fed...but we no longer visit Terra." He steepled his fingers together, his eyes inexpressibly grave. "Now, the Laikas and the Lottery only have one purpose: hope. Once every twenty-five years, we send some of our own out to die, and their sacrifice allows the rest of us to believe in something better."

Will wished she knew how to tell if that sorrow in his eyes was *real*. Xavier was a master of his craft. His regret sounded genuine, but how could Will ever believe him again?

"You must be shocked. Horrified, even. I know I was, when my father first told me the truth. It seems so bleak. So brutal. But please, believe me when I tell you it is necessary."

His words were rhythmic. The cadence familiar. He was giving a speech, Will realised. He'd prepared these words. These expressions. Hadn't he coached her through a thousand of her own?

"I spoke of a duplicate Eden: well, the Eden was not the only space station put into orbit by the elite of Old Terra. The Paradise was launched at the same time, sent to Saturn, and built using materials mined from the meteorites in the Belt. Both stations began with the same system: the Founders became Nobles and led the populace. Both utilised the white lie that there were terraformers out there preparing a new home for some distant generation. But while Eden's Nobles followed the plans laid out by the Founders, within a generation or two the Nobles of the Paradise wanted to come clean and tell their people the truth about the situation on Terra."

The barest glimmer of a smile. "I would have called the result unsurprising; the public psyche cannot take a blow like that. At any rate, there was a revolt. At first protesting, and then civil war. You know how fragile our ecosystem in the Eden is. Warfare cannot be sustained in a place like this without something going terribly wrong. The Paradise's final communication, sent seventy years after Eden's founding, told us that the hull had ruptured and the airlocks were blowing one by one. Multiple points of failure. Nothing they could do to stop it. The Paradise died, and so did all three thousand six hundred of its people."

"Our ancestors decided that we could not allow the Eden to follow the same path. So we committed ourselves harder than ever to the fiction of the terraforming. The Lottery and the Laika ships provide a focal point. A lie, but a very necessary one." He pulled in a deep breath, the first pause he had taken in a long while. "Given time, Wilhelmina, I hope you can understand. These facts are your inheritance as an Arrex. Your birthright and your burden to bear for the Eden."

The bad news done with, a smile now flickered at the edges of his mouth. "But I want to be very clear with you, Wilhelmina, you are not going to die. I have found a way to save you."

Will leaned forward, enthralled.

"We have survivors every Lottery: the Trojan ship, we call it. Someone's idea of a funny little joke, I suppose. I wanted yours to be the one retained, but the Noble Council...overruled me. They said there would be questions. Some of them," and here his lips thinned dangerously, "felt that a Noble willing to enter the Lottery in the first place was *dangerous*. I believe 'radical' was the word Zeko Oriel used. So another set of pilots was selected as the Trojan, and I have taken other measures for you without the Noble Council's knowledge."

"Your ship has extra fuel, larger thrusters, a real navigational system. My technicians tell me it was a dicey thing to install in the time frame we had, but it should be enough to bring you home alive. You aren't going to Mars. This is the first ship that has been given a full run in a long time, so we will be sending you somewhere more useful. You are going to Terra. To old Earth." There was a gleam of triumph in his eyes now, cold and deadly. "If you can bring back real, usable footage, then it will be enough for us to bring the Noble Council round. When they wheel out their own survivors, they can't publicly object to more."

"You'll be going to Luna and slingshotting around Terra onto the correct trajectory to get you home. You'll need to do it manually, and use as little fuel as possible. According to my team's calculations, you should be home in less than a year and a half from the day of your launch."

His expression turned steely. His voice was powerful, each word a command hammering itself deep into Will's brain. "You can do this, Wilhelmina. You have the skill. You can make it home." He paused, and as he looked into the camera it was like he was looking into Will's very soul. "I will see you again soon."

Then the vidscreen went blank, and Will's breath rushed out of her as the world returned.

Relief. Pure, sheer, heady relief.

She was not going to die. Her father had come through for her. He was going to save them.

Will looked across at Paige, a smile ready on her face, her arms opening to hold her. They were going to *live*!

But there were tears on Paige's face, and for a moment Will couldn't understand why. They were going to live. Surely that was all that mattered. She reached out again, but the other girl snatched her hand away.

"Did you hear him?" Paige asked, and her voice was strangely hollow. "The elite of Old Terra. They were all Nobles. All of them—all of us, I suppose."

"It makes sense," Will said cautiously. Who else would be able to afford to buy a place on the Eden? Or the Paradise, for that matter. How bizarre, to think that there had once been two stations.

A snort from Paige. Her face still oddly blank. "You *would* think that."

"What do you mean?" Will asked, beginning to feel nettled. There was no need for Paige to be so hostile. *Will* hadn't been the one to make any of these insane decisions. And—and what did the wealth of the original Eden citizens matter? The ordeal was over. No one was going to die. They were going home.

"You're all alike." Paige waved a hand at the vidscreen, her expression turning sour. "You think you can buy your way out of anything. Just like your daddy bought you a way out of *this*, when we were supposed to die like the others."

"That's the way the world works, Paige," Will said, fighting to maintain her even tone. She didn't want to have another anti-Noble fight. Not now. They should be celebrating.

Paige shook her head. "You don't get it. He *paid* to save you from this. Back then, they paid to save themselves. They didn't care how many billions died back on Terra because they were too *poor* to buy a ticket." She sighed. "Just like your father didn't care about the other Lottery losers. He just...let them die."

There was a pause. The silence stretched. Will searched for something to say, something to make it better, and came up empty-handed. It was true. Apart from the two anonymous pilots on the Trojan Laika, Xavier and the Noble Council *had* left them to die. Thune and Loysa and even Panset, all of them likely doomed to suffocate or freeze or starve to death. Whatever horrible malfunction the Laika technicians had built into the ships to kill them off at the end of the five years.

"And the worst of it is," Paige said with a little laugh, "it means I'm one of you. My ancestors were just like all the rest. Only caring about themselves. *Nobles.*" Hate dripped from the word, so raw it took Will aback to hear it. Such anger didn't seem like it *belonged* on Paige's face.

"Paige—"

Will reached out a hand, but Paige jerked away violently enough that Will shrank back. "Paige," she whispered, but Paige was already on her feet.

Stalking away from Will, placing one foot directly in front of the last, like a tiger, like a panther, every curl crackling with barely restrained anger as it bounced against her back. She reached the door to her room, and Will strained for eye contact, hoping Paige would look back, just once—

But the door slammed shut, and Will was left alone.

A cold and lonely night, the first time in days Will had slept alone. When she emerged she found Paige seated at the table, a mug of watered-down coffee in front of her.

Cautiously, Will approached. "How did you sleep?" Maybe, just maybe, it would be over now. Maybe Paige would have gained a new perspective to match a new day. Maybe they wouldn't have to fight.

But the answer, when it came, was delivered in a voice so small, so suppressed, that the hope of reconciliation died at once. "I didn't."

Will swallowed. An angry Paige was terrifying, incandescent in her white-hot rage. When sad, she was heartbreaking. But the Paige before her had passed through those extremes of emotion and into the dead zone beyond. Now she was just empty.

"What have you been doing?"

"Thinking."

Her heart contracting, Will crossed the cabin to join Paige at the table. "You should have woken me."

Paige looked at her, and her eyes were flat. Dead. There was no life left in them at all.

Will tried again. "Paige—"

"You *lied* to me."

It was happening. Exactly as she'd feared. She had to explain, she had to—

"I didn't, I—"

"We have to get to number fifteen, you said. Don't ask questions, you said. You knew this ship was different."

"Father told me to make sure we got it, but I—"

"You knew what was going to happen." The accusation was as flat and cold as Paige herself.

Will almost got on her knees right then and there. "I didn't, I swear I didn't—he told me that I should get into this one but I didn't know why—"

"You're a clever girl, Will; you really couldn't put it together? This ship was different because *your* father made it different, with your Noble fucking power and your Noble fucking money." Paige choked out something that might have been a laugh, in another life. She shoved her chair back and stalked over to the sofa. "If I wasn't your co-pilot I'd be dead, wouldn't I? Just like all our friends are dead."

"Not all of them," Will said desperately, clinging to that magic number. Four survivors, not two.

"A Trojan ship," Paige said bitterly, savagely twisting a handful of her own jumpsuit. "They pick two of us to live and leave the rest to die. They think they're *gods*." Her grip tightened on the fabric, almost throttling it now. "How do they choose?"

"Oh," Will said, raising a hand to her forehead. *"Oh."*

"Oh *what*?" Paige growled.

"Hrue Lipson came to see me, in the Training Centre. Told me to choose someone biddable."

Air hissed through Paige's teeth, low and dangerous. "So they *did* warn you?"

"No! They—he—I had no idea what he was trying to tell me. But he must have meant that they were thinking of choosing me for the Trojan ship. If I...if I picked someone..."

"Someone they could order around." Paige's voice was more bitter than ever. "Someone other than me."

"Oh, Paige," Will said softly. "It's not..."

"I *don't* think it's my fault," Paige snapped. "Don't even go there. It's your *father's* fault. Your stupid Noble Council's fault. It's nothing to do with me or anyone else. We're just...cogs. Little pieces on a chessboard."

"We have agency," Will murmured, not sure how much she believed the words she was saying. "There's no one around for a thousand miles. We're in control."

Paige huffed. "But you're thinking it too, aren't you? You think it's my fault we're out here instead of safely in the hangar."

Will nudged her, trying to bring some levity back. "You have no idea what I'm thinking."

"But you do think that."

"I *don't.*"

"If I were...quieter, if I were *biddable*, that pile of old farts wouldn't have sent us out here to die. The only reason we even have a *chance*, is that your dad is richer than Mammon."

"Than who?"

"Forget it. Just tell me one thing. Was all of *this* a lie too?" Paige was growing louder again. "A way to pass the time until you get back home and go back into your mansion and leave me behind?"

"*No*," Will said despairingly.

Why couldn't she understand? *Xavier*, and not Will, had been the one to make this decision.

But Paige was mid-flow and would not be stopped. "Because even if we *do* make it home, I don't expect I'll be allowed to live long, will I? They have to know who I am, what I stand for. They'll have read my psychological profile."

That was enough to floor Will. "What do you mean?"

Paige shrugged. That same horrible, uncaring shrug from the morning of the first message. "I'll be silenced. When we get back, we'll dock, we'll disembark, and nice and quietly, they'll slit my throat, and then off to Recycling with me."

"No—no, no one would do that." Will was aghast. "My father wouldn't."

Paige stared at her in disbelief, and then began to laugh. "You didn't think of that, did you? You really thought they'd let us both off?" She leaned in, and her face was suddenly cruel. It was like looking into a mirror. "This was never about me. It was about you, Will fucking *Arrex*, the Noble who shits gold and lives among the stars while the rest of us crawl in the dark like worms." She sneered. "Shame you got attached to your little pet, isn't it? I was never going to survive this. No matter what number ship I got on to."

And while Will stammered and gasped, trying to come up with some sort of rebuttal, Paige jumped to her feet and stalked away. The door to her room slammed for a second time in as many days, and Will was, once more, alone.

CHAPTER 20

Laika 15 – Day 65 – 09:01

Will was twelve years old, and it was Tarrant's birthday.

Prowling into the classroom after a painfully dull lunch hour, frustrated that the table beside her own had remained so determinedly empty, she stopped short at the riot of colour that met her eyes.

Paige was beaming, grinning so widely her eyes were reduced to little half-moon crescents of happiness. She was laughing, and she was dancing with Cara Sutsu, with Garth, with Erntz and Joss and Lysse Abbeia and anyone who would join her. She was spinning and whirling beneath the banner that bugled the occasion—*HAPPY BIRTHDAY PAIGE*—and the room rang with her joy.

There was a second's pause when Will entered, and only Cara smiled in greeting. More of a reflex than a genuine emotion. Lysse moved her mouth in a similar fashion, but even then it didn't seem to reach her eyes.

"Nice little gathering you've got here," Will said, and her voice was cutting. Her eyes swept across the paltry decorations: the home-made banner, the paper streamers, the porta-vidscreen blaring out music, and the sad little nutribar with an LED candle stuck in the top of it.

They had gone out of their way not to include her, so she would show them how *small* their efforts really were.

She had been ready for some return fire, for some attention—but Tarrant just laughed. "No one invited you anyway, Arrex."

As Will sat with her back resolutely turned on the festivities, she wondered what it would feel like to smile that wide. To be unconscious of the way you looked or the impression you gave or how it would reflect on your family. She wondered what it would be like to have friends who threw her a party. To be one of them—to see Tarrant turn that smile her way.

"Don't listen to her, Austyn," Tarrant said, a grin stretching across her face from ear to ear. "This is *amazing*. You guys are the best."

"Wish I'd been able to get a cake," Garth replied, voice breaking awkwardly as it wavered between tenor and treble, and Cara patted his arm to reassure him.

Tarrant giggled. "Who cares? Even a nutribar looks better with a candle on it!"

Will had considered it, turned the question over in her mind as the afternoon's lessons began. By the time six o'clock rolled around, she had reached a decision.

It hadn't taken much. Just a single one-line message to Tunis, an order followed up with a single qualifying statement. *Make sure it's a big one.*

And as Will swept from the classroom, leaving her six classmates chattering behind her, she had seen the delivery man headed down the corridor, carrying a brightly coloured box that took both arms to hold. She had paused at the corner, just out of sight, but just within earshot of the squeals of delight when the box was opened. As the singing began, she crept away, a small, satisfied smirk on her face.

It had been a perverse sort of victory: one to be enjoyed in private, not flaunted in Tarrant's face like others were. The knowledge that she had done *Tarrant* a favour—that Tarrant, had she known, would have been obligated to be grateful to *her*. It had made the celebration of her own birthday a few weeks later—a quiet affair at home, a cupcake shared with Tunis before the formal dinner with her father's supporters and staff—a little sweeter.

The memory faded slowly away. Will was seventeen years old, and until Xavier's video she had not believed she would live to see another birthday. Now she knew better—but still, somehow, she had been happier before. Two days ago, before that video, she had known what it was to have the light of Paige Tarrant's smile on her. She had known what it was to be valued. Perhaps even...loved.

And now it was gone, the light withdrawn, and she was plunged back into the darkness.

When we get back, we'll dock, we'll disembark, and nice and quietly, they'll slit my throat, and then off to Recycling with me.

Those words echoed in the chambers of her mind. With an effort, Will twisted the loneliness into something more. Resolve. She would not just lie down and give up.

All she needed was to offer Paige a spark of hope. Something to reignite the flame inside her. Once lit, it would blaze back up into that patented Tarrant inferno, and Will would be safe again inside its warmth.

She clambered out of bed and padded into the larger room outside. She spared a glance for Paige's door: still sealed, as expected. A brief check on the control room showed that little had changed. The thrusters were still firing. Her father's protection was still with them.

Will turned to the kitchen. Paige was fond of food, fond of the things they cooked together. A special breakfast—something beyond the usual fare of porridge and dried pear—yes, that could be the spark Will wanted. She looked past the cupboards and packaged nutribars to the kitchen table, where Arthur sat in his pot, thin branches spreading out a new crop of leaves. Beneath the largest cluster sat a small, lumpy brown thing, no bigger than the upper half of Will's thumb—Arthur's best approximation of a real pear.

Fresh fruit. Now there was an occasion. Something unusual in their limited little world.

Will reached out and gently probed its surface. Too hard, not even half-ripe—but if she chopped it finely, or perhaps even blended it in with the porridge, it wouldn't matter. The flavour was what counted. It didn't need to be perfect. Paige would see what Will was trying to do for her. She would understand.

With fingers that shook only slightly, Will reached out and twisted the lumpen little thing off its stalk. "Thanks, Arthur."

Her knife skimmed across the pile of greenish-yellow flesh, dicing it smaller and smaller with every pass. Scraped it carefully into a pan; not even a sliver left behind.

All her life Will had known exactly who she was. How to wield herself like she wielded the blade in her hands. Sharpened to a point, without an ounce of superfluous feeling.

Since the kiss, everything had changed. Since *before* the kiss. Since the night Paige had appeared in the hallway to take Cara's place. All it had taken was one taste, and Will had changed forever. How could she now change back, when that taste was withdrawn?

She cooked the porridge slowly, meticulously, raising the heat little by little. It had to be perfect today. Two bowls, side by side on the table, porridge poured carefully in, and Arthur's offering was sprinkled in a little swirl in each bowl's centre. A single leaf plucked from the sapling and torn into shreds added a dash of colour to each bowl, and some of Will's dwindling stock of honey sweetened the taste.

Stepping back from the table, she surveyed her work with satisfaction. On the Eden she had never prepared any dish more ambitious than a slice of toast; Tunis had always been there, ready to help. But she was learning. She was becoming more than Xavier had raised her to be, and she...didn't hate it.

She straightened the spoon beside Paige's bowl and then headed towards the bedrooms to gather the final ingredient: Paige herself.

"You up?" Hesitantly, she knocked at the door. Her tone was casual; there was no waver to her voice. As though the last words to pass between them had not been *Shame you got attached to your little pet, isn't it?*

No answer.

She swallowed, tried again. *Keep it easy, keep it light.*

"Paige, are you awake?"

Another pause, and then a few rustling sounds. Then the door hissed open, and Paige, rumpled and dour, stared out at her. It wasn't quite a glare—Will might have preferred it if it were. Glares were old, comfortable territory for them. Almost like a greeting. This expression was different. Blanker.

Still, Will put on her best smile. Her *the cameras are pointing this way* face.

"I made you some porridge. Arthur's pear's finally ripe." A small lie, but a harmless one.

Paige eyed the breakfast laid out on the table with something less than pleasure before brushing past Will. She headed for the kitchen and Will followed at her heels, heart thrumming with relief. Paige wasn't talking, but she was complying. She would take her seat at the table, and they would figure this out.

"It'll be wonderful to have something fresh, for a change," she said, the first audible inflection of nervousness entering her tone. If only Paige would *speak.*

Instead of pausing by her chair, Paige crossed to the kitchen counter and pressed the button on the food-fab to produce a nutribar. "I think I'll stick with this."

"Paige, come on." The sour taste of desperation began to fill Will's mouth. "I...I worked hard on this."

Only two days ago, they had laughed together. Embraced. It didn't seem possible, that one little video could change so much.

With seeming carelessness, Paige spread her hands. *Doesn't matter to me,* she was saying. *You don't matter to me.*

There had been the same level of detachment the evening after the first video. The sense of inevitable doom, of the futility of struggle. Paige had sat in the gyroscope, rocking back and forth, and her voice had been the exact same sort of empty. But at least in that moment Will had been her *ally.* United by their shared fate. There was nothing left of that now.

"Paige, you can't just—you can't just cut me off. We're...you're my..."

You're all I have, she wanted to say. It wasn't quite right; Paige would think she meant that they were co-pilots, *obligated* to support one another. But Paige had been all Will had long before they ever boarded this ship.

One hip cocked, Paige almost sneered. "What, Will? What are we?"

It was a challenge, and as Will looked at Paige across the table she had so lovingly set, she did not feel prepared to meet it.

"Us," she replied helplessly. "This."

Paige turned abruptly away. "*This* was a huge fucking mistake."

Will tried to move forward again, but Paige's hand sliced through the air between them like a knife. Severing whatever fragile bond had sprung to life between them.

"Leave me alone."

"Paige, please. Just come try it. It's fresh, like we used to have back in the Training Centre."

"I don't *want* your stupid pears! I'd rather eat what people like me are *supposed* to eat." Paige thrust the nutribar out before her like a weapon. "And I'm *sick* of porridge, anyway."

Her parting cut delivered, Paige wheeled away—but Will's hand snapped out to catch her wrist, yanking her back. She would not be shut out again. Not this time. There were things that needed to be said. Open wounds could only be left to fester for so long.

"Wait."

"Let me go." Paige's voice was cold, steely.

"You have to listen first."

"I don't *have* to do anything."

The impetus gone, Will uncurled her fingers. "No...but I'm asking you to. Please. We can't carry on like this."

Paige remained silent, but at least she had stopped trying to flee.

Will pressed a little closer. "Paige, I'd...I'd *never* let them hurt you. You have to know that."

Her eyes lowered so that those long lashes almost swept her cheeks, Paige raised one shoulder and let it fall. "Wouldn't you?"

Funny, how two such small words could cut so deep. Doubt wounded more than accusations ever could. This time, when Paige pulled her hand away, Will let her go.

For weeks Will had been trying to argue herself into complaisance. To believe that her worst fears were only that. And she had come so *close* to succeeding. Now at last the truth was out. Through everything, Paige had held on to that old distrust, kept it simmering away beneath the surface.

With lips that felt strangely numb, Will managed to shape one single word. *"No."*

Resuming her interrupted path to her room, Paige tossed one last thought over her shoulder. "I don't think you'd get much of a say either way."

That subtle suggestion was what snared Will anew, set hope bubbling up again. Paige did not believe her *wholly* a monster.

She hardly knew what she was doing—but there was a deep, instinctual feeling that if she let that door close behind Paige right now, it would never open back up again. And Will had never wanted anything even *half* as much as she wanted to keep Paige Tarrant.

She dove forward and blocked the door just as it was about to seal.

Fresh anger sparking in her eyes, Paige spun back. "*What?* Haven't you had enough?"

"No," said Will, almost panting. "No."

A toss of the spiralled curls. A weariness beneath the bravado. "What's left to say?"

Will fished for something. Anything to keep her talking. A memory surfaced, the same one that had occurred before she left her bed. "When we were twelve...do you remember your birthday?"

Now uncertainty crept in at the edges of the anger. "Of course I remember my own birthday."

"The surprise party that Garth organised."

"Austyn definitely didn't invite *you*."

"It was in our classroom. I couldn't exactly miss it." Will's temper finally reared its head again, a little flash of life to restore her flagging spirits. "Remember the cake? The big one with the pink icing?"

Paige blinked. "I'm *certain* you weren't there for that."

Folding her arms, Will tried to keep the triumph from her voice. "Exactly."

"No." Paige shook her head. "No. Papi sent that cake."

Feeling a slight pulse of satisfaction that it had taken only one word for Paige to grasp her point, Will smiled. They were in sync, just like always. That had to mean something.

"Are you certain?"

Floundering for a moment, Paige crossed her arms tight against her ribcage. Like she was trying to hold herself together. "Even if that were true—one cake doesn't fix anything. It doesn't alter the fact your family are *murderers*. That Loysa, Grigor, Panset, *Thune*— they're all going to *die*. Because of the Nobles. Because of *you*."

"Two of them are going to live because we chose each other. We're out here and they're still safe at home. Paige, have you never thought that I might be—I don't know—*different*?" Her heart twisting, Will fought to keep her face neutral. At least they were talking. At least the door wasn't shutting in her face.

This time, Paige's denial was immediate. "You spent your whole life trying to fit that mould."

"Because—because I didn't have a choice," Will said, her voice cracking at last. Why couldn't Paige *see* that? How could she believe even for a moment that Will would *want* their fellow pilots to die? "I didn't know *this* was happening."

"So you say."

Will took a step forward, searching Paige's eyes. Looking for something there. Something she could hold on to. "You know that's not true. You know me."

Paige's gaze flickered down. "I don't know anything anymore." She retreated into her room, sinking down onto the bed, nutribar dropped onto the sheets heedless of the crumbs.

Will followed her, heart in her mouth as she braced for the next rejection. "You do know me," Will insisted. "And you can trust me. I—I *care* about you."

It was as close as she had ever come to admitting the truth to Paige. The words that had been circling in her skull for a long time now.

Paige scoffed, but she rolled towards Will, and suddenly, she reached over to place her hand on her cheek. As she looked up at Will with the old stony eyes, the rival's eyes, Will wondered if Paige was going to slap her.

Her face inches from Will's, Paige paused, and then she laughed. A dry, aching little laugh. "We're dead either way. It doesn't matter."

And before Will could protest, before she could argue that Paige wouldn't die, she wouldn't *let* her die—

Paige's lips were on hers, moving with bruising force, teeth scraping at her skin. Kissing Will as she had *never* kissed her before, hands moving as they had never moved before. Insistent and angry and *needing,* and all coherent thought vanished from Will's mind. She didn't understand what was happening, why it was happening—but it didn't matter. All she knew was that Paige needed this, needed *her*, and she would do anything, give anything, be anything. Anything, for the girl before her.

Paige was fumbling with the zips of her jumpsuit and Will scrambled to help. Fingers moved across her flesh, the touch no longer tentative and ghosting, but rough and almost cruel in the way they twisted and pulled.

Was this *real*? Was this really going to happen? Will's heart was thudding in her chest, painful in its intensity. She had wanted this for so long, she had dreamed of this every night for months. But for it to happen *now*, after a fight like this—

"Paige, I—I—"

"Shut up." And Paige kissed her harder, harder, and the words were lost.

I love you.

Paige's nails raked through her hair, sharp against her scalp, and Will gasped at the pain of it. She tried again, to speak the words that she had never spoken before and would never say to anyone but the girl in her arms, *this* girl—but Paige bit her lip so hard that blood was almost drawn, and then Will was flipping her over, pushing her down, tearing at her clothes. Like this was a battle, and they were both fighting to win.

When it was over, finally over, they both sprawled on the bed, staring at the ceiling. Will lay beside Paige, sweaty and unclothed, and wondered if she would vomit. That her passion, her love, would have brought her to this—that *this* was how she would be with Paige for the first time—it made a sick sort of sense. Anger had always been their default state. The kindness and the calm had only come later, and had been the first things to go.

But she tried to find the bright side of it. Paige had chosen to pull Will towards her, rather than push her away. It was—it was progress, even if it made her guts twist like living things.

And Paige was beside her, squashed in on the narrow twin bed. Staring at the ceiling, eyes blank but still beautiful. She would listen, and Will would talk, and slowly, she would bring it back to how it had been. They would reach Terra, a team once more, and they would make it home.

And with Paige at her side, what could Will not do? She would make her father listen. He would be Lord Captain before long, and when he led the Noble Council the Lottery could finally be undone. Loysa, Thune, and the rest—it might be too late for them, but Will and Paige could make sure that they would be the last. No more children would be sacrificed on the altar of *hope*.

Will looked at Paige, sweat darkening the roots of her coiled hair and beading the expanse of her chest, and she summoned all her courage.

Together they would be able to climb to heights undreamed, but first Will had to get Paige's feet on the ladder.

"Paige."

A slight tilt of the head, but no eye contact. No answer.

"I've been thinking, and—well, if we make it back, we can change things. We can go public. Tell people." She waited for a response, but none came. "You and me, if we work as a team, we can fix the Lottery. Stop it. Put resources towards another Eden, instead, like Father said in the video."

Paige turned her face away, towards the wall, and Will's teeth came together in a way that was almost painful. *Don't leave me.*

"If that were feasible, they'd have done it hundreds of years ago." The response, when it came at last, was muted. "It's not going to be as simple as two Laika pilots making it back and telling everyone."

Will swallowed. "We could make it that simple."

"They'll shut us up. You—well, they'll work on you. And me..."

Will didn't need to see Paige's face to read the subtext. Paige still believed she wouldn't make it past the Eden's airlock.

"Paige, it won't happen. I-I *know* it won't." In her eagerness, Will almost stumbled over the words. "No one's going to hurt you. You're my—my co-pilot."

Paige shrugged, and all the anger from before was gone. Only emptiness was left. "Die here or die there, Will, what's the difference? At least I'm dying with my own kind here. The way I was meant to."

A lump rose in her throat, and the hope began to ebb away. By the time she got the words out, Will was almost weeping. "Please, Paige, you have to trust me. I won't let them hurt you."

Paige snorted. "How could you stop them?"

"I'll—I'll—" Will fished blindly, and then her grasping hit upon something at last. "I'll marry you. I'll marry you! You'll be an Arrex! Once you're one of us you'll be untouchable. My father will protect you just as fiercely as he protects me."

That was enough to finally make Paige turn back towards Will. For a few moments, they stared at one another, stunned into silence.

Paige recovered first. "You want to *marry* me?"

"Of—of course!" Will stammered.

And—and to her surprise, she found it was true. She'd hated Paige before the Lottery process began, or she had believed she did. But being with her, watching her, finding the person beneath the gigantic brain—it had changed so many things. Paige Tarrant was loyal. She was kind. She was self-sacrificing and open. She was everything Will wished she could be.

She *loved* her.

Yes, she wanted to marry Paige. Or she would have done if their relationship had been left to develop naturally. Once they had been together longer. She cared for Paige in a way she had never cared for anyone. *Yes.* It felt right. She would have wanted to marry her even if Paige's life wasn't on the line. It was genuine. What harm did cutting out the intervening time do?

"Yes," she repeated, more certain this time. "I do."

Paige scoffed again, rolling back towards the wall.

Will's blood ran cold. Even after the fighting of recent days, this was not the sort of response she would have hoped for after a question like that. "Paige, I—"

Her thought was cut short before it reached its end.

"What makes you think I'd ever want to marry *you*, Arrex?" Hate dripped from Paige's tongue like acid.

"Paige, please."

Paige swung back towards her, sitting up, sheets falling away from her, Will shrinking back as she advanced.

"Why would I tie myself to someone like you? You think I would ever want to be *one of you*?"

She lunged forwards as she spat those last few words, and Will tumbled awkwardly out of the bed and onto the floor. The metal was cold against her naked flesh, the impact hard enough to shake the breath out of her, and she knelt, pleading. "Paige, you have to see—"

"A *Noble*. A puffed-up, parasitic waste of oxygen, sitting on Eden's back and leeching the *life* out of us."

Will fell back, stunned by the sheer force of the vitriol.

"If it wasn't for your kind we could have done something about—about *all* of this! We could have built another station, *invented* some bloody terraformers—anything rather than just building Laikas and sending kids out to die."

"I—I don't want to argue," Will pleaded, striving for eye contact. Trying to reach Paige, beneath the shield of her anger. "Will you...will you just think about the possibility of—"

"I would rather die here than *ever* touch you again," hissed Paige.

Pulling in a stuttering breath, Will fought for control. She would not react. She would not. "You don't have to touch me, not ever, if you don't want to. But if you were my wife—"

"I am not yours!" Paige spat the words so forcefully into Will's face that tiny globules of saliva peppered the air between them, floating for a fraction of a moment, suspended like jewels. Like tears.

"No," Will said at last, watching the fire burning in Paige's eyes, watching her chest heave with fury. "No, I know you aren't."

Clutching her clothes to her chest, Will retreated to her bunk to face the wall and try as hard as she could to muffle her sobs, praying that Paige would not hear her cry.

The days that followed were cold and empty. The ship, tiny as it was, grew huge and cavernous with the gulf that separated them. It echoed with the absence of Paige's laughter.

Every morning Will made two bowls of porridge, and every morning one was scraped uneaten into the waste chute. Discarded just as Arthur's great effort had been. The UV light tilted, and Will did not bother to fix it. Arthur began to wilt. With every day that passed, Will felt that she had more in common with the miserable little tree.

The worst of it was that Paige didn't seem to *care*. She drifted through the Laika, an empty vessel herself, eyes vacant. If Will spoke, she would shrug or sigh, or more often just leave the words to hang there unanswered.

Compared to what had gone before it was a living hell.

It was nonsensical, that the most fun Will had ever had was when she was locked on a spaceship with her worst enemy, on a one-way trip to a grisly end. She had been happy, in that brief, beautiful time. But now...not even the worst days on the Eden could compare to this. No matter how exhausted she was, how many lessons she had to slog through—no matter how awful Lauron was—it was all a thousand times better than *this*.

There were moments when Will thought that she would rather lose the next ten Surveys in a row than suffer another *minute* on the Laika.

"Would you like a cup of tea, Paige?"

"Do you want to watch a movie, Paige?"

"Paige, come look at this!"

"Are you hungry? I could cook us some dinner."

"Paige, can we...can we talk?"

All met with the same unending silence. Paige had exhausted herself in one last, convulsive burst. She had pulled Will close, closer than ever before, only to thrust a blade between her ribs and set her adrift again.

I would rather die than ever touch you again.

Left alone with that sentence reverberating in her skull, Will began to understand.

This was Paige's final victory, in a way. In all her years of frantic effort to beat Will, to find a putdown that would *keep* the win safely in her hands, she had never come close to a blow as crushing as this.

And so Will finally just...stopped. Stopped asking. Stopped trying. She had sought out the warmth and the light, and she had been burned for it. Safer not risk it again.

She began to keep separate hours to Paige. Away from the Eden's diurnal cycle there was no real reason to keep the same schedule. Will kept herself hidden in her room while the gyroscope rattled, the vidscreen played, or water ran in the sink. Only when the door to Paige's bedroom hissed safely shut did she stir.

Days passed, and Will saw nothing more of Paige than a few curly hairs left on the armrest of the sofa. It was lonely, but it was a better sort of loneliness than having every word you said left unanswered.

By the third day without contact, Will thought she was beginning to understand how Loysa must be feeling.

She played Xavier's message over and over, telling herself that she was looking for hidden messages, codes, clues. To hear his voice as much as for anything else. His words looped, and she looked into her father's eyes and tried to understand.

But please, believe me when I tell you it is necessary.

The slaughter of children, *necessary.*

She tried to do the maths. He had been in power twelve years; this had been his first Lottery as head of the family, but he would have been thirty at the time of the last. Old enough to know. And the Lotteries that came before him, under her grandfather and her great-grandfather and her great-great-grandmother. How many children had her family murdered? A line of Arrexes stretching back as far as the Eden itself—a great and glorious crowd of them, with silvery hair on their heads and crimson blood on their hands.

Excelsior.

A Lottery every twenty-five years, beginning seventy years after the Eden's founding when the Paradise fell. Sixteen Lotteries...five hundred and seventy-six children. Even without the thirty-odd survivors of the Trojan Laikas, the number was staggering. More than a sixth of the Eden's current population. It was an almost *unimaginable* number, and her father thought it *necessary*.

Only caring about themselves. Paige's voice, scorn dripping from every syllable. *Nobles.*

Why was it that the cruellest things Paige said were those most deeply inscribed in Will's memory?

If Xavier believed he was making the best choice, if Lord Captain Galba Chassiron and all her predecessors believed that, then Paige was *right*. They weren't shepherds or caretakers or stewards, or anything Will had believed. They weren't even leaders. They were *butchers*.

And Will was one of them. Xanthe was one of them. Everyone, from that traitor Carroway to little Lord Gotho Chassiron, barely eight years old. All of them murderers, or doomed to become murderers. From the Founders onward, rotten to the core.

No wonder Paige hated her. She hated *herself*.

The words on her lips, ready to be said, the truth finally ready to be unveiled. *I love you.* And the answer she received. *Shut up.* Teeth on her skin, biting and bruising. *Shut up.*

You knew what was going to happen, Paige had said. And the worst of it was—maybe she *had* known. She had entered the Lottery, never thinking for a moment that her ticket would be drawn. Laika training, leaving the Eden—that was something that would happen to someone else. Not to *her*.

And no matter how many times she replayed the conversation in her head, trying to find a way she could make Paige see she wasn't a villain, that she was worthy—it always came back to the same thing.

Paige had said it best: *This was a huge fucking mistake.*

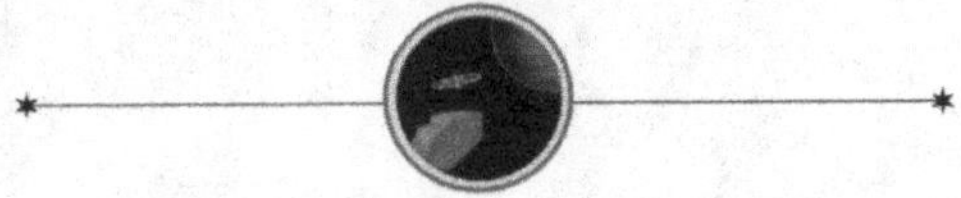

Will sat on the sofa, waiting. It was futile, but...every day, her treacherous heart managed to wring out a few more drops of hope. *Today might be the day.*

Footsteps behind her. Paige, come out to claim her nightly nutribar.

Another meal alone, another hour spent looking at the empty chair opposite. A lump rose in Will's throat.

God, I miss you so much.

But she didn't say it, and she never would. Because she knew the response she would get, and she had *some* pride left.

She lowered her head, not wanting to see even the slightest glimpse of Paige choosing to shut her out, and she waited for it to be over.

Silence.

Then there was a *whumpf*, and the cushion beside her deflated as a second weight suddenly hit.

"I'm so tired," said Paige, in a very small voice.

It took a second, two seconds, for her to believe it was real. And then Will felt tears spring to her eyes. *Salvation.* It coursed through her veins, pure and strong.

"Yeah," she whispered. "Me too."

Then Paige's head came to rest on her shoulder, and Will's tears welled up and began to flow.

CHAPTER 21

Laika 15 – Day 120 – 10:23

Once they had their starting point, things began to improve. Through many missteps and careful corrections, Will found her new normal. So long as she avoided painful subjects, kept out of the woods and stuck to the paths marked as safe, Paige was willing to let her back in.

Mealtimes were safe, movies were safe, games too. Banal, everyday things. Nothing that touched on risky topics. Night was her favourite of these new safe zones. Paige had always been at her grumpiest in the mornings, but Will had not been in a position then to appreciate the softness that evening brought. There had been the movie nights, the subtle touches of skin against skin, the rustle of curls against the sofa cushions, but that was where it had ended.

Things were different now. When Paige was tired, she would pull Will along with her, and the two of them would tumble into the same bed—it hardly mattered which anymore—and fall asleep in a tangle of limbs and copper-tinted curls. At those moments, late at night, on the edge of sleep, safe from the need to say anything, there was nothing to fear. Just the sweet smell of strawberry shampoo and the soft fabric of Paige's pyjamas against her bare arm.

It was not the same as it had been. Perhaps it never would be. But for now, this was...good. Will learned to be grateful. Not to push too hard, to take what Paige would give her without asking for more. It was enough.

Anything Paige could give her would be enough.

The subjects of the Eden, their fellow pilots, Will's family and the other Nobles—all of those were dangerous. There were topics that Will learned she must handle alone, like the upcoming slingshot manoeuvre around Terra. Xavier's technicians had left instructions, and Will was left trying to teach herself how to pilot a spacecraft with only her father's dossier and the trumped-up training the Laika Programme had given them. It was a long way from ideal.

She would have felt more confident about it if Paige had been on board, but...no. She would not jeopardise their fragile peace. Once they were back on the Eden, she and Paige would become what they'd always had the potential to be: an unstoppable team working to right wrongs instead of wasting their efforts against one another. For now, Paige needed her to handle this. And for Paige, she would.

So when Paige rose from the breakfast table and headed for the gym, Will stood too.

"See you in an hour?"

"Maybe a bit longer. I want to really stretch my legs."

Will nodded assent and headed to the control room.

As the rattle of the gyroscope began, she seated herself in the worn grey chair and ran her fingers lightly over the array of buttons. She pulled up the file that showed the trajectory she would have to follow. An arcing loop following Terra's orbit, peeling away at just the right moment to set them on course for home. A much slower return journey, with fuel mostly expended, relying on the speed they had built up on the trip out.

The diagram was so detailed it had to have been made by someone on the inside of the Laika Programme: an actual engineer or navigator. It would have made her life a hell of a lot easier if they had loaded it directly into the ship's autopilot, but it seemed that Professor Clark had been telling the truth about at least a few things; complex manoeuvres with real-time adjustments had to be performed by the pilot, not by the computer.

She tried to rehearse it, as best she could. Fingers hovering over the switches she would need to flip, brushing against the dozens of keys that had to be pressed to perform what her simplified glider had done with a twitch of the joystick. But her thoughts kept turning back to Paige. Like a racer out among the stars, no matter how high she might fly, she always came back to the Wheel in the end.

If they'd been at home, if Paige had her support network around her—well, Will knew what would have happened. Paige would have shut her out for far longer. It would have taken a while, but eventually things would have fallen back into the old pattern of sniping. A few jibes, perhaps an explosion or two on either side, and all would have been forgiven.

But here there was no one else. No alternative. Hard to forgive, when you cannot forget. When you can only find solace in the one who wronged you.

It was scary, how well Will could see inside Paige's head these days. It was hard to remember the times when the girl beneath the fire and the fury had seemed such a mystery. But when you cut them down to the core, an Arrex and a Tarrant were not so different.

And as time passed, the pressure was beginning to ease. She could not broach the subject, but Will thought that maybe Paige was starting to believe her again. To understand that she *would* do the right thing. She would not sweep the deaths of their friends under the rug. She would not let them be forgotten.

She was Wilhelmina Arrex, scion of a Noble family, but that was no longer all she wanted to be. She was Will, and she was different. Paige had *made* her different.

And one day, when Will suggested that perhaps it was time for them to rewatch *Ruination of Overmorrow*, the fifth instalment of Raenerillor and Urgam's epic love story, Paige rewarded her with what was very nearly the old soft-eyed smile. As she smiled back, eyes prickling, Will felt almost ready to sing with relief.

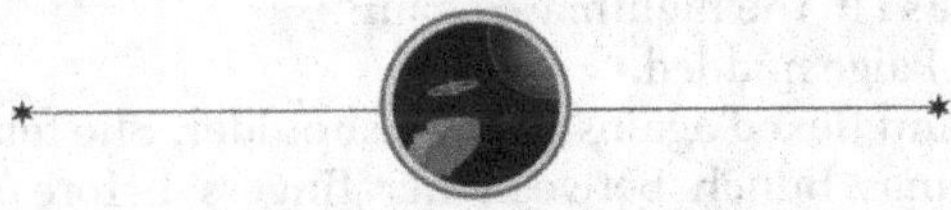

Will awakened to the sound of panting. Short, ragged breaths. *Paige.* Her heart kicking into overdrive, Will reached for her.

"Paige, it's okay."

Moving blindly in the dark, she felt her way up Paige's body, the muscles beneath the skin twitching spasmodically. Fear filled the air, rank and fetid.

"Paige, wake up. Wake up!" For one terrible moment it was like she held something dead or dying. Paige lay too still. *"Paige!"*

And then her eyes snapped open, wild and white, like a frightened animal from the old movies. She lunged upwards, clawed hands gripping Will painfully tight.

"Just a nightmare," Will said urgently, launching into the usual explanation. "You're safe. You're here with me."

Pulling in a huge lungful of air, Paige sagged back against her. "I—I—god." Abruptly, her eyes filled with moisture. "T-thank you for waking me."

"What was it this time?" Will kept her voice pitched low. Tender. The nightmares were terrible to experience, even as a bystander. Paige sometimes slipped back into uneasy slumber, but Will was always left sleepless till morning.

"Thune," said Paige in a voice thick with tears. "Thune and Cara. Trapped. And I...I couldn't save them."

"It's alright," said Will, helplessly, because it was not alright. Cara was safe, but Thune was not.

"I wish we could *talk* to them."

"Me too." Will tightened her arms around Paige. Trying to shield those hunched shoulders with her own.

"How could they *do* this to us, Will?"

"I don't know," said Will, helplessly. Thinking as always of her father, the good man, the hard-working Noble. Her father, the killer, content to let children die by the dozen so long as his own was left alone. It was a good question. How *could* he?

"A-and..." Paige's words fell slowly from her lip as the shadow of the nightmare began to pass. "Will, you're...you wouldn't..."

Her heart sinking, Will steeled herself for what she knew was coming. "Was I in the nightmare again?"

Silently, Paige nodded.

Will's hand flexed against Paige's shoulder. She felt the fabric of the pyjamas bunch between her fingers before she forced herself to relax. "What...did I do?"

"You...I *know* it wasn't you, Will, but...it seems so real. In the moment."

"What did I do?" Perhaps she was pushing harder than she should, but it—it cut deep, to know that some part of Paige believed her a monster.

Shamefaced, Paige looked away. "You were...pressing the launch button."

Funny. No matter how many times the same accusation was made, it never ceased to bruise.

"It's just a stupid dream," Paige said, her voice tight with strain. "I'm sorry."

"Don't apologise." Did she sound wooden? She didn't mean to sound wooden. It was so important to be *present* in these moments with Paige. Every failed performance risked another retreat, and Will could not bear any more distance. Will swallowed, lowered her voice, and tried again. "You have nothing to apologise for. I promise."

Paige looked up at her from under lashes still clumped together with sleep. "You...you *wouldn't*, though, would you?"

"No," said Will, injecting her voice with all the earnestness that her oratory tutor had worked to give her. "I never would." Perhaps, if she could find the right wording, the right tone, she would be able to convince them both.

"And you didn't—you didn't *know*, did you? They never said anything, or did anything that might have..."

It was endless. Exhausting. It would never be over. She wanted back what she had lost: the affection, the *trust*. But it was broken, and how could she ever repair it?

She loved someone, and she haunted their nightmares.

"I wouldn't ever hurt you," she whispered, her voice suddenly more brittle than old bone. "Please."

Please forgive me.

Her hands were shaking, and she pulled abruptly away from the embrace, before Paige could see. She hunched forward, covering her face, trying not to sob.

Paige was leaning over her. Saying her name. "Will, Will, I'm sorry. I'm so sorry. I know you never would. It was just a stupid dream. I'm sorry."

Pulling in one choking breath after another, Will tried to focus on Paige's warmth against her back. *Stay calm. Control yourself. You're an Arrex; the cameras are always on you.* It only half-worked, and when she spoke, her voice cracked with emotion. "Please, I don't—I can't fight anymore."

Paige sniffed hard, and pushed her wet face against Will's. Made a sound that was almost a laugh. "Y-yeah. I think...I think that's a pretty good idea, Arrex."

"We're a team," Will insisted. Maybe if she said it enough, she could make it true.

"A team. And when we get back—" Paige cut herself off again.

"Go on," Will whispered, fisting her hands in Paige's hair.

"I want to make the world *better*. Into somewhere I *want* to live. Would you..."

The question tailed off, but Will understood. "You can trust me. I'm on your side."

"A-and what do you want?"

An impossible question. Will wanted so many things. To go home, to fix things, to *live* instead of striving to do what was expected. *And most of all—more than anything—I want you.*

Will wanted to be *safe*. She wanted to wake with the certainty that today would not be the day she lost Paige again. She wanted Paige to be hers, really and truly. To be Paige's in turn. To *belong*. If she could not be an Arrex, could not be a Noble, she wanted to be something else. Something secure. She wanted to stop being afraid that the ground beneath her feet would split asunder, leaving Will to fall and fall forever as Paige looked at her with the old contempt and spat out *I'd rather die than ever touch you again.*

She said none of those things, of course. She said what Paige wanted to hear—still the truth, or just enough of it. Keeping that gaping maw of fear and need tucked safely away inside, where it belonged.

If she ruined this, as she had ruined so much else, there would be nothing left.

"I want that too. I want to do it with you. Together."

"Good," said Paige, a shaky exhalation. "Good."

And later, when Paige slept again, Will watched her with that old possessive terror. *She's mine, she's mine. I can't lose her. She's all I have.* The thoughts circled in her head, a horrible litany. She was hungry, when she looked at Paige like this. She was ravenous.

I won't lose her.

In a world of shifting sands, where nothing and no one could be relied on, Paige was all that remained.

Will wanted to shake Paige awake, to hold her and never let her go. *Promise me,* she wanted to say. *Promise me you're always going to be mine. Even on the Eden. No matter what.*

Promise me.

But Paige was finally resting peacefully, her expression calm, freed from the nightmares. Will could not wake her. So she just watched, and breathed, and tried to shore up the crippling terror inside of her.

I won't lose her.

"Can you pause it?"

The request came just as the big solo number was about to commence, but Will hopped up from the sofa to tap the vidscreen anyway. The long-awaited *Soft Blows the Breeze* could wait a little longer.

But when she turned back to look at Paige, Will's good mood evaporated. "What is it?"

"How is...*this*...ever going to work?" Paige sounded so fragile. A breath away from shattering. Fingers fluttered in her lap like butterflies at rest.

Dropping back into place beside her, Will searched her face. "What do you mean?"

"Us. How can we..." Paige tailed off, visibly unsure of her own question.

Covering those slender fingers with her own, Will took a moment to marshal her words. She had to get this right. "We've always been...similar, right?"

"A year ago I'd have said you were my opposite."

"In views, maybe. The way we act. But not in personality, in...in who we are. And even if we *were* opposites...maybe sometimes you go so far apart you end up meeting back in the middle."

Paige gave her a very small smile. "Maybe. If someone had told me back then I'd be dating Will Arrex...I probably would have called the Lawkeepers and had them committed."

Excitement flooded through Will. *Dating.* The first time Paige had ever defined what they were. The first time any mention of it had been made. A week ago, peace between them had been more than she dared hope for. But this was better than mere peace. This was *progress*.

Slowly, cautiously, she tightened her hand on Paige's. "Are we dating, then?"

Paige's mouth twisted wryly and she bumped her shoulder against Will's. "Don't be weird about it, Arrex."

"I won't be," promised Will, her heart singing. Her smile threatened to become a grin stretching from ear to ear. "I'm relaxed. I'm cool."

"You're *not*," said Paige, but she was laughing, and Will was suddenly overcome with a delightful certainty that they were *flirting*.

It was still close to the old sparring, the squabbling. It felt familiar, but there was something in Paige's eyes. A light, a glimmer, that had not been there on the Eden. Before the moment could pass, before she could think too hard about it, Will dredged up all her courage and leaned in. For the first time since that beautiful, terrible night, their lips brushed. Paige shuddered as though she had been electrocuted—and then she was kissing her back, like she was burning, like she was dying—like she was drowning and Will was air.

Her hands were everywhere, and Will had to fight not to pull back.

Bruises, bruises on her skin.

I'd rather die than ever touch you again.

"Paige," she whispered into the other girl's neck. The word was a sigh. A prayer. "Paige."

Slowly, Paige stilled. "What's...what's wrong?"

Will pulled back, and they looked one another in the eyes. Green and brown, ice and fire.

"Please," Will said softly, fearing that if she spoke any louder one or the other of them would fracture and break. "Let's go slowly."

Pushing her tangled hair back, Paige regarded her with an unreadable expression. Then, finally, it softened into a smile. "Alright," she murmured. "We'll go slow."

And then there was the familiar pressure of kisses on Will's skin, fingers ghosting along her arms, raising goosebumps in their wake. Limbs intertwining, hearts beating—names whispered like secrets into the dark.

They were together, and finally, Will was whole again.

"Come on, open it!"

Laughter bubbling up at the childish enthusiasm, Will ripped into the paper.

The makeshift envelope fell open to reveal a drawing. The lines were slapdash, but the colouring was painstakingly neat. A blonde elf and a green giant, holding one another close, cartoonish grins on their faces. Raenerillor the elf cradled the burly Urgam in his arms, spindly legs looking comically close to collapse. A banner hung over their heads, reading in large block capitals, *HAPPY BIRTHDAY, PUNY MORTAL.*

Will's face split into a grin that felt almost too wide for her face. "Paige, this is incredible."

Sounding pleased, Paige giggled. "It's good, right?"

Will laughed. "I'd frame it if we had any frames. Honestly, you should rethink the Terran history thing. Be an artist instead."

Paige slapped her on the arm. "Asshole."

"No, I mean it!" She snickered. "You've got real talent here."

Paige blew a raspberry. "Whatever. Now, come on. This is the best bit."

Producing it seemingly from nowhere, she thrust a parcel into Will's hands. Blinking at it, Will felt her smile grow even wider, to the point where it almost hurt. When was the last time she had received a present? Not since the day she left home. A lifetime ago.

Carefully, she opened the wrapping paper. They could reuse it; Paige had brought reams of the stuff, but there were limits even to her stockpile.

Then it finally fell into her hands, and she let out a little *oh* of surprise.

It was wonderful. A tiny fish, folded from paper carefully coloured with white flowers set against a pink background. Were those potato and carrot blossoms? The same flowers that had managed to make even the sim room look pretty for the launch party. She'd been supposed to dance with Paige that night.

Every flower was hand-drawn, rendered with loving patience. The fish itself was precise, mathematical: every line of it exact. Slender fins and a forking tail, a flower lined up perfectly to serve as its eye.

Will wondered how many failed attempts it had taken to produce something so flawless. How long it had taken to colour the paper. She felt her face growing hot, her eyes growing wet. She never used to cry, but these days it seemed like it was happening all the time.

"You like it?" Paige was smiling anxiously. "It's shockingly hard to get someone a present when you live in a sealed box with no new materials inside."

"I...I love it, Paige."

Always *it*, not *you*. One of these days she was going to slip up, and...well, she didn't know what would happen then. Perhaps if she waited long enough, Paige would say it first, and then the doubt would be over.

Paige was already turning to the side, producing the next part of her surprise. "Now the *actual* best bit."

When she saw the plate in Paige's hands, Will's threatened tears finally became real. "You made me a cake?"

Paige's answering smile was as watery as her own. "Of course I did. It's your birthday, stupid."

It was only a nutribar with some sugar sprinkled on top—but it was ten times more delicious than any of the birthday cakes Tunis had purchased from the best bakers on Spoke Six.

Perhaps neither of them needed to slip up and be the first say those three crucial words. Sometimes it felt like they didn't need words to say it at all.

"That," Paige said, grinning as she rolled her neck, "was not as awful as I thought it would be."

"See? You ought to trust my judgement more often."

Hands held up in surrender. "I'd never dispute the right of the birthday girl to choose the movie, obviously. But I really did think that one was going to be bad."

"On what basis? You prejudge *everything*."

"On the basis that the title is *Six Men, One Woman, and a Baby*—come on, that's not a good sign."

"A film doesn't have to be about the fracturing of Old Terran nations to be good." Will tossed her head. "Romantic comedies are art too."

"Being in a polycule feels like it would be hard work, though." Paige moved on from stretching her neck to rotating her arms, shaking out the cramp from an hour and a half of sitting still.

"One of you is exhausting enough." Seeing it inbound, Will made the joke before Paige could. Stealing the punchline earned her a glare, but it wasn't *her* fault if Paige was going to leave such low-hanging fruit around.

Paige raised her eyes skyward and spread her hands beatifically. *"Agis mecum iniuste et mundus me iniuste tractat."*

Will gave a low whistle. "Damn! Not an error in there."

"I do listen sometimes." Paige preened.

Leaning back on the sofa and winding a strand of hair idly round her fingers, Will's thoughts returned to the film. "I think the *real* hard work of being in a polycule would be getting *seven* people through their Parental Aptitude Tests."

A shudder from Paige. "Can you imagine?"

Will looked at Paige, at her shining eyes, and tried to imagine a life beyond the Laika. It had not been mentioned in a long time—one of the no-fly zones—but Will still hoped that it was there, just out of sight. Solidifying with every day they spent together.

Returning home. Seeing her father. Dealing, *somehow*, with the Lottery. And then on to the rest of their lives. A professorship for Paige, the Surveys for her. Perhaps, eventually, a visit to Eloise in a professional capacity at the Parental Approval Clinic.

Then the words came slipping out of her before she could stop them. "Do you want one?"

"One what?"

For a moment Will considered dialling it back. It was a risky topic...but it was her birthday, and Paige was happy. There was no better time to ask.

"A kid?" Never *kids*, of course. A Noble had one child, and one child only.

Paige blinked. "Really? You want to have the kids talk?"

"Come on, humour me."

"Fine." Paige ran an idle hand up and down Will's arm. "Yeah, I think so. You?"

A little surprised by the reversal of the question, Will shrugged. "Of course." There wasn't much passion in the statement; a child was not optional for an Arrex. Will had always known one lay in her future, no matter what she might want, so it hadn't been worth wasting thought on other options.

"What would we name them?"

Her heart singing at that casual, far-future *we*, Will strove for casual. She pursed her lips. "Well, it depends. Boy, girl, or enby?"

Paige shrugged. "Pick a name for each. I know what mine are."

"I thought this was a discussion!" Will laughed as she protested. "And you've already decided?"

"Go on," Paige said, smiling. "I want to hear what you'd choose."

"Paige Junior for a girl, obviously," grinned Will. "And, uh, Carr for an enby kid? Make your dads obsessed with them right off the bat."

"Be serious," Paige admonished her, but she was still smiling.

"Javier, then, for a boy," Will said, without much thought. "Nothing wins Surveys like a Founder name."

There was a beat of silence, and Will realised she had misstepped.

"You'd want our child to run in the Surveys?" Paige sounded... shocked.

Why would it come as a surprise? Will spread her hands. "They'll be a Noble, Paige. They'll have to."

"We're going to be working to change the system though, right?" Paige was still smiling, still easy, but there was an edge to it now. "By the time we pass the Parental Aptitude Test there might not even *be* Nobles and Surveys."

Now it was Will's turn to push out a laugh, making sure she sounded as good-humoured as she wanted to sound. "Yeah, maybe not."

An elbow to the ribs was followed by a closer snuggle. "Come on, have some faith. We're more efficient than a *maybe*."

"What are your names, then?" Fair was fair: there had better be a *Will Junior* in there.

The smile faded slightly from Paige's face. "Lain, obviously. Loysa for a girl. Maybe Thune for an enby, it's not really a gendered name."

And then Will finally grasped her error. This conversation had been a test: a very subtle one, perhaps not even a conscious one, but a test nonetheless.

"I think those are great names," she said, taking Paige's hand in both of her own. "I really like the sound of Lain Arrex. Or Lain Arrex-Tarrant—who knows what the laws on names will be after we're done? Either way, it's much better than Javier Arrex. There's been at least nine of them, and none of them were any fun."

Paige clearly did not want to spoil the day any more than Will did, because she let herself be mollified by the Arrex-Tarrant thing. "What gender would you want, then?"

Picturing a little boy with the inevitable Arrex gene editing, Will shuddered. Far too close to Lauron for comfort. "A girl, definitely."

"That was quick off the mark!" Paige was laughing again, and Will grinned back, almost reflexively. Paige's happiness had a way of infecting you, pulling you along with her.

"Boys are...ugh." An exaggerated shudder to pull out another laugh from her audience of one. "Don't think I'd know how to raise one."

An answering chuckle from Paige. "They're not so bad. Cara was my best friend even before she was a girl."

"Probably because she *was* a girl before you knew she was. Like I said, boys are *ugh*."

"And *that* is why you're not mature enough to be discussing whether or not you want children." Paige giggled and reached for another few crumbs of the questionable cake.

Will yawned and stretched. "So what now?"

"How about a bit of schoolwork?" A devilish grin.

"On my birthday?"

"You can't start slacking now, Will! It's only—" she made a show of counting on her fingers, "eleven months till the Academy!"

Will pouted. "Yeah, but it's my *birthday*."

"Come on, when did you ever take a break on your birthday before? I didn't even know when it *was* till my papi started going to the fancy banquets as part of work."

"Aren't you meant to be the radical anti-Noble reform girl? You can't abolish the office and insist the work ethic stays."

A flash of a pink pointed tongue as it was stuck out at her. Then Paige settled back against Will's shoulder, their heads just touching. "Imagine it, though. All those people in the dorms. All that *space*."

Will tried. Being home. By the time they got back, there would be very little left of their final year at school. The Academy would come around quickly, and then they would both be free of Spoke Six, the Arrex mansion and all the associated baggage.

They would spend their days in lectures, playing frisbee in the gorgeous parks in Centre. Or lounging in Paige's dorm room. Nobles bunked in a special wing of the Academy, and all of Will's ingenuity would not be sufficient to get her a room on Paige's corridor. A near-permanent sleepover would suffice, and Will would see little of her fellow Noble students. Especially Carroway. She would avoid *him* like the plague.

She would live with Paige, just as she did here—but with their friends to accompany them as well. Cara and all the rest would be Will's friends too, now. A whole Academy of people for Will and Paige to meet, and after what would be almost two years locked in a single room, they would both be ready for some serious partying.

The vision of it was so strong she could almost taste it. It was almost real; another few hundred days and it would be.

"I can't wait."

For the first time in a long while, Will was excited to see what the future held.

CHAPTER 22

Laika 15 – Day 193 – 20:45

The days passed. The stars slipped by like pebbles in a stream. Visible through the porthole, Terra grew. The brightest light in the sky, turning slowly but surely into a recognisable planet.

With every passing day, Will huddled closer to Paige. The end was coming, whether they wanted it or not. It *had* to be faced, but it was almost too vast to contemplate.

Terra. The homeworld.

"Come look," Will called through the open door of the control room. "Luna's visible."

There was no answer from Paige. The control room was still a step too far for her.

Will turned her attention back to the vidscreen. The white sphere was now joined by a second one, much smaller. Twin stars. In a matter of days—a fortnight, perhaps two—the surface would be visible. Blasted by war and nuclear winter, but still the continents and shapes that Will had grown up knowing. They would be able to see all eight mega-nations, blackened and dead. Maybe even the ruined cities—Rome! Paige would like that.

"Paige, I swear you want to see this." Her second attempt met with the same stubborn silence.

Will sighed and headed back to the door to look at Paige, seated on the sofa, books piled high on every side. The closer they got to Terra, the further she retreated into academia. As though if she wrote enough essays on Roman aqueducts and hypocausts—both of which Will had been forced to absorb far too much information on—things would somehow be fixed.

There was a shadow inside Paige now, something that had not been there before the Laika. For months Will had tried her best not to draw that shadow out, to let it lie fallow while she distracted them both. She laughed, and she smiled, and twirled Paige into dances that left them breathless. She had been relieved when

Paige let it happen, let Will spin them both a shiny cocoon, the pale white silk so much prettier than the dark beyond the Laika's walls.

Soon they would no longer have that luxury. Terra was waiting.

She leaned against the doorframe, and the metal bit into her flesh. "Why won't you help me plan, Paige?"

A heavy sigh. The book was lowered, but the scratch of pen on paper continued. "I just...I don't see the point, Will. The controls won't even *work*. Why would they hook them up? It's just another part of the lie."

"They'll work." Will didn't elaborate. Her father's name was another of those hot-button topics she preferred to avoid; for her own sake as well as Paige's. Paige hated Xavier, plain and simple, and Will...she had not yet figured out what to feel.

"If they do, it's...it's more corruption. We weren't meant to survive."

And Will had no answer for that.

Silence descended, and Paige fell back on her usual defence for when things became a little too real: she changed the subject. "I think I might re-read Tacitus this week. Do you want to borrow Cicero?"

Her heart twisting, Will reached for Paige's hand. "Paige, we ought to be getting ready."

Head cocking, Paige raised and lowered one shoulder in a crooked shrug. "What's the use? We can't believe anything this ship shows us."

"But..." After only a moment's hesitation, Will played one of her biggest cards. "If it works, we could go and get the others. We'll be in time to save them."

The pen finally fell still. Eyes darkening with anger, Paige jerked to her feet. "You're living in a fantasy! They're dead, or as good as. There's no way to rescue any of them. The only one who walks out of this alive is—"

—Is you, Will.

That she had cut herself off before declaring—again—that Xavier or the Noble Council would have her killed as soon as she walked through the Laika's door was a concession. But Will was not about to let it slide. Casual references to Paige's death were not something she was *ever* going to let slide.

"Is *both* of us."

"Fine." Paige waved a hand, conceding the point without bothering to argue. "Look, do you want to borrow Cicero or not?"

The urge to tell her where to stick her Cicero was strong, but Will gallantly restrained herself. "No; I'm trying to plan how to survive the next month. There's a ton of maths to go over, and it would be great if you could help me check some of it."

"And I told you I don't see the point!" flared Paige. "What's the good in staving off death for a month, six months? When we're going to die either way?"

"Because maybe we *won't*. It's not—you're not being *logical*. We might die at any point. The others might be dead, or they might be alive. If we just give up, we're losing all hope of ever being able to help them."

"We're never going to be able to help them no matter *what* we do. The Eden is *broken*, Will. Humanity's messed up the last chance it had."

It always circled back to the Nobles. And no matter how many times she told herself that she was no longer one of them, it was still hard not to rise to the bait. Swallowing that defensive urge down, Will gritted her teeth. "If you could get out from behind your giant bloody martyr complex for a minute you'd realise your argument doesn't make any sense."

"Oh." Paige's voice oozed with sarcasm. "I'm sorry I'm not being perfectly *logical* about the *death* of thirty-three of our friends."

The thirty-*three* was a deliberate slap in the face. Lain was already gone, and Paige used him like a weapon.

Her mouth opened, a biting response ready on the tip of her tongue—but...getting angry wouldn't make Paige engage with their situation any faster. With an effort that felt almost superhuman, Will pulled in a deep, calming breath and forced her anger to dissipate. "Thirty-one," she corrected wearily. "The Trojan ship. But...fine. If you need me, I'll be going over the trajectory maps again."

She rose, hesitating in case Paige had anything else to offer, but the sound of the pen was already resuming. There was a beat, and then without looking up, Paige extended her free hand. With a small sigh, Will took it. A brief squeeze, and then it was over. A simple code with a simple meaning: *I don't hate you.* It was a new thing, but...at moments like this, it did help. A little.

"And if I hit...this..." Will counted the buttons across from the left and pressed the fifth, praying that the manual—finally unlocked, after Xavier's modifications activated—was not the lie Paige still thought it was. "Then we should get a clearer picture."

The narrative of her actions received no reply. Paige was in the gym, running like all the hounds of hell were baying at her heels.

There's no point, she said, whenever Will tried to raise it. Over and over, the same thing. *No point.* When Paige Tarrant got something stuck in her head, it was impossible to dislodge it.

And when Will tried to imagine taking control, the autopilot disengaging...well, it was difficult not to believe in what Paige kept saying. *We're dead either way.* Flying the ship for the first time in real life while trying to perform a complex manoeuvre that their lives literally depended on was a terrifying prospect. She hadn't even had access to the training sims for the last seven months.

The Laika ships were fit for purpose, given that the purpose was to carry two pilots a safe distance from the Eden's radio range before letting them die. But as ships they were a poorly designed joke. Will was all too conscious that both her life and Paige's might be the punchline.

"So we turn the dial like so," she said aloud, trying to force her thoughts back on track, "and then..."

The cameras on Laika Fifteen's exterior rotated and locked on, and then the picture began to magnify. The white sphere, a hint of black tinting one end, grew rapidly. Will leaned in, riveted. *Terra.* The first glimpse of the planet witnessed by a human in nearly five hundred years.

The sphere grew until it filled the screen, the white fading away, replaced by smears of red and black. They were well past the orbit of Mars now, only thirty million kilometres or so distant from Terra. A matter of days until arrival.

The pixels on the vidscreen slowly resolved themselves into a more coherent picture. A reddish-black marble, whorls of muddied colour just visible. If Will squinted hard enough, those smudges of red might be recognisable as blurry versions of the continents she knew.

She sat back in her seat, letting out a breath so long that it was almost a whistle. Terra—*Earth*. Her eyes flickered over the image before her, but they kept returning to the door. Will was seeing Terra for the first time, and only one thought kept recurring. *I wish Paige was here.*

"Don't you think we owe it to them to survive?" Will said one night, as Paige was watering Arthur. "To change things, once we're home?"

Paige sighed. She turned away, focusing on the leaves and the soil of the plant before her. Just like always, she didn't want to have this conversation. But it had to be said, no matter how painful it was. Time was running out.

Moving around to the other side of the table so that Paige was facing her again, Will reached out and put her hand on the other girl's face. Forcing her to meet her eyes. *"Paige."*

She lowered the cup of water she held to the table and pushed Will's fingers gently away. "We're...we're not going to live because of anything special we did, Will. It's just...an accident. An accident that you happen to be who you are, and your dad happens to be rich enough to twist things the way he wants them. It's not because of *us*. We don't deserve it."

Trying hard not to flinch at that—it was so easy to read that *we* as *you*—Will crept a little closer. "But we've been given a chance. Don't we owe it to them to take it?"

"You could just as easily say we owe it to them to *die*, same as they're doing."

"More pointless deaths aren't the solution."

"But perhaps it's what's right."

Will felt, as she so often did, that she had come up against a stone wall. Paige's moral convictions were firm and unshakeable, and also completely *insane*. How did one argue that it was ethical not to commit suicide? She didn't even know where to start.

Maybe there was another angle to come at this from. What was Paige's weakness? What would make her do something she didn't want to do?

When you put it like that, it was an easy question to answer. Paige's weakness was the exact same as Will's own: *spite*. She would do almost anything to spite her enemies. Just to show them that she could.

When Will was a child she had travelled to Centre, up to the Command Module where the Summits were held, and she had faced off against the other young Nobles in a debate competition. It was streamed live to every vidscreen on the Eden, giving the people a chance to get to know the leaders of tomorrow.

Will fought her way through round after round. Xanthe, Carroway, Dalcifer Danis—all of them had fallen. Then came the final bout. Nico Chassiron, fresh off his victory over Lauron and a full three years older than her, arguing that Lawkeepers should not be subject to the justice system. Defending the position that no one should be immune to the law, Will had argued that Nico was trying to conflate the Nobles themselves with their right hands, the Lawkeepers, in a dangerous move that could spiral into chaos and societal breakdown. In the end, the judges had awarded the victory to Nico—but Will could still remember the words they had used. *A special commendation to Lady Arrex, for her hard work and attention to the rules of debate.*

Second place under those conditions had hardly been second place at all. Defeated narrowly by a boy who was both three years older and a Chassiron, descended from the first Captain—that was a bearable loss.

But when she returned to school the next day, glowing with triumph, Tarrant had given her a sly, foxlike little smile, and then raised her hand and suggested that they have a debate contest right here in class.

Beaming with delight at the initiative her students were showing, the teacher agreed, and the morning's lesson was abandoned in favour of debate. And it was not done like it had been in the Command Module, with formalities, assertions, and rebuttals. They were split into teams, and Will was weighed down by Erntz and Lysse, who spent the entire time cracking jokes. In the meantime Tarrant led her team from one wild leap in logic to the next. She didn't even *try* to prove her assertions. It was all feeling, all emotion—nonsense, basically, and a complete flouting of the rules of debate—but the teacher called it *powerful* and awarded the victory to Tarrant.

Will's near-victory had been forgotten entirely, and Tarrant had been celebrated for the entire week for winning their stupid little amateur contest, with no judges, no points, and no adherence to the rules.

She would never forget that horrid gleam in Tarrant's eye as she accepted the round of applause from their classmates. The way she met Will's gaze and smirked, as though to say, *See, you were proud of this, and I did it better than you.*

As a result Will had doubled her sessions with her debate tutor for a month and used funding from her father to start a debate club for the entire school. And there, with the professional judges shipped over from the Academy, she had defeated all comers. Students years older than herself, cleverer than herself—she had even beaten *Lauron*, the one time he bothered to show up. But Tarrant never came, and Will knew that *that* was a deliberate decision, too.

Yes, spite was a powerful way to motivate them both.

"What if we're not doing it because it's right?" she asked, carefully.

Eyes wary, Paige glanced up. "What do you mean?"

"What if we're doing it because...because they tried to kill us, and we're showing them they failed? We *beat* them." She was warming to her theme now. "Professor Clark, the Laika Programme, the Nobles, they all wanted us dead. And we're still alive."

Paige began to shake her head, but Will ploughed onward.

"Even my...f-father," she stumbled over the word, "even he only wants us alive to fit into his plans. He wants his heir. But what if we don't *give* them what they want? We'll survive this, Paige, and then we'll go back there and we'll ruin everything for them."

She still wasn't sure, in her own head, whether revealing the secret was the correct course of action—they might effect more *real* change by working *with* the Noble Council rather than against them—but she would worry about that later. Paige wanted it revealed, and she *had* to get Paige on board with coming home. There was no other option.

"Think about it," she whispered, her voice seductive. "We won't play the parts they want us to."

And this time, when Paige looked up, there was a small, almost vindictive smile on her lips, and a light in her eyes that had not been there before.

A flame.

"Is that...?" Letting out a breath that was almost a sob, Will pressed her fingers to the vidscreen.

The view was so much clearer now. It wasn't an empty, blasted rock, destroyed by nuclear war. It was...it was *alive*. The oceans were much smaller than on the maps Will knew, a muddy grey instead of blue, but it was unmistakable. There were threads of emerald near the edges of the desertified continents.

Green.

Life.

Was it possible? Had the earth somehow begun to heal itself, even without the aid of the fabled terraforming tools?

"Paige! *Paige*! Get over here!"

Unable to resist the urgency, for the first time since Xavier dropped his bombshell, Paige was in the control room. And as she absorbed the image on the vidscreen, what it *meant*, there was no shadow over her features now. Just a smile, bright as the sun.

It was the first real smile Will had seen on her face in weeks. Months, perhaps. In those minuscule slivers of green, there was what the Eden so desperately needed; what *Paige* so desperately needed. What the Lottery had been meant, in a twisted way, to provide.

Hope.

She turned to Will, and she beamed. "They...they were wrong."

Her heart soaring, Will nodded. "It's not uninhabitable."

Paige turned back to the vidscreen, hands clenched too tightly over the back of the chair in front of her. "There could be anything down there—nuclear waste, no oxygen, god knows, but—"

Will pressed her fingers over Paige's. "But there's *life*."

With a little hiccuping laugh, Paige shook her head. "This...this is what happens when you lie and kill people instead of actually investigating. Hundreds of years, and we never knew. We never even checked."

"I know," Will said, eyes still on the vidscreen.

Paige's head was still turning from side to side: in anger or wonder, Will could not tell. "They're so *stupid*."

Sidling a little closer, Will slipped an arm around the other girl's waist and Paige leaned into her. Together, they watched the slow turning of the planet beneath them, pointing out mountain ranges, what had once been coastlines, the vast craters from the Last War.

It was a moment that could have been only seconds, or could have been hours. It was like an insect trapped in amber, that shining moment in time, suspended and perfect, wings sparkling like diamonds.

It ended when the vidscreen beeped and two hidden panels in the console peeled themselves away to reveal what was hidden beneath. The autopilot was finally giving up control. A wheel with smaller dials and turntables built into it. Circles within circles: a dizzying array unless you knew exactly—as Will *hoped* she did— what you were doing.

With a hand that trembled only slightly, she reached out and touched the metal. Shockingly cold beneath her fingertips.

Paige moved with her, so close the flyaway hairs that escaped the main body of curls still brushed Will's cheek.

"Are you...are you ready?"

Her fingers skimming feather-light against the wheel, Will looked into Paige's eyes. A universe of warm umber, with golden stars speckled across the sky.

"I'm ready," she said, and her fingers tightened into fists.

Paige took her place in the second chair. Hands spread like wings over the array of buttons. "Then let's go."

CHAPTER 23

Laika 15 – Day 221 – 14:37

Leaning with the wheel, Will banked. It wasn't so different to a glider, if she made an effort to ignore absolutely everything about the reality of what she was doing. She just needed to stay calm. Keep a light touch. Nice and easy. Staying securely on the blinking blue path her father had laid out for her. Luna was on her left, its dark side outlined in blazing white by the planet beyond it.

It was all going according to plan.

Paige was—inconceivably—drowsing in the chair beside her. Over halfway through their nine-hour lap of Terra, and somehow, adrenaline had given way to fatigue in Paige's system. Will wished she could take the same opportunity.

But the autopilot was off, the wheel was in her hands, and Xavier's icy blue path overlaid the images on the vidscreen, calling her onwards. To follow in his footsteps, just as she always had.

What would her life have been, if she had not taken Paige's words to heart? *This isn't something that will ever affect you.*

She would have continued at school, a quieter and darker place without the presence of Tarrant. She would have gone to the Academy, studied political thought or something similar. And in a few years, when Xavier was ready to retire, she would have faced off against Lauron in her first Surveys. And that would be it. The rest of her life, following the well-worn tracks laid down by her ancestors. Not a foot out of place, not one original thought in her head.

And no Paige.

Paige would have been here, partnered with Loysa or someone else, drifting through the great empty void for her allotted five years, until her time was up. Will's eyes flicked to the girl sprawled back in her chair, legs splayed out before her, and felt a tidal wave of raw emotion rising up, threatening to swamp her. No. She did not regret disobeying her father. She did not regret a single thing.

She felt the wheel drifting left beneath her fingers and tightened her grip. Something flashed crimson on the vidscreen, a jarring colour after the blackness of the vacuum and the muted browns of Terra.

WARNING: 3° OFF-COURSE. IF TRAJECTORY CONTINUES—

But Will did not read the second line of red text; she was already correcting, hauling the wheel back to the right. Her attention had slipped, but it had only been a momentary lapse. It was recoverable. One second of distraction in almost six hours would not be their undoing.

But her movement must have been too violent, because the little white arrow that represented the ship tipped in the wrong direction—back on course and then sliding off the other side.

Xavier's blue path pulsed red now as well, furious at her. *Why don't you listen to me, Wilhelmina?*

WARNING: 5° OFF-COURSE. ADJUST IMMEDIATELY.

The ship stated it aloud this time, in a dull mechanical monotone, as though *that* would help her to fix the mess she had made.

With a jerk that sent her sprawling from her chair, Paige started awake. "Will! What's—"

And as Will heaved the wheel left again, opening her mouth to gasp out a response, the sirens began to sound.

It was no longer anything at all like piloting a glider.

Alarms blaring. A klaxon shrieking, right in her ear. Her skin slick and sweaty against the smooth wheel as she strained against it. And through it all, the red warning flashing on the vidscreen, superimposed over the earth with its little spatters of green.

ADJUST COURSE BY 13°.

Will's breath was rattling in her throat. The wheel was juddering in her hands, fighting her like a living thing. The gravity felt strange—Will was almost floating in her chair. The ship was spinning too fast.

ADJUST COURSE BY 17°.

Paige was trying to tell her something, her face distorted as she screamed the words. Objects floated past the door, coffee cups and books and strangely, a pear sapling.

Something slammed into Will's temple and the world wavered.

ADJUST COURSE BY 29°.

The sirens sounded tinny, now. Distant. Will could barely see the vidscreen. Her vision was blurring. She saw...she saw the school canteen, somehow.

The table where she sat alone was moved from its usual spot. Instead of sitting snugly beside Paige's table, it was shoved against the wall, all askew, and in the centre of the dining hall was a stage with a man gleaming with moisture under the hot lights. Hrue Lipson. The corners of his mouth crawling up his cheeks in a slow, deliberate smile as his fleshy lips shaped the words that would end her life. *The sixth ticket: Lady Will Arrex.*

There were hands on her shoulders now, pulling at her wrists. Digging into her flesh.

But Hrue was tapping his porta-vidscreen again to summon another name, and Will could not pull her eyes away.

Paige Tarrant.

No. *No.*

The vidscreen in Hrue's grasp grew larger, closer, Paige's fate spelled out in gigantic red letters, flashing and flashing. There was a view of Terra on the screen behind the letters, desert and dried-up oceans, and it was spinning crazily. Will regarded it with a strange, detached sort of horror—and Hrue Lipson opened his mouth and the screams of the siren flooded out.

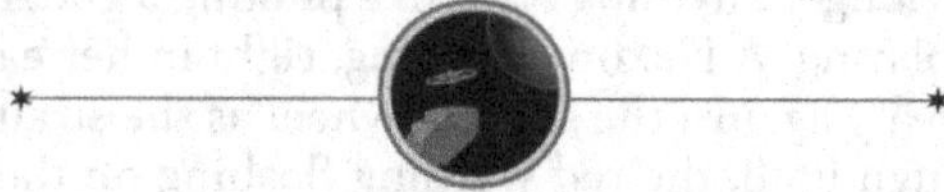

It was pitch black, and Will was utterly disoriented. In its usual night mode, the Laika left on some dim blue lights: enough to give a sense of where you were. But now there was nothing, and the Laika was plunged into darkness so complete that Will had no idea where she was.

The gravity must be malfunctioning too, because she was floating. Flying like she was a child again, playing in one of the Eden's anti-grav gyms, before her father had told her that perhaps there were more dignified pursuits for a seven-year-old Arrex.

She was suspended in inky black, nothing to see, nothing to touch. Will ran her hands over her arms, checking that she did, in fact, still have a body.

"Paige?" she whispered, and her voice sounded horribly loud in the dark.

No answer came.

She reached out at random, and set herself spinning wildly. Vomit rose, her stomach roiling, and she clamped both hands over her mouth. The only thing worse than spinning out of control would be spinning out of control in the middle of her own fluids.

Her spine collided with something, a collection of thin rods and cushioned surfaces, and she grabbed it eagerly. A chair. Aimlessly floating, just as she was. She hung on to it, but didn't try to move again. It wasn't worth the motion sickness.

Light flickered—agonising after the black. The vidscreens in the control room coming back to life. Then the gravity came back on, and Will slammed head first into something far harder than her skull.

White. Bright, blinding white. Everything Will felt was pain.

The world felt...wrong, somehow. Slanted. There was something wet on her face, obscuring her vision. When she touched it and peered blearily down at her fingers, they were all coated in red. Blood. Whose blood? Her own, or Paige's?

When that thought finished worming its way out—far too slowly to be normal—she sat upright. *Paige.* Where was Paige?

She tried to push herself up, but her arms wouldn't support her weight. She was shaking, and the blood was dripping down her chin now. Where was Paige? She called her name, her voice horribly quiet in her own ears. She tried again, screaming it this time, and it was the same—like somebody else, calling from down a very long tunnel.

With trembling limbs and a spinning head, Will crawled towards the control room door. Still ajar. "Paige?" she croaked. "Paige, are you alright?"

Her clawed fingers fastened on the doorframe, and she hauled herself forward.

Her vision was still oddly blurry, but she turned her head from side to side, attempting to make sense of the out-of-focus shapes. The blue-grey colour of the sofa, the brown of the kitchen table, both of them thrown on their sides. A sad scattering of green where Arthur lay, trunk snapped in two. The cream of the cupboard doors, hanging askew, plates and bowls scattered everywhere. And there, beneath the vidscreen that they used for their movie night...a shape clad in a familiar shade of iron-grey, mantled with a cloud of chestnut hair.

"No." The word choked her. "*No.*"

Somewhere, she found the strength to stumble onto hands and knees and stagger across the room. Collapsing by Paige's side, hands hovering over her, afraid to touch. Her curls splayed across her face, and her arm bent at an angle that no arm should bend at. There was blood, staining the grey of the jumpsuit black. Filling the air with that hot-metal coppery tang.

"*Paige,*" whispered Will, agonised. "Paige, no, no, no."

A lexicon of only two words, a litany repeated over and over as she desperately, gingerly brushed the hair away, peered into her face. The constellation of freckles that Will knew by heart stood out starkly against the pallid skin. The bloom was gone.

"*No,*" sobbed Will again, a great ugly hiccuping sound. "Please, *please*, no."

She pressed her fingers against that velvety skin, not yet cold, and she began to keen.

And then Paige opened her eyes. Searching brown eyes met Will's, and the tears falling from above onto the freckled cheeks became tears of joy.

"Paige, oh, god, I thought you were—" She couldn't even say the word.

"What...what happened?" Paige tried to sit up and winced, cringing over her twisted arm. "*Ah!*"

"Don't move it!" Will sprang into flurried motion—*Where is the goddamn first aid kit?*—and stopped short as the dizziness overwhelmed her again.

"*Fuck*, it hurts."

"Just...just give me a second, we can—we can bandage it—" Will was back on her hands and knees, crawling towards the jumbled pile of things from the kitchen, climbing over Arthur's broken trunk as she went.

"I think it's...broken. *God*." Paige hissed the last word between her teeth as she probed the wounded arm with one finger. "Bandages...*ah*...aren't going to do much."

Rummaging frantically through the disorder, Will tried to keep herself upright. "Hold on, hold on."

The familiar green box sent relief flooding through her system. White cross on the lid, medkit inside. What else would she need, what else? A knife, a snapped leg from a kitchen chair for the splint, a sheet from the laundry cupboard to bind it.

Her treasures secured, she crawled back towards Paige.

"You're bleeding!" Paige sounded alarmed, but Will waved it aside. Paige's injuries were more important. Her own could wait.

She reached out for Paige, but her treacherous hand went astray, hitting the wall to the left of where she had thought Paige was. Her vision was playing tricks on her, and she *needed* it right now.

Paige grabbed her hand, touched the plum-sized lump that throbbed on Will's temple. "Seriously, Will, I think you might be concussed."

"You first," Will muttered, dropping the load she had gathered in the kitchen. "Then we'll clean it."

"If you're sure," Paige said. "I can't do much for you with my arm like this anyway."

Working together, they got Paige into a sitting position.

"You've...you've got to get the bone aligned before you can put that on." Paige stumbled over the words, pointing at the splint with her good hand.

"What?" Somehow that didn't make sense. Will had been to the same first aid courses as everyone else at school. The treatment for broken bones was simple. Call the medical response team, and if that wasn't possible, splint, bandage, and get to the hospital.

"You've got to push it back together," Paige ground out.

"I...I..."

"You're *definitely* concussed," said Paige, with a dry, horrible sort of humour. "Come on. Just put your hands here...and there...and for god's sake do it quickly."

"Three, two, one—" Will's hands moved convulsively on Paige's wrist and elbow, but she could not do it. She could not hurt her.

Paige was pale, sweaty, strands of hair slicked down in little streaks against her forehead. "Will, for fuck's sake, just do it!"

Will looked up into those wild eyes, the whites clearly visible, the pupils mere pinpricks of terror, and her breath came too quickly. "Paige, I can't—"

"*Do* it!" screamed Paige, right into Will's face, and with a sudden spasm of movement, Will obeyed.

The bones ground into place with an audible crackling, and Will rocked back onto her heels, almost incoherent with fear. "Are you—Paige, a-are you—"

"I'm...fine," answered the other girl in a strained voice. "Come on. Splint it."

With shaky, uncooperative fingers, Will did her best to obey. It took too long, and Paige had to bite down onto the flesh of her other arm to keep from crying out, but finally, Will tied the final strip of torn sheet, and slumped against the wall. Safe at last in the knowledge that Paige would be okay.

But Paige's five unharmed fingers were already prodding at her forehead, sending spikes of pain hammering deep into her skull. Will moaned incoherently and tried to turn away, but Paige was determined. Will's wound was cleaned, examined, and finally bandaged, and then Paige was half-carrying her towards the bedrooms.

"Go," said Paige. "Sleep. I'll wake you in an hour or two. It'll take me that long to reboot the computer and figure out what the hell went wrong."

And for once, Will was too exhausted and bewildered to argue, and she simply obeyed. The mattress in her room was upside down on the floor, but she could not summon the strength to fix it. She simply sank to her knees and dropped onto it, face first. A fresh burst of pain from the wound on her head, and then merciful blackness claimed her.

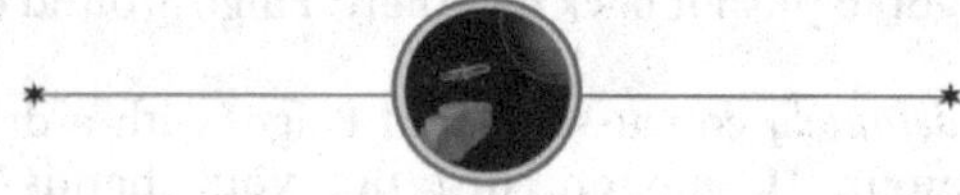

Slowly, painfully, they made sense of what had happened. Nearly sixteen hours had passed since the initial incident. The thrusters had ceased firing as soon as Will's hands left the steering wheel, and they had continued in Luna's orbit, contained by it like an earthworm in a SoilGro bed. The chance to complete the lap of Terra and break away back towards Jupiter was lost.

Their speed had fallen to almost nothing. Laika Fifteen was now a stationary satellite of Luna, and all the fuel they had used to get up towards escape velocity had been wasted.

"What can we do?" Will whispered, through lips so numb she could scarcely feel them.

"There's only one thing we can do," Paige answered. "We have to go round again."

All her earlier determination to die alongside their fellow pilots had vanished. Now the prospect of remaining here, stranded amongst the rest of the space junk that the ancient humans had filled their sky with, made her almost as pale and bloodless as Will.

Hopelessly, Will indicated the fuel gauge, flickering red in the vidscreen's corner like so many of the other sensors. "We don't have enough."

"We will." Paige swallowed hard. "Just. But there won't be enough for course corrections on the way home. This...this will be our last chance."

Those last few words sounded dim to Will's ears. As though Paige was speaking from a great distance.

"Will it work?"

"We'll lose a lot of speed, but hopefully it'll still be enough."

"And if it isn't?"

Paige looked at her, lips tight. "It'll have to be."

Coffee stained the dashboard; perhaps the cause of the malfunctions earlier. But Paige was typing, her fingers flying over the buttons, the engines humming to life beneath her touch. Xavier's path sparked into existence again. A crystalline blue promise of what awaited, if they could get this right.

A future.

The wheel emerged once more, and Will closed her fingers around it after only a moment's hesitation.

"Do you think you should—"

"No," said Paige decisively. A small flourish indicated her bandaged arm, the splintered end of the chair leg still protruding. "You're the one who trained for this. You can do it."

Her words were brusque, but they rang with conviction, and Will took courage from the sound. She could do this. She *would*.

Forefinger extended, Paige stabbed a key, and Laika Fifteen groaned and shook with the force of its own thrusters burning. Up on the vidscreens, the shadowed craters and peaks of Luna began to slip past them once more.

It was a mess; everything was a mess. They were closer to death than they had been since Xavier's video threw them that first lifeline, but Will was *happy*. When the world was at its worst, she and Paige were at their best. Things fell apart, and the two of them came together again. They were a team, working in synchrony.

When Paige believed in her, anything was possible.

CHAPTER 24

Laika 15 – Day 515 – 13:35

"Anything?" Will stuck her head through the doorway to ask, but she saw the answer in Paige's tight-curled fists on the radio receiver before the other girl ever opened her mouth.

"Not yet," replied Paige.

Handing Paige her seventh cup of coffee that morning, Will flopped into the seat beside the other girl and draped an arm across her shoulders.

"Surely it won't be long now."

Jupiter filled the sky before them now, and over the past few days, the Eden had been growing steadily to dominate the vidscreen. Blazing silver against its backdrop of red and bronze.

"Five days out was when we lost signal last time," Paige replied. "We can't be much further out than that now."

Five days. Five days until the door hidden behind the gyroscope would open once more. Will tried to imagine life beyond these four walls, but it felt like make-believe. A movie for the two of them to watch before they curled up to sleep.

What would Xavier look like, now? Maybe his steely-blonde hair would have greyed, faded to white at the temples, new wrinkles carved into the skin around his eyes. Would she recognise him, when she saw him in the flesh once more? Perhaps, if she had not been an Arrex, her first instinct might be to embrace him. But he would expect a smile, a stiff handshake, a clasp of the shoulder for the cameras. His own muted version of affection. But how could she accept that from him, knowing what she did now? He was her father, and she loved him—and he was a killer.

She glanced sideways, at Paige. What would Paige do, when the doors of the Laika closed again, and they were on the outside? She would run to her parents, of course, enfold herself in their arms. But what came next?

What if—what if, once she was free, she no longer wanted Will?

It was an old fear, resurfacing from the darkest parts of her mind. The sort of thing that jerked her awake in the dead of night, reaching blindly for Paige.

But it was only a fear. Not a reality. Over and over again, Paige had chosen her. The Laika had changed them both, and nothing could separate them now. They had begun as opposing magnets, but now they both pointed to the same true north. Locked in orbit like binary stars.

Impulsively, she leaned over, pressing a kiss against Paige's cheek.

With a laugh, Paige pretended to fend her off, but then returned the kiss. "What was that for?"

"Nothing," lied Will. "I just...I might miss this, in a way."

"I get what you mean," answered Paige. "Things are easy here."

Will's heart plummeted. *Easy.* Uncomplicated, without the barriers of Noble and non-Noble to separate them. It would not be easy on the Eden.

"Just the two of us," Paige went on, oblivious, "but I suppose there'll still be times like that at home, won't there?"

"Y-yes," said Will, shakily, making a conscious effort not to let her hug become a death grip. *There'll still be times like that at home. Just the two of us.* Words to learn by heart. A promise to treasure. "Yes, there definitely will."

Balancing her coffee on the dashboard before her, Paige leaned over to try again. "Come in, Eden Station. Come in, Command. Do you copy? This is Laika Fifteen returning. Do you copy, Command?"

And then, finally, for the first time in almost two years, the radio crackled.

"This is Command," said a distant voice, shocking in its strangeness to Will's ears. "Please...please repeat."

Her throat bobbing, Paige swallowed hard. "This is Laika Fifteen," she said. "We're coming home, Command. Please prepare to receive us."

There was a moment of silence. Of disbelief. The profound, deep-rooted *doubt* of a person paid a pittance to staff a radio station only so that the cameras and concerned parents could see them sitting there. A radio that would usually crackle only with the voices of ghosts.

Will knew what he was going to say before he said it.

"You...you were never *meant* to come home, Laika."

Will lay beside Paige, breathing in her presence and her essence and that same old ridiculous smell of artificial strawberries. It was the last night. Their very last night.

"I love you," she whispered into Paige's curls. "I love you, I love you, I love you."

She had thought Paige asleep, but she wasn't altogether surprised when those slender brown fingers threaded their way through her hair and tangled in the white-blonde strands.

"I love you, too."

A sense of wholeness, of completeness, blossomed inside Will then. It took root in her heart and grew up and out into every limb, every finger, every toe. It bloomed, like a white flower on a pink origami fish, like a new leaf on a splintered sapling bandaged with the same care as a broken arm, and all was right with the world.

She was home.

No matter where she was, Laika or Eden, as long as Paige was there too, Will was home.

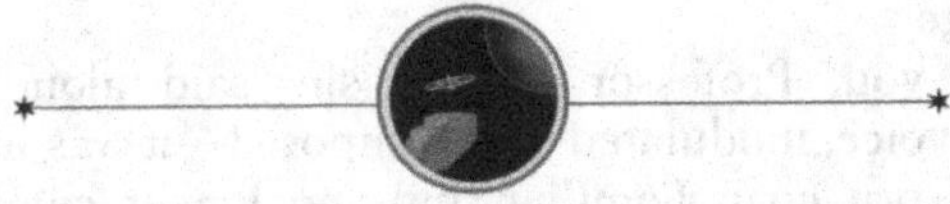

"Welcome home, Lady Arrex, Pilot Tarrant." Professor Clark's voice flowed smoothly from the speakers. Calm and unruffled. As though the return of two of the teenagers she had smilingly sent to their deaths was something she had *expected*.

Well, mused Will, perhaps she *had* been expecting them. Xavier had not achieved any of this alone. Even someone as highly placed as Professor Clark would have their price.

And what of the second surviving Laika, the decoy? The Trojan Laika stored as a matter of course in the mass accelerator, the two pilots locked inside believing they were adrift while never leaving Eden's walls. Who else had survived, Will wondered. Who had Professor Clark and the Noble Council deemed...what was the word Hrue Lipson had used? *Biddable.*

"I want to speak to my dads." Paige's response was immediate. Her fingers were clenched so hard around the radio receiver that the knuckles were pale and bloodless.

"They'll be a part of the welcoming committee this afternoon, of course," Professor Clark replied. "Lord Captain Arrex feels the return of two of our treasured pilots is a moment best captured for posterity by a professional camera crew, and an authentic family reunion is a key part of that."

Lord Captain Arrex. How odd to hear that said aloud. Everything she had worked for, the culmination of all her ambition. The very reason she had done this. It was strange, how little emotion it provoked in her.

She's lying, mouthed Paige, the words silent despite the fact she was no longer pressing the button to transmit.

Will nodded. Professor Clark might well be pretending that she had told their families and the press, planning to catch them as they disembarked and bring a swift end to the whole mess. But she didn't think it likely. There was no way Xavier hadn't placed two or three well-paid informers in Professor Clark's department, and he had to be in the loop by now. Perhaps he would have even told Grayson, if he was still a member of the Cabinet. If Professor Clark tried anything, Xavier would make her regret it. And as for Xavier himself—the Noble Council—Will could handle them. She would protect Paige.

"Thank you, Professor Clark," she said aloud. The old diplomatic voice, modulated and composed—it was like slipping on a well-worn coat. Familiar, but...no longer comfortable. It pinched, now. She had outgrown it. "We're looking forward to it."

"Of course, Lady Arrex. We're all thrilled to welcome you home."

"We're so excited to be back," replied Will, stressing the plural. "*Both* of us."

"She's lying," repeated Paige, as soon as it was over. "She's planning something—"

"It doesn't matter what she's planning," said Will calmly. "My father will stop her. He's...he is what he is, but he'll protect us now."

"But—"

Again, Will knew what was coming. *He'll protect you, not me.*

"Did you see the glider-racing this morning?" she interrupted, before it could be said.

Paige nodded. Like a swarm of colourful insects, the bright little ships had circled the Wheel. Catching the light in a way that made them flare brighter than shooting stars on the Laika's vidscreen.

"There's no way they didn't see us. They know a Laika ship is coming. *Everyone* will know. And a Laika ship..."

"...Has two pilots," Paige finished, almost reluctantly.

She was so anxious, she almost didn't *want* a solution. Will regarded her, and smiled. The worries were fading, and she would make Paige's fade too. They *knew* each other. *I love you too*, Paige had whispered, into the purple darkness of the night.

There could be no undoing the ties that bound them.

The radio hissed, spitting static once more. A new voice. "Laika Fifteen, come in. This is Command."

"We copy."

"Please prepare for landing, Laika pilots. Retrieval drones are en route, and the mass accelerator bay doors are opening to receive you."

Will pulled in a breath, and her ribs seemed to tighten around her lungs. *Home.*

We're home.

Any second now the door would slide open. Will's fingers curled and uncurled, nails biting into her palm until their movement was arrested by a touch of soft skin. She glanced across at her co-pilot, and a small smile flickered on her lips as Paige slipped her hand into Will's.

The journey ended exactly where they had begun. Standing side by side in the corridor of Laika Fifteen in the orbital mass accelerator, down in the bowels of the Eden. Facing their future side by side, just the two of them.

"So—what now?"

Will understood the question. Double-checking. A request for reassurance. "We do what we said we would." The Arrex creed was less important to her than once it had been, but one part still remained. Will Arrex kept her promises. *All* of them.

Paige squared her shoulders, pushing her jaw out and tightening her fingers over Will's. "We tell them the truth."

Will smoothed her thumb over Paige's soft skin. "We fix things."

"You're with me?"

"I'm with you."

And she was. The final door hissed open, the blinding lights of Eden and the cacophonous thunder of voices hitting them all at once, and they huddled closer together. Paige recovered herself first and stepped abruptly forward, tugging Will along with her.

For a moment Will almost resisted, but then she stopped. It was time to be brave—again—and, for the first time, to do the right thing. Just as Paige always did.

Will steeled herself, and she followed the girl she loved into the light.

ACKNOWLEDGEMENTS

This book would not exist if not for Laika, the dog who, like the ships I named after her, was never meant to come home. Her sacrifice, and that of many other animals, led to humans ascending to the stars. The beauty and tragedy of her story gave me the original idea for this one.

For the human contributors, I first want to thank my partner James, who is always my first reader and my work's biggest supporter. I also want to thank my writing group, who hosted a short story competition for which I wrote the prologue and first scene of a story titled 'LAIKA 15'. They are a wonderful group and some of my closest friends.

I owe a lot to the entire team at Tiny Ghost Press, who have been wonderful throughout this process. First was Tom, the editorial assistant who first saw the promise in the manuscript and advised me that my initial (very enthusiastic) 150,000 words was a little too long. My copy editor Dana spotted all the little errors I had missed over my dozens of re-reads. My editor Joshua was a delight to work with, and his brilliant suggestions helped polish the work into the final product you're reading now.

Next up is my cover artist Annabelle (@avendell as she's known online) for the most beautiful cover art. She brought Will and Paige to life exactly as I imagined them and implemented every ridiculously detailed tweak I asked for.

I'd like to thank my older sister and the immensely helpful team at the Society of Authors who helped me understand the impenetrable legalese of the world of contracts as a first-time author.

And finally, thank you to my readers for picking up this book and giving it a shot!

THE AUTHOR

Shannon K. English grew up amongst the windy moors of northern England. She is inspired by mythology, fantasy of every stripe, and powerful tales about characters struggling with terrible choices. As an asexual and panromantic author, she tries to tell the representative sci-fi and fantasy stories she loves to read. Her favourite writers include Ursula K. Le Guin, Shannon Hale and Jack London.

A ROMANCE TO HOWL HOME ABOUT

TAKE HOME THE BEST SELLINH
THE ALPHA'S SON
SERIES...OUT NOW!

AVAILABLE IN PRINT, EBOOK, & AUDIOBOOK

WWW.TINYGHOSTPRESS.COM
@TINYGHOSTPRESS

www.ingramcontent.com/pod-product-compliance
Lightning Source LLC
Chambersburg PA
CBHW010340170726
18283CB00009B/2886